From Barcelona,
with Love

Also by Elizabeth Adler

Elizabeth Adler

From Barcelona, with Love

St. Martin's Griffin

New York

FROM BARCELONA, WITH LOVE. Copyright © 2011 by Elizabeth Adler. All rights reserved. Printed in the United States of America. For information, address St. Martin's Press, 175 Fifth Avenue, New York, N.Y. 10010.

www.stmartins.com

Design by Patrice Sheridan

THE LIBRARY OF CONGRESS HAS CATALOGED THE HARDCOVER EDITION AS FOLLOWS:

Adler, Elizabeth (Elizabeth A.)
    From Barcelona, with love / Elizabeth Adler. — 1st ed.
        p. cm.
    ISBN 978-0-312-66835-8
    1. Private investigators—Fiction. 2. Missing persons—Fiction. 3. Cold
cases (Criminal investigation)—Fiction. 4. Murder—Investigation—Fiction.
5. Mothers and daughters—Fiction. 6. Barcelona (Spain)—Fiction. I. Title.
    PR6051.D56F76 2011
    823'.914—dc22

                                                                    2011005081

ISBN 978-1-250-00826-8 (trade paperback)

First St. Martin's Griffin Edition: July 2012

10 9 8 7 6 5 4 3 2 1

For Red and Jerry Shively,
dearest friends and the best companions,
with whom life is never dull

Acknowledgments

Thanks, as always, to my dedicated, and fun, St. Martin's team, especially Sally Richardson and my editor, Jen Enderlin—simply the best. To my lovely agent, Anne Sibbald, and the wonderful team at Janklow & Nesbit Associates. The list could go on, like winners at the Oscars thanking their mothers and fathers, wives, children, great-aunt, and friends, but I'll simply cut to the chase and let you get on with . . . Barcelona. . . .

Prologue

Los Angeles, California

You could have heard a pin drop in that courtroom the morning the police informed the judge that they had insufficient evidence to prosecute Isabella Fortuna de Ravel Peretti, whose stage name was Bibi Fortunata, for the murders of her lover and the lover's new "mistress," who, by the way, also happened to be Bibi's best friend.

Then came the shocked intakes of breath, followed by shouts, jeers, screaming, yelling, chaos in the courtroom, the judge banging his gavel and calling for order and the sheriffs on duty attempting to keep it. But there was no holding back the press, they were out of there like the legendary pack of wolves baying into their cell phones, and the paparazzi, shoving forward, pushing aside all those in their way, jostling cameras up and over to get that money shot of Bibi Fortunata's beautiful face.

Bibi was crying as she was hustled, head down, into the back of the black Range Rover where she sat, knees together like a perfect lady, handbag shielding her face, and was driven away through the surging crowd.

Everyone knew Bibi. She was the hottest ticket in town: singer, songwriter, actress, celebrity, the woman they claimed every woman wanted to be, and every man wanted. Except, it seemed, for Bibi's husband, and also the lover, who had also cheated on her.

She had been good to that lover, had paid his way, introduced him to people who counted in show business, got him acting jobs. It must have gone to his head because, as with most affairs, proximity to a new woman made it easy, especially when it was offered "legs open and available," as Bibi said when she confronted her "best friend" Brandi about it. "All he had to do was knock on your door and there you were, beckoning him in, naked but for a black lace thong."

"How do you know that?" Brandi had asked, startled. She'd thought it was private between her and the lover and that he would never tell on her. But he had delighted in doing so, complete with details. "Bastard," Brandi said, grinding her teeth.

"Bitch," Bibi said, crying.

And that, Bibi had told the police later, was the last time she had seen her best friend, Brandi, gulping down a glass of white wine—a "Two-Buck-Chuck" Sauvignon Blanc (the two-dollar white wine from Trader Joe's that privately Bibi also thought was very good) while leaving rose-colored lipstick prints on the rim and managing to sneer at Bibi's naïveté at the same time. "I always thought you were dumb," Brandi said in a parting shot.

That night, the lover, Waldorf Carlyle, was alone at the wheel of Bibi's silver-blue Bentley when it went out of control, spun out over Mulholland, and down into the canyon. It took two days to get the wreck up that steep rocky slope, riddled with earthquake faults and loose rocks. He was dead, of course, and the Bentley was a write-off.

That same night, Brandi was also found dead, long after Bibi had departed leaving her own wine undrunk. Brandi was in her own bed. And, for once, alone.

Bibi became front-page news in a way her publicist had never dreamed of. She went into hiding in her Hollywood Hills mansion, canceling all concerts and appearances. After weeks of investigating, expert witnesses declared the Bentley's brakes had definitely been tampered with, but then were unable to explain exactly how. It was only a suspicion, they said meekly, taking a hefty fee for that noninformation.

"Peaceful," was how the tabloids described the best friend's death, though how they knew that remains a mystery. As did who took the picture of her that appeared on the Internet, looking eerily beautiful, as if she were simply sleeping, though admittedly her jaw had dropped open and her exposed teeth gleamed too whitely against her now-greenish alabaster face.

Her death, the coroner said, was due to "an overdose of prescription drugs."

Isn't it always? people asked cynically, wondering if she had taken them deliberately after a fallout with the lover because he wouldn't leave Bibi for her. Or was it the angry Bibi who had slipped the pills into the wine they had shared just an hour before she died? The popular tabloid vote went to Bibi as the killer.

In all this Bibi's Italian husband, Bruno Peretti, a writer, kept out of the scene, holed up in his Palm Springs mid-century-modern house, blinds closed over the windows. There were more windows than walls in that house with views onto the desert and the mountains, beautiful in winter capped with snow, with the palm trees silhouetted black against them and the hard blue of the sky. Instead, he took solitary walks with his new pup, a pale Rottweiller-type with the kind of warning shifty look in its eyes that kept the media at bay. Peretti hung out at Melvyn's, his favorite bar, drinking martinis but always with a designated driver, male of course—he wasn't about to mess around with women at a time like this, though he was certainly a good-looking man, all hard chiseled cheekbones and strong nose, thin and fit, and with the same look in his eyes as the Rottweiller.

Nobody understood why Bibi had married Peretti in the first place. Bibi, with her flame-red hair, her pale lake-green eyes, her delicate freckled skin and slender sensuous body. Her looks were as off-beat as the songs she wrote, which were all about a woman finding out who she was; about the way life dealt you one blow after another then suddenly sent you happiness; about loneliness and the intimacy of lying in bed with a man; about making love and delicious calm afterward; about the glass of wine too many and the harsh words spoken that never should have been. Bibi, in torn fishnets and platforms and silver bustiers; or in slender, sensuous sparkled green chiffon, or in plain jeans and a T-shirt, Bibi sang about her own life and everyone knew what she was saying, and every man recognized her passion and, every man, it was said, imagined himself in that lover's place. So why not the husband?

Bibi had asked herself that question many times. Beauty and success is no compensation for loneliness and Bibi knew only too well what loneliness meant: a too-big house staffed with too many assistants, housekeepers, nannies, chefs, stylists, musicians, trainers . . . Which still left her all alone. She and the child, that is.

The identity of the child's father was Bibi's secret. It was certainly not Peretti; he had merely taken on that role, adopting the daughter when he'd also taken on the role of Bibi's husband. There were rumors, though, that the child's father was a Russian ballet dancer, a star who had absconded from the Kirov on a European tour that included Barcelona. Nobody seemed to remember anything about that, but Barcelona was where Bibi came from, though she rarely went back there.

After the double murder, suspicion hung over her head for months. And then suddenly it was over. There was no evidence

against her, but the damage had been done. Her reputation was
in shreds. The Italian husband, who was in Palm Springs alone
with his dog at the time of the killings and who, in all this, was
scarcely mentioned or seen, abandoned both Bibi and her child,
Paloma. Who could blame him? Her fans also abandoned her, they
were already on to the newest and the next, whose glamorous lifestyle they could aspire to. They wanted "role models" but not this
type. Murder was not good for the box office.

Bibi's fame disappeared like smoke. She realized there was
no secure life for a child whose mother was branded in people's
eyes as a killer. Ruined by the scandal, breaking her heart, she
gave up Paloma, and sent her to live with her family in Barcelona.
Then Bibi, too, left for Europe, where she quite simply disappeared.

The case was kept open but no one had taken the blame for
the double murder.

A couple of years passed. It was as though Bibi had never
existed.

Part One

Chapter 1

Malibu

Much later, when Mac thought about it he realized the story had not begun in Barcelona, but at his own funky Malibu beach house, a pistachio-colored wooden shack built in the thirties by an adventurous would-be movie actor who'd never made it. It was rumored to have been lived in by sex goddess Marilyn Monroe, in her early Norma Jean days, and had ended up like a small green barnacle stuck on the end of a row of expensive houses owned by mega-moguls and billionaires, whose sea-view decks took up more space than Mac's entire home.

Anyhow, he happened to be sitting on his own, smaller deck, with his dog, the three-legged, one-eyed Pirate, whose underbite gave him a permanent smile and whose ragged gray-brown fur looked as though the moths had been at it. Mac had rescued him one dark rainy night driving over Malibu Canyon, stopping to scoop up what he thought was a dead mutt, only realizing when it opened its one uninjured eye and looked gratefully at him, that it was still alive. He took off his shirt, wrapped the dog in it, and drove straight to the emergency vet in Santa Monica, where they'd performed a miracle of surgery. The dog lived, and of course he had become Mac's dog.

He'd named him Pirate because of the eye patch the dog had worn, Long John Silver–style, until the eye socket healed, and Pirate was now his best buddy. Mac loved that dog and the dog loved him.

"And never the twain shall part," misquoted Sunny Alvarez, Mac's fiancée. Well, she was his fiancée *again,* after the debacle in Monte Carlo the previous year. At least Mac hoped she was. But that was another story, and anyway, she was right about the dog.

He remembered the evening the Barcelona saga began perfectly. He'd propped his feet on the deck rail and was watching waves crashing onto the sand, comfortable in shorts and a favorite old blue T-shirt, dark hair still wet from the shower and combed hastily back, eyes narrowed against the flame of the setting sun, with not a thought in his head other than that Sunny, his girlfriend—his lover—his on-again fiancée—was busy in the kitchen. She had gone to fix "something to nibble on," while they drank what she called "the good stuff," which meant the bottle of expensive champagne she'd bought to celebrate their reunion.

They had been apart too much these last few months but were now as passionate about each other as ever, though Sunny still maintained it was Mac's PI work—and his inability to ignore a ringing phone that they both knew usually meant "trouble"—that had caused the rift. As well as Mac's calling off the wedding, one more time, due to "work," of course, and that's when Sunny had run off to Monte Carlo. But Mac wasn't about to bring that up now. They would simply drink their champagne and make a toast to "true love."

Mac had been sorting out other people's lives for a lot of years now. He had a sixth sense for "trouble" and a double-six for bad guys, no matter how charming and plausible they might appear. In the past few years, as well as his PI "day job," he had become

TV's super-detective, with his own show, *Mac Reilly's Malibu Mysteries*, appearing on your screens Thursday nights in real-life docu-drama style, reinvestigating old Hollywood crimes, with Mac looking extra-cool in jeans and the black leather Dolce & Gabbana jacket Sunny had bought him and that had somehow become his trademark. It was typical of Mac that when Sunny told him the designers' names he had no idea what she meant. "Dolce" sounded like Italian ice cream to him. And after all, he was more usually to be found in shorts and T-shirt hiking up Malibu Road to the supermarket, or breakfasting in Coogie's, than decked out in black leather.

Anyhow, the show had brought him unexpected fame, though of course it was all relative, but the money was good, which had made a change.

So, there Mac and Pirate were, that glowing sunset evening, with Sunny in the kitchen fixing something to go with the celebratory champagne, when he saw the child again, walking along the otherwise empty beach. In fact it was Pirate who spotted her first. He was up on his feet—all three of them—in an instant, pointing like a hunt dog ready to retrieve.

The girl was maybe eight or nine years old, whippet-thin, wearing clumsy black granny boots, clomping along at the edge of the waves. It wasn't the first time Mac had seen her; she'd taken to walking by his place several times a day for the past week, always in the same gray hoodie, always with the hood partially covering her face, and always alone. And she always slowed down opposite his house, casting quick sideways glances his way before hurrying on.

Sunny had noticed her too. "She's probably just starstruck and wants your autograph," she'd said.

But Mac didn't think so. There was just something about this child, something in the stoop of her thin shoulders, the sheer vulnerability of her sticklike legs and the huge shadowy eyes that spelled trouble. Watching her now, coming down the beach one more time, he wondered what was up.

Sunny caught sight of her too, from the open sliding doors leading from the kitchen onto the deck. Not that she was really thinking about the child, she just sort of took in her presence in a passing glance. The sun was going down and Sunny was already in her pajamas, cream satin boy-shorts and a cami with taupe lace over the appropriate bits, plus she had on her tall black sheepskin Ugg boots, her favorite softies. A girl needed to keep her feet warm on these cool Malibu nights.

It was only six thirty but Sunny had felt like an early start to love and life tonight, with a little grilled cheese sandwich because all she could find in Mac's fridge was an ancient lump of Monterey Jack. Still, along with the fizz and "just a little lovin'" as Dusty Springfield so wisely put it on the CD wafting from the tiny living room, it should be a wonderful night.

Looking at Sunny, you would never think she was a great cook—which she certainly was. Nor would you take her for a Wharton School of Business graduate and owner of her own PR company, which she also was, though you might have caught a glimpse of her former wild-child days if you ever saw her tearing down Pacific Coast Highway on her Harley, hair streaming from under her helmet, and her Chihuahua, Tesoro—the "fiend on four paws" Mac called her—tucked into the saddlebag.

Sunny was a golden-limbed Latina with a fall of long black hair Mac once told her, romantically he'd thought, was as glossy as a Labrador's coat emerging wet from the sea. She had amber eyes under brows that winged up at the sides, a longish slender nose, and a mouth that defied description. Sufficient to say it was generous and infinitely kissable, especially as she always wore a bright red lipstick only she could have gotten away with. And she smelled delightfully of her own warm skin and Guerlain's Mitsouko, a rich old-fashioned scent because, as she always said, at heart she was an old-fashioned girl.

The champagne was already cooling in an ice bucket out on the deck and Sunny grabbed a pair of flutes in one hand and the plate with the sandwich in the other and went to join Mac.

The girl had stopped opposite the house and was skimming pebbles across the waves, which had picked up speed and height and were slamming onto the shore and covering her in spray. She didn't seem to care—or perhaps she didn't notice. She looked small and somehow so alone on that long empty beach, that Sunny was puzzled. Children her age usually ran around in groups, laughing, yelling, pushing each other, there was always movement, noise, laughter, life.

It all happened in a moment. Pirate gave a sudden warning high-pitched whine then hurled himself down the wooden beach stairs, just as the giant wave licked over its own top, unfurled in a green glaze, and came crashing down on the child.

Mac was down those steps in a flash, wading into the swirl, aware of the fierce pull of the sudden riptide, reaching out for the girl with one hand and the struggling dog—her would-be savior—with the other. Kicking powerfully, parallel to the undertow, he dragged them both back to shore, emerging several yards down the beach where he flung himself, spent, onto the sand beyond the next wave's reach.

Sunny was already running to them. She dropped to her knees and began thumping the girl's back, getting her to retch up what seemed like half the Pacific Ocean, while Pirate shook himself all over her cream satin pajamas.

"I'm calling the paramedics," she said.

"No." The girl lifted her head, panicked. "No, please don't. My aunt wouldn't like it."

It crossed Sunny's mind briefly to wonder what kind of aunt would not want to call the paramedics to make sure her niece was not half drowned, but then the girl insisted she really was okay.

On his feet now, Mac stared worriedly down at her. The child's voice was rough from all that choking. The gray hoodie had been ripped off by the wave and she lay exhausted, on her back, arms and legs splayed, looking like a stranded starfish. Her huge chestnut brown eyes were anxious, her pale face was dotted with freckles, and her terrible cropped thatch of carroty-red hair looked as though it had been shredded by a runaway electric razor.

"Thank you." She spoke at last. "I'm Paloma Ravel," she added in a small voice, as though, Sunny thought, she was embarrassed to tell them her name. Then Pirate came up and sniffed her, looking anxious too, and Paloma sat up and put her arms round him.

"I love him," she said, burying her face in his sodden fur. Wet, Pirate resembled the proverbial drowned rat, skinny as the girl, and Sunny wondered if that wasn't one of the reasons Paloma loved him. They looked alike.

"He tried to save me," Paloma said, kissing Pirate's wet inquiring nose. "I will always love him. You're so lucky . . . you know, to have a dog like that," she said, looking up at Mac.

"I know," he said. "And I know he barked to try to warn you. You're a lucky girl, Paloma Ravel. But, since there seems no need to call for help, you'd better come into the house and let Sunny dry you off before I take you home." He hauled her to her feet. "I'm Mac Reilly," he said, looking down at her.

"I know," Paloma said, blushing as Mac took her hand and

walked with her back to the house she had been casing for the past week. It was as if her dream had come true. "Thank you, Mr. Reilly," she added, remembering her manners and that she was glad to be alive.

Chapter 2

Paloma felt strange actually being *inside* Mac Reilly's house. She had viewed it so often the past few days from the beach and now she was surprised to find it so small. The Malibu house her aunt Jassy rented, a mere half mile away, was enormous compared with this, and even then Jassy had complained, saying beachfront property was always skimpy because of the location and the cost. But looking at Mac's low-slung living room that also acted as dining room and front hall, with the dog-hairy blanket covering the comfy sofa meant for lounging in front of the old-fashioned white brick fireplace, it did occur to Paloma, who'd been brought up rich in whichever of her many lives so far, to wonder if Mac was as successful a detective as she had previously thought.

A small tan-color Chihuahua bared its teeth in a snarl and threw itself across the floor at her, skidding to a stop only inches from her black granny boots, that squelched, waterlogged, as she jumped, about two feet in the air.

"Tesoro!" the beautiful woman who seemed to be Mac Reilly's girlfriend yelled.

Paloma observed the pink heart-shaped diamond ring and decided she must be his fiancée. Lucky her, she thought enviously, though she had never yet, in all her nine years, even thought about having a crush on a boy. But Mac Reilly was different, and besides, he had rescued her from a watery grave and she had gone rapidly from "crush" to "idolizing." She had read somewhere about watery graves and they did not sound too appetizing; you got all green and puffed up and didn't even look like yourself. If she had really drowned her aunt Jassy probably would not even have recognized her and that would have been annoying.

"Tesoro!" Sunny yelled again, and the dog, who'd been sniffing Paloma's boots suspiciously, retreated backward, keeping a warning growl just behind its teeth. "That's my Chihuahua," Sunny told the shivering child.

"The fiend on four paws," Mac explained. "But you don't have to worry, he only bites me."

Eyes still fastened nervously on the dog, Paloma wondered about that. But then the fiancée, who told her her name was Sunny Alvarez, said it was true and the Chihuahua was only defending its territory because it had a thing about Pirate and the two were always at war.

Paloma noticed Pirate, still lurking outside on the deck, and said anxiously, "Oh, poor, brave Pirate." Then she looked more closely at the dog and said, astonished, "But why does he have only one eye? And what happened to his other leg?"

"It's a long story," Mac said. "But don't worry, the Chihuahua didn't do it."

Paloma silently thanked God for that; but then Tesoro bounced toward her, jumping up and down, gazing adoringly all the while into her eyes.

"How sweet she is." Paloma bent to pick up the tiny dog but Tesoro didn't like her cold, wet embrace and quickly wiggled away.

"Come on, Paloma Ravel," Sunny said, putting an arm round

her thin shoulders, regardless of the sopping T-shirt. "We've got to get you out of these wet things."

She showed her to the bathroom, handed her a large towel, then told her to take off her wet clothes and put them in the plastic bag she gave her. She told Paloma to take a hot shower, then dry herself thoroughly, *really* scrubbing with the towel, to get her circulation going again.

"You're looking a bit blue," she said, still worried, watching as Paloma took off the boots, and handed them to her.

Sunny tipped them upside down over the sink and little rivers of water poured out.

"Will you look at that," she marveled. "I thought you'd swallowed half the Pacific and now here's the other half."

She pulled out the sodden gym socks Paloma had stuffed into the toes, and added, surprised, "These boots are *way* too big, you even had to stuff the toes. So, why are you wearing them? Most kids wear flip-flops on the beach," she added. "In fact, I do myself."

Paloma felt herself blush again. She turned her face away, wishing she didn't do that. It always revealed her true feelings, which were usually that she was nervous or embarrassed, like now.

"It's . . . well . . . the boots are my mother's," she said. Which was sort of true. They had belonged to her mother once, but Paloma could not bring herself to say they "*were* my mother's." She hated to speak of her mother in the past tense, and still thought of them as belonging to her mom. She was only keeping them for her until she could return them.

"Oh my God." She clutched at her wrist, drooping with relief when she found the gold bracelet with its seven jiggly charms still there. "I thought I'd lost it in the sea. *Ohh!*" She'd just remembered her iPhone was in the pocket of her lost hoodie. "My iPhone's gone," she said, stunned. "My aunt bought it for me."

"I'll bet your aunt will be so pleased you are still alive she'll buy you another," Sunny said. "The bedroom's right across the hall. Meet me there when you're ready."

Paloma stood looking around at the famous detective's bathroom. It was very masculine with white oblong-shaped tiles like the ones she'd seen in city subways in New York and Paris, all the way to the ceiling, which was painted a very dark blue. Blue like midnight, Paloma thought, impressed.

There was an oversized claw-foot tub, a white pedestal sink with a mirrored cupboard over it that Paloma, who knew about such things because of her sophisticated aunt Jassy, thought must be Art Deco, and a walk-in shower with an unframed clear-glass door that, if you were not aware, you might easily walk into and smack your nose. The shower had lots of jets at various heights as well as an overhead rain shower, and Paloma threw off her wet T-shirt and shorts and her sodden underwear, opened the heavy glass door cautiously, turned on the faucet that she hoped was only the overhead one because otherwise she'd get drowned all over again. She waited till she saw she had guessed correctly and the water was coming down just hard and hot enough to bear, before she stepped under it.

The one thing about having short hair—*scalped* hair Jassy called it—was that you didn't have to fuss with it. Under the shower, out again, towel it off, and it simply dried in minutes. "Wash and wear hair," Jassy had said, laughing at her.

Paloma's aunt Jassy laughed at her a lot, though only in a nice way, of course. Well, maybe sometimes it wasn't so nice, like the Crème de la Mer incident. That had been difficult. But Paloma didn't want to think about that now.

The hot water finally penetrated the chill and Paloma turned it off and dried herself with the big blue striped towel Sunny Alvarez had given her.

She thought about Sunny's last name, wondering if she was Spanish, like her, though of course Paloma was only half Spanish. On her mother's side. Though nobody seemed too sure of that since nobody had ever met Paloma's real father, and nobody seemed to know *exactly* who he was. Which was disturbing, but she'd decided long ago not knowing was a lot better than knowing the *step*father she'd hated.

"Paloma?" Sunny was calling her from outside the door. "Are you okay, there, *chiquita*?"

She'd called her *chiquita*! Sunny *was* Spanish after all!

"Coming." Paloma wrapped the towel tightly around herself, embarrassed by her nakedness and, careful that no spare inch of flesh should show, only her shoulders and arms, and her legs from the knee down, she opened the door.

Sunny had changed into jeans and a sweater and was leaning against the wall opposite the bathroom, arms folded. "Hey, that's better, kid," she said, sounding all-American now and making Paloma wonder if she'd got it all wrong about the Spanish thing.

"Come with me." She took her by the hand but Paloma still clutched the towel fiercely against her chest with her other hand. Of course Sunny understood her childish modesty; she had been the same at that age.

She said, "Here's a T-shirt of mine and a pair of yoga pants. They'll be too big of course, but they'll do to get you home with. You'll have to go without underwear for the moment though."

Paloma blushed again at the mention of her underwear, but Sunny tactfully turned her back while she struggled to change under the towel, the way she'd seen bathers change out of their swimsuits on the beach without anybody so much as catching a peek of anything important. Not that she had anything really *"important"* yet; not even a hint of anything, but she still didn't want anybody to see. Not even Aunt Jassy.

"Okay," she said, when she was ready.

Sunny turned and inspected her critically.

The pants were huge. She knelt to roll the legs up, then took a multicolored scarf from a peg behind the door that Paloma—who knew about such expensive designer things because of her aunt Jassy, who was a clotheshorse if there ever was one—realized from the bold zigzaggy colors must be Missoni.

Sunny hauled up the yoga pants and tied the scarf around the child's skinny waist. "That should do it," she said, smiling up at her.

Paloma was momentarily dazzled. She thought she'd never seen anyone more lovely than Sunny, in quite a different way from Aunt Jassy, who was also a beauty but much more glossy. Sunny Alvarez seemed to Paloma to have a golden glow about her, a simplicity combined with something else—an earthiness. She wondered if that was the right word. Whatever, Paloma thought Sunny was lovely, and impulsively, she told her so.

"Well, thank you, sweetheart." Sunny hugged her and Paloma could tell she was pleased. And then Sunny took an apple green J. Crew cardigan from a drawer and helped stuff Paloma's arms into the sleeves, and buttoned it up over her chest.

She took a step back and regarded the girl seriously. She said, "Paloma, what happened to your hair?"

She asked the question very gently but even so Paloma was mortified to have to explain that she'd been having a bad day, that her hair was too wild and curly and she had cut it all off on an impulse because she'd simply got fed up with it. "Besides, it's *red*," she added, unhappily, because the other kids all teased her about her carrottop, and besides she knew it looked terrible and that she would have to live with the results of her action for a long time.

"It'll grow," Sunny said, encouragingly.

"Are you Spanish too?" Paloma spoke Castilian Spanish, which was different from Sunny's Mexican. The "s" sounds were pronounced "th"—as though with a slight lisp. The reason Spaniards came to speak that way was because in the old days their king at the time had a bad lisp. Out of respect his courtiers, and later all his subjects, copied their king's lisp so he wouldn't feel bad about it. Paloma knew that from history. But then Sunny replied in the Mexican Spanish accent Paloma knew well from living in California.

"My father is Mexican," Sunny said. "He's a rancher out near Santa Fe. And my mom's a blond hippie flower-child he met on vacation, so I'm kind of half-and-half."

"I wonder if I am too," Paloma said, looking thoughtful and puzzling Sunny. Still, Sunny could see the girl had been traumatized and knew better than to pry right now.

No questions asked, she took Paloma by the hand and led her back into the living room and out through the sliding glass doors and onto the deck, where Mac was sitting with Pirate right next to him. Tesoro had taken up a cocky stance at the top of the steps to the beach. The bottle of champagne listed in an ice bucket on the old white wicker table; the ice had half melted by now, leaving a puddle around it. The two flutes Sunny had dumped there before she ran to help were next to the now wilted grilled-cheese sandwich. Still, the sandwich made Paloma's mouth water, in spite of the fact it looked well after its sell-by.

"Come and sit here." Sunny pulled up a chair for Paloma,

then catching the girl's hungry glance, she handed her the plate with the sandwich and a fancy blue linen napkin she'd intended for her own little private champagne party. Then she went back to the kitchen and got a Diet Coke for Paloma, came back, opened up the champagne and poured a glass for herself and one for Mac. She flung herself onto a floor cushion, lifted Tesoro onto her lap, and gave Mac a look he knew meant, "Okay, Detective, she's all yours now. Make of her what you will."

Chapter 3

Paloma took a grateful slug of the Coke. It felt good going down her ravaged throat, though she did think all that seawater had given her voice a thrillingly deep edge. She sounded almost grown-up, like her friend Cherrypop who lived on the Ravel vineyard in Spain. But that was scary; she didn't want to be grown-up yet. Not until her mom came back.

Mac Reilly was giving her that same keen, narrowed-eyed look she'd seen him give on TV when he was sorting out criminals and con artists and abusers. Of course, her aunt didn't know Paloma watched such an adult program; she thought she still watched *Mary Poppins,* for God's sake. She did, but not that often anymore, and she would never admit to it anyway, in case the other kids at school thought she was a wimp. That is, when she *went* to school, because more often than not she was off with Jassy and her friends, roaming the world with the latest governess or tutor in tow. She said "the latest" because the tutors never stayed long in Jassy's employ, complaining about the hotel rooms and never knowing where they'd be from one week to the next.

Mac said, "So, Señorita Paloma, now that we've saved you, don't you think you owe us an explanation?"

Paloma took a deep breath. She guessed she did but the way it often happened with her, like now, she couldn't get the truth out. She was worried Mac and Sunny would be shocked, that they would laugh at her, tell her to go on home and forget all about it. "What happened in the past, happened," Aunt Jassy had told her so often. "You just have to let it go and get on with living." Paloma knew she was right, but it was tough. In fact it was impossible.

"I know you from TV," she told Mac, blushing shyly again, squeezing the Coke can so tight it crunched and Coke squirted all over the yoga pants Sunny had lent her.

"Ooops, sorry," she muttered, embarrassed, mopping it up with the Missoni scarf. "Jassy always says I'm clumsy."

"My mom always said that about me too," Sunny said, kindly, because the child was so obviously embarrassed. "And I'm glad you caught Mac's show. Tell me, what do you think of him?"

Paloma stared gratefully at her. "I think he's just wonderful." She turned to gaze at Mac, all worshipful brown eyes.

Sunny sipped her champagne trying to hide her smile. Of course, the child was a fan; she'd known all she'd wanted when she'd haunted their house that week was an autograph. "Some of us feel that way about him," she said, giving Mac a wicked little smirk. "Wait here, sweetheart, and I'll get you an eight-by-ten glossy of the master detective. I'm sure Mac will sign it specially to you."

Sunny departed in search of the photo, and Mac looked keenly at Paloma and said, "So, what else is up?"

Paloma squinched further down in her chair; she wanted so badly to say *All I want, Mac Reilly, is for you to find my mom, I want you to bring her home to me, please oh please, let her come back, let everything be all right again, let things be the way they were. . . .* But she still couldn't bring herself to say it because Jassy had told her you never could go back and things could never be the same and she was afraid that's what Mac would say too. He would tell her the truth and her hopes would finally be destroyed, and she would be left alone in the world. Abandoned. All over again.

"I think you're wonderful," was all she managed to say before Sunny returned with a really good photo of Mac, looking casual, leaning against this very deck rail.

Mac threw her that quizzical glance again, before signing it, and Paloma knew she had not fooled him. He was too smart for that.

"Come on then, sweetheart," he said, taking her hand. "I'll walk you back home."

Sunny kissed her goodbye and gave her a hug, a true, close-to-the-heart hug, arms wrapped almost twice around her.

"I'll send back the clothes when they've been washed," Paloma promised but Sunny said not to worry, they were hers to keep, which almost made Paloma cry, she was so pleased, and she got to thank her all over again. She kissed Tesoro on her button nose and stroked her sleek fur.

And then there they were, just the two of them, her and Mac Reilly, walking hand in hand along the beach where she had so nearly drowned. Pirate limped behind them, weaving from side to side as though herding sheep.

Aware of the warm clasp of Mac's hand, Paloma tried to re-member what it had felt like, being rescued by him, but she couldn't recall a thing, only a lot of green water in her face.

"Did I really almost drown?" she asked.

"Nah!"

She glanced up. He was laughing.

"Just next time don't get too close to the water. It's a big ocean out there, and unpredictable."

"I know. Riptides," she said. She'd heard all about them but this was her first experience. Even though she couldn't quite remember it, she knew she didn't want it to happen again. "I'm actually quite a good swimmer," she volunteered. "My aunt was a champion swimmer in school and she taught me."

"Good for her," Mac said, thinking it was a pity she hadn't also warned her about walking alone on the beach.

"Anyway, I'll bet you are," he added because he could see she looked downcast.

Paloma stopped at a flight of steps leading up from the beach to a rather grand house, all white with severe modern lines and a bank of massive windows that made Mac flinch, thinking about the eternal sea spray, the blowing sand and the clinging mist, and the price of the endless window cleaning involved. He knew though that people who lived in such grand houses never stopped to consider the cost.

"Well, this is it," Paloma said, not quite knowing how to say goodbye, and not wanting to, because really, truthfully, she still wanted so badly to ask for Mac's help. It was the whole reason she'd *haunted* him all week. But now she knew he was way out of her reach; a TV star; a famous detective; she couldn't afford to pay him and he wouldn't waste his time on her . . . but she wanted to tell him, she wanted to, so badly. . . .

"Mac . . ."

"Yes?"

He was still holding on to her hand.

"Ohh . . . Nothing."

"Sure there isn't something you want to tell me?"

"Just that we're leaving tomorrow. For Barcelona," she added. "That's basically where we live."

"Basically Barcelona?"

Paloma shrugged. "We live all over the place, wherever Jassy chooses at that moment."

Mac handed her the manila envelope with his photo in it. "I've put my card in there, Paloma Ravel," he said. "If you ever decide there's something you want to talk about, you call me. Okay?"

She stared at him, shy, bug-eyed, speechless. Then Pirate came and shoved against her legs and she bent to pat him but also to hide her tears.

"Okay," she said, then she turned and ran up those steps. Back to Aunt Jassy. And back to Barcelona.

By the time Mac got back the sun had disappeared and a mist hung over the horizon. Sunny had abandoned the fetching look of the satin pajamas for the more practical jeans, the Uggs, and an old green cashmere sweater of Mac's, a particular favorite because she loved the way it smelled of him.

"Kiss me, my hero," she said dramatically, throwing her arms wide. But she meant it. "After all you did just actually save a child's life," she added.

"What about Pirate? He got to her first."

Sunny kissed the still-wet dog. "Braveheart," she said and the dog gazed adoringly up at her, until the Chihuahua, fresh from sleeping on Mac's warm bed, hurled herself at him, bared teeth gleaming. Sunny caught her mid-leap.

"Little bastard," Mac said mildly. "Attacking the hero of the hour."

"Oh, just pour me some more champagne, will you," Sunny said, "and tell me what you think of our Paloma."

He got fresh chilled flutes from the refrigerator, filled them, and handed her one. "A toast to Paloma," he said, "who, I suspect, is in some kind of trouble."

"What? A little girl like that? In trouble?" Then Sunny remembered the look in Paloma's wide chestnut eyes. She recalled uneasily how some girls had looked like that, when she was at school. It was the look of an outsider, of someone who wasn't quite in touch with her life . . . a loner.

Mac said, "You realize she's Bibi Fortunata's daughter."

Sunny gaped at him, the glass halfway to her mouth. "No!" she said. Then she remembered Paloma's red hair, her freckles, her long delicate body. "*Oh my God,* of course she is," she said. "The long-lost Bibi."

"Who simply disappeared," Mac said. "Gone forever, I guess. Though how she could leave her child behind I don't know."

"I do," Sunny said. "Bibi was in such a mess, condemned as a killer by the media and the public, even though she never had a trial. How could she bring up a child? How could she be a normal mom, picking her up at school, going to all the school activities? Who would want to know Bibi's little girl? It's tragic, but I believe Bibi did the right thing."

Mac went and sat next to her on the garden swing with the striped awning he'd inherited when he bought the house, all those years ago. Arm around her, swinging gently back and forth, he looked out at the darkening band where the ocean met the night sky, and said, "I got the feeling she wanted to talk to me."

"So what are you going to do?"

He shrugged. "Nothing I can do. If Bibi wants to hide from the world and her family, that's up to her."

"Maybe you're wrong and Paloma was just starstruck," Sunny said, because after all Mac was by way of being a "star."

Still, Mac wondered what was up.

"I wonder why she lives—basically—in Barcelona?" he said, looking thoughtful.

Part Two

Chapter 4

Barcelona

There's a tall stone house, tucked away from all the traffic and the noise, the cafés and the crowds at the end of an alley in the historic area of Barcelona known as Las Ramblas, a kaleidoscope of narrow streets crammed with shops and churches, bars and clubs and small hotels.

The house has a high shabby wall and a pair of iron gates, painted blue. An old man holds guard over these gates, sitting day by day in his small stone guardhouse, a bright blue beret over his white hair. The beret matches his eyes, blue and still young, though the rest of him is falling apart. A dog sits beside him. A sleek little black-and-white dog, a would-be Jack Russell but with Spanish ancestors.

The old man speaks only Catalan, the language of Catalonia, which is where Barcelona is located, and if you attempt to talk to him through the gates wanting to know if this is a museum and can you see round, you will be given a growl by the dog and a glare from the old man and told the Catalan equivalent of fuck off.

The now neglected courtyard once bloomed with carefully tended garden flowers, as well as heavy-scented jasmine and bougainvillea and hibiscus, because Barcelona is on the Mediterranean and enjoys that special climate, hot in summer but never too cold in winter, to need more than an overcoat when the north wind whips in. Now the garden is overgrown and wild.

Today is different though. The old man is on the alert, his eyes watchful. For today the gates of the Ravel family townhouse are to be opened again. The Matriarch is expected. The last time those gates were opened were for her husband's funeral, ten years ago.

The Ravel name has been known for more than two centuries for the fine sherries they produce in the fertile, chalky land of the Jerez region, but are also known now for the vineyards and bodega in Penedès, south of Barcelona, where the Marqués de Ravel red wine is made, a wine that is rapidly climbing its way to become one of the most popular Spain produces; less weighty than a Shiraz, less tannic than a Chianti, softer than a Californian Cabernet. Its popularity also lies in its price point: not too high, not too low.

The pricing was the decision taken by Doña Lorenza de Ravel, the widow and grand Matriarch of the Ravel family. What the Marquesa de Ravel says goes—and her family, with their inheritance in mind, does her bidding uncomplainingly. Or at least they do not complain in front of her. Not too loudly anyhow. Only one of her four stepchildren has ever disobeyed and that was Bibi and she was a rebel right from the day she was born, and, possibly, too, until the day she died.

Today, the grand townhouse has been cleaned, dusted, aired. Doña Lorenza has summoned a family meeting. She intends to sort out the past. Finally.

The white-haired old man pushes back the iron gates, removes his beret, bows his head respectfully as the black BMW X5 swings into the short driveway and parks in a sputter of gravel. The driver's door opens and a pair of long legs emerges, feet encased in red python four-inch-heeled Jimmy Choo heels, followed by their owner. Very tall, curvy, rampaging black hair, fuchsia lipstick on her wide mouth, black eyes that take in everything in one wide comprehensive glance. No silver-haired grande dame this. Forty-one-year-old Lorenza de Ravel, the Matriarch, is *hot*.

Lorenza was the third wife of Juan Pedro de Ravel. She'd married him eighteen years ago when she was only twenty-three and Juan Pedro was sixty-five. Widowed for ten years, she is the main inheritor of his fortune and his lands, his vineyards, his bodega, and his famous sherry business. The Ravel name is known worldwide, but it was Lorenza who turned some of those inherited vineyards into wine-producing, Lorenza who oversees the business; she who made the decision to go for the popular market instead of taking on the small and very competitive upper-crust wineries; she who decided the quality and the price point that have made it a success.

Lorenza slams the car door shut and stands for a moment, taking in the old house where she had come as a young bride, far from blushing and virginal but with a handsome silver-haired husband who adored her and was rich enough to satisfy all her whims. She is beautiful now, but then she had been truly lovely, a softer, rounder, thrillingly sexy young woman who enjoyed nothing more than making love to her husband, or him making love to her, or them making love. Whichever way they did it she loved it. Right up until the day he died, not in her bed, thank God, though he was—also thank God—in her arms, and she had been able to say goodbye to him.

He had died, right here, in this house, on a sunny autumn evening with the long library windows still open to catch the breeze and Magre, who was Juan Pedro's beloved old black cat, curled on his knee. The cat was named Magre—"skinny"—as a joke because you never saw a cat as fat as this one. Juan Pedro had said he felt a chill and pulled a sweater over his shoulders. Sitting in her big yellow wing chair opposite, Lorenza had glanced up from the glass of wine—the new vintage they were tasting—and, surprised, thought her husband suddenly looked his age.

Juan Pedro smiled at her. He lifted the cat and put it tenderly onto the sofa next to him. "Come here, my *guapa* Lorenzita," he said, holding out his hand to her. She liked it when he called her *guapa,* "pretty one"; it made her feel like a teenager. She went and took his hand and he pulled her onto his knee. She put her arms around him, leaning back a little, smiling into his eyes. *"Guapa,"* he whispered again, and then he exhaled deeply and all the life went from his brown eyes, leaving them pale as beach pebbles.

Lorenza did not scream, nor did she call for help. She knew it was too late. Instead she held him close to her warm body, loving him for loving her and hating him for leaving her.

Everyone thought Lorenza Machado had married Juan Pedro de Ravel for his money and his prestigious name. The truth was Lorenza had married him because she had fallen madly in love. He was only the second man she had loved in her entire life.

Holding him, she'd wept silent tears until Magre's piteous yowl brought her back to her senses. The cat's steady golden gaze held hers. Juan Pedro's cat knew what had happened. Cats always understood those things. It was as though Magre was saying "We loved him together, now I am yours." And because of that Lorenza removed her arms from around her husband's neck, she pressed his eyelids over his blank eyes and kissed his mouth. Then she picked up Magre, who must have weighed all of seventeen pounds, and went to fetch help.

She left the de Ravel house in Las Ramblas the day of Juan Pedro's funeral, vowing never to return. How could she? Without him? It was their place and now it was ended.

Of course the entire family had shown up for the funeral, not one of whom believed Lorenza had married Juan Pedro for anything other than his money. "Well, now she's got it," they muttered to one another in the crypt of the great temple of Sagrada Familia, Gaudí's architectural gift to the city of Barcelona and still unfinished all these years after Gaudí's accidental death in 1926. Genius did not stop you from getting run over by a tram, even if you were one of the great architects of the world, as well as one of the poorest. And one whom Juan Pedro de Ravel had revered, which was why his funeral service was held there.

The ornate spires, the curlicues, the colorful mosaics, the sheer fantasy of the immense temple were in such contrast to the quiet, reserved husband Lorenza knew, she wondered why he'd stipulated that his funeral service should be held there. One of the reasons had to be because it was big enough to hold everyone and had a joyous feel to it, even if it was in the crypt and you were tripping over ongoing works and bags of cement. So many people had packed in, friends, relatives, business acquaintances, wine dealers, children, grandchildren, ex-mistresses (none since his marriage to Lorenza but they still cared because he had always taken care of them), workers from the estates and the vineyards. They came from around the world to say goodbye to him.

Lorenza had already said her private goodbye to her husband. She retreated to the oldest of the Marqués de Ravel vineyards in Penedès, southwest of Barcelona, and the ancient house that had begun as a small whitewashed stucco building, thick-walled, Spanish style, against the winter winds and with small windows that kept out the cold, but also kept out the summer's heat. When it was first built it was not a comfortable place, but the original had been added on to, growing over the years in a Dutch Colonial style that would have been more at home in South Africa's vineyards than in Spain.

The white house was beautiful, special, with its blue gables and dormers and the long row of tall windows on the ground floor that let in all the light and sunshine. The view was lovely even in winter, when the vines curved in spiky leafless rows up the hills and over and down, into infinity it seemed. Then came the spring, and leaves of such a tender green it touched the heart because it meant life was coming back to the Ravel land. Of course with summer the place became alive with itinerant workers, and come the late September–early October harvest, depending on the weather and the exact ripeness of the grapes, white for the grassy-scented Sauvignon Blanc, and Tempranillos and Cabernets, there seemed to be more people at the vineyard than in Las Ramblas.

The stone-faced bodega would smell of crushed grapes and also of the food set up outside on planked wooden tables, good hearty food for the workers, with wine to drink after a long day's picking, and maybe a de Ravel sherry or two afterward to wash down the good bread, baked that morning by Lorenza's own cook who had been with the family longer than Lorenza herself.

Until Juan Pedro died, Lorenza had never lived at the bodega, only visited. Now it was her home, her domaine, her life. It was also the symbol of her success.

Lorenza had become a force to be reckoned with and that was why, today, after reading the shocking letter from the American lawyer over and over again, she had called a family meeting. It had finally become necessary to sort out the past and secure the de Ravel future.

Chapter 5

Lorenza's housekeeper's name was Buena. In fact, her real name was Maria Carmen but her response to any question or comment was always *buena*—"good"—and so she had become known by that. Buena had been sent on to Barcelona a week earlier to open up the house. She'd called in plumbers and electricians to make sure everything worked, and had employed a team of cleaners and window-washers and repairmen, because after all, nothing had been touched in ten years. The "wake" Lorenza had held after her husband's funeral, for family and the closest friends, had left her big *salón* in an after-the-party mess, which Buena had cleaned up then, but now she saw to it that everything was put back clean and tidy. Only the master bedroom and the small library that opened onto the courtyard garden, the room where Juan Pedro died, though they had been cleaned too, were exactly as he had left them. On Lorenza's orders, nothing had been moved.

The front door was a single slab of solid chestnut, twelve feet tall, carved from a tree on the Ravel estate, felled in a freak hurricane a century ago. The door knocker was solid brass in the shape of the Hand of Fatima. The fingers were worn smooth with use and had once again been polished to a dull gleam.

Buena heard the car and ran to open the door, flinging it back so hard the knocker rat-tatted against the groove it had made in the wood. She pushed back the gray hair that somehow always straggled out of its bun, skewering it with a long hairgrip, adjusted the horn-rimmed glasses that always slid down her long nose, straightened the blue cotton housedress, worried that it pulled over her plump hips, and beaming with pleasure called out, "*Bienvenido, Señora.* Welcome home."

Standing next to the car, Lorenza saw her and laughed. "It wouldn't be the same without you here, Buena." She walked across the gravel, careful in her high red heels, took the single wide step in one stride, and flung her arms around her old friend.

"How many years has it been since we were first here?" she asked into the tangle of hairpins above Buena's left ear.

Buena said, "Must I remind you again that *I* was here first. I arrived the day before you, yourself, came. The bride."

Of course Lorenza didn't need to be reminded. Buena's had been the only welcoming face she'd encountered that day. The others—Juan Pedro's family, his children, had stared sullenly at her over their glasses of chilled Ravel Manzanilla sherry, then had kissed the air next to her cheek.

"You were so lovely, Señora," Buena said, stepping aside so Lorenza could enter. "All in white satin, with a long train embroidered with pearls and a white orchid in your hair."

"And Juan Pedro's gold ring on my finger. The family didn't like that then, Buena. And you know only too well, they don't like it today. To them I was always the interloper, stealing their mother's thunder, even her name. Of course, I understood. She died too young. But I was young too, and it was my wedding day and I was damned if I was going to knuckle under and wear a beige dress and a hat. I wanted Juan Pedro to see me as his bride."

Lorenza's dark eyes crinkled with laughter as she met Buena's. "After all, he had to see he was getting his money's worth, didn't he?"

She looked around her house. It had started life a couple of centuries ago as a tiny theater, dedicated to operetta, the only reminders of which were the two ornate little boxes curving out from the mezzanine, one each side of the wide marble staircase. Their red plush upholstery had faded to a silvery blush, entwined cupids blew golden trumpets across their stucco fronts, and pairs of narrow wooden doors, pale green and gilt, enclosed their privacy.

Naturally, there had been stories of a shadowy "diva," a ghostly lady in an elegant wide-brimmed hat and a gleam of diamonds. She was, so the story went, still waiting for the lover who never showed up.

"Then she should get herself up and out and get another lover," practical Lorenza snapped, when Juan Pedro first told her the tale. She had no time for ghosts. Of course she had never seen her. "That's because no 'other woman' would dare show her face in Lorenza's house," her husband had said, laughing. And that was probably true.

To the left was the *salón,* used only for formal parties, and later for Juan Pedro's memorial. His "wake" as Lorenza preferred to call it, because she liked the way the Irish gave a party to say goodbye to the dead instead of a somber meeting.

To the right was the formal dining room, painted on her orders, a glowing yellow that at night reflected the candlelight like sunshine. They had held dinner parties for twenty there, with her favorite old-fashioned Coquille St. Jacques—scallops on the half shell—for starters and chocolate/sherry soufflés for dessert, served with the local Catalonian white wine with its slight fizz known as Txakoli, as well as a good deep red from Rioja.

Looking round, Lorenza now said to Buena, "We built memories around that table."

"And you will again, Señora," Buena said firmly, following her as she walked down the hall to the library.

The door was open and Lorenza stood there, looking into her past, seeing herself and Juan Pedro, him on the sofa with the cat lolling against him, and she opposite, long legs tucked under, listening to Joni Mitchell singing about tearing down paradise and putting up parking lots, or else the soft Brazilian sambas of Bebel Gilberto, and sometimes Schubert's Unfinished Symphony played so loud her husband would cover his ears, groaning. She'd watch him reading the morning papers, catching up with the news, checking his messages on the laptop he hated because he was old enough to prefer things on paper that he could handle, and not messages winged at him through thin air.

He was still so good-looking; those fine wide cheekbones held his face firmly, his chin had only a hint of fullness—she would never call it "sag"—his deep-set eyes under the heavy brows, his sensual mouth that often she would get up just to kiss. In their year of courtship—seduction, she always called it, making him laugh—and their eight years of marriage, she had never tired of making love with her husband.

"You know why I look this good?" she would ask, curled up next to him in bed at night, or very often in the afternoons, because making love was what she said a Spanish siesta was really for. "It's because I'm a woman who gets fucked a lot." His snort of outraged laughter made her laugh too. "Well, what else can I call it?" she asked, licking his mouth that still tasted of her. "People can tell, you know. I have that kind of glow about me."

He sat up and looked at her. "That you do," he said solemnly. "I don't know if I can keep up with you."

"Don't worry, I'll help you," Lorenza remembered saying, making him laugh again.

"I always was a sexy bitch," she'd added, and Juan Pedro had put his hand over her mouth to stop her. "Don't tell me," he'd begged. "I don't want to know about the others."

So she had told him nothing about her past, other than her childhood on the Iberian island of Majorca, and of being sent to a strict convent school in Brussels at the age of thirteen, and then breaking all the rules in a glorious few years of newfound freedom at university, in Florida.

Now, alone, she walked into their library, their "special" place, and took her usual seat on the big pale yellow wing chair opposite Juan Pedro's sofa. She'd had the walls painted when she moved in, a pale azure, hand-rubbed to a smudgy softness. She'd always liked the way her yellow chair looked against them. The sofa, though, was amber linen, indented on the side where Juan Pedro always sat. The cashmere sweater he had thrown over his shoulders the night he died lay where she had left it across the back of the sofa, neutral color, soft, the sleeves neatly folded together.

"I wonder," Lorenza said softly, to herself, "I wonder if I can really ever come back here."

"Your room is ready, Señora," Buena said from the doorway. "And the children will be here soon. Better hurry. You know how impatient they always are."

Lorenza sighed. Didn't she just?

Chapter 6

Lorenza walked upstairs and into the large sun-filled bedroom she had shared with her husband. She stood for a moment, sniffing the air; she could swear she still smelled him, and if she closed her eyes she knew she would see him, lying on the bed waiting for her, the gray silk coverlet thrown back, naked but for his shorts and with a sheaf of papers in his hand because Juan Pedro never wasted a moment, he was always working.

Sighing, she gathered herself together. She put her handbag down on the ottoman at the foot of the bed, a habit that always annoyed her husband—he said it got in the way of his feet. He was very tall but even so, Lorenza told him that was just plain ridiculous. He simply liked everything to be put away in its rightful place and not scattered around "his" room. It's *our* room, she would remind him.

She went and stood by the window, arms folded over her chest, gazing down at the quiet courtyard, thinking about the past, and then about the future. About what was to come.

There was no love lost between Lorenza and Juan Pedro's children. They'd resented her from day one and they resented her even more when their father left her the controlling shares in the Ravel sherry business, along with the estates and the other vineyards and houses that went with it. Of course they had all been amply taken care of, earlier, with handsome trust funds as well as shares in the business, even though none of them had even the remotest interest in the family wineries. Things had changed, though, since Lorenza was in charge.

Expected today were Juan Pedro's only son, Antonio, and two of his daughters, Jassy and Floradelisa, all by his first wife, and all of whom stood to inherit from Lorenza, who had no children of her own. And then there was Bibi of course, the youngest, the daughter of his second wife, who died when she was born.

Turning from the window, she sat at the gilded Venetian satinwood vanity table that Juan Pedro had complained was out of place in this heavy-beamed Spanish room, with the hint of stone exposed through the pale creamy paint.

"The stone is to let reality in," Lorenza told him solemnly when she'd done it. "Just in case things go wrong and we have to return to that old Ravel stone cottage." Of course that had made him laugh; "There is no old stone cottage anymore," he'd said. "This is it. And it's all yours." And now it was.

She ran a comb through her mass of shoulder-length black hair, bemoaning the fact that it was totally uncontrollable. Always had been. It floated around her face in a movable dark cloud and God help her if she were ever caught in a wind because then it stood on end and she looked ready for takeoff. Her hair, she decided, was not her best feature, though others felt differently. And indeed it gave her somehow too-round face character, as did the widely set dark brown eyes, and the too-big mouth she colored again with Lancôme's fuchsia lipstick. Beauty was in the eye of the beholder, she thought, amused, and she had never seen herself as that.

She wasn't bad though, for forty-one, thinner than she had been at twenty, still bosomy, though now trimmer from hard work and the stress that also showed on her face. She turned away from the too-revealing mirror. The truth was anyone but the owner of that face would have called her lovely. A lovely woman, Doña Lorenza de Ravel. And a woman to be reckoned with.

She went and checked herself in the long mirror: plain black suit, skirt just to the knee, pearls at the neck. The grieving widow, she thought with a pang.

Nervous, she pulled at her three-strand pearl choker, suddenly feeling as if it were strangling her. Juan Pedro's beautiful gift had once upon a time belonged to a famous French aristocrat whose head had been chopped off, come the revolution and the guillotine, while those *tricoteuse* knitted away, screaming with delight. Lorenza had been relieved to hear they had not been on the poor woman's pretty neck at the time.

"There's no blood on these pearls," Juan Pedro told her, seeing her stricken look. "She was young, and, they say, quite lovely and I have no doubt she would smile to see you wearing them." Sometimes though, in moments of stress, like now, those pearls seemed to tighten up on Lorenza's neck.

Tires spun on the gravel. She went to look. It was Antonio, Juan Pedro's only son, his eldest child. In fact Antonio was almost exactly the same age as Lorenza, something that had certainly not pleased him when his father had introduced her as his new wife-to-be.

Of course, Antonio *would* be first to arrive. Lorenza would bet he couldn't wait to hear what was going on, hoping she was going to give it all up and hand over the reins to him. We'll see, she thought, as she walked down the stairs and took a seat on one of the two cream-brocade sofas fronting the empty marble fireplace, that instead of crackling logs held a haphazard display of flowers hastily flung together by Buena.

She did not get up when Antonio strode into the room, but she did smile and hold out her hand, while thinking that Antonio never simply "walked" into a room, he always "strode." He was tall and dark, not handsome but with his father's compelling eyes and beaky nose.

"Lorenza," he said, in the same hearty tones that made you understand he was very much a presence. "Good to see you," he added, not meaning it, as he bowed over her hand, then took a seat opposite.

"Good to see you too, Antonio," she said, not meaning it either. It had hurt once but no longer mattered, except that he was Juan Pedro's son and now ran the sherry business. Lorenza had handed him that job a year or two after she'd inherited the vineyards, after she had learned all she could about vines and grapes and terrain, and also made the decision to make wine as well as sherry. Antonio had been reluctant at first, though now he did a good job, even though he was a playboy who liked the good life and the clubs and cheated on his wife.

Antonio's home was, of necessity, in Jerez, in Andalusia, where sherry is produced, and where the Ravel family vineyards had existed for a couple of centuries. With easy access to the playgrounds of Marbella, and the Costa del Sol, where Antonio was a well-known figure, always with a pretty woman—who was definitely not his wife—the location suited him just fine. Anyway, he knew he was better off away from Barcelona and Lorenza's long reach and knowing eye.

"You look beautiful," he told her now, insincerely. "As always."

"Why, thank you, Antonio. I wish your father could have been here to hear you say that. He always believed you thought me vulgar and too sexy for my own good. Or his."

"Oh, God, Lorenza." Antonio rolled up his eyes and fiddled

with his Hermès tie, a pattern of tiny green turtles running on a pink background, a frivolous contrast to his impeccably cut dark blue pinstripe suit.

"I like your tie," Lorenza said, with a flash of mischief. "I've never figured out why men hate wearing ties when really it's the only pretty thing they're allowed. A touch of color, you know. Though," she added, eyeing him up and then down again, "somehow I've always envisioned a winemaker as a man of the earth. You know, in khakis or blue jeans, an old plaid shirt. A man comfortable with himself."

Antonio had been given his hardworking grandfather's name, plain and simple, but there was nothing plain and simple or hardworking about the grandson. He smoldered, silently now, thinking about his stepmother. He had never, ever, referred to Lorenza as his father's "wife," eliminating her any way he could from "the family" even though she now *owned* that family. Right now, Antonio felt like killing his stepmother but contented himself with a dark glare that, had Lorenza been looking, would have told her so. Before he could make a stinging reply the doorbell rang and Buena, who had been lurking behind it, quickly flung it open.

This time Lorenza got up to greet her guest. She had always liked Floradelisa, Juan Pedro's eldest daughter, and she believed the daughter liked her. At least she thought Floradelisa cared, and of all Juan Pedro's children she was the simplest and most "real."

She was plump, and as dark as Antonio, but with blue eyes and a face as pale as a ghost, which was the reason her father had named her Floradelisa. With her pale skin, he said she reminded him of a lily flower. A *fleur-de-lys* or a *Flora de lisa*. Now, though, hugging her, Lorenza worried that her pale stepdaughter never saw the light of day.

"Floradelisa," Lorenza said.

"Lorenzita," she said. And they both laughed at how silly it sounded.

"You're working too hard, I can tell," Lorenza said, knowing it was true. Floradelisa was a chef and owner of one of Barcelona's most avant-garde restaurants, where she was known for her outrageous menus with desserts of vaporized berries, re-formed into miniature works of art, served with a chocolate skin so fine and thin it crackled in the mouth; and fusion sauces that were mere froths of nitrogenated cream; and tiny exquisite lamb chops that were three mouthfuls of melting delight, as well as other unrecognizable delicacies that diners flocked to try—or at least to say they had been there and eaten the latest thing. Floradelisa did not serve her family's popular and inexpensive red wine at her restaurant, only the finest of Riojas, or Bordeaux, or Burgundies would do. Though of course the de Ravel sherries—the chilled Manzanilla and the rich Oloroso—were served as aperitifs, or to complement special dishes.

Her restaurant, Floradelisa's, was outrageously expensive, super-chic, and almost impossible to get into, and it ran its owner's life. Short, untidy, and frustrated, with no man in her life, Floradelisa's home a mess and her kitchen immaculate.

She trotted—at full speed, as usual—over to the sofa to kiss her brother, who made a halfhearted attempt to get up to greet her. She gave him a push back down. "Don't bother, I can see you're comfortable."

She plumped next to him and he eyed her, frowning.

"Couldn't you at least dress up just a little?" he asked.

Floradelisa looked down at her outfit. She was wearing her usual chef's white jacket, liberally stained with some kind of purple sauce, her hideous black-and-white-checked polyester chef's pants, and the usual work clogs.

"I came straight from the kitchen," she explained. "I have to get back there as soon as possible."

"Of course you do, Flora." Lorenza always called her Flora, finding she tripped over the longer name, though no one else ever did. "I was just telling Antonio I expect people who work to look like what they do, what they *are*. You know, a vintner, a chef . . ."

Flora smiled, amused, and Lorenza thought she really had the prettiest blue eyes, startling in her pale face, but now two spots of color burned her cheeks.

"You look hot, your cheeks are pink," she said as Buena came in bearing a tray with a silver coffeepot and the platinum-rimmed cups Lorenza hated. They had been a wedding present from someone, she couldn't remember who, and were too fancy for her taste. She guessed Buena had thought this was a "fancy" occasion; three of Juan Pedro's children under the same roof. With *her*.

"It's from slaving over a hot stove," Flora explained, stealing a long thin biscuit from the plate before Buena had time to hand them around. "And I'm starving."

"You don't look it," Antonio said, unkindly, taking in his plump sister once again. "You should lose some weight."

"Oh, shut up, Antonio. You have my job and try to lose weight. I'm always having to taste something . . . a bit here, a bit there. . . ."

"And a bit everywhere else." He refused coffee and slumped sulkily back against the sofa cushions.

"You look tired, Flora," Lorenza said. "I know you're at the market before dawn, and then you work all hours, God knows what time you get to bed. But I do think you should take time out to go for a walk, get your hair cut, and maybe a manicure every now and then. A girl should keep up with those things."

Flora burst out laughing "Oh, Lorenza, there are girls like me, and there are girls like you. I simply don't have the time. . . ."

"Nor do I," Lorenza said sharply. "We must *make* time, Flora."

"So what time is Jassy coming, anyway?" Antonio glanced impatiently at his watch, his father's old Patek Philippe, gold on a thin alligator strap.

Lorenza thought the watch probably qualified as an antique by now and was probably worth a small fortune. She almost wished she hadn't given it to Antonio, but it had belonged to his father, who had worn it every day, and it was only right it should belong to his son. Pompous prick though he was.

"Let's hope Jassy'll be here soon," she said. "I'd like to get this over with."

"*What* 'over with'?" Flora took another biscuit. Lorenza moved the plate away from her, though why she bothered she did not know, after all Flora was a chef and consumed food all day long.

"You'll see," she said, just as the door opened and Jassy breezed in.

Chapter 7

Jazmin de Ravel, known as Jassy, brimmed with energy and a sheer pleasure in life that drew everyone who ever met her, into her orbit. She was a force field, Lorenza thought, a magnet; always on the move, always seeking someplace new, some*one* new. Tall, with the wide shoulders of an athlete—she had been a champion swimmer at school—narrow hipped with racehorse legs, a rounded behind set like twin small melons on her slinky frame, with breasts that almost matched, and, in the towering heels she always wore, Jassy was a cross between *Playboy* and an haute couture model.

Today, her blond hair swung smoothly over her shoulders and down her back, a river of gold. Other days she wore it softly curled, framing her face in twists and strands, sweet as an angel. And sometimes she piled it up on top and put on her pointed horn-rimmed glasses—she was terribly shortsighted—looking like a fifties vixen secretary, the kind always out to get the boss.

Jassy had been baptized Concepçion Eldorado Mercedes Jazmin, which, when added to de Ravel, was quite a mouthful. The "Eldorado" was because she had been conceived after an epic "battle" between her parents, which one of them had obviously scaled the heights and won, hence the baby daughter. Mercedes was a traditional Spanish family name, though most of the world thought it was a German car. In fact Mr. Benz had named his car for his Spanish wife whose name was Mercedes—therefore Mercedes Benz forevermore. So, from Concepçion, Eldorado, Mercedes, and Jazmin, Jassy had chosen to be "Jassy," though she had long ago decided she could be anybody she darn well pleased; she could do anything she wanted; go anywhere in the world she liked. She had the money, the looks, and the capacity for making friends and having a good time.

"Hi," she beamed now, taking in her brother and sister and Lorenza in one quick shortsighted glance.

"You should wear your glasses," Lorenza said. "And you're late, Jassy."

"Sorry." Her myopic blue eyes met Lorenza's. "Allergies, I couldn't get the contacts in today and I couldn't find my glasses, it was too late to look for them. They're probably under a sofa cushion somewhere."

Sure they are, Lorenza thought, accepting Jassy's kiss, breathing in her scent. Jassy was a Dior Poison kind of woman. Exactly *whose* sofa? she wondered.

"You look lovely," Jassy said, taking in her stepmother, head to toe. "I always loved those pearls. Isn't it time to get out of the black though? After all, it's been . . . well, how long has it been exactly?" she asked, walking round the coffee table to kiss Antonio and Floradelisa, and managing to knock over a cup of coffee with her voluminous white voile skirt. "Ooops, look what I've done now," she said with a grin. "Never could take me anywhere."

"It's being without those glasses," Antonio said. "You'll kill yourself one day, walk under a bus, or fall off the pier or something."

"Oh, there'll always be somebody there to save me." Jassy was nothing if not confident. "Hi, Floradelisa, how's business?"

"Hot," her sister replied.

Jassy winked at her, and laughed. "Oh, you mean in the *kitchen*! Come on, Floradelisa, it's time you hooked up with a guy, some young chef as hot as you and your kitchen."

Floradelisa blushed, uncomfortable. "I don't have the time."

Lorenza said, "Jassy, I thought you were bringing Paloma with you."

"She's in the kitchen, Buena's feeding her cookies, I suppose. She'll spoil her to death."

"Well, *somebody* should take care of her," Lorenza said briskly. She was still not quite sure how it had worked out that Bibi's daughter lived with Jassy, though in fact it was Lorenza's own fault because it was she who had asked Jassy to fly to Los Angeles and bring Paloma "home" to Spain, while Bibi was under suspicion of the murders.

When they'd got back Jassy told her how Paloma had cried when she kissed her mother goodbye, such loud tearing sobs it had almost broken Jassy's own heart.

Jassy still remembered that journey vividly. She'd torn Paloma away from her mother, driven her to the airport in a rented bright blue Porsche followed by a squadron of motorcycle paparazzi that she'd dodged like an expert, simply dumping the car outside Arrivals and calling the rental company to come and pick it up.

She'd dragged the reluctant seven-year-old into Starbucks, bought her a chocolate frappucino and a giant chocolate-chip cookie, taken her into the store and stocked her up with teen magazines and candy, bought her a gray sweatshirt that said FLY *L.A.* in pink fluorescent script on the front, tied the laces on her red Converse high-tops for her, held the frappucino and the rest of the stuff while Paloma went to the bathroom, then fled into the Admirals Club where she ordered a large vodka martini and tried to take her mind off her niece's sobbing, as Paloma gulped down the frothy iced drink.

"Listen, *chiquita*," Jassy had said finally, when she could bear it no longer. "I'm your aunt. I'm going to be taking care of you until your mother gets back."

Paloma's soulful, red-rimmed eyes, shiny as autumn chestnuts, sought hers. "Come back from *where?*" she'd asked. "*This* is home."

For once Jassy had been lost for words. What could you say to a child whose mother might well be going to jail for murder?

"Well, anyway, you're going to live with me until Bibi gets back," she'd said finally. "And that's that. So, let me mop up your tears, and I'll tell you all the fun things we're going to do together. You're going to love living with me, Paloma, we'll travel the world, you'll go to all the parties, you'll know *everybody.*"

"What about school?"

"I'll get you a tutor . . . a governess, she'll teach you to speak Spanish properly."

"I already speak it a little," Paloma said. "Mom never does, but our Mexican housekeeper always speaks to me in Spanish."

"Then all we have to do is polish it up a bit." Jassy beamed her wonderful smile, drawing little devastated Paloma into her magic circle. "Don't worry, I'll look after you," she'd said, hugging her.

And Paloma, breathing in Dior's Poison, thought she might quite like that.

Later, Jassy regretted promising to take Paloma under her carefree wing, but despite Lorenza insisting Paloma go to live with her at the de Ravel bodega, nothing could change Paloma's mind.

"I want to live with Aunt Jassy," she'd said firmly.

So that's where Paloma had lived for the past two years, ever since she'd left her mom, frightened. Even though then-seven-year-old Paloma had not understood why she was frightened—at the big Hollywood Hills house, with the photographers parked outside the gates so Paloma couldn't go to school, where anyhow the kids all talked behind her back and the teachers frowned at her.

But that final image of her mother had never left Paloma, or Jassy. Bibi had looked so small and alone and Paloma felt as though somehow their roles had been reversed; somehow she had become the mother and Bibi the child. It haunted her days and her dreams, even while she cruised the Mediterranean on millionaires' grand yachts with Jassy, and attended parties with rock stars in Bodrum, Turkey, and summered on South of France beaches, or traveled to L.A., or New York. She went with Jassy to buy clothes in Paris and London, and flew wherever and whenever Jassy wanted. Paloma always tagged along. Nobody even asked anymore what's that kid doing here? They just accepted her as part of Jassy's life, and some even suspected she was Jassy's own child by a married lover.

But Jassy never minded what anybody said. And that's why Lorenza could never put Jassy down as a totally superficial spoiled beauty, sensual, wicked, and at thirty-seven still playing around in the resorts of the world. Paloma lived an extraordinary life in the grown-up whirl of social activity that fueled her aunt's life. Lorenza knew it was not suitable and it certainly was not right, but without removing the child and breaking her heart a second time, there was nothing she could do about it.

Chapter 8

Paloma had followed Jassy into the big stone house in Las Ramblas and suddenly realized her boots squelched. It sounded extra loud in that big empty hall, kind of echoing to the rafters and those funny theater boxes that were plastered with small cupids. Or were they cherubs? Or possibly little fat gold angels, because she saw now they had wings. Small and not too fluffy, but definitely wings. Plus they had pink mouths pursed in what looked suspiciously like kisses. *Angels blowing kisses?* What kind of naughty place was this anyway? And this was her *grandparents'* house.

It was the first time Paloma had been inside the Barcelona mansion. Of course she'd passed it many times quickly on her way to some massage appointment in Las Ramblas with Jassy, where Paloma would have to wait patiently, playing games on her iPhone, or submitting to reflexology until her feet ached from the pressure. Paloma was definitely not keen on massage, but she was concerned about her boots.

She was just glad they hadn't floated off her feet and been lost in the Pacific. They were all she had of her mother. That, and the narrow gold charm bracelet she always wore, despite convent school rules against the wearing of jewelry. One of the few times she actually went to the school in Paris, she wore it tucked up under her shirt sleeve, or else in summer when short sleeves were the rule, attached to a thin gold chain round her neck, when everybody assumed it was simply a gold cross, the same as almost everyone wore. She disguised the telltale bump carefully, with the school tie, or a scarf, or else tying her sweater sleeves around her neck. Nobody was going to part Paloma from that bracelet, or from those boots. She would run away from school first, run like her mother had. Run away and no one would ever see her again, never know where she was. She just wished she were older than nine. Twelve would be good. You could do so much more, get away with more when you were twelve.

Jassy had disappeared into the *salón* and Paloma wondered, with a pang of loneliness, whether anyone would even miss her if she simply left now. Her aunt was always so frantically busy with her own grown-up business and friends; always on the move, though she was really good about including Paloma in everything. But Paloma was sensitive to Jassy's moods; she understood there were times when Jassy would rather be on her own. In fact, just last year, Jassy had left her for *two whole weeks,* at the Ritz Hotel in Paris.

Paloma was eight then, and Jassy had simply told her to amuse herself while she went to visit a sick friend in the South of France.

"Call room service for anything you want," she'd said airily, hugging her a quick goodbye. "You understand this is urgent, and anyhow I know you'll be perfectly okay on your own. It's just a couple of days, after all."

Paloma had guessed she was going off for a "romance" with her latest passion. Johnny, his name was, and she'd had no choice but to get on with being alone. At first, it had definitely been scary.

She'd thought about calling Lorenza, but that would have been telling on Jassy and Paloma would never do that. She *loved* Jassy. Jassy had saved her when she was scared out of her wits with her mother going crazy, locked up in that awful house in Hollywood that used to be home. Her lovely home, with her lovely mom, and her lovely life. Just like normal people. Except of course Mom was a star but that didn't alter their home lives.

So she'd stayed on alone in the big suite in the Ritz, ordering up room service, mostly the grilled ham and cheese sandwiches the French called Croque Monsieur, and spaghetti, and lots of ice cream. She'd even ordered a bottle of champagne because she liked the grown-up way it sounded. She told room service her aunt was throwing a little party. Of course she hadn't drunk it; she'd tried that before, sipping from untended party glasses, and didn't really care for the taste. She went for lonely walks all over Paris, and she thought a lot about her mother. Remembering. Waiting for the day she would come back.

Loneliness, Paloma had decided then, was a sad thing. She had never been lonely when Bibi was around.

Bibi was the best mom. She'd cooked Spanish empanadas and churros, and American mac-and-cheese, or sent out for Mulberry pizza or sushi. They would eat together in front of the enormous TV with their bare feet propped on the big tufted black leather ottoman, swigging back Diet Cokes and giggling at SpongeBob SquarePants or the latest Disney or animation feature. Later, her mom would make sure Paloma showered and she always helped her wash her hair that was definitely not like Bibi's. It was lighter, carrot-color, and Paloma thought hideous, and besides it was *wildly* curly, which was one of the reasons she had cut it all off.

Bibi would drag the comb through her damp hair, trying not to pull, but there were lots of *ow*s and *ouch*es. Then, both in their pajamas now, they would sip herb tea—chamomile because Bibi said it made you sleep better. Then it was teeth brushing, and if she had school the next day, Bibi made sure Paloma had her schoolbag packed. If not, she would tell her she could lie in luxuriously until she absolutely wanted to get up, and when she did, if Bibi was not working, they would breakfast together and maybe play tennis. Paloma wasn't very good at tennis, "clumsy with the racquet" her mom said; or they'd swim, or go to the beach, or horse ride out at Malibu, though Paloma wasn't keen on that either. Sometimes, they would shop, but Bibi always got recognized and caused too much of a commotion with the paparazzi, and it wasn't fun. So instead the stores sent things over for her to choose from, brought by very smart young women who were even skinnier than Paloma—and *she* was a skinny kid. In fact those girls were so skinny Paloma sometimes wondered if they were really her own age and just playing dress-up.

In the evenings, Bibi often had things to do and Paloma would have friends for a sleepover, or she would go stay with them. Maybe they would go bowling, or dance a bit to some wild punky music they liked, bouncing up and down and throwing their heads from side to side, arms flailing, legs like pogo sticks, but *they* still called it dancing. Or sometimes Bibi would take her out to supper, at Geoffrey's on the ocean at Malibu, where you could hear the waves whisper and the wind held moisture that collected in tiny crystal drops on the strands of her long red hair, and the maître d' and the waiters all made a fuss of her. Being Bibi's daughter was fun sometimes, but sometimes it was a pain, when the public clamored for autographs that of course Bibi always gave, though never at dinner. *That* was not allowed.

Paloma and Bibi were close as two sisters, except, of course, Bibi was always "mom." It was Bibi who patched up Paloma's scraped knees, Bibi who found the Band-Aids, got her tonsils removed, got her shots on time, took her to the dentist. Bibi was a hands-on mom, except when she had to be on tour or making a movie or something, and then the Mexican housekeeper took over, as well as all the other "satellites" who were always in the house; the entourage, the assistants, the secretary, the PR; the personal trainer, the musicians, the staff, the gardeners, the pool guys, the tennis pro. Life in the Hollywood Hills was one long nonstop event. Until it all came to an abrupt end.

And that's why the boots were so important. Black leather, soft and supple as silk, they reached to just above Paloma's ankles, hitting just at that space between where ankle stopped and calf began. They laced loosely up the front with a tongue that always scrunched down a bit because Bibi had always left the laces dangling, which made Paloma worry she would trip over them. Bibi never had.

But, standing there, in that sunny front hallway of the Hollywood Hills house on that final morning when Jassy had come to collect her and take her away forever, Paloma heard her mother scream. She screamed and screamed—and kicked her legs. Those boots came right off and landed at Paloma's feet. She grabbed them, clutching them to her chest, wailing, as Jassy tugged her out the door. Jassy shoved her into the passenger seat of the bright blue Porsche and slammed the door. She ran round to the driver's side, hitched a seat belt first over Paloma, then herself, gunned the already idling engine and took off, out through the electronic gates that barely had time to open, past the mob of faces and cameras pointed at them, winding too fast down the hill, heading for the 405 freeway and, though Paloma had not realized it at the time, for LAX and a flight—with a change of planes in Dallas—that ended up in Barcelona. Where Paloma had never been before.

And that's why the boots were so precious. Paloma had de-spaired of them ever coming back to life, that Malibu evening a few weeks ago when lovely Sunny Alvarez had pried them off her feet and tipped them upside down and the seawater had splashed out like a mini-fountain. The boots were still wet when she got back to Spain, and she put them on the terrace in the sun, at the Marqués de Ravel bodega in Catalonia, where they had gone to stay with Lorenza.

In fact it was the second time those boots had gotten a good soaking. The first was when Paloma was in the South of France with Jassy and she fell into the swimming pool, still wearing them. She put them out to dry on her hotel room balcony but by the time they had, they looked shrunken and withered, as though they had died or something. That was when she had a brainwave.

She went to Jassy's room and took her big pot of Crème de la Mer. She dug her fingers into its rich depths and smothered the boots with it. She rubbed the cream in tenderly, the way she'd seen Jassy do with her face. Then she polished the boots with an old T-shirt, spitting on them and polishing some more because that's what she'd heard soldiers did. She rubbed in more cream, until the pot was almost empty and the boots had regained some of their suppleness. Unfortunately they hadn't really shrunk and Paloma still had to tuck socks into the toes, but she wore them whenever she could, despite Jassy and Lorenza's protests. They thought they made her legs look even skinnier. She thought maybe she looked a bit punk. Like a Hollywood chick. Hopefully.

And anyhow, how was she supposed to know that Crème de la Mer was only the most expensive face cream probably on the whole entire planet? When Jassy found out she shrieked *"shit"* then clapped a hand over her mouth because she never cursed in front of Paloma. Then she really told her off, but later she burst out laughing and it had become a whole big joke—one Paloma often heard Jassy repeat to her friends—about Paloma polishing her boots with Jassy's pricy Crème de la Mer. Everyone thought Paloma too funny for words. *Quaint little kid,* was how she heard someone describe her; *a bit odd,* another said; and *Are you sure, you know, like, she's all right?*

Paloma was outraged. It was like asking was she *nuts?* When all she was, was missing her mom and trying most of her time to figure out how to find her, and wondering if she would ever come back.

I mean, a girl was *entitled* to worry about her mother, who just happened to be the best mother in the world. And her mother was the reason Paloma had stalked Mac Reilly's Malibu beach house, trying to get up the courage to actually speak to him and ask him if he could help find her.

She had never met a detective before, only seen them on TV and in movies—but somehow she'd known Mac Reilly was the only one who could help because on his show he seemed like a real person, and she just knew he was totally, absolutely *honest.* Which unfortunately Paloma herself was not. Sometimes she fudged the truth because it sounded better, and anyhow the truth was not always fun, especially when other kids asked about Bibi, and all that Hollywood stuff.

"Ohh, she's just gone on a long trip," she would lie airily, while inside her stomach clenched into about sixty-five knots and her mouth went so dry it was hard even to speak.

And that's what happened when she finally met Mac Reilly and Sunny Alvarez, and almost drowned and that funky, darling, three-legged, one-eyed dog she fell instantly in love with, leapt into the Pacific Ocean to try to rescue her. And so did Mac

Reilly. And the words got stuck in her throat and she'd almost died all over again of shyness, and all she could manage to say was thank you, because she was so choked up with saving her long story about Bibi and about how she simply had to find her mother and could he help her or she really would go out of her mind. *Truly out of her mind this time*—you know out there in space somewhere. But she just could not get the words out.

Mac even asked her what was up, and she'd said, oh nothing. Now it was too late, and anyhow there was this big family meeting, here at the house in Las Ramblas she had never even seen before, and somehow she got the feeling it was going to be about her. Right now, she would like to be anywhere but here. She'd much rather be at the Ravel bodega with her friend Cherrypop, who, anyhow, she couldn't wait to see.

But then she spotted Buena, peeking her head out the kitchen door, smiling at her, and she left Jassy to it, and ran to see her old friend.

Chapter 9

Buena had a big welcoming smile and her gray hair was straggling out of its bun in the way that always sent Paloma's fingers itching to put it straight, and she'd run right to her.

"I'm off to talk to Buena," she'd called over her shoulder to Jassy, racing down the hall and into Buena's welcoming arms.

She'd settled on a high stool at the marble island with its stainless steel prep sink and a rack of copper pans floating somewhere over her head and with a tidy row of colorful bowls arranged down the center.

"Do you know why we all are here, Buena?" she asked. "Nobody ever comes here."

"Not since Don Juan Pedro passed on." Buena's face was solemn, remembering times past as she took milk from the refrigerator, poured some into a tall glass, and pushed it over to Paloma. "Your grandmother Lorenza couldn't bear to be here alone, when she had been so happy here with Juan Pedro."

She handed Paloma a little basket full of cookies. "*Polverones,*" she said, smiling. "Remember? The kind you like."

"Dust biscuits." The word *polvo* meant "dust" and when Paloma bit into the cookie it disintegrated and left a fine white sugary dust

all around her mouth. She laughed, blowing it away, making Buena
laugh too.

"Buena, did my mom like it here?" she asked, taking a second
bite and then demolishing the whole thing because there was no
neat way to eat this kind of cookie and it had already crumbled
in her hand.

"I only met her once or twice, Paloma, you already know that.
She lived all those years in Hollywood and only stopped by here
when she was on tour. That's when she would see her father."

"And Lorenza."

"And Lorenza."

"Did my mother like Lorenza?"

"They liked each other well enough. And for the Lord's sake,
Paloma, why did you go and cut off all that wonderful hair? Do
you want to look like a boy or something?"

"Nope." Paloma took a second cookie. "I just want to look
like me."

"Like yourself?"

The child drank the milk, looking at Buena over the top of
the glass. Buena noticed her nails were bitten.

"Just myself," she agreed. "That's all I am. Myself. Trouble is,
though . . . Buena, mostly I don't know *who* I am. And sometimes
I think I never will. Unless I can find my mother and then she'll
tell me. Won't she?"

Buena nodded. "Mothers always know these things. And I
hope so, Paloma, I surely hope so."

But the truth was Buena did not think so. She thought Paloma
would need to work out her life all on her own. That was just the
way life was. You had it in your grasp, all was well—then suddenly you no longer had it and everything went wrong.

Tears threatened as she looked at the scrawny child, with her cropped red hair sticking up in tufts like a Shetland pony's, still worrying about her mother as well as about what was going on in the *salón,* and why all the family was here, at the old Ravel house that no one ever came to anymore. Buena wondered too.

Chapter 10

In the salón, Jassy had thrown herself onto the sofa. Ignoring the coffee she had spilled, she fluffed her skirt over her long thighs and said brightly, "So? Why are we here? What's up?"

Lorenza took a napkin and mopped up the coffee. "I should have used your skirt instead," she said, irritated. "After all, that's what caused it."

Jassy shifted her long blond hair languidly over her shoulder and gave her a smile. "Go ahead," she invited.

Lorenza gave an exasperated sigh. Jassy had made her life difficult from day one.

Jassy sighed back. She had always been jealous of Lorenza, she'd hated her father's attention being taken away from her, and she was the first to threaten to sue when the will was read and it was discovered that Juan Pedro had left Lorenza everything. Well, not *exactly* everything. He'd also left his youngest daughter, Bibi, one-third of the valuable vineyards and the income to be held in trust for any children she might have. Now, Lorenza controlled that trust for Paloma.

Jassy refolded her skirt, glancing at her brother, who was sitting up straight now, arms crossed over his chest, head thrust aggressively forward. Antonio was, Jassy decided, quite a good-looking man; well, maybe not so much good-looking as striking. Commanding. Like her father. While poor Floradelisa, hunched tiredly on the edge of her seat, looked like the hired help, though Jassy would never have hired her. She was too untidy, scruffy, even. Her sister needed grooming lessons and even so she doubted she would ever catch a man. Good thing her restaurant was doing well, so well in fact that she was now famous. Floradelisa's had won all kinds of awards, though her food was not Jassy's style. Personally, she was a caviar and champagne woman. Add a salad and some chocolate and that could be her chosen last meal before execution. And speaking of execution, she wondered which one of them was going to get the ax today, because this meeting had the feeling of doom about it.

"So?" Antonio said this time. "Exactly *why* are we all here, Lorenza?"

"Well, first, I thought it would be nice for you to see the house reopened. I hoped it would bring back memories of your father."

"Of course it does." Antonio was impatient. "*And* of my mother," he added pointedly.

"Of course."

"I love this house." Floradelisa poured herself more coffee.

Of the three, Floradelisa seemed the most at ease. Leaning across the table she took another biscuit from the plate Lorenza had removed from in front of her earlier.

"One of my strongest childhood memories is of walking to school from here, out those blue iron gates, skipping down the street, stopping to buy churros on the corner . . ."

"Well, you *would* buy churros, wouldn't you," Jassy said nastily, eyeing her plump body up and down.

"Of course I would. So did most every other Spanish kid. That bit of deep-fried pastry dusted with powdered sugar, sometimes even dipped in chocolate, was the best thing I ever tasted. Until I grew up, that is, and learned to appreciate other things."

"How different we are," Jassy mocked. "You'd never know we had the same mother."

"Or father," Antonio added.

Lorenza had watched these verbal battles for years. Nothing ever changed, except that now, the fourth child, Bibi, was not here.

Bibi's mother was Juan Pedro's second wife. She had died giving birth, leaving Juan Pedro devastated, but then his new baby had unexpectedly taken over his life. He adored her from day one. She was a star from the minute she was born, he'd told everyone proudly, though the truth was she was a spoiled brat, indulged to the hilt because of her poor motherless state.

Bibi's baptismal name was Isabella Fortuna, but she had older siblings who were learning to speak English and they called her simply "the baby." Her first words were not "Mama" and "Papi," but "the baby"—or as she said it in her charming infant lisp, "the bibi." And from then on, she always spoke of herself in the third person—as in "The bibi wants churros," or "The bibi loves Papi," or "The bibi is crying." And so Bibi she became.

Lorenza took a sheaf of official-looking papers from a canvas supermarket bag (she was very eco-conscious), thinking how sad it was that Bibi's own daughter was left in that same motherless state. Of course Paloma had always been fatherless, since at first Bibi claimed she didn't remember who the man was. Didn't *remember*! Lorenza hadn't let her get away with that one, for Paloma's sake, and later Bibi took it back and said it was too personal to tell. It was her secret and one day maybe she would tell Paloma, but no one else.

Then, Paloma could make up her own mind about what to do. Meanwhile Bibi would be mother and father to her.

The Italian husband had certainly never acted like a father to her. Anyway, no one had ever liked Bruno Peretti. And that was what this was all about.

"Jassy," Lorenza said. "Please call Paloma in from the kitchen. She needs to be present at this meeting."

Jassy looked surprised, but she got up and went out and yelled, "Paloma. You're wanted."

Paloma slid from the high stool, hitched down her short skirt, retied her boot laces, smoothed her plain white T-shirt over her meager chest, patted her gold charm bracelet to make sure it was still there, then with a worried smile over her shoulder at Buena, walked reluctantly from the kitchen.

"Poor little thing," Buena murmured, watching her go. "When will she ever face the truth and realize she will never see her mother, that *wild* woman, again?"

She did notice, though, that on the back of Paloma's white T-shirt was written in large purple script, *You can go home again.*

Jassy had flung herself down again, this time in a chair away from Lorenza, who was now looking expectantly at her.

"The kid heard, she'll be here," Jassy said, just as Paloma appeared at the entrance, and stood, small and skinny, all big eyes and cropped head.

"Jesus!" Lorenza exclaimed, stunned. "Whatever did you do to her, Jassy?"

Jassy shrugged. "She did it herself. Cut it all off, then had a go with an electric razor."

"All that wonderful curly red hair," Floradelisa moaned, staring at her niece, who still stood in the doorway, as though ashamed to enter.

Instead, Lorenza walked over and took her into her arms.

"Sweetheart," she murmured, "I've missed you."

"I've missed you too," Paloma said. "I wish you could have come to Malibu with us."

"Perhaps next time."

There were no more comments from anyone about her hair, merely a groan from Antonio, who shifted his eyes away from her and gazed, exasperated, up at the ceiling. His family got on his nerves. Including his wife and his own two children.

Lorenza had to admit that Jassy was very good about Paloma, and very good about allowing her her individuality. And when Jassy remembered, she was truly affectionate, buying Paloma presents and expensive clothes she never wore because, like most kids her age, all she wanted were jeans and sneakers. *Red* Converse sneakers.

"Come, *guapa,* sit next to me." Lorenza took Paloma's hand and led her to the sofa. "You are nine years old now, old enough to participate in a family meeting. Especially," she added, "since this concerns you."

Paloma sagged onto the sofa, legs sticking straight out. She looked like Raggedy Ann with the stuffing taken out. She'd guessed this "talk" had to be about her mother and didn't want to hear it. She stared sullenly at her red sneakers.

Sighing, Lorenza looked at her stepfamily, gathered in the great shadowy *salón* where for two centuries the Ravels had gathered on memorable occasions. The pearls were threatening to choke her again and she tugged nervously at them. She hoped her plan would work. If it did not, it could mean the end of the Ravel empire.

"I am about to throw a bombshell into the works," she said finally. "And it's about Bibi."

Chapter 11

"*It's also about* your stepfather," Lorenza added and Paloma looked up at her, shocked. "Stepfather" was not a word she had ever expected to hear again.

It was typical of the child, Lorenza thought, that she did not ask "What about my awful stepfather?" She simply sat there, looking traumatized all over again, but Lorenza had seen the fear flicker in her eyes, and pitied her. This was not going to be easy but it must be done.

"I have here a copy of a letter I received from Bruno Peretti's attorneys in Los Angeles, plus copies of another letter sent by his legal representatives in Madrid." She handed copies to each of them. "I think you're going to be very surprised by what Peretti has to say."

Nervous, Paloma edged closer to her grandmother, and Lorenza reached out and patted her hand.

"Don't worry, *chiquita*," she whispered, while the others took the letters and began to read. "Everything will work out, I'll make sure of that."

Antonio read quickly, then threw the letters onto the table. He glared up at her. "*My God. Has the man gone crazy?*"

"He's out of his *mind*," Floradelisa said, looking worried.

Jassy was reading more slowly, and very carefully. She read it once, then read it again. Then she screamed, "*No, no, no, noooo . . .* he cannot take Paloma. I will *die* before I part with her."

Paloma jumped up and ran to her. "Jassy, Jassy, what do you mean? I'll never leave you," she said, throwing her arms around her. Paloma's face only came up to Jassy's hard rib cage, which was a bit painful when she squeezed but she didn't care. "Tell me I don't have to go."

"You are not going *anywhere*." Lorenza's voice was firm. "I will make sure of that. And, you seem to have missed the point, Jassy. It's not Paloma Peretti wants, it's the Ravel properties. He's only using Paloma as a way to get them, and get his hands on Bibi's money."

"Bibi's money," Antonio repeated. A pang of fear slipped through him, a mere sword flick, but it was there. Bibi had been legally married to Peretti. Could he have a real case against them?

Lorenza said, "Peretti claims that since Bibi has been missing and can be presumed—" She glanced at Paloma and could not finish that sentence but everyone got that she'd meant "presumed dead." "—he is entitled to Bibi's one-third share of the Ravel estate. He's claiming Bibi's third of all our vineyards, a third of all the monies that have accrued from that, as well as from the sherry, and all the other Ravel enterprises; the cork business, bottling, other products, the lands and buildings. He's even claiming ownership of this house, which he claims was left to Bibi. Which, in fact, is true. It was. And now it should be Paloma's."

She sighed as she looked at Paloma. She was only her step-grandmother but she had always considered herself Paloma's *real* grandmother.

"There's worse," she said. "In an attempt to bolster his case, Peretti wants custody of Paloma. It's true he is her legal stepfather, he adopted her right after he married Bibi, though after the . . ." She hesitated looking for the right word. "After the 'events' he abandoned Paloma. He wanted nothing to do with her.

"Now he claims to be concerned for her welfare, he's worried about her rattling around the world with Jassy, who he declares is 'unsuitable and immoral.' He wants to raise Paloma himself, take care of her financial interests. He says he doesn't trust the Ravels not to cheat her with no parent around to look out for her. And unfortunately, he is *legally* Paloma's parent. Of course he knows that under the trust, she will inherit her mother's share when she turns twenty-five. And that's what he's after."

"If he hasn't spent it all by then," Antonio said angrily. He knew Peretti's type only too well. When Bibi had introduced him he'd told her Peretti was a shit, told her to get real, and anyhow why did she need a guy like him. "You've only to look into the man's eyes to know where he's at," he'd told her. And he'd been right. Look at the way Peretti had dumped Bibi when the scandal hit; look what he was trying to do now.

"I have the replies from our own family lawyers." Lorenza handed round more papers. "They're not admitting it, but the problem is they think he has a viable claim against the estate, especially if he regains custody of Paloma."

"Oh, God." Jassy was crying now, fat tears slid down her face and splashed on the top of Paloma's head. Paloma still had her arms twined round her and her face buried somewhere in Jassy's middle. She covered her ears with her hands, she couldn't bear to hear any more about Peretti taking her away.

Jassy said, "What do we do now?"

"First we must prove his claim is worthless," Lorenza said. "And there's only one way to do that." She paused and looked at them. *"We have to find Bibi."*

Even though her hands were over her ears, somehow Paloma

heard that. She untwined herself so fast from Jassy, she almost fell on the floor. She wasn't crying but she was breathing fast and her hands trembled, sending the little gold charm bracelet she always wore, clinking. "You mean . . . *find my mom?*"

"That's exactly what I mean. And it won't be easy. We've already had detectives looking for her, but . . ." Lorenza clutched at her pearls again, wondering if that poor little Marie Antoinette courtier had felt like this when they came to take her away to the tumbril, because that was exactly the strangled way she felt now. "As you know, they found no trace."

Antonio said, "It's hard to believe, in this day and electronic age, a woman could disappear so completely. Unless . . ." Jassy threw him a warning glance and he paused in mid-sentence. The words "dead or alive" hung in the air.

"There's more," Lorenza said. "The Ravel wine business cannot continue the way it is. To keep up with the world market we must expand. To do that we need money. We need Bibi's permission, in writing, to sell off the less profitable part of the sherry vineyards. This will enable us to buy our neighboring vineyard in Penedès. I'm sure you understand that since the wine is where we are making our money, this is what we ought to do. The owners, the MacGuires, are willing to sell, and since their land is contiguous with ours, it would be a perfect acquisition. They have told no one else that their bodega is for sale yet, and out of respect to Juan Pedro, who was their friend for over fifty years, they've given me first option at a favorable price."

Shock, then anger, registered on Antonio's face. He'd had no idea Lorenza had meant to sell off some of his sherry vineyards, though of course he knew the Oloroso land at the mouth of the Guadalquivir River had not been producing the way it used to. He suspected Lorenza blamed him. That woman knew too much.

He wondered if she'd had detectives tailing him too, catching how little time he actually spent in Jerez, and how much more time in Marbella with an *amiga,* a "friend" who, in fact, he was quite fond of, not the least because she was tall and sun-tanned and had a sexy look always in her eyes when they rested on him. Which they had been doing frequently of late. *More* than of late; for over a year if the truth were known. He got the feeling now that Lorenza knew what was going on.

"The MacGuires' land is more clay than the Ravel," he reminded her, figuring attack was his best defense. "It's not been profitable for years—which I suppose is why they want to unload it on us. Pass it on at some inflated price giving us first chance, letting us think we're getting a bargain."

Lorenza threw him a pitying glance. The fool was ruining some of the best vineyards in Jerez and he dared to criticize *her* capability, *her* knowledge of what the land was like. The MacGuires were an old Irish family who had immigrated to Spain two centuries before. They had been the first to welcome Lorenza back to the Ravel bodega after Juan Pedro's death. They were honorable people. No way would they attempt to cheat her, nor she them.

"A fair price has been agreed," she said, ignoring Antonio and handing round another set of papers. "I intend to buy this vineyard. In order to do it we need money. And to get that we must find Bibi."

"What if Mom's dead?" Paloma's small voice cut suddenly through all their business talk.

There was a shocked silence, then Jassy said, "Don't talk like that, *chiquita,* it's not true."

"But how do we *know*?" Paloma persisted. "For *sure,* I mean?"

Lorenza said, "We don't know, but we must be prepared for the truth, whatever it is. It's time. Don't you agree, sweetheart?"

Paloma rubbed her burning cheeks. "Is it the best thing?" she asked, worried. "Best for my mom, I mean."

"It's the *only* thing, child," Lorenza said quietly. "The time has come when we must know the truth and whatever it is, we will deal with it."

Antonio folded his arms across his chest. "I want no part of it. And no part of selling off any of my vineyards either."

"I'll remind you those vineyards are *not* yours, Antonio. The major share belongs to me and to Bibi, in trust for Paloma. You were given and accepted your separate inheritance by your father when you were twenty-five. The vineyards, in which you then had no interest and no desire or will to run, were excluded for exactly that reason. You are only employed in Jerez in your capacity as manager of the estates. Floradelisa, you are in a similar position. You wanted to have your own life, to own your own restaurant. Your father saw to it that you were amply taken care of. As for you, Jassy, you took your share of stock and money and chose to live your life as you pleased. I'll remind you all of something else. That if it were not for me, by now there would be *no* Ravel family vineyards. *No* Marqués de Ravel wines. And certainly no more Ravel sherries. Without me, everything would have had to be sold off by now, exorbitant taxes would have had to be paid, and your lives would have gone on without any of this. Without this house and without the bodegas."

"And without *you*," Floradelisa said.

Lorenza inspected their cold faces closely. "That's true, too. I must admit, though, I've always wondered what all of you really knew about Bibi," she added shrewdly, and saw Floradelisa blush, while Antonio stared at the ceiling again, and Jassy hid her face in her hands.

"Listen carefully now," she added. "I'm prepared to make you a deal. I am ready to make over *half* of my own personal stock in the Marqués de Ravel wineries to be shared by the three of you. The condition is you have to find Bibi. Whichever one of you finds her will get the major share."

They were silent, but she knew she had their full attention.

"It's my belief one of you knows where Bibi is," she added. "Now, we'll find out."

Lorenza didn't know this, she just *thought* one of them did, and in order to find out she would put the pressure on.

No one said anything and Lorenza guessed why. No one wanted the scandal of the double murders to come back again. No one believed Bibi was innocent. To them Bibi was a lost soul and they did not want to see her again. Except, of course, for Paloma, whose love and belief in her mother had never failed, even though Bibi had abandoned her.

"And how do you propose we do that?" Antonio put the responsibility squarely back on Lorenza's shoulders. He certainly wasn't going to do anything about Bibi, because anyway now he intended to get his hands on his stepmother's shares just as soon as he could prove her incompetent. She had *told* them the business needed money, and it wasn't just because of his sherry. Lorenza might think she had her hands full with Peretti's claim but just wait till he got his claim in. *Then* she'd have something to keep her busy. In fact she might just be forced to look for another rich husband.

Lorenza said, "As I mentioned earlier, I employed detectives to look for her, with no result. Now, it's up to you three to figure out how to find her."

"I know someone who can find her," Paloma said.

They turned, astonished, to look at her.

"I met him in Malibu. I wanted to ask him to help me then

but I just couldn't. I thought he would laugh at me, but now I know he won't."

"And who exactly is that?" Jassy asked, wondering who Paloma could have met in Malibu that she didn't know.

"Why, Mac Reilly, of course. The famous TV private investigator."

Lorenza sat up straighter. She looked thoughtfully at Paloma. "You know," she said after a while, "the child might have a point."

Chapter 12

Lorenza patted Paloma's hand. "I believe we've probably all seen Mac Reilly's TV program," she said.

"What program?" Antonio only watched TV for horse racing or golf.

Floradelisa shrugged. "I don't have time for TV. I'm always at the restaurant."

"She's just too *busy* in that kitchen," Jassy said. She was getting a bit sick of Floradelisa's work ethic, and maybe a bit jealous of her success. "I've seen Mac Reilly's show," she said. "I know who he is, but what I want to know is how Paloma met him."

Paloma blushed to the roots of her red hair. "He lives near where we were staying, in Malibu. I'd pass his house all the time when I walked on the beach."

"And exactly *how* did you know it was Mac Reilly's house?" Jassy asked.

Paloma fingered the bunny charm her mother had placed on the gold bracelet on her first birthday. It was an Easter bunny because Paloma's birthday was around Easter time. One floppy ear was pinned down with a tiny diamond. Bibi had told her it looked as though he was begging for a treat and his treat was that now he knew he belonged to her. Paloma had made Bibi repeat that story a hundred times, she'd even named the bunny Treat. She rubbed him now, for good luck, knowing she was in trouble because she was going to have to tell the whole story, about almost drowning, before they heard it from Mac Reilly. Which they would if they talked to him.

She said, "I got caught in this big wave on Malibu beach. Mac's dog came running to help me and Mac swam out and got me out of the riptide." She looked apologetically at Jassy. "That's when I lost my iPhone. It got swept away. I'm sorry."

Horrified, Jassy thought of what might have happened if it were not for the unknown Mac Reilly. "*Oh my God,* Paloma, why didn't you tell me?"

"I was scared, I thought you'd be angry."

Jassy rolled her eyes, spilling coffee and tears again as she hastily got up and grabbed hold of Paloma. "*Chiquita, why* would I be *angry*?"

"Because you didn't know I went walking on the beach alone." Paloma took a deep breath. "And anyhow because I was really stalking Mac Reilly."

"*Stalking* him? Whatever for? We could have just invited him over for dinner."

"I wanted to talk to him alone."

"About Bibi." Lorenza understood, immediately.

"Has the kid gone crazy too, like her fuckin' crazy mother," Antonio said. Floradelisa gave him a hard nudge with her elbow that sent him gasping for air. "*Bitch,*" he whispered.

"No more bitch than the one you keep in Marbella," she whispered back.

Antonio rubbed his sore ribs. It seemed he had no secrets anymore. Everybody knew his business. Little Paloma was a dark horse though, stalking a TV detective. Like mother like daughter, he thought.

"Nobody's mad at you, Paloma," Lorenza said quietly.

"Did you tell him Bibi was your mother?" Floradelisa asked.

"I didn't have to. He knew."

"The resemblance is there," Lorenza said. "Anyone can see whose daughter she is."

Floradelisa glared at Antonio, she knew he was choking back the words "what a pity." Sometimes her brother was such a bastard she wondered how he could be Juan Pedro's son. Wouldn't that be funny, she thought, as the idea took hold in her mind. What if Antonio was really *not* Juan Pedro's son? What if their mother had had a little fling, or maybe more than one? After all there were three of them, and each one looked completely different. And none of them looked like either parent, apart from Antonio's beaky nose, but that was typically Spanish. You only had to look at the court portraits in the Prado Museum to see that. And just *perhaps* that was the reason their father had not left any of them the Ravel estates, and had been able, legally, to leave everything to Lorenza and Bibi.

Weary, Floradelisa pushed back her heavy dark hair; *she* was getting crazy now; *things* were getting crazy. "Are we all going nuts?" she asked, biting into another biscuit and daring Lorenza with her eyes to say something about it. "Are we seriously considering asking some American TV detective Paloma met on Malibu beach to find Bibi for us?"

Lorenza said firmly, "If you have any other suggestions I would be delighted to hear them. This concerns *all* of you, I'm asking for your help and so far all I'm getting is objections. Or silence."

"Speak now or forever hold your peace," Jassy quoted from

the marriage ceremony, glaring at her siblings. "At least Paloma tried to do something about it, and I think hiring Mac Reilly's a great idea, especially since it almost cost her her life."

"Saved, of course, by the *famous* Mr. Reilly." Antonio heaved himself up from the depths of the overstuffed sofa, looking round at them as he buttoned his jacket. "Of course Lorenza will do whatever she wants, as always. All I ask is that you let me and my lawyers know what that is, so I know exactly what action to take."

Lorenza thought Antonio was nothing if not predictable.

She said, "For God's sake sit down and listen for once, Antonio," in a tone Juan Pedro would have recognized as her "not to be messed with" voice; soft but touched with steel. Antonio must have recognized it too because he unbuttoned his jacket again and slumped abruptly back into the sofa. He put his head in his hands.

He said, "So go on then, tell us what we are all going to do to save the Ravel bodegas and find the poor, long-lost murderer, our dear half sister, Bibi."

Jassy leapt to her feet again. "How can you even *say* that in front of Paloma? How *dare* you?" Antonio lifted his head and gave her a smirk. Her hand shot out and she smacked him right across his smug face. "Bastard," she snarled.

"Oh, Jesus." Floradelisa turned away. She walked over to the window and pushed back the swagged silk taffeta curtain. "Oyster-colored like the winter sky" she remembered Lorenza telling her when they had bought the fabric together. Staring out at the empty courtyard in the house she recalled as being full of life when she was a child, she asked herself what was happening to this family? She thought longingly of her kitchen and her staff, waiting for her. Her busy, pressured restaurant seemed almost peaceful after this scene.

Paloma hid her face in Lorenza's shoulder, and Lorenza said, "There's no need for all this ugliness. I'll explain the situation again. First, Peretti is claiming Bibi's share of the Ravel estate. He plans on getting custody of Paloma to reinforce that claim. He's forcing us into a corner. We cannot allow Paloma to go to that man. Second, the Ravel business cannot continue unless we either find Bibi or find out what has happened to her, because we also need to sell off some of the sherry vineyards, less profitable thanks to you, Antonio, to expand by purchasing the MacGuire bodega.

"I've already told you, I'm prepared to hand over half of my own shares to you. Whichever one of you finds Bibi will get the major share, plus a bonus that I will not even talk about right now." Her dark glance collected them once again. "I said, I've always believed one of you knows where Bibi is. Now maybe we'll find out." She watched to see what reaction she got, but Antonio remained stone-faced, Floradelisa stared out the window, and Jassy seemed lost in her own thoughts.

Then Jassy said, "Paloma, did you ask Mac Reilly to find your mother?"

Paloma shook her head. Looking at her, Lorenza thought she seemed to have shriveled into herself, looking somehow even smaller, thinner, like a fallen angel in a Titian painting.

"I just couldn't, I really wanted to but I couldn't do it. I couldn't talk about Bibi. . . . I was . . ."

"You were too shy," Jassy finished her sentence.

"Too afraid, more likely," Lorenza said. "You wanted to know—but you didn't want to know." Paloma nodded. "In that case this meeting is closed." Lorenza put her papers back in the canvas bag. "I'll think about Mr. Reilly, consider what he might be able to do to help us. After all," she added thoughtfully, "he was probably in Hollywood when it happened."

"That's what he does," Jassy said. "Solves old Hollywood murders and brings criminals to justice."

"You must all think this over," Lorenza said. "Meanwhile, I insist Paloma comes to stay with me at the bodega."

"Oh, but . . ." Paloma stared longingly at Jassy.

"No 'buts' this time." Lorenza was in charge. "I don't want that stepfather and his lawyers claiming Jassy is an unfit guardian. You are coming to live with me. We'll leave right away." She looked at her stepchildren, wondering what they would do next. "You can think about this, then call me and give me your suggestions. If you have any."

"Not me." Antonio turned his back on her and strode out into the hall.

Watching him go Lorenza wondered when he would ever learn.

"I have to get back to my kitchen," Floradelisa said, and Lorenza submitted her cheeks to be kissed, first the left, then the right, then left again.

"Three for love," she said, hoping to catch an answering gleam of understanding in her stepdaughter's eyes.

"I'm not sure I've always believed that," Floradelisa said, moving away to kiss her sister, and then Paloma.

Lorenza wondered exactly why Flora was behaving so resentfully when all they were trying to do was find out what had happened to Paloma's mother and to save the Ravel family business. She wondered if Floradelisa—and Antonio—knew more than they were saying.

She watched Floradelisa pat Paloma's shoulder as she said, "When are you going to come and help out in my kitchen, *querida*? I'll teach you how to cook."

Paloma's plain face lit up. "Can I use that blowtorch thing you burn everything with?"

Floradelisa laughed. "You'll have to ask your grandmother's permission for that." She waved goodbye as she trotted, fast as always, out into the hall. They heard her talking for a second to Buena, then the sound of the great door slamming.

"So, Jassy? What about you?" Lorenza didn't really need to ask. She knew Jassy was a devoted, if sometimes neglectful aunt. Her heart was in the right place, even though she gave it away too quickly, and too often, to other people. *Men,* Lorenza meant. But that was simply the way Jassy was. In and out of love and in and out of bed.

"I'll do whatever needs to be done," Jassy promised and was rewarded by Paloma's first smile of the day.

Still, Lorenza wondered about Jassy too. One of the three siblings knew something, she just knew it. The question was, which one? And why wouldn't they tell?

"Come on, Paloma," she said, taking her stepgranddaughter's hand. It felt hot and she hoped the girl wasn't getting a fever, her face was quite flushed too.

"So what about Mac Reilly?" Paloma looked hopefully at her. Mac was her last hope.

"We'll have to think about that," Lorenza said.

Chapter 13

Malibu

Sunny Alvarez lay on her stomach on the old Wal-Mart chaise lounge on Mac's deck, listening to the roar and hiss of the waves while reading a travel brochure for Mauritius. Tesoro was curled very neatly in the small of her back, lifting gently up and down with her breathing, while keeping a slightly bulging eye out for Pirate's return. And Mac's, of course. It was Sunny's belief that Tesoro secretly adored Mac, though so far the dog had done little to prove it.

The fish soup Sunny had prepared earlier simmered gently on the stove and the aroma of the rouille she had made, a saffron and garlic red pepper mayonnaise that later she would spread on croutons and float on top of the soup, lingered temptingly.

Her menu was inspired by the two books she'd been reading in bed the previous night: Patricia Wells's *The Provence Cookbook* and Roger Verge's *Cuisine of the Sun*. So inspired, in fact, that that morning, she'd gotten on the Harley, buckled Tesoro into the saddlebag, and sped off to Santa Monica Seafood to pick up the necessary fish. Everything had to be fresh. Cleaned, scaled, whatever good fish they had, plus a few shrimp for the broth. Mussels would have been overkill, though she was tempted, but an authentic Mediterranean fish soup contained no mollusks.

She'd spent her afternoon chopping onions, tomatoes, and garlic, sautéing and seasoning. Saffron turned her soup yellow, then the tomatoes turned it coral, and now the whole was blending beautifully. Add a fresh baguette, a green salad dressed with a goodly slurp of light olive oil, Italian balsamic vinegar, from Modena of course and of course aged at least ten years, a twist of black pepper, and dinner was ready. A bottle of Mac's good Montrachet was chilling in the fridge and she couldn't wait for him to get home.

A glance at her watch told her he was late, though her rumbling stomach had already informed her of that. It wasn't unusual for Mac to be late, but what was unusual was that he had not called her.

It was seven o'clock and the sun was already sliding down into the ocean. Time for a sweater. Time to dab Mitsouko behind her ears, brush out her hair, add a touch of her "evening" lipstick, the slightly bluer red Chanel she always used at night. Time also to light a romantic candle or two, because she had a brilliant idea that she meant to discuss with Mac over the special dinner, about a vacation in Mauritius, an island in the crystalline Indian Ocean, where the food was an enticing mix of Chinese and Indian and Creole. There were beautiful hotels, where she felt sure they would serve those delicious holiday rum drinks complete with little umbrellas. She and Mac could swim and snorkel; they could sit in—or more probably *out of* the sun, eat divine food, sip divine drinks and—she was sure of this—make divine love. All she needed was for Mac to take a week off—and that was the difficult part. Still, he hadn't taken a break in months, and now she was working on it.

She sniffed the soup and hoped the Mitsouko would win out over the garlic. She was looking forward to a wonderful evening.

She dabbed on the lipstick—she never smoothed it on, you

couldn't do that with red, it looked gloppy—and took stock of herself in the bathroom mirror. Why, she asked herself, do women act all girly when they want something from their man—the perfume, the candles, the good dinner, the beautiful wine. Because we're clever, she answered herself smugly.

"Hey, babe." Mac's voice was followed by the slam of the front door.

"In the kitchen," she called, running back there because she knew it looked good when a man came home and found his woman busy at the stove. Grabbing a long spoon she began to stir the soup. She lifted the pan lid, burned her hand, let out a yell, and dropped it. Then the spoon fell into the soup and Tesoro jumped up onto the counter and knocked the baguette onto the floor and the bowl of precious hard-slaved-over rouille teetered on the very edge of the counter.

Mac grabbed it just in time, as Pirate came sauntering over. The dog sniffed the baguette, gave it a tentative lick, decided it wasn't for him and looked up at Sunny, hoping for steak.

"And I thought you were a big shot in the kitchen," Mac said, laughing. "A Miss Culinary-Know-it-All."

"In my *own* kitchen, I am, not in this apology for a cupboard you call by that name."

"It works for me. Anyhow, love-of-my-life, I picked up pizzas for dinner. Pepperoni for me, margarita for you. I know your taste."

He leaned in for a kiss but she pushed him back with a glare. All her carefully laid plans were going awry . . . the beautiful dinner, the wine, the candles, the white shirt buttoned just to "there," the pale cashmere sweater over her shoulders, the soft, full skirt, the bare gold sandals that brought to mind summer beaches. . . .

Mac looked at her, puzzled. "What's wrong with a good pizza? I thought we'd celebrate."

Uh-oh—he realized something must be up; they usually fell into each other's arms, even if they'd been apart only five minutes, but tonight Sunny hadn't even kissed him, yet. She had not even made a move toward him. In fact Sunny was standing there with her hands on her hips and a glare in her eyes that told him, somehow, he was in trouble.

"I hate pizza." She took the dish of rouille from him and put it back on the counter. She picked up the pan lid, rescued the drowned spoon from the soup, then ran her singed fingers under the cold tap. She realized suddenly what Mac had just said.

She turned to look at him. "*What* are we celebrating?"

He sniffed the air. "Something smells wonderful." He sniffed again. "Fishy."

Sunny put the lid back on the pan and leaned against the counter, hands on her hips. "Celebrate *what*?"

Mac took the chilled bottle of Montrachet out of the fridge. "How about a glass of wine, Sunny Alvarez?" He inspected the label. "Hmmm, very nice. Tell me, is this from my cellar? Or did you buy it specially?"

Sunny snorted. Mac's "cellar" consisted of three metal wine racks stashed in a cupboard next to the front door, though she had to admit it did contain some pretty good stuff. Of course her own "cellar," back in her stylish condo overlooking the boat-slips at Marina del Rey, had custom-built refrigerated wine storage. Well, it was a cupboard too, *really*, that kept the wine perfectly, though she had to admit Mac's choices were better than her own. She was a risk-taker where wine was concerned, buying names no one had ever heard of, though always from good areas, known for their excellent product.

"Actually, it is your wine," she admitted. "I didn't have time to shop at the wine merchant as well as cook this special, and very wonderful dinner."

Mac clapped a hand to his head, as it dawned on him. "Oh my God, I brought pizza and you've been . . ."

"Slaving over a hot stove . . ."

"All afternoon . . ."

"You didn't even call to ask did I fancy a pizza," Sunny complained. "And I can never get you on the phone when you're working . . . and well, it was all just meant to be a surprise." She sighed, melting, and said, "Oh, the hell with it, let's just have that glass of wine."

One step toward him took her from the stove to the kitchen door and into his arms. And then Mac did kiss her, and he did smell her perfume and not the garlic and the fishy soup.

He kissed her some more, hands flat on her back against her ribs, pressing her to him. Her softness, her scent, her amber eyes, her golden skin made her the sexiest woman in the world.

The kiss lasted a long time. It made Sunny's knees tremble. In the back of her mind, though, she was wondering why Tesoro wasn't snapping at Mac's ankles, or any other part of him her jealous little dog could reach.

She leaned back, happy again. Laughter lurked in her eyes. "Pour that wine, baby," she murmured. "I vote we have it in bed."

For a regretful second Mac thought about the pepperoni pizza, still hot and spicy and perfect. Fortunately for him, he did not voice that thought and anyhow it only lasted a second. He had the Montrachet open in a flash and was pouring the wine into the glasses Sunny had taken from the cupboard when she remembered.

"Mac? Exactly *what* are we celebrating?"

"The show's going on hiatus. I've gotten two weeks off."

Her eyes rounded with surprise. Then she smiled. She kissed him again. Lightly this time, but on the lips. She lifted her glass to him.

"Perfect timing for our vacation," she said, thrilled.

And then the phone rang. Didn't it always?

Chapter 14

Stuck with a wineglass in each hand, Mac hesitated at the bedroom door. His cell phone was in his shorts pocket. He gave Sunny a "should I answer it" kind of look. She looked stonily back at him.

She did not offer to take the wineglasses so he could free his hand and answer. Instead, she walked past him into the bedroom, unbuttoning her white shirt as she went. She turned and gave him a look. He was still standing there. The phone was still ringing. He was still holding his very nice crystal glasses full of wine.

Eyes linked with his, Sunny slid the shirt off her shoulders. She unhooked the floaty white skirt and let it slide onto the wood plank floor that sloped toward the window because it was warped by the damp sea air.

The phone kept on ringing.

"You need voicemail," she told him, naked but for her Hanky Panky turquoise lace boy-short underpants and the gold wedge heels.

"No contest," Mac said, looking at her. For once, he ignored the ringing phone, and walked over and handed her a glass.

"*This* is our *real* celebration," she murmured. The glasses tinkled pleasingly in a toast, which set Tesoro off barking. And for once Sunny scooped her up and dumped her in the hallway and shut the bedroom door.

It would be just the two of them tonight.

"*You know what?*" she said, a few hours later. "I have a great idea for your two-week hiatus."

Mac had his own idea for that hiatus. He lay back, watching lazily as she brushed her long dark hair, smoothing it with her hand after each stroke.

"It shines like a blackbird's wing," he said admiringly.

"That's an improvement on a black Lab still wet from the ocean."

"I should write a song about it." He sat up and took a sip of white wine. Even warm, it tasted good.

"Somebody already did. Paul McCartney, I believe. Anyway he wrote something about a blackbird, maybe not its wings. But I'm getting away from the point." She gave him that long slow under-the-lashes look that made Mac's toes curl all over again.

He reached out and pulled her to him. She fit so neatly into that space just beneath his shoulder, with her cheek pressed against his chest and her leg flung over him. He said, "Better tell me what's on your mind, Sonora Sky Alvarez"—he called her by her real name—"and what else we're celebrating tonight, besides my hiatus."

"That's just it. *I* don't have a hiatus yet. I have to be in Napa this weekend for the wine festival. I've worked my butt off getting publicity for Ewan Mallow and Mallow wines, and this weekend will be the culmination. He's getting an award, plus a great rating from Robert Parker for the latest vintage."

"Ah, that's right. I kinda forget you work too."

She punched him and Mac groaned.

"My PR company may be small, but it's very good. All my clients are doing well, thank you very much."

"All ten of them. Two of whom are failed actors."

"They are so *not* failed." Indignant, she pushed him away. "Marcus is in Paris making a movie with Charlotte Gainsbourg . . ."

"Marcus has a *small part* in a Charlotte Gainsbourg movie," Mac corrected her. He loved to bait her, she was so passionate about what she did, and in fact she was very good at it. Her company was doing well and she was making quite a name for herself.

He said, "What about the other actor?"

"Well . . ." Sunny shrugged. "Okay, so maybe he has failed, but now he's writing songs. You'll see, he'll become the next John Mayer."

"He might want to rethink that," Mac said, "publicity wise."

"That's because men need a woman like me, to keep them on the straight and narrow, publicity wise. Whatever any of my clients think, they know to button their lip and not say a word to the press without my approval."

"Quite the little tyrant, aren't you." He nuzzled the smooth hollow under her collarbone. "So, you're telling me I'll be all alone this weekend, is that it?"

"Unless you want to come with me?"

His eyes told her that, despite how much he loved her, he did not want to spend a weekend in Napa meeting and greeting wine folk and testing their product.

He said, "I'd rather go fishing."

A high-pitched snuffling wail came from behind the closed bedroom door.

"Oh my God. I forgot the dog." Sunny ran to open it.

He watched her appreciatively. Then he saw the Chihuahua crouched outside, saw the little dog giving Sunny that "how could you leave me" look, saw it roll over, paws in the air, playing the "helpless little mite."

Mac sighed and reached for the wine. He couldn't win with that dog. The little bastard beat him every time. He spotted Pirate lurking outside the bedroom door and called to him.

"Tell me," he said to Sunny, "why *my* dog should wonder if he can come into *my* bedroom, when yours considers it her territory." He reached out to stroke Pirate's shaggy ears.

"Oh stop it," Sunny said, not wanting to get into the Tesoro/Pirate thing. It was an ongoing situation and besides it was not *exactly* what she wanted to talk about right now.

"So. Listen." She settled next to him on the bed, clutching Tesoro to her chest.

Looking admiringly at her, Mac said, "*Portrait of a Naked Venus with Her Toy Dog* . . . very Boucher. That's a French artist," he added for her benefit.

"I *know* who Boucher is, but *this* Naked Venus would like to get a nice suntan, frolicking with her beloved in the aquamarine waters of the Indian Ocean . . . so clear, so translucent, so gently warm and inviting you won't believe it."

He said, "You've been there, then?"

She looked, exasperated, at him, head on one side, long hair cascading over her shoulder. "Well, not exactly *been* there . . ."

"You mean you just read the holiday brochure."

Sunny beamed. She squeezed Tesoro so tight the dog yelped. "You got it," she said, excited.

"No, I don't." Mac didn't want to hear about the Indian Ocean. He wanted to hear about the fast-running waters of Oregon's Rogue River and the steelhead he could catch there. He wondered if this time of year you had to use lures and not fresh bait. He'd have to check on that. Maybe he'd buy a new tent, a bigger one. That would make Sunny happy.

Sunny put her dog down and leaned enticingly over him. Her hair tickled his chest and her eyes—those long-lashed eyes—smiled right into his. "Think about it: Chinese food, Indian food, Creole food, fish fresh from the sea. Think low-rise hotels on white sugar-sand beaches, a turquoise sea, and those drinks with little umbrellas. They grow rum there you know."

"Nobody 'grows' rum."

Sunny shoved him, impatiently. "So what about those rum drinks with little umbrellas then?"

"I was thinking more along the lines of an ice-cold Bud and a fishing rod, and the taste of *my own* freshly caught fish, with smoke curling from my barbie . . ."

"And the gnats biting my butt!"

"I'll tell them to bite mine instead."

"Hah, even *you* can't control bugs."

Mac laughed. "Babe, I can't even control you, and you're my very own bug, I'm bitten, caught, addicted."

"Addicted to love," Sunny sang the Robert Palmer line in his ear. "Just think, we can sleep under the stars with the sound of the Indian Ocean in our ears, and I'll bet they have mosquito nets. Just the two of us . . ."

"What about the dogs?"

Sunny beamed. This was the clever part. Women always knew which button to push. "No Tesoro this time," she said. "Roddy can come here and take care of the dogs." Roddy was Mac's assistant.

"He understands Tesoro, and he adores Pirate. He adores you too, Mac. You know he'll do anything for his 'boss,' even at short notice. Like, for instance, in a couple of days' time."

"You'll love it, fishing," Mac said.

Just as the phone rang. Again.

Chapter 15

"Oh my God," Sunny cried, suddenly remembering her soup, left on a low light hours ago. The smell of burned fish came from the kitchen and she leapt out of bed and ran for the door.

Mac gazed after her; unsure whether she meant oh my God it's the phone again, or oh my God it's the soup. The bedside clock told him it was 10:25 P.M., but there were no time limits in his line of work. You did what you had to do at any hour, even though it might be rough on your private life. Sunny understood that. At least he hoped so.

He picked up the phone. "Reilly," he said.

"Is this *Mac* Reilly?"

It was a woman's voice, light, pleasant, and with a trace of a lisp on the "this." Cute! Mac had to resist the urge to copy her lisp when he agreed that yeth he wath Mac Reilly.

"Mr. Reilly, may I call you Mac? You see, I feel I already know you."

Mac was surprised; he quite definitely did *not* know *her.* Still, everybody had a story and he got the feeling she was about to tell him hers.

"Go ahead, Mac it is," he said. "And what shall I call you?"

"Jazmin."

He nodded. "Pretty name. Is there another to go with it? Just, y'know, to give me a clue as to exactly *who* you are, and how you got my number, and why you might be calling me at—" He glanced at the bedside clock. "—at exactly half past ten on a Wednesday evening."

"It's seven thirty A.M. here. And if I can call you Mac, you may call me Jassy."

She was flirting with him and he didn't even know who she was, though he knew from the time difference she was calling from Europe.

"So, Jassy, you want to tell me what this is all about?"

Sunny had come back and was standing by the bedroom door. There was a stricken look on her face and a blackened fish pan in her hands. Mac got up and walked round the bed still naked, took the pan from her, kissed the stricken look from her face and whispered, "There's always the pizza."

She threw a dagger look at him and then at the phone still held to his ear.

He sighed. The smell of burned fish did not bode well. Not only that, now Pirate had the baguette clamped between his jaws. He made a quick and wise decision not to get involved and returned to his phone caller.

"I apologize," he said. "A slight distraction. Now, Jassy . . . you were about to tell me your real name?"

"Jassy *is* my real name. Jassy de Ravel."

He remembered now. "Paloma's aunt."

Sunny was still standing by the door with the burned fishy pan in her hand, next to the dog with the baguette still in its mouth. She was listening.

"I am," Jassy said. "And I'm calling because Paloma told us

yesterday—in fact she told *the whole family*, you saved her life. You, and *your dog*, she said."

"I believe Pirate got there first."

There was a tremor in Jassy's voice as she said, "I'm so ashamed, almost in *despair* when I think of what might have happened. I didn't know Paloma walked alone on the beach, I would never have allowed it . . ."

"Of course not," Mac said, but he was thinking Aunt Jassy should have paid more attention to the child she was supposedly in charge of. "When you are the one looking after a child, that's what you're supposed to do," he said coldly, because he had not forgotten it had been a close call and Paloma might very well have drowned. "You're supposed to look after them. *You* are the child's life-support system."

"I'm sorry, and you are right to be angry. And I am calling, very humbly and gratefully, to say thank you."

"Then I'm glad you called." There was a silence. Jassy seemed to have nothing else on her mind, so Mac said, "No need to say thanks, I would have done the same for anybody. Say hi to Paloma for me." Then he remembered the anguished look in the girl's eyes, the urgent feeling she'd wanted to tell him something, and added, "And tell the kid to call me if she wants to talk. Thanks again for the call," he added, about to ring off.

"Don't go!" Jassy de Ravel's voice held a note of panic. "*Please,* don't cut me off. I have something else I need to talk about."

Mac guessed what her call was really about. "You mean about Bibi."

There was a pause, then Jassy said, "Of course I mean Bibi. We have to find her. I mean, Paloma needs to know if her mother is dead or alive. *There!* I've finally said it. Nobody else here dares even mention those terrible words. *Dead or alive.* And they're afraid to say well, if Bibi *is* alive, why has she abandoned her child. Do you realize Paloma was only seven when I went to L.A. and dragged her away from her mother and took her to Spain. *Seven years old*, Mac Reilly! I want to tell you, I've done my best but I am not this child's mother. And the fact is I'm not really suited to be *any* child's mother. Still, I've never left her—well, a couple of times, but only for short visits. And I'll tell you something else you need to know, Mac Reilly, I *love* that child. So, whatever you are going to find out about Bibi, and that terrible husband who also abandoned the kid he'd adopted, and about Bibi *murdering* her lover and his . . . his *bitch* . . . whatever it is, I for one am prepared to face it."

Mac grinned. Jassy de Ravel was a take-no-prisoners kind of woman. He said, "Tell me, did Paloma know you were going to call me?"

"She did not. No one knew. The family Matriarch, Lorenza de Ravel, called a meeting yesterday. Lorenza and Bibi inherited most of the Ravel vineyards and estates. You may have heard of our family?"

Mac most certainly had. The Marqués de Ravel wines had claimed a goodly share of the American market, and their sherries had ranked alongside Sandeman and Domecq for a couple of centuries.

"Anyhow," Jassy continued. "We have a set of circumstances here where it is imperative to find out, finally, exactly what has happened to Bibi. Bruno Peretti is Paloma's legal stepfather. Now he wants to get his hands on Bibi's one-third share of the estate, and legal guardianship of Paloma. He's trying to take that child away from me, and I'm not going to allow it. And nor is the Matriarch. *Over our dead bodies will that awful man get Paloma.*" She stopped for a moment, thinking, then added, sadly, "As well as maybe Bibi's."

Mac said, "Then you really think Bibi is dead?"

There was a long silence, while Jassy seemed to be thinking about it. "I don't want to believe that," she said finally. "But if she's not dead then how could she *not* have come back to get her daughter?"

"She didn't come back because she's an accused murderer. She never went to trial but the blame still sticks. And, far as I remember, no one else has been arrested for those crimes."

Jassy said, "Look, Mac Reilly, I'm prepared to fly out tomorrow—*today*—to meet with you. Please, *please,* tell me you will help us. I'll be on the next flight, I'll even *charter* a plane, I can be there in just hours. . . ."

Mac thought quickly about his hiatus; about his plans for a fishing holiday, and Sunny's plans for a vacation in Mauritius. He saw his long slow days alone with the woman he loved disappearing like smoke from that barbeque; and if he closed his eyes he could almost hear the distant muted slurp of the Indian Ocean's aquamarine waves on white sugar-sand; he could almost smell the rum and the spices, the cumin and coriander, the masala, lemongrass, ginger. . . . "Please don't do that, Jassy," he said quickly.

"You've got to help me," she begged. "Paloma told me you were the only one who would know what to do. Paloma was stalking you, you know, on the beach, she wanted to ask you to help then, but she was too shy and too embarrassed. . . ."

Mac remembered her waif's big brown eyes. He sighed. "I'll tell you what I *will* do. I'll look into the case for you here in L.A., find out what I can. It's so long I don't remember offhand exactly what happened, but it'll all be documented. I'll get the facts and we'll take it from there."

There was disappointment in Jassy's voice as she said, "Then I'll have to accept that. And I thank you again for your help, Mr. Reilly. It's very important to us, and especially Paloma. I can't let her go back to that man."

"I'll check on him too," Mac said. "And it's *Mac*. Remember?"

Jassy laughed then. Surprised, Mac thought she sounded like a pretty woman.

"Thank you, Mac."

"Tell Paloma hello. And if she wants to call me, she can."

"I'll tell her. I'm sure she'll be thrilled."

Mac closed his phone. He looked at Sunny, who was still standing in the bedroom doorway. The smell of fish hung in the air and Pirate held the baguette like a bone between his paws, gnawing happily.

"Let me guess. That was Paloma's aunt Jassy," Sunny said.

"It was."

"And I'll bet she said she's sorry she left Paloma alone and the child almost drowned."

"You got it."

"What else?"

"She and the Ravel Matriarch and the entire Ravel family want us to find long-lost Bibi."

"*Us*?"

Mac shrugged. "Well, *me*. But don't forget you are my assistant."

"Unpaid."

"We can do something about that."

"And tell me, what exactly *are* you going to do about Bibi?"

He frowned, thinking. "I don't remember the case, it's a couple of years ago. I said I'd check it out, see what was up; what, if anything, has been resolved."

"That doesn't find Bibi."

"No, but it might tell us why Bibi disappeared. It will also tell us about the dead lover and his girlfriend. And also, and most crucially—and I might add the real reason I'm prepared to look into it—and I am only *looking into it*, you know, I'm *not taking on* the case . . ."

"Just *looking*," Sunny said. It was the phrase women used when they said they weren't shopping, but they really were.

"The reason I even agreed to *look into* this case is because Bibi's ex wants her money and in order to get it he's claiming custody of Paloma."

"You mean he wants Paloma so he can get his hands on the money?"

"That's exactly what the Ravel family think. So I'll have to do a bit of looking into the husband too."

"What's his name?"

"I've no idea. I haven't even thought about the Bibi case in years."

"And now you will." Sunny saw her Mauritius paradise disappearing before her eyes.

"We can still go fishing," Mac said, hopefully.

She threw a pillow at him.

"I'd better warm up that pizza," he said, ducking past her, out the door.

Chapter 16

Bodega de Ravel, Spain

Paloma was at the de Ravel bodega waiting for her friend Cherrypop to arrive. She thought the only good thing about leaving her aunt Jassy in Barcelona and going to live with Lorenza at the vineyard was that her best friend lived there.

Cherrypop was only a year younger than Paloma, but she always seemed so much wiser, even though she had not traveled the world like Paloma, who had even spent two weeks alone at a big hotel in Paris and sipped champagne from leftover party glasses when nobody was looking. Lorenza said Cherrypop was one of those girls who seemed to have been born with her head screwed on. Paloma thought she meant that Cherrypop was "sensible." Nothing could have been farther from the truth.

Cherrypop had acquired her name as a small child when an indulgent cook had fueled her addiction to a syrupy cherry soda. It was said that the child's first words had been to demand "cherrypop," which the smiling cook had given her, straight from the plastic bottle with a bright pink straw that matched the color of the soda. The child had sipped her cherrypop endlessly through that straw, until the sugar finally wore a little hole the exact same round shape of the straw in her two front baby teeth. She had been called Cherrypop ever since, though her proper name was Monica, and never a drop of soda had crossed her teeth from that day to this. Much to her chagrin.

Now, eight-year-old Cherrypop had perfect new front teeth. She had long blond hair worn in a thick braid that swung down her back and that Paloma envied. She was small and chunky and with the narrowest prettiest feet Paloma had ever seen, except for Jassy of course, but then Jassy had a pedicure every week and had feet any ballerina would envy. Cherrypop had a cute little snub nose and innocent blue eyes and knew how to behave herself when she had to. And how to misbehave when she didn't. Which was one of the reasons Paloma liked her.

Paloma's room was on the second floor of the big white house and had two windows, each overhung with a blue tiled gable. Paloma thought they looked like eyebrows, and they created areas of shade that made her room seem mysterious and very private.

Lorenza told Paloma always to remember that even though she had so far not spent very much time there, this room was hers. Nobody else would ever be allowed to sleep in it, even when the house was filled to the rafters for the after-harvest party, or Christmas, or holidays. Lorenza wanted Paloma to understand that even though she might travel the world with Jassy, *this* was her true "home."

Paloma missed Jassy, but now she was looking forward to seeing her friend. She sat with knees under her chin, on the window seat, watching, waiting. The seat cushions were made out of some soft peachy-gray fabric, silky stuff that felt good under her bare legs, and were not at all "little-girly" or cute.

"You are definitely not the girly-cute type," Lorenza said, when Paloma asked why she couldn't have pink gingham and a fluffy pink feather boa to wind round her four-poster, like Cherrypop did.

She'd said, "My dear little Paloma, you are much too good for feather boas. And that's something you should remember when you are a grown woman."

Paloma had wondered what she'd meant by that last bit, but she knew the first part was true. She was certainly not cute. Or beautiful. Unlike her mother. She wondered how it could be that a child could resemble her mother and yet not? That she could have the same coloring, the same characteristics, and yet appear so different, so plain. Besides, she wished she could have had pink.

She did have *one* pink thing. The telephone. Barbie pink, it sat on the small desk placed under the second window. The desk was made from wood hewn from hundred-year-old vines, gnarly and gray with age. It stood there, on sinewy-vine legs with little darker-gray circles where branches had been chopped off; with her schoolbooks dead center and the pink phone on the right.

That phone looked old-fashioned, like something out of a Gidget movie. Paloma knew about Gidget from watching old movies on TV with Jassy, who adored all that fifties, early sixties surfer stuff—but in fact it was a replica and was as fast, if not faster than her iPhone. Jassy had replaced the one lost in the Pacific Ocean. Of course Paloma had not told Jassy exactly *how* she had lost it until yesterday, when the whole story about almost drowning had come out. Anyhow, now the pink phone rang and she leapt to answer it.

"*¿Diga?*" she said.

She expected it was Cherrypop, who should have gotten her message by now, that she was here and dying to see her.

But it was Jassy, who said, "I called him."

Paloma drew in a shocked breath. She didn't even have to ask who. She crossed her fingers hopefully. "What did he say?" Praying it was "yes."

"He said he would look into the case."

Her *mother* was just "a case." "What does that mean?"

"It means he'll check the police records, check out everyone, including your stepfather, and get back to us."

"Is that good?"

Jassy thought about it, then said tactfully, "He said you could call him, any time, if you want to talk."

"Thank you." Paloma knew she would not call. She hadn't even been able to speak to Mac about her mom right there in person on Malibu beach. Even when he'd *asked* her, for God's sake.

"Anyway, *chica,* I offered to fly there right away to talk to him, but he said no, he'll just check it all out."

"He'll find her," Paloma said, suddenly filled with the kind of confidence that had no basis in reality. But then she wasn't dealing with reality. She was dealing with the possibility that her mother was a murderer.

She had discussed this with Cherrypop, who'd told her all that murder stuff was just crap. Cherrypop's mom was from the projects in Brooklyn so Cherrypop had a good command of American vernacular. She knew every curse word there was and she also claimed to know what they meant. Paloma didn't always believe her; Cherrypop just threw stuff out at you and you had to sift truth from lies . . . something Paloma also knew about, though when *she* told fibs—well no, damn it—(or "fuck it" as Cherrypop said when she was showing off) she told real *lies*. Downright deliberate *lies*, not stupid little fibs, but they were only to cover up the stories about her mother. It was Paloma's way of protecting her.

Jassy said, "Paloma, are you going to call Mac?"

"But he said he'd get back to *you*."

"Yes, he did."

"Then I guess I'll just wait and see." Paloma thought for a minute, then added, "But Jassy, if all he is going to do is look up the records and see what really happened, why can't *I* do that?"

"Because Mac has access to certain information we don't. We'll just have to wait and see what happens. I'm sure he'll call soon. Meanwhile have a lovely time with your grandmother. I'm going to miss you, *chiquita.*"

"Me too," Paloma said, as Jassy rang off.

The door was flung open and Cherrypop stood there wearing copycat red Converse sneakers like Paloma's, her long blond plait swinging over her shoulder, her oh-so-innocent round blue eyes taking Paloma in.

"Love the hair," Cherrypop said, and Paloma laughed. Cherrypop was such a liar.

Chapter 17

Malibu

Mac's big-screen computer took up most of the space on his desk, an old wooden rolltop model Sunny had found on one of her scrounges around the local flea markets and which, like the dining table with the bulging legs, she assured him would qualify as "an antique" someday. *When,* she wasn't exactly sure, but Mac put his trust in her and also put up with the old ink stains and the fact that the desk was totally unsuitable for electronic equipment and a large man with too many papers, most of which were piled on the floor, to be transferred later to his "office," a single room in Santa Monica with a frosted glass door with his name on it. *MAC REILLY PI.*

That door satisfied all Mac's remembered images of the great "private eyes" from the past: Dashiell Hammett and Raymond Chandler, Perry Mason and Ellery Queen. And after all, a simple office was all that was needed because a detective's work took him out and about in the world of thieves and thugs, sleazy streets and smart restaurants and worldly women, just the way it had in those old movies.

In fact the office was a bit of a joke. A nice woman came in once a month to file papers, and dust a bit, but his real office was at the studio and functioned perfectly, with a real staff; as well as his assistant, Roddy, bleached-blond, and gay, gorgeous, and sometimes outrageous, and totally devoted to Mac. Roddy had been with him five years, since the beginning of TV's *Malibu Mysteries,* and knew everything there was to know about him.

Nowadays though, information came easy, with Google and *Huffington Post* and *The Daily Beast.* It was, Sunny told Mac, scarcely worth his effort to go hunting for it anymore when they offered it right there in the privacy of your own home.

Nothing about Bibi Fortunata was private, though. Her life was up there for anyone to see, including a couple of topless photos snapped by some too-enterprising paparazzo who'd climbed a tree next door and aimed his zoom lens directly into her bedroom window. Bibi had won that court battle; such invasion of privacy could not be tolerated and the tabloid concerned had paid a hefty price in compensation and damages, but the photos were still out there. Nothing could ever be gotten rid of in this electronic age.

Mac thought about that as he sat in front of his computer. His own life, anyone's life, had become an open book. Privacy had become a privilege instead of a right. So why, then, had Bibi not known that her so-called best friend was a call girl, albeit the "expensive high-class" sort.

"You know the ones," Mac said to Sunny, who was hanging over his shoulder reading all about it. "The escorts. You see them in the big hotels all the time."

"You mean the good-looking women always dressed better than I am, in a fancy cocktail outfit at three in the afternoon. And always, I'll bet, with a pair of clean panties in their Vuitton bags."

Mac laughed. He knew some of those women; they weren't *all* bad, they simply wanted to make money and were prepared to put up with anything to get it. Well, *almost* anything. The top girls drew up their rules and the men abided by them, or else paid extra. Which meant really big money. A good dominatrix did not come cheap in this town.

"Everybody has to make a living," he said, dodging Sunny's whack.

"*I* make a living," she reminded him, as he turned to kiss her.

"That you do, my love, and I know you'll be able to keep me in my old age, in the style to which I've become accustomed."

"Then you'd better behave yourself and forget Bibi and her best friend and take me to Mauritius. I have the hotel all picked out. Ten whole days of peace and love and good food on an island in the Indian Ocean, that's about as far away as we can get from all this 'trouble.'"

Mac looked at her. "I believe Paloma's in trouble," he said, suddenly serious.

"I know," Sunny sighed. "I saw it in her eyes too."

"Poor kid."

"Poor little girl. In those old boots of her mom's. And the charm bracelet. It's all she's got left." Sunny heaved another sigh. How could she compete with a nine-year-old with a broken heart?

Mac said, "All the reports tell the same story. Bibi's best friend and neighbor—her lover's 'mistress'—was known as Carly Malone. Her hooker name was Brandi."

"Why are they always called Brandi?" Sunny complained. "They have to use so much imagination on their job, you'd think they could come up with something better than a stripper name."

"Guys like stripper names, in that context, I guess." Mac was still scanning the screen. "And she was still a working girl, even when she was going out with Bibi's lover."

"*Going out with!* Now there's a euphemism if I ever heard one."

"The report is that the lover, who went by the name Waldorf Carlyle, real name Jimmy Skeener from Knoxville, Tennessee, never took Carly/Brandi out alone, not to dinner, not to parties, nowhere, unless Bibi went along, and then Carly/Brandi simply played the role of the best friend."

"Playing footsie with Bibi's lover under the table in the restaurant," Sunny guessed.

"Or worse," Mac agreed. "She was that kind of woman. Anything goes, and she knew how to do it."

"Excite a man, you mean?"

"The lure of the forbidden appears too regularly in my line of work. Wives are spurned for it. Murders are committed for it." He shrugged. "And that's what so interesting about this case. Both the lover and his new mistress . . ."

"His 'bit on the side,'" Sunny corrected him, thinking of the betrayed Bibi.

"*Both* the lover and his bit on the side were murdered."

"The police couldn't prove *he* was. That Bentley could have just gone out of control."

Mac gave her a skeptical glance. "Have you ever known a Bentley to go out of control?"

"Well . . ."

"Rarely, I'd say. I'd also say it was a wild coincidence if, in fact, that is what happened."

"Then you don't believe it?"

"I do not."

"And what about the bitch best friend?"

"The autopsy found cocaine and 'prescription drugs' in her stomach and her bloodstream. Oxycontin, Percodan . . . like that."

Sunny had heard too many similar descriptions of the tragic deaths of young celebrities. "What about in the wine though?"

"Only in her lipstick on the rim of the glass. Not in the actual glass itself."

"So no one slipped a pill into her wine?"

"They were unable to prove that."

"And unable to prove that the car going over Mulholland was not an accident."

"Cars have gone over Mulholland before."

"And what about that little satin pillow? Found next to her dead face, it says here."

"That's the tabloids' sensationalist reporting. They would say that. Again that's something that was not proven. She was not suffocated."

Mac clicked off the computer and turned to face her. "And that's why now I have to do what Raymond Chandler would have called some 'leg work.'"

Sunny stretched out a long leg for him to inspect.

Mac said, "A beautiful leg, a very, very lovely leg, but not the sort I'm thinking about." He ran his hand along her smooth thigh though and their eyes linked.

"I know." She sighed again. "You're thinking about the Beverly Hills PD."

"I am."

"You're going there now?"

Mac knew it was late but there were no regular office hours in his job. "Right now, baby," he said. "But first I'm calling Lev Orenstein."

Sunny groaned. If Lev was involved she knew her holiday was a lost cause. Mauritius was out. Lev Orenstein was only the best bodyguard known to man. He was fortyish, bald as a coot, and always wore aviators and a Tommy Bahama flowered shirt with jeans and sneakers. He was six-one and in good enough shape to take on all comers. He was also a triple black belt in karate and had worked with the Israeli Special Forces. He organized corporate and round-the-clock surveillance with his team of personally trained men; he was one of the greatest shots ever and he knew the watering holes of the rich and famous like his own bald handsome face in the mirror. He also knew a lot of their secrets. Lev was a man known for his loyalty and for always being on the side of honor.

Paloma Ravel was going to find she had a new friend. Sunny was sure of that.

Chapter 18

Mac occasionally had Sunny act as his impromptu assistant. She had been known not to throw a faint when a body fell out of a refrigerator in a villa in Tuscany, or scream when a withered hand emerged from the desert sand, though she could scream pretty good when she saw a spider or a snake. But that didn't happen often, and anyhow she knew it made Mac feel macho rescuing his "damsel in distress."

Still, Mac wasn't sure he wanted her to be involved. A child might be in danger, a murderer was still on the loose, and a well-known woman had simply disappeared like smoke from his barbie, the one on which he was supposed to be cooking steelhead fresh-caught from the Rogue River in Oregon. For a moment he regretted the fishing trip, but then he remembered Paloma's anxious eyes.

Of course Bibi's story was an excellent scenario for his *Malibu Mysteries* show. The perfect format. The only difference was that this time he knew the people involved.

"Bibi's got to be somewhere," he said to Sunny.

"Right." She could see his mind was made up. "No Mauritius then." It wasn't a question and he knew it needed no answer.

"No Rogue River," he said.

"It's Bibi instead."

"It's *Malibu Mysteries* . . ."

"With yours truly, Mac Reilly, coming at you, Thursday nights in person and in living color."

Sunny knew how popular Mac's show was, and how good Mac was at what he did. Looking for a killer was not unusual; this was Mac's game, this was what he did, seeking out murderers and con artists, abusers and pedophiles. The only trouble was the show had brought him the kind of fame she knew Mac wasn't sure he wanted.

Sunny also knew how much the public loved him: they wrote in and told him so. They loved his rugged slightly unkempt look; that dark hair that even though he was in his early forties, was, thank God, still thick on his head, and through which he had a habit of running his hands when talking. They wrote in to say they loved the way his dark blue eyes crinkled when he smiled, though Mac insisted that it was caused by too many days on the beach and too many nights spent propping up bars in his mis-spent youth. They also said they loved the way his eyes narrowed when he looked directly into the camera, as though he was talking to each viewer. They wrote in and said how sexy they thought his stubble was, though usually it was because he'd been too busy even to think about shaving and anyway he hated TV makeup.

They e-mailed and twittered how much they loved his casual outdoors look, acquired from his beachside lifestyle, and his lean six-foot body, always clad on TV in jeans and a T-shirt, usually old and well-worn, because Mac wasn't into clothes, and anyhow he always wore the soft, easy, black leather jacket Sunny had bought him in an effort to smarten him up. The jacket had become part of his identity both on-screen and off. Like him it was a bit worn-in, a bit beat-up. Looking at him now, though, Sunny thought that was just her Mac.

He was already on the phone.

Lev answered on the first ring.

"How're y'doin', friend?" Mac asked, hearing Lev's throaty chuckle in response.

"You want something," Lev said. "It's the only reason you ever call."

"Where are you?" Mac knew Lev could be anywhere in the world. He protected movie stars and celebrities, heads of corporations, rich men, richer women, and even royalty, in their homes and on their travels. He saw trouble before it arrived and knew exactly how to stave it off. Mac always said Lev could stop a vampire in his tracks. Forget the stake in the heart, all he'd have to do was hold up a hand and the devil's representative would shrivel to a heap of ashes. He hoped Lev could do that now.

"I'm in New York," Lev said. "Actually, right now I'm at Teterboro, New Jersey, about to board a chartered Gulfstream 5 heading for Shannon, Ireland."

"I'll bet I know who with," Mac said.

"I'll bet you do."

Movie star Carole Brightwater was with a man who was not her husband, and with Lev's help, was traveling incognito. Or almost incognito, because before she'd hired Lev to take care of things, she had been photographed departing LAX with a well-known golf pro, en route to New Jersey. "A golf holiday," she had told the press hastily, though when Carole Brightwater had ever played a game of golf was a mystery.

"Each to his own," Mac said.

"Ain't that the truth," Lev agreed, yawning.

"I hope you're not too tired to take on a bit of trouble," Mac said.

"Shoot," Lev said.

"You remember Bibi?"

Lev whistled. "Sure do."

"I have to find her."

"Why you? And why now?"

"Her kid needs her mom," Mac said.

"Jesus," Lev said. "You know this kid?"

Though Mac couldn't see him he knew he was running his hand over his bald head, a habit he had when thinking.

"I saved her from drowning in the Pacific just last week."

"Jesus!" Lev said again, stunned. "The kid wasn't . . . I mean she didn't try to . . ."

"It was an accident. I saw it happen, that's how I managed to fish her out. Meanwhile, you recall the case?"

"A suspected double murder, and Bibi was the suspect who got off the hook."

"Well, now all we have to do is find out who did it, and find Bibi."

"That means you don't think *she* did it?"

"I surely hope, for her kid's sake, that she did not."

"How old is she?"

"Around nine, I guess."

Lev said, "What's your next move, besides corralling me, I mean."

"Checking with the Beverly Hills PD, then a little visit to Palm Springs to meet the ex who's claiming custody of Bibi's little girl in an attempt to get his hands on the family fortune. The *de Ravel* family. You may have heard of them."

Lev whistled again. "Old money and new money as well. It's not a bad wine, y'know."

"It's not bad money either, and one-third of it rightly belongs to Bibi, if she's alive, and if not, then to little Paloma Ravel."

"I know a member of that family," Lev said. "Socialite, great looking, a bit crazy. I bump into her in odd corners of the world."

"That would be Jassy," Mac said.

"Right. Jassy."

"She's Paloma's aunt. She's looked after her since Bibi left."

"What about the grandmother? The Matriarch. I hear she's a force to be reckoned with."

"So far it's just Jassy. I don't know anything about the Matriarch."

"Okay, I've got to get on this plane. Ms. Hot-to-trot Carole is getting irritable because her security is missing. Like I only have three other guys surrounding her. You couldn't get to Carole if you brought in the cavalry. So, what d'you want me to do?"

"Use your contacts, ask around, especially in Europe. Bibi has to have left a trail. And my guess is if she's still alive, she won't be too far away from her kid. She was a good mother, she'd be concerned, be looking out for her child."

"Got it," Lev said.

Mac nodded. Lev knew every underworld contact, as well as the top social ones. He would not let him down.

Chapter 19

The next phone call came from the Ravel family lawyers in Barcelona and took Mac by surprise. The man introduced himself as Felix Montrin, then got right down to business.

"The Ravel family Matriarch personally asked me to get in touch with you, Mr. Reilly. She is aware of your reputation as an investigator. She needs help. This whole family needs help, especially the child. And here's why."

Montrin outlined the situation with Peretti. "He's not even a *blood* relative," he said, in his somber perfectly English-accented voice. "The man is only after her money. So you see, Mr. Reilly," he concluded, "why this family now asks for your help. You are there, in Los Angeles, where the 'events' took place. And you see that now," he added, "it's essential Bibi be found. . . ."

Again the dreaded words "dead or alive" hung silently in the airwaves.

"I'm already making inquiries," Mac told Montrin. "I'll get back to you when I have something to discuss."

There was silence for a few seconds then Montrin said, in the tone of a man unhappy with what he had to do, "Mr. Reilly, the Matriarch would like to meet with you personally."

"In the hopes of persuading me to take on the case?"

"Probably." Señor Montrin was deadly serious. "I have taken the liberty of booking you a first-class seat on the Delta flight leaving for Barcelona on Monday. You have a suite at the Méridien hotel, where I am sure you will be most comfortable. The Marquesa de Ravel asks only for a fraction of your time. One day, in fact. You are booked on a return flight Wednesday. And of course, should you agree to take on this case, the Marquesa asks me to tell you that your fee will be whatever amount *you* stipulate. The Marquesa *insisted* I tell you, Mr. Reilly, whatever figure *you* suggest, she will agree."

Mac said, "The Marquesa is very trusting, but I'm not in the habit of stiffing old ladies and children out of their inheritance."

He heard Señor Montrin's answering sigh. The lawyer was obviously not happy with his client's open-ended financial offer but had no choice but to go along with it.

"Can I assume you will be on the Delta flight Monday, Mr. Reilly?"

The man was talking about tomorrow! Mac thought about Sunny and their vacation plans. Rogue River? Mauritius? But he'd only be gone a couple of days and anyhow Sunny was up in Napa. Remembering Paloma's frightened brown eyes, he told Montrin he could assume he'd be on that flight.

Barcelona beckoned.

First though, he would go meet the villain of the piece. The ex-husband, ex-stepfather, Bruno Peretti.

Chapter 20

Palm Springs, California

Melvyn's is the kind of old-fashioned watering hole patronized over the years by a multitude of stars: Sinatra and his Rat Pack, Tony Curtis, Rita Hayworth, John Wayne, Tracy and Hepburn, Garbo and Dalí. Tom Cruise, Madonna, Trump, and Travolta. Like that. It's still buzzing with stardom today, thanks to the owner, your host, Mel Haber, who knows how to keep his customers happy and constantly laughing.

His small hotel in Palm Springs is known as the Ingleside Inn and has traditional bungalows with green lawns and a multitude of flowers. The food is also traditional, and good, and who knows, you could still be sitting next to that movie star or celebrity at the long dark bar, where they know a good bourbon from an indifferent one, and the waiters have been there forever and a day, and will be there forever after, because surely there is a Melvyn's in heaven.

Mac knew the place from way back, before he was *Malibu Mysteries* and was just another private eye on the scent of a trail of wrongdoing. After all, the desert is a big empty space with plenty of room for trashed weapons and hidden corpses, though now it's mostly rolling green golf courses and coral-roofed houses half hidden under tumbles of vivid bougainvillea, with smiling retirees happy to have left winter back in Minnesota or Alberta. There were still, though, Mac noted appreciatively, sitting up at the bar, a lot of good-looking women around. Women with tanned legs and long hair, keeping a keen eye out for that rich older guy on the prowl for a new lease on life.

Mac had already scouted out Bruno Peretti's house, located at the very end of a narrow road that wound round the foot of a mountain, emerging into a plateau with a view of the dark valley floor atwinkle with lights, and a sky that matched. The desert had its own clear-eyed beauty, still innocent after all these years of being hit on by developers and tourists.

Mac got out of his car and took the time to breathe deeply. The night air was warm in his lungs, with a velvety texture on his skin that sent a shiver of pleasure through him. He wished Sunny could be with him, but she was still in Napa sipping wine and no doubt being chatted up by rich vintners.

He looked at Peretti's house. A blank wall faced the sandy street, sand-colored too, and low enough for Mac to see over it without making an effort. He leaned against the car, arms folded over his chest, taking in the scene. It was very quiet. Not even a car or a dog's bark. There were other houses farther back down the road but Peretti's stood alone in a fair-sized bit of land. A long, narrow lap pool gleamed turquoise to the left of the main building, which was classic mid-century modern, low-slung and with a lot of plate-glass windows. A large sign over the wrought-iron gate warned visitors to beware of the dog, and as if to clarify that threat, a large wooden kennel, the size of a big kid's play-house, occupied the space next to the front door, over which a spherical amber lamp glowed. A light also shone from the windows on either side of what Mac took to be the hall, and in another room which fronted, he guessed, onto the pool area. Maybe Bruno Peretti was home after all.

He walked across to the gate, put his thumb on the electronic buzzer and left it there. No one inside picked up the answer-phone demanding angrily to know what the fuck he thought he was doing. No dog barked. Mac checked the security camera aimed right at him, and the sign that said this property was guarded. There was nothing to be gained for him here; he needed the man himself. He needed to ask him a certain question, the answer to which—or merely his reaction to it—would give Mac a clue as to where exactly Peretti stood in this case.

And that's why he ended up at Melvyn's where, those in the know had told him, Peretti could be found six nights out of seven. Nobody seemed to know what Perreti did on the seventh night but Mac was pretty sure he wasn't just resting on the Sabbath and dedicating himself to God.

He realized his informants were correct about Peretti and Melvyn's when he spotted the Rottweiler-type dog sitting in a silver Corvette, its snout stuck out the open window, tongue lolling and a nasty look in its red-rimmed eye. He asked the valet-parker about it and was told that Mr. Peretti always parked his own car because the dog was trouble and nobody would go near it.

"I'll bet," Mac said, carefully skirting the parked Corvette and walking under the small arched awning and through Melvyn's welcoming doors.

The dining room to the right was almost full, not bad for notoriously slow Sunday nights, and the bar was doing good business. Peretti was there, a martini glass in front of him. The seats on either side were taken and Mac stood in back of him, waved a hand at the barkeep, and ordered a Diet Coke. He never drank on the job. At the far end of the bar was a small dance floor where a couple of gals gyrated slowly to the music from the local piano man, who Mac thought played a good tune. He'd always liked a bar with a guy who sang and played, it brought things up a notch from just a place to down a drink after a long day.

Hearing Mac's Diet Coke order, Peretti turned his head slightly. He glanced at him out the corner of his eye, then went back to his drink.

The light was dim, the wooden counter sufficiently old to have a history, and the black-and-white autographed glossies of four decades of movie stars glimmered with memories. Mac thought this would be a nice place to bring Sunny some weekend when they could both shake free.

Talking of free: the blonde with the oversized behind outlined in tight yellow capri pants got up from the stool next to Peretti, collected her friend, and departed. All Mac had to do was slide into that still-warm seat. He did not like the way it felt and wished he were somewhere else. Then he thought of Paloma de Ravel's troubled eyes and remembered he was not on vacation.

"How're y'doing?" he asked Peretti, raising his glass to ask for another Diet Coke.

"Good."

Mac wondered how it was possible that a single word could have an Italian accent.

Peretti hadn't asked, but anyway Mac said, "Me too."

Peretti stared face-forward at the bar.

"Nice place they've got here," Mac pressed on.

"It is popular."

The shrug that accompanied these words was Italian too, a contemptuous lift of a shoulder, a curl of the lip.

The barkeep noted Peretti's almost empty glass and without asking mixed him a fresh martini: Bombay with a lick of vermouth, straight up, two olives.

Peretti lifted the glass and looked at Mac. "*Salute,* Diet Coke," he said, with a glint of mockery in his narrow light eyes, whose color Mac couldn't quite define in bar gloom. Peretti fished out the olives and placed them on a saucer, then took a hearty gulp of almost pure gin, throwing back his head and sighing.

Mac thought it must have hit him like a bolt of lightning. He remembered the Corvette parked outside and wondered if Mr. Peretti intended to drive home, up that winding sandy road with the valley all atwinkle on his right and a mountain looming on his left. He kinda hoped the dog could drive.

Peretti was staring straight ahead at the bar again. "I know who you are," he said, without looking at Mac.

Mac nodded. "And I know who you are. So I guess there's no need for introductions."

From his black linen shirt pocket, Peretti took a bunch of notes folded into a silver money clip, removed a fifty, and slapped it on the counter. "I'll bet fifty I also know why you're here."

Mac said, "'Fraid I'm not a betting man, especially when the odds are stacked. And since you know why I'm here, maybe you can help me out with some info. Like why all of a sudden you want custody of the stepdaughter you gave up two years ago."

Color crept into Peretti's handsome face, with the hard chiseled cheekbones and the same dangerous look in his eyes as his Rottweiler-type dog. It was the only sign that he was rattled. He did not down his drink and snarl at Mac, he simply said, "Since you seem to know all about my business, Mr. Reilly, there's really no need for any discussion."

Mac shrugged too, copying Peretti's contemptuous little lift of the shoulder. "What I really wanted to know, Peretti, was whether you murdered your wife's lover? Or was it really just a slip of the brakes?"

In one quick move Peretti rose from his bar stool and punched

Mac, who, for once taken by surprise, slid to the floor, while the bartender yelled at them and the other patrons backed off in alarm. And then the waiters came running and so did the Palm Springs cops.

And that was sort of that, for the night," Mac told Sunny, on the phone, driving back to L.A. in the dark, with the windmills sucking up that desert air at the side of the 101, and with a black eye and a jaw that hurt like hell. "Well, almost," he added, thinking of the phone call from the Ravel family lawyer he had received earlier.

"That guy can surely pack a punch," he said, touching his face tenderly. But Sunny only laughed.

"I'll kiss it better when I get home," she said.

Mac put on his indicator and changed lanes to get away from the trucks that seemed to take up the entire freeway at night. "And when will that be?" He had a good reason for asking.

"Oh, Monday night, I guess."

"That's too late," he said.

"Too late for what?" She sounded puzzled.

"Too late because by then I'll be in Barcelona."

Chapter 21

Napa Valley, California

When Mac called her, Sunny was lying in bed in a small green and white room at a little inn someone had recommended and that, surprisingly, had turned out to be charming. For once she had left Tesoro home. Actually she'd left her at the beach house to be looked after by Roddy. Outside her glass doors was a balcony that overlooked a grassy slope with a chinaberry tree tossing in the freshly-up night wind and an almost full moon lighting the backdrop. Even though Sunny had left the curtains open because of this enchanted view, she could not see it because she was wearing a cashmere eye mask, as well as the matching cashmere bed socks. *Pink,* for God's sake, a Christmas gift bought by the currently unemployed actor in Rome, when he'd been flush from a small role in a Cinecittà epic, when he'd worn a toga and breastplate, as well as a sinister frown that he'd complained later needed Botox injections to remove the almost permanent creases. He'd even questioned whether or not he could charge the movie production company for the shots and had been quite miffed by Sunny's laughter.

Anyhow, when she was alone in bed her feet were always cold and she missed Mac, so the bed socks came in handy. And the mask was soft against her tired eyes, though sleep was still elusive, which was why she was still awake when Mac called.

She ripped off the mask and sat up straight, though, when Mac said "Barcelona."

"Tomorrow!" she exclaimed. "You cannot be serious." She stared blankly at the moonlit tree. The wind had started to howl and the branches tapped against the window. Suddenly nervous, she wondered if there were any other guests at this charming inn, or whether, like Janet Leigh in *Psycho,* she was alone.

"Barcelona?" she said, feeling loneliness creep over her, plus the flush from several "tastings" of her client's latest vintage—a Cabernet, and really quite good, though she was more of a white wine person herself. Of course she would never tell her client that, only that his red was one of the best, and since it had just gained ninety-four points on Robert Parker's list it seemed it was true. And *she* was the one whose promotional ability had taken it from an unknown to a name. Well, the beginnings of a name, but then everyone had to start somewhere. And that wasn't Barcelona.

"What about Mauritius?" she asked.

"What about Rogue River?" he said.

"Monday, you'll be in Barcelona."

"And you'll still be in Napa."

"You forget, I return Monday."

"And I return Wednesday."

Hope glimmered, she could almost see that white sugar-sand beach and crystal Indian Ocean. "We could leave Thursday . . ."

"Pack the tent, baby."

"Mac Reilly, I have never—*never*—slept in a tent. And I am not about to start now."

"Why not?"

She could hear laughter in his voice. "Because my feet get

cold and I refuse to allow you to see me in these ridiculous pink bed socks."

"You could always take 'em off . . ."

There was a phony leer in his voice and despite herself, Sunny giggled. She missed him terribly, though he could not have liked what she had managed to do to the room. Her version of unpacking was simply to take everything out of the cases and drape it over chairs and tables where she could see it. The blue dress she had worn was on the floor where she had stepped wearily out of it an hour ago, and her lace panties and bra led in a trail to the shower. In a haze of perfumed oil, she had thrown herself into bed, missing Mac like crazy, head spinning from all that red wine. No, not simply *red* wine, she corrected herself. After all, she represented a vintner. It was a *Cabernet Sauvignon.*

"You failed to ask," she said with a touch of frost, "since you are so caught up in your own affairs and your black eye and poor hurt jaw, but yes, thank you, the presentation of my client's new vintage did go well this evening. People seemed to like it a lot and I believe I've managed to gain him some valuable friends in the media."

"I've noticed a good red will always gain friends," Mac said. "Meanwhile, baby . . ."

"Meanwhile . . ." Sunny slipped farther down into the pillows, pressing the phone to her ear, wishing it could bring Mac closer.

"Meanwhile," he said, "I'd better bring you up to date on the Ravel family. The Matriarch says Bibi has to be found and she believes I am the one to find her."

"And are you?"

He hesitated. "Maybe not. But then I think of the kid's frightened eyes and that bastard Peretti who might get custody of her, so he can lay his hands on her inheritance. And so then again, I think maybe yes."

"So you're giving the Matriarch a shot."

Sunny could almost see Mac's shrug. She heard the loud honk of a truck's horn and his curse in response. "Bastards," he muttered. "These truckers think they own the road, three abreast on the freeway, can you imagine?"

Sunny didn't want to. She said, "All I want is for you to say 'I want to run away with you, Sunny Alvarez.' Anywhere but the Rogue River, hip deep in steelheads."

His laugh was deep and affectionate. "I miss you, baby," he murmured.

She closed her eyes listening as he told her how much he missed her, and yes he wanted to run away with her, and Mauritius was sounding better and better. . . .

"Though Spain might not be a bad vacation spot either," he added, sounding thoughtful. "Should events take a new turn."

Sunny got up and walked to the window. She closed the curtains, shutting out the nervously tapping tree branches and the moon and the night.

"Bastard," she whispered, and heard him laugh as he said goodnight. And that he loved her.

Chapter 22

The nice woman at first-class check-in at LAX gave Mac an amused grin. "Looks like maybe you didn't win this time, Mr. Reilly," she said, handing him his boarding pass.

"A mere flesh wound," he said. "You should see the other guy."

She leaned closer, elbows on the counter. "I'll bet he doesn't look as good as you."

"Worse." Mac waved a hand at her as he turned away. Then he turned back. "Actually, he got off scot-free. I never even touched him."

"Never mind," she said, laughing. "The best man always wins."

"Let's hope so," Mac said.

The guy at immigration gave him the once-over, though, staring at his passport photo then staring at him, then back again, checking info on his computer. "Thanks," he said finally, handing the passport and boarding pass back. "Have a good trip."

Shoes off, and his belt with the silver buckle—a mustang rearing its elegant head—his wallet and change, his old Timex steel watch, his loafers, and his small carry-on bag all placed in the plastic tray, Mac stepped through the metal security barrier, eyed warily by three uniformed men, who quickly signaled another couple of guys over.

Reinforcements, Mac thought, sighing as he held his arms up while one wanded him.

"How d'ya get the eye?"

The man's glance was remote and to his surprise Mac felt guilty. "A guy in a bar took a dislike to me," he said.

"D'ya hit him back?"

"I did not."

"Then you should have, Mr. Reilly." There was a grin on the guy's face now, and Mac guessed he'd been set up.

"Next time I'll be sure to," he said, high-fiving, then stopping to sign a few autographs for the small crowd that had gathered, before heading quickly for the lounge, where, over a beer—a Stella Artois, a European beer; he was getting into the mood—he called Sunny again and got her voicemail.

He said, "So I'm here, at the Tom Bradley Terminal, without you, and I just wanted to tell you I wish I was on my way to Mauritius. *With* you. Love you, Sunny Alvarez. And don't you ever dare leave me again. And don't tell me, well, I am the one leaving *you*, because I'll only be gone for two days. With the time differences maybe make that three, and then I'm taking you on that holiday." He paused for a second then added, "Promise."

Hours later, after a stopover in Atlanta, the first-class steward on the international leg of the Barcelona flight fixed Mac an eye pack and then a Jim Beam on the rocks. "A good combo," Mac said wearily.

With the ice, the eye began to feel better, well at least numb, which he guessed was better. Sipping his bourbon, he chalked up another bad point to the ex-husband, which led him to wonder anyhow what the ex-wife was really like.

It was odd no one had ever talked about Bibi as a woman,

only about her child, and about the murders, about the lover and the Italian husband, and that she'd been missing for over two years. All Mac knew about Bibi was her music. Of course he knew her face from a thousand photos; a calm, composed face, a woman in charge of herself, emotions under control, careful smile judged to the inch for the camera. Her pale greenish eyes looked back at him from those photos, half-lowered lids possibly veiling her true feelings.

Sipping his bourbon, ice pack clamped to the eye, Mac allowed himself to consider the fact that it was possible Bibi Fortunata was guilty of murder. After all, she was the classic woman scorned. A famous woman, publicly humiliated by her lover and her best friend. A situation like that, anything could happen. And might. Plus if Bibi Fortunata *was* guilty of the murders she was never charged with, she would have a very good reason to disappear, and reason also to give up her daughter. A woman—especially a famous one—could not simply disappear with a kid in tow. She might be able to change her own appearance but never the child's. And besides, kids talked. Anyhow, the murder case was still active, which meant there was always the chance the police might come up with new evidence linking Bibi to the crime.

Mac slugged back the bourbon, refused the meal, surrendered his empty glass, and reclined his seat. Ice pack propped on his eye, he reminded himself to ask Lev, when he got to Barcelona, if he knew via the gossip why Bibi had married Peretti. Lev worked with the kind of people who knew these things; he knew more stories about everyone than anyone else.

He ditched the ice pack and closed his eyes—painfully. It had been a long twenty-four hours from Palm Springs to somewhere over the Atlantic Ocean. He was wondering about Barcelona and the Matriarch when he fell asleep.

At Barcelona's El Prat airport, the Immigration officer stared suspiciously at him. He was getting used to it. He waited patiently while his passport was checked, then his face and his purple eye. The passport was checked again; he was checked again.

"Your profession?" the officer demanded.

"I'm in TV." He wasn't about to go into the private investigator stuff here. His head was throbbing and he was thinking he should not have drunk the bourbon on the plane.

The passport was stamped, he was waved on, only to be stopped again walking through the green light at customs. A black eye would do it every time, he realized. He surrendered his small Tumi duffel; all he needed for a couple of days was in there. Then Security arrived with a dog who sniffed in a desultory fashion at his legs and the bag, before he was waved reluctantly on.

Welcome to Barcelona, Mac thought, wondering wearily if his journey was really necessary.

A small dark-haired man in a blue pinstripe business suit, jacket buttoned, dark glasses over his eyes, was holding up a card with Mac's name on it. He seemed to recognize Mac immediately and hurried toward him.

"Mr. Reilly," he said, in his carefully accented English. "Felix Montrin, the de Ravel family attorney. We spoke on the phone."

"Of course." Mac shook his hand. "Good of you to meet me."

"The Marquesa de Ravel asked me particularly to greet you and bring you safely to your hotel."

"Safely? Is there any danger I should know about?"

"No. Oh, no, nothing like that. It's just that the Matriarch was concerned that you did not have to wait for a taxi, and Barcelona's traffic is notorious, unless you know your way around it. She was simply concerned for your comfort."

"That's very kind of her." Mac found himself being as courtly and formal as the lawyer, who pointed out various monuments and buildings as they surged impetuously through the thick traffic with seeming disregard for their own safety. Mac was beginning to think he would have had more chance of getting to the hotel alive in a taxi than with Señor Montrin driving. The man just seemed to expect everyone else to get out of his way, and somehow they did. Maybe he could learn something from Señor Montrin, Mac thought as they weaved their way to the Ramblas area and pulled up in front of the Méridien hotel.

Señor Montrin told him the Matriarch would expect him at six that evening. A car would pick him up at exactly five fifty. "You have much to discuss," he added, getting out of the car and shaking Mac's hand.

"Then you will not be joining us?" Mac was surprised, he'd thought the attorney would want to be in on any discussion, even if only to make sure the Matriarch, as the man so pompously referred to her, didn't overstep the bounds and offer him a few million to find Bibi.

"The Matriarch insisted on seeing you alone."

It was clear the attorney was not pleased about the situation. Mac didn't blame him. The Matriarch was obviously a strong-willed woman used to getting her own way.

His suite was spacious with windows overlooking the noisy Ramblas, though, thank God, it was soundproofed. A bottle of his favorite bourbon, and also a bottle of dark rum, awaited. *Compliments of the Marquesa de Ravel,* the card said. There was a bowl of fresh fruit and a plate of just-made churros, scented with cinnamon sugar.

Mac got out his iPhone and e-mailed Lev, asking him for all the info he had on the Bibi/Peretti relationship. As an afterthought he asked if Lev knew, anyway, why Bibi had taken a lover? After all, she'd only been married for a year.

Then, feeling guilty about leaving Sunny, he gave up on his idea of the tent, the Rogue River, and the steelheads. Instead he e-mailed Roddy, and asked him to find out about flights to Mauritius. And where the fuck was Mauritius anyway?

He flung off his clothes, stepped into the shower, and let the journey wash away. After five minutes he got out and took stock of himself in the mirror, patted his flat belly, combed back his hair with his hands, and groaned at his purple eye. Sunglasses were probably not appropriate to meet a Matriarch but he had no choice.

Wrapping a towel round his loins and eyeing the big fluffy white bed, he wished Sunny were here. He sank into the sofa, bit into a churro, and checked his iPhone. There was an e-mail from Lev. "Apparently Bibi was lonely," was his reply to Mac's query.

Seems Peretti came along just at the right low moment. Why do women always go for the bad boys when things get tough? Word was he didn't want her sexually. Don't ask me why, probably was into something else. Just hoping it wasn't little girls. Word also was "the lover," Waldorf Carlyle, was good at "his job." Hey, make a woman feel like a woman and she's happy. With all that talent, all that fame, all that money, you'd think she wouldn't need to grab on to a cheap fucker like that. But he was right there, he was available and hot for her—and that's all I know. I'll keep you posted.

Mac ate another churro. So. Bibi was lonely, unfulfilled, and probably emotionally at the end of her rope. Things did not look good for Bibi.

He e-mailed thanks back to Lev, wanted to call Sunny but,

taking into account the nine-hour time difference, decided against it and e-mailed her instead. *Lot of traffic here, you're not missing a thing, but me,* he wrote. *Love you.*

He called the desk and asked to be given a wake-up call at five, then fell into the big wide white bed and immediately to sleep.

When the call came he got up, refreshed, showered again, put on his clean jeans and, in deference to the Matriarch, a white linen shirt. He slung on his black leather jacket, ran his hands through his hair, refused to look in the mirror at his eye, put on his sunglasses, and took the elevator down to the lobby.

"Mr. Reilly, the Marquesa's car is waiting for you," the manager himself told him.

Mac half expected an ancient Rolls, bright yellow like something from a fifties movie, but it was a BMWX5 SUV, black and shiny. Not a speck of dust, despite the Barcelona traffic.

"Señor Reilly." The driver, a thin young man, sprang to attention when he saw Mac. He opened the back door with a flourish.

"Thanks, but I'll sit up front with you." Mac walked round to the passenger side and got in. The interior smelled faintly of some flowery perfume.

The driver said his name was Carlos, and that they were only minutes away from the house where, he told Mac, the de Ravel family had lived for two generations. "The winery, what we call the 'bodega,' is even older, of course," he added.

Mac wondered if he might get to see the winery that, thanks to the Matriarch, had improved the fortunes of this family over the past few years. Not that they'd needed it. He checked out the tall stone house as the car swept through the iron gates, motioned in and on by an old man with a face like a pickled walnut under a bright blue beret.

Family retainer, Mac thought. That's what this family was all about. Wealth, position, and history. The Marquesa de Ravel was going to have a lot to live up to.

The massive wooden door stood slightly open. The driver got out, waved Mac up the steps, pushed the door wide, and ushered Mac inside. Then, with a polite *"Buenas noches, Señor,"* he departed, leaving Mac alone in the hall.

Mac was surprised not to be greeted by a butler, or at least a uniformed maid. On his left was what he guessed would be called the *grand salón* with its cushioned brocade sofas and crystal lamps; and on his right a dining room with a long table set as though for an imminent dinner party for twenty, with golden chargers and yellow plates, long-stemmed wineglasses and amber water glasses. A simple butter-yellow linen napkin was at each place, and a low gilded metal trough filled with pots of fresh herbs ran down the center. Mac could smell the basil from where he stood. He'd bet before he died old Juan Pedro and his Matriarch had held some great parties here.

He stared up the sweeping staircase at the twin fantasies of the theater boxes with their faded rosy velvet curtains and the gilded cupids tooting their trumpets. Somehow, he'd expected the conventional Spanish home of an older couple with heavy dark furniture, lowering beams, and half-drawn drapes, and what he'd gotten instead was an operetta, a theater set. It was all so fantastical it made him smile.

Still no one came to get him. Mac wondered uneasily about Montrin saying the Matriarch was concerned he got there safely. "Safely" was not a normal word to use. Could there be danger here?

Suddenly impatient, he walked through the hall toward the back of the house. His footsteps rang loudly on the marble floor. The house felt empty, as though no one actually lived here.

At the very end of the hall an open door led into a kitchen. Copper pans gleamed on a rack over a center island. To his left was another door. Curious, he opened it and peeked in. This was obviously the heart of the house, where the real living took place. Sofas still bore imprints of where people had sat; a sweater was flung across the back of one, and a folded newspaper waited to be read. French windows led onto a courtyard where an unseen fountain tinkled lazily. Two walls were lined with books and, curious about the de Ravels, Mac walked over to take a look.

Head bent, he read the titles: English and French as well as Spanish. Obviously the de Ravels were an international bunch.

He heard a light footstep in back of him, smelled that same faint flowery scent from the car. He straightened up, and swung round to look.

She was standing there, in a red dress, by the open door, looking back at him. She smiled when she saw his black eye. He'd had a black eye the night she first met him.

"Well, Mac Reilly," the Matriarch said. "Nothing much has changed, has it?"

"Not much, Lorenza," Mac agreed.

Chapter 23

Miami

She was Lorenza Machado when he first met her. Nineteen years old and delicious as a ripe peach, with the thickest Spanish accent that made the words "I love you and ohh how you do that thing . . . how I love it . . . oh make me feel that some more," sound even more erotic to the young detective he had been then. Plus she had dark eyes that promised excitement and a smile that would haunt Mac's nights for years to come. He had fallen instantly and completely in love. And so, Lorenza told him, had she.

It happened in a club in Miami. The Havanita, it was called. A muggy Florida night, a low palm-thatched room leading onto a tiki-torched courtyard, crammed tables, waiters bearing trays of potent rum drinks over the heads of the dancers; a band—an even more potent mixture of Cuban and Puerto Rican—driving the Latin rhythms into the hot bodies on that dance floor. The very air seemed to throb around Mac, propping up the bar, drinking a Coke, a craggy twenty-three-year-old rookie detective, sporting a black eye from a fight a couple of nights before; dark hair a little too long for his own good, dark eyes too blue for women's own good, a body honed without the slightest effort on his part, and that was perhaps too good for both him and the women, who seemed to spot him a mile away, or even across a bar, and like iron filings to a magnet, were drawn to his tough young looks.

Mac had had his share of affairs, he'd even had a few weeks' fling with an "older woman," all of forty-two and on the lam from an erring husband, but he had never before fallen in love.

Lorenza Machado was ravishing in short red chiffon that moved with her body as she danced barefoot with a handsome, flashy Cuban who had eyes only for her, and who wore his large gold Rolex over the cuff of his custom-made white guayabera shirt, and whose expensive Mercedes convertible was parked, by the well-tipped valet, right outside the club's red-carpeted entrance.

Lorenza's eyes linked momentarily with Mac's. She hesitated, missed her step, almost fell. The handsome Cuban caught her, laughed, offered her another drink.

"But I don't drink," she said, looking back at Mac. He was still looking at her.

She excused herself, threaded her way through the dancers, came and stood next to him.

It was as though Mac had been struck by lightning. "I didn't know what it meant to be in love until I saw you," was his opening line. It came from his heart.

She smiled her soft-lipped sensual smile, then reached up and touched his blackened eye. "Pobricito," she said, her sweet voice full of sympathy.

His eyes drank her in.

"You have hot eyes," she murmured, never having been devoured by a man's eyes before.

"Only for you," he said. And then he took her by the hand and led her back onto the dance floor. He slid his arm around her, holding her in that place just above the waist so she was pulled toward him. His eyes never left hers. She leaned away, looking at him as they danced to a soft, light, romantic Cuban song, oblivious to the other dancers, to the waiters bearing trays aloft, to the handsome man she'd been dancing with, flirting with, just minutes before.

Mac moved his hand up her back, he touched the soft nape of her neck where her thick black hair swung as they moved, feeling the heat of her there, the hint of sweat. He leaned in to her, his face close to her ear. He could smell her flowery perfume, her skin.

"I'm in love with you," he murmured, just loud enough for her to hear, through the soft blare of trumpets, the guitars, the hypnotic rhythm.

Her body relaxed in his arms, soft as only a sensual woman could be. Her head drooped.

"Yes," she said, so quietly Mac could barely hear. But he understood. Love had struck them both.

"Where are you from?" he'd asked, still holding on to her hand.

"Gainesville," she replied.

He stared at her astonished, then he laughed. "I thought you were going to say heaven."

"No. Oh, no. That's why I'm here. In Miami. I've run away from college."

Mac had driven through Gainesville once or twice. In those years the university seemed to be all the town consisted of, set deep into the flat swamplands of northern Florida. He understood. She didn't belong there.

She was looking down at their clasped hands. A current seemed to run between them. It was so strong it almost had a color. Blue.

She said, "I'm a sophomore. I miss my home. I feel better here, in Miami. The food, the people, the music. Closer to my family, in Spain."

Mac, who'd practically raised himself alone on the streets of Boston's rough North End, wished he had a family to miss. But suddenly it didn't matter. He asked her name, told her his.

Then, just like when he was in junior high, he said to her, "Will you be my girl?"

"Of course," Lorenza said.

And she was. For three passionate months, heady with love and sex, she traveled up and down Florida to be with him. But a young detective was expected always to be there, and Mac was dedicated. His schedule was tough, his time not his own.

Finally, that was what caused the end of the affair, though not of their love. "That will be forever," they'd told each other.

"All good things must come to an end," she'd said, sadly collecting her few possessions from his cheap studio apartment that certainly did not come with a Miami ocean view, only of a rough parking lot dotted with Corollas and old Ford trucks, one of which was Mac's.

Lorenza had been summoned back by her family to Spain, actually to the island of Majorca where she had been raised like a young lady. "Or at least they tried," she'd once told him with a giggle as she lay wantonly naked in his arms after making love for the third time that night. The nights were so long then, so filled with each other's needs and emotions, so sensual, so hot they could never get enough of each other.

But it was over. For good. They could not survive the pressures of her family, their youth, their parents, and his ambition. "Love," as they knew it then, was at an end, though it would live on in Mac's heart, a wonderful memory. As it did in Lorenza's.

They both realized young love like that could never be repeated. Never forgotten. In fact not only had Lorenza been Mac's first true love, she had been his only true love. Until he'd met Sunny.

Chapter 24

Barcelona

"*So?*" *the new* Lorenza said, standing in front of him, barefoot and wearing a red chiffon dress, exactly the way she had when they first met at the Havanita. "Do I get a kiss?"

"You mean for old time's sake?"

Arms folded across her chest, head tilted to one side, Lorenza looked deep into his eyes. "More than twenty years, Mac, and you still remember 'old times'?"

Oh, he remembered. Now, in that red dress, in the soft evening light, she might have been the young girl he had known then. Her body was still slender, the face she'd always complained was too round, was still smooth; the big dark eyes that always reminded him of Goya's court portraits still held a hint of unrestrained fire. She looked so very Spanish, her cloud of dark hair swept up at the sides with tortoiseshell mantilla combs.

"I don't have to try to remember," he said simply. "You never left me."

She came toward him, held out her hand. He took it in both of his. She said, "They say first love is the one you always remember."

"Then they're right. But you had the advantage, you were expecting me."

She laughed. "Surely it must have crossed your mind, since

you remember me so well, that the woman in Spain with the name Lorenza, the woman who contacted you, might just be the same? *You*, the famous private detective."

"I simply thought you were Paloma's grandmother. The family boss."

"Stepgrandmother. I was married to Paloma's grandfather."

"Juan Pedro de Ravel."

Their hands were still clasped.

"People thought I'd married him for his money and position. It wasn't true. I loved him very much."

"I'm sure you did."

"Not the way I loved you, Mac. This was different, but still wonderful."

"I'm glad," he said.

Then Lorenza stepped into his arms and kissed him. And time stood still.

Her perfume, ginger lily and dark amber, was in his head, the faint citrusy scent of his skin in hers; a paradise revisited, youth reclaimed in a single long embrace. He felt her bones beneath his hands, the way he had when he'd held her on that dance floor, the pliable swing of her body as she finally took her mouth from his and leaned back studying his face.

"Mac Reilly, you have not changed," she murmured. "Even the black eye is the same. You were always in trouble, even before I met you."

"And for the same reason," he said. "A guy in a bar I picked a fight with."

"For a *good* reason, I'll bet."

"For Bibi," he said. "It was her husband."

In an instant the past was left behind. Lorenza disengaged herself, took a step back, folded her arms over her chest again.

"Ah, Bibi," she said. "Odd, isn't it, that my husband's famous

daughter should bring us back together?" But what Lorenza was
thinking was how strange fate was. Fate, Lorenza believed, never
left anything to chance. Fate was preordained. And Mac had not
changed . . . he was the same, oh, he was the same . . .

She shook her head, cleared her thoughts, pulled herself together.

"I'm forgetting my manners," she said lightly. "I've not even
offered you a drink. Come with me."

She led the way across the hall into the big kitchen whose
square-sash windows overlooked a neglected side garden. Weeds
and tall grasses had overtaken the roses and she lifted open
the windows letting in the scent of jasmine and the sound of birds
singing their evening song. The sky had darkened, rain suddenly
spattered.

Mac leaned against the counter, arms folded, legs crossed at
the ankles, watching her. She was the same. Oh, yes, she was the
same.

"Rain is such a wonderful sound in hot summer." She removed a bottle of champagne from the refrigerator that kept it at
exactly the correct temperature for serving. Mac took it from her,
stripped off the wire cage, and slid the cork smoothly out without even a pop, merely a wisp of smoke.

"Remember, we used to drink rum and Coke." He poured the
crisp elegant Krug into crystal flutes. "It was all we could afford,
and barely even that."

"Young and poor." Lorenza lifted her glass to his in a salute.
"Sometimes I think those were the best times of our lives. Remember, Mac?"

Oh, he remembered it well. Somehow youth and love and sex
had overcome their perpetual state of poverty, surviving as they
did on take-out rice and beans from the nearby Cuban café,

splurging on proper dinner at a bistro or an evening at a club when he got paid, or when she got her allowance from her parents, which stopped when they realized she was no longer attending college and summoned her back home.

There was something magical in the optimism of young love that could never be repeated. Then life moved on. The years added up. More than twenty now.

"Did I tell you, you look wonderful," he said, leaning back against the counter again, keeping his distance.

She laughed and pointed to her face. "Look closer, Mac, and you'll see *I'm* no longer the girl you knew. And you are not the young man *I* knew." She studied him for a minute, then took a taste of her champagne. "I must say, though, like a good wine, you've aged well. In fact I think you look better than ever, with all that success and experience on your face, in your eyes."

Dangerous ground lurked between them. Mac thought of Sunny, of Malibu, of Pirate and his TV show. His real life. It was time to move back to reality.

He strolled round the large kitchen, glass in hand, inspecting shelves stacked with heavy pottery dishes in vibrant reds and blues and yellows. He looked at the large landscape painting of an English garden on the wall opposite the window, took in the copper-colored walls, the yellow window shades, the deep blue of the big Dacor stove. Lorenza had always loved color.

"You know I don't live here anymore," Lorenza said. She took the bottle of champagne from the cooler and refilled their glasses. "I haven't offered you anything to eat," she added, "because after our business discussion I want to take you to my stepdaughter's restaurant." She threw him a challenging glance from the corner of her eye. She knew Mac was a hamburger-and-ribs kind of guy. "Floradelisa's is one of Barcelona's most daring restaurants, known for its . . ." She hesitated, looking for the right word. "Shall we say *adventurous* food."

"Then I'll look forward to the adventure," Mac said. "And tell me, why don't you live here anymore?"

"This was our home, Juan Pedro's and mine. I was lost without him."

"I understand."

"I live at the vineyard, south of the city. I love it there." She laughed. "I'm the boss. I can keep an eye on everything, and everyone. Nothing gets past me. I'm a tyrant."

"But you get the results you want."

"You know about my winery?"

"Now I do."

"I never remember you drinking wine."

"I couldn't afford it," he said. "Or at least not the kind I might have wanted to drink."

"Well, now you *can*. My wines are aimed at exactly that market, at people who want a decent wine at an affordable price."

Mac listened as Lorenza told him how she had learned her trade, traveling through Spain's Rioja country, through France's Loire and Burgundy, Saint-Émilion and Bordeaux.

"It took me four years of nonstop learning," she said. "And it took my mind off my loss. I was too busy for grief."

Mac thought that was a pity. Grief was necessary; without it life went on unfinished.

She poured a glass of her red and held it out. "Taste," she said, looking at him. He knew she wanted his approval.

He tasted, thought about it. Tasted again. Considered.

"I'm a man who knows wine now," he said. "I have my favorites, I know what I like and a lot of it is too expensive. So when I tell you this is good, Lorenza, you know I'm not simply flattering you. This is a good, decent, homely red with a flowery aftertaste that somehow reminds me of you."

She threw back her head in a delighted laugh. "Coming from you, that's indeed praise."

He put down the glass, slid onto a bar stool at the counter, and for the moment put the past where it belonged.

He said, "Okay, Lorenza, you got me here. Now, let's get down to business. I want to hear the whole story and the real reason you want me to find your long-lost, and possibly murderous, step-daughter."

Chapter 25

Malibu

Sunny was on her way to Mac's place. The Napa trip had been stunningly successful; not only had she gotten her client a lot of publicity, she'd also been approached by two other wineries. Business was looking up. She might even need a third assistant, someone like Mac's Roddy, who was babysitting the dogs and the house while they were away.

California was undergoing one of its periodic heat waves. Even Malibu seemed to be melting under the sun. The ocean glimmered smooth and gray-green and the air pressed heavily on her shoulders as she turned her convertible into the Colony, waving hi to the gatekeeper, who knew her well. She made a right at the T-junction and drove along the only street. The large houses to her left were on the beach; the ones to her right had shady gardens, and all were expensive. Except Mac's, of course, though Sunny guessed he'd probably get a good price for it now as a teardown. The drive from the airport had been one long traffic hell and now here she was, parking outside Mac's place, and he wasn't even here to greet her.

Barcelona! she thought, frowning.

She slammed the car door shut, calling hello to a neighbor

and waving to the guy who detailed the neighborhood's cars, pointing a finger at her own and mouthing *Tomorrow?* He waved a chammy cloth back and mouthed *Okay.* A few days of parking at LAX had left a film of grit over Sunny's brand-new white four-door Porsche Panamera. Everybody else in L.A. seemed to drive black cars, despite the heat. She didn't get it. It was just one of those L.A. things, like Botox, or pumped-up lips, or boob implants. Sunny thanked God she had no need to follow those fashions; nature had given her very satisfactory breasts, a good body, full enough lips, and a so-far unraveled brow. And a white car. Long may it reign.

She leaned against the car, taking in Mac's little house, the scene of their love affair, with its pale sea-greenish paint job, its fretwork trim, its white door that led directly into the living room. The ficus tree in the small side yard was getting too big for its boots, and its branches were spreading onto the tiled roof. She'd remember to tell Mac to do something about that.

It was so comfortingly familiar; the house where she and Mac lived together. Well, most of the time they did. Her own home was out at Marina del Rey, a modern condo with floor-to-ceiling expanse of windows, pale walls, white sofas, and a perfect—albeit small—stainless-steel kitchen where, as chef-in-residence, she cooked for the two of them, and sometimes their guests. Her bedroom was usually a chaos of half-unpacked suitcases and strewn clothing, since she was always somehow halfway between there and Malibu. Her untidiness drove Mac crazy but she bargained her way out of it by cooking him great food and she always said proudly he could eat off the floor of her kitchen. If Tesoro would allow him, that is.

She opened the gate to the narrow sandy path leading to the beach.

Mac was in Barcelona. Without her. Damn it, why couldn't he have waited? They could have gone together, made it into a holiday. She would have given up Mauritius if he would have given up the fishing trip. They had never been to Spain and she would have loved to see the city where Picasso was born, explore Gaudi's fabulous church and the Güell Park and the museums, maybe visit the coastal village of Cadaqués where Dali had lived and worked with his scary wife, Gala. And then there was Seville and Granada, the beauty of the Alhambra with its famous gardens and courtyards . . . damn it, why hadn't Mac waited for her!

She had no idea what was happening with Bibi and Paloma. There had been only one message from Mac. *You're not missing anything but traffic and me,* he'd said, or something like that. Well, she was also missing seeing Barcelona.

Tesoro heard her footsteps and came flying toward her followed by an irate Roddy, golden blond, spray tanned, blue eyed, and gorgeous.

"Goddammit, dog," he was yelling as he rounded the corner, almost colliding with Sunny. He put out his arms to stop himself and she fell into them, laughing.

"I might have known it was you," he said, hugging her. "That bloody dog never moves so much as a whisker unless it's to attack Mac or try to kill Pirate, or else run to her mama."

"Don't you call my baby a bloody dog," Sunny said, bending to scoop up Tesoro, who whined pathetically. Ears flattened, she licked Sunny's face, letting her know how terrible she was to have abandoned her.

"Don't you worry, my precious," Sunny murmured, kissing the dog's glossy little nose. Tesoro weighed in at just about three pounds and "Could," as Roddy said now, "easily be squashed flat under a careless footstep. *Like maybe mine,*" he added grimly. The dog had driven him to distraction, yapping and whining, and biting at Pirate.

"Nobody's that careless," Sunny said, taking Roddy's hand as they walked together onto the deck overlooking the beach.

"Overlooking" was not quite the right word; Mac's house was actually *on* the beach, built on old wooden pilings driven into the sand. The deck stretched the width of the house—small but fairly deep so there was room for a couple of chaises and a covered garden swing, a table, four chairs, and a couple of dog beds. Pirate was fast asleep in the one at the far end.

"You look upset," Roddy said, checking out Sunny as she flung herself onto one of the two old Wal-Mart chaises. It creaked ominously, and she noticed it had definitely developed a list to the left.

"Not that you don't look wonderful, as always," he added, leaning against the deck rail and taking in her narrow white Gap pants, black James Perse tee, and Chanel flats. No jewelry except for the small gold hoops, hair pulled on top with a scrunchie, not a speck of makeup.

"Goddammit, Sunny, I don't know how you do it," he said admiringly. "All the way from northern California and you look fresh and beautiful as a daisy."

"At least you didn't say '*goddamn*' daisy."

She grinned at him and he apologized. "It's the dogs, they've driven me to cursing," he said, reaching out to pat Tesoro, who gave him a baleful look and a curled lip.

"You see what I mean? That dog can drive a man insane."

"That dog loves her mama, don't you, darling-heart?"

Roddy wafted a dismissive hand. "You must be dying of thirst. What can I get you?"

Sunny looked at the sullen silent sea, at the oddly threatening sky and the relentless sun. Even under the shade on Mac's terrace with the fan turning the air around it was stifling. The beach was almost never like this.

"Do we have any Pimm's?" she asked, suddenly inspired by the thought of the cool, summery English drink.

"My dear, of course we do." Roddy beamed, delighted. He smoothed down his sleeveless black wife-beater tee and black satin swim shorts and clapped his hands delightedly together. "My dear, I even have *fresh mint* for it. Stole it from next door's terrace when they weren't looking. Just stay right there and get comfy. Won't be a sec."

"Roddy," she called as he disappeared through the sliding glass door into the kitchen. "Any news of Mac?"

He popped his head back out. "Only that he's in Barcelona. And that he has one of the blackest eyes you ever saw."

"Purple?"

"Probably turning yellow and green by now. Trust me, sweetheart, you would not want to see him."

Oh but I would, Sunny thought sadly. *Barcelona!* Oh, Mac! Lonely, she wondered what he was up to.

Chapter 26

Barcelona

Lorenza and Mac were sitting at the small kitchen table by the open windows, listening to the rain. Lorenza's heart was still pounding from the thrill of seeing him again and she still felt his kiss on her lips. The sudden transition from personal to business had taken her by surprise; she had expected more from Mac. Then, she'd asked herself, more *what*? More past? Some present? Maybe even a future?

She was a fool even to think like that. More than twenty years had passed. She was no longer that sexy young girl he'd known, though her body still remembered him, and that kiss had triggered a response. But obviously not for Mac. He was all business now. Love, past or present, was forgotten.

"So, Mr. Detective," she said, pulling herself together one more time. "Tell me about yourself."

Mac got up and fetched the champagne. He poured the last of it into their glasses. "I'm willing to bet you already know most of it," he said, meeting her glance across the table.

"Hollywood's TV detective, famous, fashionable, and successful."

"I'm good at what I do."

She bit her lip, sorry she had mocked him. "I remember when you were just starting, I remember how dedicated you were, and how good you were at your job, even then."

"I hope I'm good enough to unravel the Bibi mess, for Paloma's sake as well as yours. So, Lorenza, why don't you tell me *exactly* what's going on."

She told him everything, including the deal she'd made with the three siblings. "I wanted them all to go out there and hunt for her, but somehow I get the feeling one of them might know something. . . ."

"You mean one of them might know where Bibi is? Or knows if she's dead?"

"I really don't know what I think." She gave a helpless little shrug. "It's just a gut feeling."

Mac got up again, thrust his hands in his jeans pockets, prowled the kitchen floor silently. After a few minutes he turned and looked at her. "Lorenza, do *you* have any idea where she might be?"

"No." She hesitated. "Again it's only a gut feeling, but because Bibi was a good mother, I think if she's still alive she would not be far away from her daughter. In case Paloma got sick or was in some kind of danger. It's a mother's instinct, to be there to protect her child."

"Then you think Bibi's here, in Spain?"

She nodded. "Somewhere in Spain." She spread her arms wide, a bitter smile on her face. "But who knows where to begin to look?"

Who indeed, Mac thought. Especially him, who knew almost nothing about this country and where a woman might go to hide out. Would Bibi choose a big city? Barcelona even? Or a mountain retreat? A seaside resort? And anyhow, where was she getting the money? The more he thought about it, the more he began to believe Bibi must be dead. Death was the last resort of a desperate woman.

Lorenza said, "I know none of her bank accounts has been touched and none of her investments have been sold. Bibi has not seen a penny of her own money since she left the States."

"Then how could she survive?"

"I always wondered whether one of the sisters, or even her brother might have funded her, if only to keep her out of the way. They wouldn't want a murderer in the family."

"A *suspected* murderer," Mac corrected her.

"So tell me," she said. "If Bibi did not do it, then who did? And why? The police had no other suspects. And after all, she had a motive, the wronged wife."

"Bibi was not a 'wronged wife.' She was a wronged *lover.* There's a big difference, Lorenza."

"Why? Don't lovers kill too?"

Mac stopped pacing. Hands still thrust in his pockets, he turned to look at her. "I guess to find the answer to that we have to ask Bibi. And I suggest we begin our search with the brother and sisters. Find out what they know."

"You'll meet them all tonight, at the restaurant. You really think they'll tell you?"

"No, but I'll put them on their guard, then wait and see who makes a move."

He took the chair opposite her. Hands folded on the table, he looked at her again. Really looked at her, in her red dress, rubies dangling in her ears, the narrow platinum wedding band her only ring.

He reached across, took her hand again. "You loved Juan Pedro very much, didn't you," he said gently.

She nodded, sending her ruby earrings swinging.

"Is there anyone else?"

She stared down at their linked hands. "There have been . . . some." She glanced up and smiled. "After all, I am a woman."

"You're beautiful, Lorenza, and special. You'll make some man very happy."

She took her hand away, rested her chin in it, half smiling. "But not you, Mac."

She was asking him, straight out, telling him she could go there, be back where they started all those years ago.

"Lorenza . . ." He hesitated and she held up a hand.

"Of course there's somebody else, I should have realized. I'm sorry."

"You needn't be sorry. It's the finest compliment you could have paid me."

She was a fool, the words had simply tumbled out of her mouth. God, was she really that lonely, that man-less? But it wasn't that. It was that Mac was special. He always would be.

"I'm sure she's wonderful," she said.

"Her name is Sunny, and yes, she is wonderful." Mac looked intently at her. "And you know something else, Lorenza, she's a lot like you."

"Then she must be a wonderful wife." She was laughing at him now.

"We haven't quite gotten to that point yet."

He wasn't married after all. Lorenza picked up the champagne flutes and carried them to the sink. "You shouldn't have told me that, Mac Reilly," she called over her shoulder. "Don't you know 'all's fair in love and war.'" Then, laughing, she added, "We must be going. Floradelisa's waits for no one. I'll go and powder my nose."

Mac watched her walk away. She was beautiful. Sexy. Still had great legs. Restless, he got up and prowled some more. He thought about Sunny. She must be back from Napa by now. She might even be in Malibu. Where he should be. With her. Not in this emotional sensual minefield. How could he have known the past was going to catch up with him?

He'd better find Bibi and get out of here. Fast. Safely back to Sunny.

Chapter 27

Floradelisa stood by the swing doors leading to her kitchen, waiting for Lorenza and Mac Reilly. A pretty young hostess was at the front desk, chic in a specially designed Gaultier suit, black of course—what else? But with dozens of ropes of glittering red-quartz beads slung around her neck and red suede heels that exactly matched the restaurant's in-your-face red walls. The floors were black, the tablecloths traditional starched white linen, the flowers simple low bowls of massed deep-red carnations, with no scent of course because that would intrude on the flavor and aromas of the food. And at Floradelisa's the food was everything.

Floradelisa had changed from her stained work clothes and wore a pristine white chef's jacket with her name embroidered in scarlet. Her dark hair was tucked under a loose cloth cap—no token chef's hat for her—and of course she wore the ubiquitous clogs. White.

Spotting her stepdaughter from across the room, Lorenza waved. She thought Flora could have been a scrub-nurse prepared for surgery. And in a way, she was.

Floradelisa waved back, threading her way past the full tables, smiling here, shaking a hand there. She noticed that Mac Reilly was holding Lorenza's elbow in a familiar sort of way, yet he was only the detective summoned to find Bibi. She wondered how come they were on such intimate terms already as she gave Mac a quick once-over.

She had to admit he was attractive, even with that shiner that somehow only added to his bad-boy good looks. She groaned inwardly, praying they had not made a mistake and that Lorenza was not going to fall for Bibi's detective. This family had enough problems without adding romance to them. The words "fortune hunter" came to mind but she dismissed that idea quickly. After all, it was Paloma who had found the detective, Lorenza had only agreed, as they all had, to hire him. That is, all with the exception of Antonio, who was in no position anyway to protest too much. Antonio was a shit and everybody knew it. Except his poor wife.

The truth was Floradelisa herself had only agreed under pressure. In her opinion things were better left as they were, with Paloma living with Jassy, Lorenza safely out at the vineyard, Antonio in Jerez, and her taking care of business in Barcelona. And there was no doubt in Flora's mind that with the threat of a murder charge still hanging over her head, Bibi was better off out of Paloma's life. Not that she would ever say so to Lorenza, or to poor little Paloma, but in her opinion that child had enough love coming at her from her Ravel family to take care of her the rest of her life. Floradelisa had no doubt this was the best way and she would stick to that view, regardless of any queries from any private detective, famous or not. The only problem was this detective came with the reputation of being clever and very good at what he did, and she wasn't sure the Ravel family was ready for the truth.

"Lorenza," she said, quickly kissing her stepmother, and being kissed rather more firmly back. She noticed that the detective, who'd been holding Lorenza's arm so proprietarily, had stepped back and was watching them. He was not smiling, and Flora was surprised. She'd expected him to be a bit obsequious, wanting to insert himself into the family scene. After all, he was a hired hand, and Lord knows what Lorenza had agreed to pay him.

"I'm Floradelisa," she introduced herself, and Mac shook her hand briefly.

His eyes met hers. He thought her flamboyant restaurant did not describe the woman he was looking at: a plain, plump, introverted woman.

"Lorenza told me the story of how you were given your charming name," he said.

"My father was a very charming man. Anyhow, where's Jassy and Antonio?"

"Late, as always," Lorenza said.

Flora showed them to a table by the window, and Gaultier-black-clad waiters hurried to pull out the massive antique carved Spanish chairs, upholstered in deep red leather, a traditional contrast to the very modern food being served.

Rows of Philippe Starck red lucite chandeliers highlighted the cropped red carnations, and a drink was quickly brought, a tiny glass full of amber liquid, along with a white plate with a ceramic spoon holding a small coral-colored ball.

"An amuse-bouche," Floradelisa said. "A tapa, if you prefer the Spanish."

"Are we permitted to ask what it is?" Lorenza knew to expect the unexpected.

"Taste first," Flora said, folding her arms. "Then tell me what you think."

Mac bit into the coral ball, sipped the drink. Flora did not

look the least bit anxious for his approval, she was totally confident in her culinary skills.

He said, "First, I'm willing to bet this is a Mexican beer, a
Negra Modelo. And it was absolutely perfect with this wonderful
mutation, or whatever, of what I'd guess is blue crab. I don't know
what you did with it, Floradelisa, but it goes on my list of a perfect
little bit of food heaven."

Lorenza stared, surprised, at him. She had no idea what she
had just eaten, only that it was crisp on the outside, fluffy on the
inside, that it looked freaky and tasted delicious.

"You're a genius, Flora," she said. "What else can we expect
from you tonight?"

"Let's just say you are in my hands," Flora said, pleased. She
looked at Mac. "All I can promise is I won't poison you."

He nodded. "That's the good news. Now I'm waiting for the
bad."

She had turned to go back to her kitchen, but now she turned
back again. "What do you mean?"

"I mean about Bibi. What do you know that you're not telling
the family?"

Angry hot spots blazed on Flora's pale cheeks. "I don't know
what you're talking about."

Mac said, "Listen, Flora, Bibi is why I'm here. If you don't
know where she is, then I'd like to have your take on her, what
motivated her, who *exactly* Bibi was."

Taken by surprise, Flora found herself blurting out something she had always thought was the truth.

"I think Bibi, for all her success, was always a woman in
search of herself—and never finding her," she said. "And that's all
I know about Bibi," she added, turning quickly and heading for
the safety of her kitchen.

They were silent as wine was poured. A basket of tiny house-baked rolls was brought with a bowl of sweet yellow butter and a saucer of deep green olive oil. Waiters wove their dance, soft conversation hummed from other tables, there was a clean aroma of food and spices. The red room was a theater for food.

"What do you think Flora meant by that?" Mac finally asked Lorenza, taking in for the umpteenth time that evening that she looked gorgeous in her red chiffon, and her ruby earrings in her big carved red Spanish chair.

"It's a woman thing," she said. "I think she meant that for all our apparent confidence, all our formidable energy—and Bibi was formidable onstage—inside we . . . *she* . . . might have lost her strength. I know I lost mine when Juan Pedro died. And I know Bibi was undermined by unscrupulous managers who worked her to death on those lengthy world tours, and by a relentless schedule of work and recording. And worst of all by that husband. Bibi found success very young and it left her no time to discover herself. I think that's what Flora meant."

Mac remembered Lev's e-mail about Bibi . . . *make a woman feel like a woman and she's happy.* "You think that's the reason she took a lover."

"I do. And then the lover failed her too. He cheated on her."

"A crime of passion," Mac said. It seemed almost too simple.

"The others are late," Lorenza said, looking worried as Floradelisa sent out yet another tiny appetizer. "But then Jassy always is."

Mac stared, puzzled, down at his plate at what looked like a small speckled brown egg in a curlicue of white sauce. He glanced up and met Lorenza's eyes.

She smiled conspiratorially. "Spoon or fork? What do you think?"

"Oh, fingers," he decided.

He picked up the brown egg-thing and bit into it. Immediately his taste buds were hit by a pervading sweetness, than an edgy bitter undertone, then citrus . . .

"Wonderful," he said, astonished.

Lorenza smiled, wiping her fingers delicately on her starched white napkin. "One of these days, I'm hoping Floradelisa will leave all this surreal experimentation behind—food as art—and cook real food again. Spanish food. At least then I can be sure my sauce doesn't have a deconstructed pig's tail in it."

"Why don't we try a bottle of your de Ravel wine," Mac suggested. He was suddenly having a good time and in no hurry to meet the siblings.

"Flora refuses to serve it, but I'll order a Txakoli, a local wine. You'll like it, it has a bit of a sparkle."

"Like you," he said and she laughed.

"Not quite as good as those rum punches," she reminded him, as their eyes linked with memories again across the table.

Chapter 28

Antonio had arranged to pick up Jassy at her surprisingly small but luxuriously modernized apartment in an Art Deco building on a chic street in the Eixample district, and drive her to Floradelisa's. He hated her tiny cage elevator, it gave him claustrophobia, so instead of going up he called on his cell and told her he was downstairs. Jassy said she was running late and would be down in a few minutes, then kept him waiting for exactly twenty. Antonio timed it on his watch, pacing the street, glaring at the parking officer patrolling the area. He got on the phone and called her angrily, again.

"I'm right here," Jassy said, suddenly, from behind him.

Startled, he swung round. "Jesus Christ, Jassy, you almost gave me a heart attack."

"Only *almost*?" she said, mockingly. "Too bad."

"Jesus! I don't know why I bothered coming. I should have let you go on your own to meet this detective. I sure as hell don't want to meet him. I didn't want to hire him in the first place."

He held the car door open, waiting impatiently while Jassy dropped into the low-slung seat of his dark blue Maserati.

"You must have short-legged girlfriends," she complained,

pushing back the tan leather seat. "And anyhow, is this *another* new car?"

Antonio ignored her. He gave the parking officer another frosty glare before taking off, too fast, only to jerk to a stop at the red light.

Exasperated, Jassy looked angrily at her brother. The seat belt had almost choked her. She smoothed her narrow cream-colored skirt over her thighs. "You'll end up killing somebody if you continue to drive like this," she said. "And yes, I did ask if this is *another* new car. No wonder stepmother Lorenza is pissed off at you, squandering the sherry profits on fast cars and fast women."

"What do you know about my women?" Anthony turned his head and smiled at her, a true Cheshire cat smile.

"Don't smile at me like that," she snapped. "We are here on business and don't you forget it. Paloma's future is at stake and I'm warning you now, Antonio, if you know anything about Bibi and are not telling, this detective will find out."

"There's nothing to find out." Antonio's voice was cold. He was negotiating Barcelona's traffic like a race driver, after all he'd grown up here and knew it as well as he knew the route from Jerez to Marbella, only here, unfortunately, there wasn't the same alluring woman waiting for him. Only his stepmother and some small-time Hollywood detective. He knew how to take care of guys like that. But he needed Lorenza's shares in the company, so was forced to toe the line. Lorenza hadn't said what the extra reward was, but Antonio knew it must mean money, and by God he needed money right now. He'd need even more when he divorced Elena and had to pay for her for the rest of her life, plus three children to put through school and God knows what else.

"The fact that the sherry business is taking a dive is not my fault," he said to Jassy.

"The fact that the *de Ravel* sherry business is taking a dive *is* your fault, and no one else's," she said.

Antonio heaved a sigh. "I don't know why I bothered to pick you up. You're nothing but a troublemaker."

"Antonio, you make your own trouble. Have you no thought for your wife? No *respect*?"

"Mind your own business."

"The de Ravel sherry *is* our family business, and Lorenza is prepared to give us half of it to share and you're squandering *my* portion on your indulgences; cars, apartments in Marbella, boats, women . . ."

Antonio turned into the Calle Mallorca where Floradelisa's was located, pulling up with a squeal of expensive brakes in front of the valet parking stand. He turned to glare at Jassy as the valets rushed to open their doors. "Don't you dare breathe a word of this tonight," he snapped.

She glared back at him. "You're forgetting we're here for Paloma tonight, not for you, Antonio. And not so you can get another chunk of de Ravel money that, thanks to Lorenza, we still possess."

Antonio got out. He buttoned his jacket, straightened his tie—a more sober blue tonight with a small pattern of sailboats—his woman had bought it for him in Marbella just last week. He patted it fondly.

Jassy swung her legs from the low-slung car, smiling her thanks as the red-jacketed valet gave her his hand and helped her up.

"It's a great car, though," she said, taking Antonio's arm and smiling as they walked into the restaurant. After all, it was better, whatever was going to happen, to present a united family front.

Chapter 29

"Here they are at last." Lorenza spotted them coming in. She thought how good-looking Juan Pedro's two children were. Walking toward her, they looked like the perfect couple, no one would ever take them for brother and sister: Jassy so Nordic blond like her mother, Antonio the dark Spaniard like Juan Pedro.

Mac was watching them too. Jassy was a lovely woman, elegant in short black off-the-shoulder lace and enormous graduated diamond drop earrings that glimmered as she moved. Her blue eyes were made bluer, Mac suspected, by contacts. Her brother drew attention too, tall, broad-shouldered, dark and beaky, in a custom-tailored suit and expensive tie. They were smiling but the tension between them was palpable. Mac got to his feet as Jassy offered him her hand.

"How lovely to meet you." She peered at his black eye. "My oh my, somebody didn't like you."

"Or maybe he just ran into an unfriendly door." Antonio shook Mac's hand too. He did not say it was good to meet him. The antipathy was mutual.

Jassy turned to smile at the handsome young waiter who'd brought them a glass of the Negra Modelo and the delicate crab tapa. "How are you, Johannes?" she asked, nodding, pleased when he said he was well. Jassy was good with waiters, she always inquired about their health and their families.

Antonio tilted his head back and threw the beer down his throat. "God," he said, disgusted. "Whatever this is, it's too sweet for me. Give me a vodka on the rocks any time." As if by magic a waiter appeared at his side with exactly that. Floradelisa knew her brother's habits.

"It's good of you to come all this way at such short notice, Mr. Reilly," Jassy said.

"Paloma needs help," Mac said. "That's the reason I came."

Antonio said, "I'm relieved to hear it's not just for the money."

"In fact money has not yet been discussed."

Mac watched Antonio take a gulp of the martini. There was a nervousness to his movements, the too-tight grip on the stem of the glass, the sideways flicker of his eyes at Lorenza, turning his head to see who else was dining there that he might know.

"Then it's time we did talk money," Lorenza said, firmly. "And since this is a family matter and concerns Paloma and Bibi, I'm telling you now that Mac's fee will be paid by the four of us from our personal funds."

"Well, there goes my chartered yacht this season," Jassy said cheerfully.

"And my divorce," Antonio said.

The two women turned to him, horror-struck.

"*What* did you say?" Lorenza asked.

"You can't divorce her, Antonio, you simply can't do that to Elena and the children." Jassy shook her head and her blond hair glinted with a reddish shine in the light from the chandeliers, and her eyes glimmered with held-back tears. "Oh shit," she gasped. "I can't cry in a restaurant, even if it is my sister's. And anyway, I changed my mind. Yes, you *can* divorce," she said in a fierce whisper. "Only Elena should be the one to divorce *you*. She's better off without you."

"I'm sorry to inflict our family problems on you," Lorenza said to Mac. "I didn't expect this."

"I'm here *because* of your family problems," Mac said. In fact he was enjoying the scene. Antonio had showed his cards before they'd even gotten into the game. It was clear he was a complete narcissist who cared for no one but himself, and that included Paloma. He thought Lorenza had better deduct Antonio's share of his fee off the top *before* he got his hands on the reward money.

"I have a set daily fee," he said mildly. "Plus the usual expenses, of course."

"Of course," Antonio said, finishing his vodka and signaling for another, as the waiter removed their plates.

Lorenza hadn't expected Antonio to behave quite this rudely. "Whatever your fees are, Mac, they will be taken care of immediately. All that concerns us is Paloma. And Bibi, of course."

"Of course, Bibi." Antonio sounded bitter.

Mac said, "Tell me about your sister."

Antonio met his eyes for the first time. He shrugged, and raised his eyebrows. "Bibi? There's nothing much to tell. What you saw was what you got. It was all a façade, that sweet, sexy, girl-singer shit. Bibi could chop your heart out without a second thought. And if you want my opinion, that's exactly what she did with her lover and his whore. She killed 'em dead, Mr. Mac Reilly, hotshot TV detective." He turned triumphantly to Lorenza. "There, I've just cut down on our expenses. I solved the murder. And now don't you think we're better off leaving the question of 'is Bibi dead or alive' alone? And letting little Paloma get on with her life, not having to have a condemned murderer for a mother?"

Silence fell over the table. Lorenza hung her head and Jassy began to cry again.

"Oh, the hell with this." Antonio flung down his napkin and got to his feet. "I didn't want to meet the detective anyway. I'm leaving."

Mac got to his feet too. "Before you go, Antonio," he said, "I think we can cut down even more on the expenses. Why don't you save time and trouble and just tell me where Bibi is."

Had it been possible for a man so tanned to turn pale, Mac would have sworn Antonio did. He stood for a minute, staring, shocked, at Mac. Then without so much as a goodnight, he turned and walked out.

Chapter 30

"I'm sorry." Jassy sniveled quietly into her napkin. Johannes, the waiter, appeared and quickly removed Antonio's place setting. Other waiters arrived carrying large, plain white plates with a single oyster in the very center, glazed, Johannes told them, with aloe vera, agar-agar, and powdered silver.

Mac had never heard of agar-agar, nor had he ever eaten powdered silver, and he wasn't sure he wanted to try now.

Suddenly, he missed Sunny very much. He could see the two of them here together, at this extraordinary restaurant. Sunny would have enjoyed every new taste, even those she didn't like. "It's the experience that's the thing," she would have said cheerfully. Her innocence seemed light-years away from this complicated family. He checked his Timex; eleven thirty and the restaurant was crowded, with still more people coming in. They ate late in Barcelona, but it was three in the afternoon in California, and he wanted very badly to talk to Sunny, he wanted to hear her laugh, ask him how he was and did his poor eye need kissing better.

He looked at the two women. Both were staring at their plates. Neither had touched the oyster.

"I'm afraid our lovely dinner has been ruined," Lorenza said, sounding tired. "Perhaps we should call it a night."

"Tomorrow is another day," Jassy said, blotting mascara from under her eyes. She was always good for a cliché to fit the occasion.

"Please tell Floradelisa we had to leave," Lorenza told Johannes, who wrung his hands and stared, disturbed, at their uneaten oysters.

Mac handed him a hundred-dollar bill, thinking what the hell, let Antonio complain about the expenses. He apologized and turned to leave. Then he turned back, picked up the oyster, and put it in his mouth. He stood for a second, eyes closed, savoring it. Then he opened them and smiled at the bemused Johannes.

"I never ate silver before," he said, grinning as he followed the two women to the door.

Lorenza and Jassy sat in the back of the BMW and Mac sat up front with the driver. They dropped him at the Méridien first. He got out of the car and Lorenza put down her window and leaned out to say goodnight.

"Did you get the responses you were looking for?" she asked.

"I believe I did."

"Then will you come to the vineyard with me tomorrow, to see Paloma? We can talk then."

He'd meant to go back to L.A. tomorrow but he knew now he couldn't. Not even for Sunny. He was too involved. "I will," he agreed.

"I'll pick you up at eleven." Without a further word, she signaled to the driver and was gone.

Mac watched the disappearing taillights. It had been an eventful evening. What's more, he still did not have a clue as to where to begin his search. *Where* would a woman like Bibi run to? And, more importantly, *who* would help her, because she had to have had help. He wasn't sure of anything much, right now, but he was sure of that. Bibi could not have done this disappearing act alone.

Part Three

Chapter 31

Cáceres, Extremadura, Spain

You would not have recognized the plain-looking woman in the longish green cotton skirt and shirt, a beige hand-knit sweater thrown loosely around her shoulders against the cool wind that had gotten up. A wide-brimmed straw hat was pulled over her mouse-brown hair and she wore rimless tinted glasses over her dark brown eyes. There was something almost hippieish about her, as she strolled through the Saturday street market in the small medieval Spanish town of Cáceres, with her big woven basket and the hat, and those shaggy bangs half obscuring her face, and with the old dog plodding devotedly behind her.

She had parked her small Seat in her usual spot on a side street, always careful to be legal. She could not risk so much as a parking ticket.

She strolled the market, followed by her dog, buying fruits and vegetables picked that same morning by local smallholders, who greeted her familiarly, calling out *"Hola señora, buenos días."* They took the best tomatoes for her from the back of the stall, the ones they saved for special customers; they added a little extra to the bag of hazelnuts; weighed only the ripest of the new mountain cheese, first cutting a small chunk for her to taste.

The miller was there with his sacks of flour, wholemeal and also unbleached, which she preferred as it was lighter. The region was famous for its excellent bread and she took pleasure in making her own.

Her shopping done, weighed down by her loaded basket, she walked to a café on the square, where she ordered a double dark coffee and a slab of baguette, sliced across, then brushed with deep rich green olive oil and toasted on the *plancha* that still had a hint of the previous night's garlic. Buttered until it glistened, it was a treat she looked forward to all week.

Sitting alone in the café in one of Spain's most beautiful squares, Bibi felt a brief moment of content.

Time seemed to have stood still in Cáceres. As it had when, thanks to her father's friend Rodolfo Hernandez, she had changed her life and become his distant cousin, "Vida."

It had happened so suddenly, like a bolt of lightning coming at her from her past.

She was alone at the Hollywood Hills house. Jassy had taken Paloma away. Her staff and hangers-on had already departed, not wanting to be associated with a woman involved in murder, whether it was true or not. She had just dismissed her loyal housekeeper who had cared so dearly for Paloma, and whose wails as she had walked out the front door for the last time still rang in Bibi's ears. She had sent her daughter away to find a new life with Jassy and her Spanish family. She had done it because she loved her, and saw there could be no life for them together: a notorious suspected killer traveling the world with her small daughter.

Who would even want to know them? Who would even allow their own kids over for play dates at the notorious Bibi's house? Paloma must have a new start, free and clear. And Bibi would grieve forever.

She stood in the front hall, listening. There had always been music in her house: pianos, guitars, voices, laughter, children. She had turned off all her phones except the very personal one, a private number very few people knew.

The silence was profound, almost tangible; it was like a wall of fog around her, she was stifling on it, couldn't breathe . . .

And then the phone rang, the one clutched in her hand, the one with the private number. Her eyes were so filled with tears she had to hold it close to see who was calling. *Rodolfo Hernandez.* Her father's friend. She had known him since she was a child. He had called earlier, when the story first broke, said he would be there immediately to help. But she had turned him down. "I'm ashamed," she told him, "to have my father's friend see me like this."

"Call me," he said, "when you need me."

She had not called and now he was calling her.

"I heard about Paloma," he said. "I'm sending a plane for you. You will come back here, to me, in Spain."

"I need to disappear," she said.

"You will," he promised.

Rodolfo Hernandez observed her now, from his place at the open storefront bar in Cáceres. Its gray terrazzo floor was littered with discarded wrappers from the *pinchos,* the small tapas served there, succulent mouthful-sized portions on a bit of crusty bread, speared with a toothpick and handed to you on that bit of paper that always ended up on the floor. There was usually a sampling of wild boar stew or the Spanish *tortilla,* a potato omelet; there'd be a chunk of local flinty cheese and the tiny white anchovies known as *boquerones* and fresh fava beans in their skins; and the sweetly salty Iberian ham for which the region was famous. Along with a mid-morning brandy, they went down very well.

He drained his glass and tossed his paper napkin—so small and slippery it was virtually useless for its purpose of cleaning fingers messy from tapas, onto the floor along with the rest. Every now and again somebody would come out with a straw broom and sweep them up, scattering a few drops of water then mushing around an old mop, until in another half hour or so the papers and the peanut shells and the fava skins accumulated all over again.

It was a Spanish tradition, like the TV stuck high on a shelf blaring the latest soccer game, and the bottles of Soberano and the sherry; the rough red wine; the draft beers, and the *plancha*—the flat grill—and the gathering of older workmen whose place this really was, and who for breakfast and before they set off for work at dawn tossed back a brandy with a slab of oiled baguette hot off that *plancha,* the way others might have a cup of coffee and a muffin.

Rodolfo was an older man, in his seventies now, leonine with his broad brow and swept-back silver hair and with the formal manners of an earlier European generation. A longtime friend of Juan Pedro's—though he was younger—he had known Bibi since she was a child. He had stood back, watched her career take off, admired her talent and her strange beauty, watched from afar the mistakes she had made; and he had always remembered her birthday. And one thing he knew for sure was that Bibi was no killer.

Looking at her, sitting in the café across the square, Rodolfo thought no one would recognize her now, though he himself had hardly recognized the woman stumbling wearily down the metal steps from the sleek Gulfstream 5 he'd sent to rescue her from the house in the Hollywood Hills that had become her prison: ripped jeans, black sweatshirt, red hair dragged so tightly back it looked painful, large green eyes blurred with fatigue and tears.

She'd looked at him, then looked around her at the towering Sierras cutting through the dense forests and boulder-strewn hills of the province of Extremadura, one of Spain's least populated and remote areas, where life still went on at a pace long-lost to the tourist-ridden Costas. She'd looked at the lowering gray sky and the silver helicopter ready to take them to Rodolfo's country home in the dark green forest. He could tell her heart was in her boots. He knew all she wanted was to get back on that plane and go find her daughter.

He'd hardly recognized her, but Bibi recognized *him*. When Rodolfo wrapped his arms round her she felt safe. For a few moments the terrible past weeks were gone. She was free. She was home.

He took her to his house, a place he called modestly "my cottage" though in reality it was a two-story stone mansion dating back to the fifteenth century, and where the ruins in the parklike grounds were reputed to be of a hideaway built by the Knights Templar, who'd hunted in that area in the thirteenth century. To be sure the house was modernized and luxurious for a man like Rodolfo, who had been brought up with luxury. Generators powered electricity; twenty-first-century plumbing had replaced the original outhouses and now there were sybaritic bathrooms—not of marble or onyx, nothing flashy for a country house, he explained to Bibi when he showed her around. Just good Spanish ceramic tiles and the old rust-colored terra-cotta floors that had been there for what seemed like forever.

Bibi had hidden out there until, before too long, the hue and cry abated. There were other scandals, other murders, other celebrities in trouble. Bibi was half forgotten, though not by the L.A. police, who still had an unsolved double murder in their cold-case files. Unless they found the killer, Bibi would never go home again.

Instead, with Rodolfo's help she learned how to become someone else. Clairol changed her red hair to mouse; contacts changed her green eyes to brown; big skirts and loose sweaters changed her slender body to shapeless. She chose the name Vida because it meant "life," and Rodolfo said what she had was a new life. Now she spoke only Spanish, sometimes Catalan, but certainly never English. In fact if anyone she met inquired, she would quietly admit that she'd always had a block about foreign languages and had never managed to become fluent.

"It's embarrassing," she would say in her sweetly lisping Castilian accent. "But I do not travel so it scarcely seems to matter."

With time hanging heavily on her hands and a terrible gap in her heart and in her mind, with her constant thoughts and worry for her daughter, and a brain that needed occupying now she had no music, Vida learned to cook. Nothing like her sister, of course. Vida was a plain country cook, like the plain countrywoman she had become. She was, Rodolfo knew, different in appearance, but not in her heart.

And anyhow Bibi/Vida had her own place now, a couple of kilometers from Rodolfo's. Her new home. Simple. Silent. And lonely.

It had taken Bibi a long time to get to the point where she could sit in the café and watch children playing, without her heart wrenching. Finally, she had stopped trying to guess which of them might be Paloma's age and was able to watch them chasing each other round the plaza, shrieking with delight, fast and fleet of foot as little wild animals. She told herself they were simply children, free to laugh and play and lead a normal life. And *that* was what she had given her daughter. *A normal life.*

Still, a tear lurked as she quietly sipped her coffee. She missed having children around so much. They had always been an important part of her life.

Rodolfo left the bar and pushed his way through the noisy Saturday morning market crowd toward the café. Bibi saw him coming. Her face lit up and she waved. The dog recognized him too and stumbled eagerly to its feet.

That damned dog, Rodolfo thought, exasperated.

Bibi had found it living wild, lying tiredly by a stream where the forest just began and the trees were more thinly spaced, letting in the sunlight. So she had spotted his dull black shape and gone to investigate.

The dog had struggled bravely to its feet and, head hanging, looked up at her with eyes that seemed to say *This is the end of the road.* To which Bibi had added, out loud so she knew the dog heard, "For both of us, my friend."

He was too weak to walk so she picked him up and carried him back to Rodolfo's. "We are the same," she'd told the shocked Rodolfo, who'd said she must let the vet deal with him.

"He's too old and decrepit for you to take care of. *Now . . .*" he'd added. He didn't need to finish his sentence, Bibi knew what he meant. "*Now.* When you need to look after *yourself.*"

"I don't care that he's old and starved." She'd held him closer. "I'll fix him."

And she had, though of course there was nothing she could do about his age, which the vet put at around twelve years. Old, for a dog who'd had such a hard life and who was in such bad shape.

Bibi didn't care. He was her friend, and she named him "friend" in Spanish. *Amigo.*

Amigo's tail wagged slowly as Rodolfo bent to pat him. Everything about Amigo was becoming slower, Bibi thought, worried, as Rodolfo kissed her, patting her shoulder affectionately too.

"You look well, my Vida," he said, calling to the waiter for a *café solo,* then turning back and giving her an appraising look. "I might even have said, just a minute ago when I spotted you from across the square, that you looked . . . happy?"

Bibi smiled. He obviously had not noticed her tears from across the square. "I'm happy because you are here this weekend. I didn't expect to see you."

Looking at him, she thought how handsome he looked, the perfect gentleman in his custom dark blue shirt and tan linen pants, his handmade country loafers. He wore a simple round steel watch and no rings. Rodolfo had never been married, though he'd had a partner for twenty years whom he loved. His name was William and he was trusted with all Rodolfo's secrets, including Bibi's identity. The rest were confidential business secrets of Rodolfo's private financial company, based in the tax-free haven of Andorra.

He'd managed Juan Pedro's finances, and looked after the de Ravel estates, and now he also looked after Bibi. She had refused to touch any of her assets in America for fear of being traced. She'd wanted to disappear for good, for Paloma's sake. That meant she was broke, but Rodolfo had helped her.

At the café, Rodolfo threw back his coffee in a single gulp and ordered another. "And for you, *querida*?" he asked.

Bibi considered the amount of caffeine she'd already consumed, then decided the hell with it. "An espresso, please," she said, sighing at her own indulgence.

"It's spur of the moment that I'm here," Rodolfo said, sitting back and folding his arms over his chest, smiling at her. "I brought some friends with me for the weekend. I called you earlier, but when you didn't reply I guessed I'd find you here."

"Buying up all the best fruit and veg," she said. "I'll be baking some bread later, if you'd like some."

"Why not bring it with you tonight? I'm inviting you to dinner," he explained.

"Ohh, but you said you have company . . . friends."

"New friends, who I'm sure would like to meet you. And I know you would like to meet them. There's one young man in particular, a singer. You could bring your guitar, play together . . ."

Bibi's eyes flashed panic. "But I can't sing, I mean it's impossible. He might recognize me . . ."

"No need to sing, I'm just asking you to come and enjoy yourself for once, and anyhow nobody recognizes you now. You're simply my cousin. It's an opportunity for you to hear some music. I'm sure he'll sing for us, Vida. Perhaps you could play your guitar with him, try one of your new songs. Be *yourself*, Bibi, for a little while."

She had often played her new songs for Rodolfo, but never for anyone else and she was nervous. She bent to stroke the dog.

"I'm scared," she said simply. "After all we've done, all I've gone through, isn't this risky?"

"Would I ask you if I thought it were? I'm simply inviting you to dinner and to meet some friends. You've done it before. You need not play if you don't want to, but I thought the singer might enjoy hearing some of your new songs. They're different from your old ones. It will do you good. And besides, *he* is good. So? Will you come?"

Bibi took a deep breath; why did she feel as if she were burning her boats? "If you insist," she said.

"*Querida,* I insist." Rodolfo was pleased. He'd known she wouldn't be able to resist the pleasure of music. Her lifeblood.

"Anyway, who is this singer?" she asked.

"His name is Jacinto," he said. "The young singer-songwriter who's doing so well. I thought it was time to put music back in your life, even in this small way. A woman needs friends, the kind of people who understand her," he added, patting her hand, rather anxiously. He was worried about her loneliness. He hoped he was doing the right thing.

Chapter 32

Extremadura is a mere few hours' drive north of Málaga and the tourist destinations of the Costa del Sol, but it is another world, of medieval villages and Renaissance palaces, with the ruins of aqueducts and amphitheaters built by the Romans. It's a place from where the conquistadors set out to find the New World. The Sierra mountains cut through the middle. There are stony hills and deep silent forests, home to wild boar and red deer, to pheasant and ravens and to the black stork and the Spanish Imperial Eagle. Moorish walls with lookout towers encircle the ancient town of Cáceres, while outside those walls are valleys dotted with ancient stone castles and monasteries. Herds of cattle, the Iberian Avelina-black and the Casareña White, roam those valleys, as well as flocks of sheep from which comes one of Spain's most famous cheeses, the Torta del Casar. Wild pigs feed on acorns, giving the region its famous Iberian ham, and there are orchards and groves of olives and vineyards.

The first time Bibi saw the little town of Trujillo, she was with Rodolfo. It was that magical hour between evening and night, when all was quiet. The square, with its lovely Renaissance palaces and arches, and narrow medieval streets winding off of it, was floodlit and quiet. Bibi felt as though she had stepped back in time; she might have been living in another century. Outside the town the countryside lay silent and secretive, and it was that silence, that remote beauty, that drew her instantly to it. After all the noise, the flashing cameras, the screaming and yelling and her own personal agony, she needed peace. She needed that silence. She needed to be alone.

It was there she found the castle.

Small, turreted, set atop its own green hill, remote but, via small winding roads, accessible to a motorway and from there to a train or a plane that would, if necessary, take her to the place where her daughter lived. Bibi might never see her daughter again but she needed to be there, in Spain, for her. *Just in case.* She never dared ask herself what that "in case" might be. All she knew was that in a matter of life and death she would be there.

The Castillo was too old to even know its own beginnings. Gothic with ancestors from the middle ages, it had a view over the valley to where Rodolfo's own house was hidden in the trees, a mere couple of kilometers away, and where his family flag flew when he was in residence.

"Like royalty," Bibi teased, laughing. And he was.

The Castillo had been owned by a wealthy Chicago widow. It had been on the market for a couple of years, and was going cheap. Castillo Verano, Summer Castle, the widow had called it, but Bibi preferred its original name, Castillo Adivino—the Fortune-Teller's Castle, so called because a woman said to have supernatural powers and the ability to foretell the future had been its first owner.

It was love at first sight. "I have to live here," she said, making Rodolfo sigh.

"It's just like with the dog," he'd complained. "It's too old and decrepit for you to look after."

"I don't care," she said. "I need it. I can breathe here."

And seeing the glint of new excitement in her eyes, of course he'd found a way to get it for her. To protect her, he had one of his Andorran companies purchase the Castillo. Bibi's name would not appear on the title deeds.

She did nothing fancy to it, she didn't have the money, but thank God, the Chicago widow had fixed up the roof, where, to Bibi's delight, a pair of storks now nested in a chimney. The widow had also drilled a well and put in plumbing that almost worked, and electricity that worked sporadically, when the old generator felt up to it. She had also installed a couple of bathrooms, importing immense American bathtubs and gilded fixtures, with showerheads that tended to trickle like gentle rain or else drowned Bibi in one giant swoosh before turning off completely, which meant she'd be stuck with shampoo in her hair and have to run to fetch a bucket of water from the kitchen to rinse it off with.

The "country" kitchen the widow had installed had the same kind of quirks. There was a big old stove that worked on propane, delivered by an old man on a flatbed truck, rattling up the hill with the tanks swaying from side to side, until Bibi feared they might explode. The stove had to be lit with a long taper, standing well back, so she didn't singe her arms. There were open shelves with old blue gingham curtains stretched across on a wire, where she stored her new dishes, bought in the street market. The deep stone sink had enormous bronze taps that swirled crazily when you turned them. Unlike in the bathroom, though, there was always good water pressure due to the fact that it was closer to the well on the south of the hill. There was also a big rustic table and benches that had obviously been built in the house and left there because they were simply too big to ever get out the door.

There was nothing grand about the Castillo Adivino. You entered through a big wooden door studded with iron *clavos*, and with hand-forged black iron hinges. It opened with a great clanking iron key on a chain that must have weighed a couple of pounds, and you walked directly into a lofty white room topped with heavy dark beams. The gothic windows with their pointed arches had not been touched, though the Chicago widow had put in a pair of glass doors that led to a stone terrace sheltered by a grove of almond trees, long unpruned and running wild. In the spring they were covered in pink blossoms and flooded the air with their scent.

There were three bedrooms beneath the turrets, one of which, the smallest and prettiest, she'd told herself she would keep for Paloma. She was dreaming of course, but then she needed to keep Paloma's dream alive. Their windows were set in embrasures the thickness of the stone walls, with cushioned window seats and views over the valley where the lights of Trujillo twinkled in the darkness. On moonless nights when the little town was floodlit, it looked like a backdrop for some old Hollywood epic.

Bibi had done nothing fancy with her castle. All she'd been able to afford was a fresh coat of whitewash on the interior walls and flea-market finds for furnishings. She'd bought, cheap, a high-backed dark green velvet sofa and a low white table with chrome legs, very thirties and completely out of keeping but she liked the whimsical way it looked amongst all those old beams and gray stones. A couple of mismatched armchairs sat across from the sofa opposite a vast stone fireplace with a massive iron hook hanging over the grate, where in the olden days she supposed a cauldron of stew, perhaps of wild boar hunted down in the forest, would have cooked. There were a couple of lamps, a cushioned basket for the dog, and a wooden hat stand with a mirror and brass pegs on which she hung her rather battered collection of straw hats.

Of course there was a piano, not the Steinway concert grand she'd had in Hollywood, just a small upright Yamaha, but its sound echoed pleasantly from the high ceiling. Plus two guitars, one electric, one acoustic, the same ones she'd always played. A few Andalusian woven rugs, cream with patterns of blue or green, a few cushions, a CD player—a gift from Rodolfo—a small TV, a laptop, and that was it.

Her bedroom had a view over the valley and a bed big enough for two, though Bibi knew only she would ever sleep in it. She'd found a swatch of cream lace, handmade right here in the area, and draped it comfortingly around, enclosing her and Amigo cozily in the quiet of the night. There was a foggy old cheval mirror, a pine chest, a comfortable wing chair, a small desk placed beneath one of the windows, and an armoire that held the baggy tops and long skirts she secretly hated.

She had to admit she missed those snug little cashmeres, the narrow designer skirts and short dresses and the heels. After all, she was still a woman. Now, even her jeans were baggy and her sweaters were described in the catalogs from which she bought them as "boyfriend sweaters." Which meant Big.

The Castillo was a complete contrast to the multimillion-dollar over-decorated house in the Hollywood Hills, where it was always *she* who was responsible for everything and everybody—*she* who had to write the songs, make sure the next record was even better than the last, the next concert bigger and more spectacular . . . *Her* energy had fulfilled everyone's lives.

Here, alone, but for her dog, there was a kind of peace she hadn't known for a long time. Not since she was a child, living with her father at the de Ravel bodega, where Paloma was now.

Peace. She only hoped someday her daughter would find it.

Chapter 33

Los Angeles, California

Sunny's phone rang just as she was about to leave for a meeting. She checked the time as she picked up the phone. Four thirty. She was supposed to have been there five minutes ago.

"Sun, baby," Mac said.

Oh God, it was him. At last! She sagged with relief, then told her assistant to go on without her. "Say I'll be there in ten," she said, beaming. Then to Mac, "Just tell me you're at the airport and about to catch a flight home."

"Well, not exactly the *airport* . . ."

This couldn't be good. She sank into the chair behind her desk. "Why not?"

"Things got a bit complicated here."

"Complicated? Like you miss me so much you can't bear to be without me and simply have to get on the plane, or else . . ."

"Or else what?"

"Or else I'll get on a plane and come to you."

Mac laughed. Sunny always surprised him. "I'll bet you would, too."

She said, "Anyhow, what's so complicated? I thought all I was missing was the traffic."

"And me."

Sunny sighed into the phone. "And you, Mac Reilly," she said softly.

"I have to see Paloma tomorrow. Out at the de Ravel vineyard."

"Hmmm, suddenly you're in wine country."

"Sunny, Sunny, what can I say. Only that I miss you the way I'd miss a rib if you cut it out of me, the way I'd miss your thigh over mine if you didn't sleep with me, the way I'd miss . . ."

Sunny laughed. "Better stop while you're ahead."

"Okay. But it's true. This family is complicated and I was thrown right into the middle of their fights."

"Poor you, but I'll bet you're already hot on Bibi's trail."

"I met the Matriarch."

"Ah, the Matriarch." Sunny slung off her white mules and put her feet up on the desk. Twisting a strand of hair lazily around her finger, she said, "So, what's she like?"

"Actually," Mac said, "she looks a lot like you."

"You mean like me grown old?"

"Well, not exactly *old*," Mac said.

She took her feet off the desk and sat up. "How old not old?"

"Forty-one."

She caught the hesitation in Mac's voice, then he added too quickly, "In fact it turns out I knew her, years ago. In Miami. We were both so young, just kids really."

"*Knew* her?"

"I knew Lorenza."

Sunny took a deep breath, then said, "I'll bet she's beautiful."

"I told you already, she looks a lot like you. Anyway, I thought I'd tell you that," he added, a bit lamely, she thought.

"So. An old girlfriend," she said thoughtfully.

"You could say that."

"A widow."

"She is that."

"Beautiful."

"That too."

He didn't need to say more; Sunny had read between the lines. "You'd better come on home, Mac Reilly," she said quietly.

"Soon as I can," he said.

"What are you doing right now?"

"I just sent for room service."

"I'll bet it's a burger and fries."

"You know me too well."

"Sometimes," she said, twisting that strand of hair, "I don't think I know you as well as I thought I did."

She checked the clock. Four forty-five. "I'll talk to you later," she said. "I have to go."

She ended the call and sat for a moment staring blankly at the wall. Something was up, she'd heard it in his voice. An old lover. And Mac was going to be alone with her at her romantic vineyard. "She's beautiful," he'd said. "We knew each other. We were so young . . ." And now she was a young widow, not that much older than Sunny herself.

Sunny remembered Monte Carlo just last year, how tempted she had been by another man, and how much she would have lost—her life with Mac, their love—had she succumbed to that temptation.

She took her feet off the desk, sat up, and dialed the number of her best friend, Allie Ray, in France.

Allie Ray was a true Hollywood movie star and she looked the part. Long blond hair that hung straight as a die past her shoulders, wide-spaced turquoise blue eyes—truly turquoise and that's without contacts—a God-given perfect nose, and a wide, full smile of such sweetness, on-screen and off, it held men entranced. Not only was Allie beautiful, she was nice.

Mac Reilly had saved her life, not too long ago, when a demented stalker threatened her. In a way Mac had also saved her estranged husband Ron, and, then he and Sunny had gotten Ron and Allie back together. It was then that Allie had made her decision to give up her career and she and Ron ended up owning a tumble-down cottage in the Dordogne in western France not too far from Saint-Émilion, where they were now trying their hand at growing grapes and making their own wine. Only in a small way, of course, but you never knew with Ron, he was ambitious, and a man used to success.

But happiness, Allie had discovered, could be found in a country cottage light-years away from movie studios and red carpets, though she kept her hand in, occasionally accepting a role in a small French movie, for a couple of which she'd received great praise.

"Hi, sweetheart," she said now to Sunny. "I was just thinking about you. What are you up to?"

"It's not what *I'm* up to," Sunny said with gloom in her voice. "It's Mac."

"Uh-uh." There was a pause while Allie digested the implications of what Sunny had just said. It was only last year that she and Ron had hurried to Monte Carlo to help when Sunny had threatened to go off the rails with another man.

"You can't mean what I think you mean. It's just not possible."

"It might be. He's in Barcelona."

"So why aren't you with him?"

"I had to be in Napa. My client's a vintner, it was a publicity thing. Oh my God, I just thought how strange this is . . . I was at a winery, you are at *your* winery, and now Mac's at the de Ravel winery."

"De Ravel? Sherry? New wines?"

"The same. Remember Bibi Fortunata? The singer-songwriter-star-celebrity, and possible murderer?"

"Jesus. Of course I remember that story. Whatever happened to her?"

"That's what Mac's in Spain to find out. She's a de Ravel. We met her little girl on the beach at Malibu, Mac saved her from drowning. Bibi simply disappeared after the murders and the child, whose name is Paloma, went to live with a Ravel aunt. Now Paloma's stepfather is after her, he wants custody so he can get his hands on her money. So of course, it's Mac to the rescue once again."

"He never can resist."

"That's the trouble."

Allie knew what she meant. Mac's work had been the cause of Sunny's postponed marriage last year.

"Anyhow it turns out the de Ravel family Matriarch is all of forty-one years old and gorgeous. She was also Mac's lover, in their long-lost youth, in Miami."

"Oh . . . my . . . God . . ." Allie realized now what was up. "She was probably his first true love, and you never forget those."

"I'm willing to bet on it."

Allie thought for a few seconds. "Of course you can trust Mac completely. He loves you, he'd never—"

Sunny interrupted, "I heard something in his voice, Allie. Besides, he'd told me he'd only ever really loved one other woman before he met me. It has to be her."

Allie didn't have to think twice; women always knew what to do in these circumstances. "You'd better get your ass over there," she said. "I'll tell you what, Ron's in New York. He's got the Citation out at Teterboro. I'll call him, tell him to pick you up and get you to Barcelona right away. Start packing now. And remember, take some good stuff, the competition might be a little tough."

"Oh, Allie, are you sure it's the right thing to do? Shouldn't I just trust Mac?"

"You can't trust *her*," Allie said. "I'll meet you in Barcelona. Where is Mac staying?"

"The Méridien."

"Ron will make reservations."

"I'm bringing the dogs," Sunny said. She knew Mac would never give up on his love for Pirate, no matter how much temptation stared him in the face.

"Do *not* bring the dogs. Not this time," Allie told her firmly. "You'll have your hands full dealing with the Matriarch. You just have time to get your nails done. And remember, action is always the best policy. Glamorous Spanish widows have nothing on us."

Sunny hoped not.

Ron called a few minutes later.

"I'm in trouble with Mac," she said.

"Allie told me."

His voice, like the man, had a rough edge to it. Ron Perrin was of middle height, stocky, and always in a hurry. He walked with his head jutting forward as if to propel himself along even faster. He had wavy brown hair and deep-set molten brown eyes under bushy brows. He was not unattractive in a way that combined money and power, though there was always speculation as to why a gorgeous woman like Allie Ray, who could have had her pick of the most eligible men available, would even look twice at him.

Allie and Ron knew why though. Ron had not been there just

to escort a famous movie actress and play the celebrity; Ron was the one who'd found her, a girl at her lowest ebb, taken her from nothing and given her the confidence to become the woman she was now. He'd taught her how to play the star. Ron had always loved her even though they seemed to have lost that love for a couple of years, but now it was stronger than ever.

"I'll never leave you again," Ron had told her.

"And I will never leave you either," Allie had vowed.

And that's the way things stood between them now, and forever and ever, amen. And that's why Allie had just told him she could not bear to see things go wrong again between Mac and Sunny. She knew what they had was special. They could not be allowed to lose it.

"I need to get to Barcelona right away," Sunny said to Ron.

"I'm your man. I'm in the car, in the Lincoln Tunnel, on my way to Teterboro now. Let's see, door-to-door I can be with you in four hours. Meet me at Santa Monica airport."

"You're a lifesaver," she said.

"Hey, remember," he said quietly. "So are you. That's what friends are for."

Allie had been right. Sunny just had time to collect the dogs, repack her bag with the stuff she'd taken to Napa, plus a couple of more glamorous frocks and her favorite Jimmy Choos—her "goddess" shoes, the ones that fastened round the ankles with sexy satin straps—and get her nails done. She decided not to call Mac and tell him she was on her way. She would surprise him.

Chapter 34

Trujillo, Spain

It was eight o'clock on Saturday night and Bibi was getting ready to go to Rodolfo's dinner. It was still light out and the evening was sultry. A thunderstorm threatened. She'd bet Rodolfo had planned on dining on the terrace and hoped bad weather wouldn't spoil his party.

Through the open window she could hear the goats, three of them, named Uno, Dos, Tres—One, Two, Three—munching steadily on the shaggy grass, easier and cheaper than cutting it using the ancient tractor-mower, and besides the goats were more fun. And, despite the fact that she had already locked up her chickens, a rooster still crowed. She thought he'd definitely got his timing wrong. But then maybe so had she. Should she *really* go to this dinner party for the singer? Wasn't it risky?

Fresh from her bath she inspected herself in the cheval mirror, another flea-market find that reflected only half of her so she could only see herself in two parts, either from the head to knees, or knees to feet. Naked, she still looked like the old Bibi, the girl onstage in the torn black fishnets and the silver corset and the six-inch platforms, which was one of the naughty roles she'd played. Or the other soft, slinky, sensual woman with the smoky eyes in the long mermaid-sequined pale green chiffon with her wild mane of flame red hair loose around her shoulders. Or the girl-next-door with a ponytail, barefoot in jeans and T-shirt. Which one was she really? Bibi wished she knew. She had always been able to be anyone she wanted, and she had ended up no one. She was not even a mother anymore.

There was a photograph of Paloma on her nightstand, the last one Bibi had taken of her before it all began. They were at the pool and Paloma had just emerged from the water, gap-toothed and smiling, her long wet hair stuck dark and gleaming like amber ale instead of its usual carrot. It was her eyes though, that got to Bibi, meeting the camera, and her mom behind it, with all the joy the world could offer a little girl on a California summer's day, when she was safe and loved and nothing could ever possibly go wrong.

If only, Bibi thought, I had not slept with Wally Carlyle. "The lover." That's what the media had dubbed him, though he was never *in love* with her, nor she with him. She hadn't even really fancied him. Not like she had Bruno in the beginning.

People asked how could she have taken Wally for her lover, and they were right. He'd had a reputation with women and she should have known better.

But I was wounded, she thought. Bruno was unfaithful, a serial cheater, he humiliated me. He told his women he despised me, that I was cold, controlling, and sexless. "I married you for *what* you were, not *who* you are." Bruno had *said* that, standing in their bedroom, adjusting his tie, putting on his jacket, ready for a night on the town, though not with her. And she'd known then he'd married her for her position, and her money.

"You're really nothing, Bibi," he'd said, and she'd flinched at the contempt in his eyes. "And you *know* it."

Despite all her success and acclaim, it had gotten to her on a

deeply personal level. She'd almost believed him. So she left him
at the Palm Springs house with his pit bull and his vodka and
his women, and took Paloma home to the Hollywood Hills. She
moved on.

From bad, she thought now with a rueful smile. To worse.

In fact she had almost laughed when she was suspected of
murdering "the lover" and his "girlfriend." She'd only just found
out Wally was cheating on her with Brandi, and though she was
furious, it really meant nothing. In the beginning Wally had flat-
tered her into feeling good again, he'd made her feel attractive,
sexy. "Look at you on stage, he'd said. "Every man wants you.

And she'd been so wrapped up in her own world, her bruised
ego, her music, her recordings, her concert tours, surrounded by
her entourage, insulated against reality, she hadn't even realized
her girlfriend was betraying their friendship and was sleeping
with her lover. She hadn't known Brandi that long but somehow
she'd insinuated herself into Bibi's home, into her life, become
"the friend," always there to help, to offer sympathy and advice,
let's have lunch, go shopping, girly stuff.

Life, Bibi decided, was full of traitors.

Anyway, if she had been a killer, it would not have been the
lover and the girlfriend she would have murdered. It would have
been Bruno. And Bruno, she always knew, was dangerous.

Suddenly longing to feel herself again, she dragged on her old
jeans, artfully ripped at the knees. They still fit like a second skin,
the way jeans should. She inspected her lower portion in the mirror. Her butt still looked good. She put on a white cotton peasant
blouse, another street market find. It slid off one shoulder and was
gathered at the waist and had long full sleeves edged with lace and
had red flowers embroidered down the front. Kind of Hungarian-
Gypsy-looking. She peered doubtfully at her top half in the cheval

mirror. It looked okay. All that was missing, she thought, fighting back sudden tears, was a child standing next to her, dressed in something cute and girly, whose hand she would hold, and who she would introduce proudly to Rodolfo's guests. It was not to be, and anyhow Paloma would not have gone to a grown-up dinner party. It was simply another dream. A scene from another life.

She brushed out her bangs and skewered her long mousy hair on top with a Spanish mantilla comb, then wondered if she looked too contemporary, not enough the country girl, so she added the tinted glasses and a brown shawl she'd knitted herself.

She was getting quite good at knitting on those long evenings alone, with a glass of wine and only Amigo for company, and the soaring sound of the music she so missed, on the CD player. And on those long sleepless nights, trying to keep the bad thoughts at bay, she would sit cross-legged in the wing chair in her bedroom, with the dog sleeping at her feet and the night outside dark and still, playing her guitar, writing the music that would never leave her mind.

People always asked how did she do it, where did the ideas come from, how did she think of those chords? Where did that lyric, those words, those feelings come from? Her answer was she didn't know; it was simply there, in her head.

She put on her little red canvas espadrilles, thinking wistfully of those high strappy platforms; grabbed her lipstick, her guitar, and the loaf of bread she'd baked for Rodolfo, and called to Amigo.

The lights had come on, on the winding gravel track leading down the hill. The rooster had settled down and the three goats were standing on the grass, watching her. The smallest one, Tres, bleated. A pitiful sound. He was her favorite and she knew he hated to see her leave. "Be right back, guys," she called, in English, then she laughed, thinking her goats probably only spoke Spanish. As she must remember to do tonight.

She didn't bother to lock her door, nobody did around here, and anyway that key on its hefty chain was a nightmare to turn. Still, she would never change it for a modern one, she wanted her Castillo Adivino to remain the same as it always had.

With Amigo sitting in the passenger seat, his head hanging out the window, she put the dusty white Seat in gear and set off down the hill for Rodolfo's party. She hoped she was doing the right thing.

Chapter 35

Rodolfo's house was approached by a long straight cobblestone drive that swept in a circle to the front portico and that, female friends complained, was hell on high heels. In fact several sprained ankles had had to be treated by Rodolfo's longtime partner William, with cold poultices and glasses of champagne and kisses-better that always seemed to do the trick.

What Rodolfo modestly called his "cottage" was actually a large country house, not quite a *palacio* but with its ten bedrooms and many bathrooms it was still impressive, set in leveled acres of lawns and flower beds on the outskirts of a forest. The Hernandez flag, flown when he was in residence, dated from Renaissance times. The family had come to their wealth by a long route, as merchants traveling the Silk Road in the fourteenth century, then on to shipping out of Venice in the fifteenth, and later, via the Spanish court—with time out for the Inquisition—as international bankers and money managers. Today, Rodolfo's main offices were in the Principality of Andorra where he took care of the investments and tax-free requirements of some of the world's wealthiest men and women.

The "cottage," referred to locally simply as El Grande—"The

Big One"—had started out as a hunting lodge and the family had owned it for a couple of centuries—no time at all really, in those parts, where ruins dated back to the Romans, and where Fernando III had conquered the Islamic fortress in 1232, and from where one of Trujillo's greatest native sons, conquistador Francisco Pizarro had set off to conquer Peru. There is a palace in Trujillo built by his brother to commemorate Francisco. It has a magnificent window with the heads of both brothers and their Inca wives carved in stone above, and there's also a warrior-like statue of Francisco, complete with sword and armor, in the town's main square.

Tonight Bibi was surprised to see Rodolfo's driveway lined with blazing torches and the house illuminated. A local farmer from whom Bibi had bought her goats was acting as a sort of valet parker/majordomo, in his blue overalls and boots and with a black beret slapped on his bald head. Rodolfo did not go in for uniforms. The people who worked for him were all country people and he'd told them they could wear whatever they damn well pleased as long as they were clean and smiling. Rodolfo hated pretension and if his guests were such snobs they didn't like his helpers (he never called them servants) then they need never come again.

The farmer opened the car door and wafted her toward the house. "Señora Vida, how're my goats?" he demanded, taking her by the elbow and helping her up the steps, a touch of chivalry that melted her heart.

"Eating a lot," she said. "My lawn is lovely and they keep the ravens away from the chickens with their racket."

"There's no better music than the bleating of a goat," he said solemnly, and Bibi knew he meant it.

The dog padded at her side, tongue lolling in the sultry evening heat, panting slightly. She carried the loaf of fresh-baked

bread and the acoustic guitar in its case, still wondering whether
or not she would play it. It all depended on the young singer. She
was so out of touch she had never heard of him. Perhaps he was
famous. She hoped not. But then she saw the long black Mercedes
limousine parked with other cars to the left of the house. She had
never seen a limo at Rodolfo's before.

"That's Jacinto's," the farmer told her. "The singer."

Rodolfo's partner, William Bailey, met her in the hall, tall,
stocky, his once corn-blond hair now graying, a farm boy too, from
Iowa, though he'd left long ago to become a banker. He smiled as
he wrapped his arms tenderly around her.

"*Querida,* there you are." He stood back, eyeing her apprais-
ingly. "My, my, what a lovely Hungarian peasant girl you look tonight," he said. "I love the blouse but I do think you should lose
the glasses."

"I need them," Bibi explained.

"You do not. You can see perfectly well, especially with those
contacts. While I, my darling Vida—see, I remembered to call you
Vida—need these darn spectacles. It's either that or a white stick."

Bibi was laughing as a voice said, "And why should you have
to *remember* to call her Vida? Isn't that her name?"

Bibi swung round and came face-to-face with a tall man,
younger than her, and very sure of himself. His brown eyes had
a quizzical look as they searched her face. He took her hand in
both of his, then raised it to his lips.

"I'm happy to meet you. Vida?" he said, with a question in his
voice.

William stepped in. "Well, since you've now met, I'll tell you,
Vida, this is Jacinto. And Jacinto, may I introduce Rodolfo's cousin,
Vida Hernandez."

"I like your name, real or not," Jacinto said, giving her back

214   *Elizabeth Adler*

her hand. "Vida—*Life*. It seems a good philosophy, to believe in life so much it becomes your name. Your parents must have believed in you. Unless of course you chose it yourself, later."

Bibi didn't know who Jacinto was but she knew she was on dangerous ground; this was a mistake; she should not have come; she sensed he suspected something.

Pulling herself together she said, "Oh, I think parents usually manage to find the right name for a child. And I suppose yours called you Jacinto?"

"In fact they did not. My first manager chose that. He decided my real name had no showbiz ring to it."

William interrupted. "Vida must meet our other guests. Jacinto has brought some of his musicians and Rodolfo invited some people from Monaco he has business dealings with, plus a few from Holland and England."

Jacinto watched her go. He found her intriguing, mysterious, and he liked that. He also liked that she didn't know *who* he was. *That* made him smile.

Chapter 36

Jacinto was a Spanish superstar, famous throughout Latin America and now nibbling at the U.S. with his latest mix of plaintive lyrics and hard-thrusting beat. Bass-driven, sexy, and amped to the high heavens, it was impossible to resist.

He wasn't handsome in that old Julio Iglesias way, more Marc Anthony via Justin Timberlake; tall, lean, and fit with zero body fat because he used up so much energy pacing the stage with his dance moves; thin-faced—all cheekbones and beaked nose and wide, fleshy, sexy mouth; brown eyes, deep-set so they looked even darker; lowering brows and dark, dark hair long to his shoulders, and always flopping over his eyes, a trademark look that endeared him to his female fans, who claimed he was the sexiest thing on two legs. And maybe he was. He was also just twenty-two years old.

There was another side to Jacinto though; the softer side where, perched on a stool, stage lights dimmed to a narrow spot that picked up his hands as he stroked a melody from his guitar, he'd half whisper, half sing a song of love. Poetic words he'd written himself and that his audience felt came from his heart. He wooed them into silence as he ended those songs; they'd sit mute and still as the spotlight dimmed, then went out, and then the applause would finally come, and the shrieks and screams. Though Jacinto knew this was a tribute, he secretly hated it. *No screaming please,* he wanted to say. *Just listen. Hear what I have to say, take it to your hearts, let your hearts be quiet for a while.* Then, as if in rebuttal of his own words, he'd stalk that stage again, guitar wailing, bass thrusting, girls screaming.

Jacinto was a European star and now an international star in the making. A star with a talent that would never fade. It was a life of glamour and hardship, always on the road in a convoy of sixteen tour buses and a dozen eighteen-wheelers, of chefs and trainers, of managers and backup singers, of musicians and their families, kids, dogs, even a cat—his own blue Persian, Mitzi, whom he loved like a child.

The responsibility for all these people and the audience, the paying customers, was all his: he was the one who had to get up on stage every night; his energy could never be allowed to flag; his talent could never drift into the quiet, alone places he sometimes longed to be. Jacinto had realized long ago that he was a business and that the rock-star tour buses and eighteen-wheelers carrying the equipment, the lighting men, the roadies, the managers, the families and dogs and cats all depended on him for their living. That was showbiz and, though sometimes he was tired and low, he would never let them down.

It had taken only two years for him to reach this point.

He had accepted Rodolfo Hernandez's invitation to spend a weekend at the old hunting lodge, tempted by the simplicity it offered. Rodolfo was managing his business affairs and he liked the man, liked his old-world courtesy, his impeccable manners, and his ability to live the good life without being the least bit flashy.

Jacinto wanted to dip into that life even if only for a couple of days, and when he'd seen the old house in the forest with the black ravens flying overhead and glimpsed a red deer peeking through the trees as he was driven in the long black Mercedes limo up the endless cobblestoned driveway, he'd smiled in relief. He knew that here he would find peace. There would be no fans, no one wanting a part of him; no one wanting him to be "the entertainment." Here, he could simply be himself.

William led Vida and Jacinto into the great room, all done out hunting style with dark wood paneling and antiques. There were two stone fireplaces, one at each end, both filled with flowers on this warm night rather than blazing logs. A row of French doors led out onto a wide stone terrace canopied in dark green edged in twinkling white lights. A topiary hedge was trimmed into fantasy shapes. Beyond that was a view of parkland where the trees glowed with golden globes.

A long table ran down the center of the terrace, its soft white cloth trailed with vines and leaves and candles flickering in glass hurricane lamps. A couple of women helpers were putting on the finishing touches, making sure each place setting had its appropriate rough greenish glasses for the wines and water; that each piece of the antique bone-handled cutlery was exactly one inch from the edge of the table, and that each white cotton napkin was folded into a perfect triangle and set in a water glass. Nothing fancy, but everything beautiful was Rodolfo's philosophy for dining, as it was in life.

Bibi looked around and her heart sank. She wished she was back in her den, at the old Hollywood house, she and Paloma with their feet up on the ottoman, eating pizza and watching a movie. Now, she had to be someone else.

Twenty people were drinking William's specialty cocktail. He made it with Cava, the Spanish version of champagne, mixed with Domaine de Canton, a French ginger and cognac liquor that Bibi knew from experience tasted absolutely delicious. She also knew that more than one could knock her socks off. Accepting the brimming flute she decided she had better be careful.

Her heart sank again when she took in the women dressed to kill in little couture cocktail frocks, short and sexy in chiffon and studs and sequins and ankle-tied stilettos. Their blond hair glimmered like spun silk in the lamplight and they smiled glossy smiles at the men; tall men, broad-shouldered in pastel linen shirts and white pants. "No jackets allowed" had been Rodolfo's orders, though he hadn't needed to give that order to Jacinto's young musicians who anyway would wear whatever they pleased, which tonight were thin cotton T-shirts stamped with a recent tour date and the name "Jacinto."

Too late Bibi realized that the old ripped jeans, the peasant blouse, and the hand-knitted brown shawl were a mistake. She had lost all that rich successful urban gloss. She didn't fit in. She suddenly wanted to disappear. To run away.

"You can't, you know," Jacinto said from behind her.

She swung round and the cocktail sloshed over the side of her glass and onto the dog, who sniffed his wet fur, licked tentatively, then decided against it.

"Can't what?"

"Can't run away. And nor can I. Rodolfo invited us, we accepted, and here we stay for the duration. We're stuck with these people. I'm sure your mother taught you the same good manners as mine."

"My mother died when I was born."

"I'm sorry. Then I guess you didn't learn manners after all, so you *can* run away."

He was laughing at her. He stepped back, half bowing in a courtly gesture. "Señorita Vida."

"*Vida!*" Rodolfo bustled toward her, beaming. He always loved a party and this promised to be a good one. "There you are, and you've already met Jacinto."

"Vida was thinking of leaving," Jacinto said. "I'm trying to persuade her to stay."

"But you can't possibly leave. You are to stay and have a good time," Rodolfo ordered. Then to Jacinto, "My Vida is a little shy but she bakes the most delicious bread. Thank you, *querida,* for the loaf, we shall all taste it at dinner. Which, of course, is simplicity itself, as it always is out here in the country. Ah, and of course you brought Amigo."

He called to a passing helper, "Please take Amigo to the kitchen and make sure he gets some of that chicken he likes, and make sure also to chop it finely."

He turned back and smiled at Jacinto as the dog padded off to the kitchen. "I'm afraid Amigo's teeth are not what they once were."

"He's old." Bibi came to her dog's defense. "How lovely the women look," she said, glancing down at her market-stall blouse that had looked so good in the top half of the cheval mirror.

"Let me take your shawl." Jacinto's hand was on her shoulder. "It's such a warm night I'm sure you don't need it."

She turned to look at him. Their faces were almost touching and she caught his faint citrusy scent. There was something very masculine about Jacinto: tall; maybe too lean, thin face all cheekbones; a glimpse of tattoos on his forearms, on his neck; dark eyes that if it were not so "romance novel" she would want to describe as piercing; a lank mop of dark hair falling over those eyes; and a mouth . . . well, she'd better not go there. She felt that sudden thud in the pit of her belly, the sudden thrill of sexual attraction.

He was casual in narrow black pants and a loose black shirt with the sleeves rolled. He wore a gold signet ring on his right pinkie, a small diamond stud in his left ear, and no watch. He was obviously a man for whom time did not matter.

She turned quickly away . . . she didn't want to think about that mouth. And anyhow why was he always *smiling*?

"Come, *querida,* let me introduce you to everyone," Rodolfo said, and telling Jacinto he already knew everyone anyway, he took Bibi by the arm and walked her over to where the half-dozen women guests stood, decorative as wild birds amongst the solid hunting-lodge antiques that had been in Rodolfo's family for generations.

They eyed her speculatively, smiling practiced social smiles, surprised when Rodolfo said she was his cousin and lived nearby in her own castle.

"Your *own* castle?" the woman from Paris said, astonished. "But what on earth do you do all day? Out here in the wild?"

"Ohh, I bake bread." It was the only thing Bibi could think of to say.

"How *interesting*," the Monaco blonde in black said, still smiling her social smile.

"Vida also writes songs," Rodolfo told them. She threw him a pleading look but he added, "I'm hoping after dinner she and Jacinto will play for us."

"*Entertainment*," another blonde from Monaco, this one in very short red silk, complete with an all-over golden tan, commented.

All Bibi wanted was to collect her dog and get out of there. She excused herself and drifted, almost invisible, it seemed in this crowd, toward the windows.

"You're not having a good time," Jacinto said, at her elbow again.

"I don't know anyone here. I lead a quiet life. I'm not used to parties."

He came to stand in front of her. *Ohh God, she should not have come, he was too clever, he was too curious. Too sexy.*

"Why don't you take off the glasses?" he said.

"I need them."

"I heard William say you didn't."

"Then he was wrong." She was damned if she was going to take off the glasses. "Besides, my glasses are none of your business," she added, nervous.

"Sorry. It's just that you look like the before picture on the makeover. You know what I mean, the country lady turns into . . ."

"If you're thinking Cinderella, think again," she said sharply. "I like the way I look, I like my dog, I like living here."

"In your castle."

She turned away, drained her cocktail, did not answer.

"I'll bet it's haunted." He leaned into her, whispering. *"Ghosts from the past."*

"It is," she said, taking another cocktail from a passing waiter. She knew she shouldn't but she was nervous. She took a gulp then stared down into the glass wishing she were anywhere else but with this singer with his rock-star hair and questioning blue eyes and who anyway was standing far too close to her. She took another gulp.

"*I* am the only ghost at my castle," she said. "*I* haunt it. All by myself."

For a long second his surprised eyes locked onto hers, then William came up and said, "Dinner is being served, friends. Please look for your name on the table in the little silver-bird card holders. A different bird for each person. We're serving local food tonight, so expect some surprises. Pleasant ones I hope."

Jacinto was seated in the place of honor on Rodolfo's right, with the golden Monaco blonde on Rodolfo's left. A dark-haired Amazon of a woman who said she was from Sweden was placed on Jacinto's left. To her relief, Bibi was seated at the other end of the table between William and a pleasant older Englishman who only wanted to talk golf, a game about which she knew nothing, so she just listened and made an appropriate gasp of admiration whenever one seemed appropriate.

Amigo wandered out from the kitchen and settled at her feet, and local girls circled the table bearing platters.

Bibi's bread had been cut into crusty chunks and put in linen-lined baskets. There was sweet, almost white, unsalted local butter in iced silver dishes, melting now because the night had turned so warm. Bowls of a chilled tomato-and-fig soup were already set at each place; her bread was passed around; a white wine poured, a local vintage, flinty and inexpensive and obviously, Bibi thought, watching the sun-glossed women avoiding the bread and pulling faces as they tasted the wine, a far cry from the pricy vintages they were accustomed to. She had been accustomed to expensive wines herself, to the good Bordeaux and the granite-crisp white Burgundies, as well as the Californian Two-Buck-Chuck— the Charles Shaw—that was better than its title led you to believe, and that was the very same wine she had been drinking with Brandi, the night she was killed.

Caught up in the memory, she put down her spoon, suddenly not hungry.

"More bread, my dear?" The nice Englishman to her left was inquiring. "I can recommend it, it's delicious."

"Why, thank you." She managed a pleased smile. "Actually, I baked it myself."

His bushy brows rose in astonishment, "Well, now, I can't say that I've ever met a woman who baked her own bread before. Tell me, my dear, what other talents do you possess?"

"She composes," William said, from her other side. "Wonderful songs. You'll hear, after dinner."

Bibi shook her head. "Oh, no, I couldn't, I wouldn't bore you with that."

"My dear, if they are as good as your bread and as good as William says—and I know him to be an honest man—then I'm sure I'm not going to be bored."

"We'll see," she said, giving William a warning glare, but he merely smiled back at her.

The Englishman turned to speak to the Amazon from Sweden and William turned to speak to the sun-kissed beauty whose short red dress exposed her long golden thighs all the way to the top.

Bibi looked out over the suddenly-still parkland. The breeze had dropped and a spear of lightning flashed in the distance, illuminating the forest like a rock concert stage. Lighting men ought to take lessons from nature, Bibi thought, as she counted, waiting for the rumble of thunder that would follow. They said you could calculate the storm's distance by a minute for every second counted. She got to nine. Still pretty far away. Perhaps William and his weather forecaster were correct and the storm would head for the Sierras instead of Rodolfo's. With a sudden ache of longing, she wondered what her daughter was doing right now. Had she had friends over for supper? Did they watch TV and eat pizza? Had they danced their crazy wild dances? Had she missed her mother . . . ?

She looked up and met Jacinto's intense gaze.

"Don't be sad," he mouthed down the long table.

Bibi wondered how he had known.

The soup bowls were whisked away and the main course of local lamb, slow baked with plums and served with truffled wild rice and *migas,* tiny pieces of bread fried with sweet peppers and morsels of chorizo. Lightning flashed. Bibi counted to eight this time. The Monaco women picked at their food. Rodolfo went round the table pouring red wine into the heavy greenish glasses.

"A Rioja," he said, nodding, pleased at the murmurs of approval. "I thought it would go well with the lamb, and our local specialty, the *migas.*"

Forked lightning suddenly speared into the ground and the entire sky turned white, as sheet lightning flashed, then flashed again, and again. A spatter of rain crossed the parkland and a wind shook the trees. Then all the lights went out. The candles flickered dimly in the hurricane lamps.

"Not to worry," Rodolfo said, cheerfully continuing to fill glasses. "The generator will pick up in a minute."

"What a shame," Jacinto said. "Everyone looks so lovely in the candle light." He was looking at Bibi as he said it and she put a hand up to her hair, nervously adjusting the tortoiseshell mantilla comb. It slipped and her long hair came tumbling down over her shoulders.

Thunder roared directly overhead, a wind whooshed across the terrace, sending the half-full glasses crashing, and the women shrieked and leapt to their feet, running for the French doors and the safety of the big room.

"Good thing we'd finished our main course," William said, calmly rising. "We'll move into the dining room. It was all set up anyhow, just in case."

Jacinto had Bibi's elbow and was hurrying her into the house. "You look wonderful with your hair down," he whispered.

She clasped her wind-swept hair with her free hand and

glared at him. "There's no need to hold on to me, I won't blow away."

"Like the Monaco woman, you mean." And despite her need to keep him at arm's length, Bibi laughed, because just then the wind had lifted the Monaco woman's skirt, and blown her, her bottom showing, toward the house.

Everyone reassembled round the dining room table. The women cowered nervously as the thunder crashed overhead, sounding like a jet taking off.

"More wine," Rodolfo called as William closed the windows.

Jacinto took the chair next to Vida.

Somehow she'd known he would.

"You intrigue me," he said, and he meant it. "You're a mystery woman. Who knew until the wind blew it down that you had such wonderful long silky hair?" He touched a strand that lay across her forehead. He pushed it gently back, looking at her, and she smiled.

"Can you really be *smiling*?" he asked, sliding an arm round the back of her chair.

She leaned away from him. "I was."

"You don't like me? I wonder why. Most women do."

"I don't even know you."

"So why not let's practice getting to know each other. It's normal at a party, don't you think?"

Salads were put in front of them, simple greens touched with dark olive oil and a hint of balsamic vinegar. Cheeses were passed around.

"Try this one." Bibi pointed out the Torta del Casar. "You'll like it."

"If you don't know me how do you know I will?" He was looking at her and not at the cheeses. She was all big brown eyes behind those tinted glasses.

"I just know," she said simply. And somehow she did, she knew Jacinto was like her.

Dessert was brought, a local concoction of raspberry and cheese and honey called Tio Pichu, "Uncle Pichu," served in rough pottery bowls with delicate English Georgian silver spoons.

Then everyone took their cups of thick dark coffee and retreated to the big room again, settling into the deep sofas and high-backed chairs, or on big cushions on the floor. The thunder had moved on though lightning still flashed and rain still splattered on the terrace. From the open French windows came a sweet fresh breeze.

Jacinto picked up his guitar. He perched on the edge of a chair next to the piano, and began to strum softly.

"*Ahh,*" Bibi heard the women murmur appreciatively, but Jacinto wasn't singing one of his own songs, he was singing Leonard Cohen's "Hallelujah," quietly, movingly.

Drawn to him, Bibi took her own guitar and went and sat at his feet, picking up the melody. When he'd finished there was silence, then a spatter of applause, then he launched into one of his own songs about being young and knowing your world would never change . . . until suddenly one day it did . . .

When he'd finished, he turned to Bibi. "Please, play one of your songs for me," he said, speaking so quietly only she could hear. And quietly, she began to play a melody.

He leaned toward her, listening intently. "Why don't you sing it for me?" he asked.

But Bibi refused. Instead, she spoke the words, just for him to hear. Like all her songs the story was simple, yet not so simple. It was about knowing who you really were. She'd called it "Just Be . . ."

"Remember me . . ." the lyric began:

All your life
All my life
All I tried was to be someone
To be someone else . . . not to be me . . .
I see I don't need you now,
I don't need you to come back.
I don't need you to take the ice from my eyes,
The ice from my heart
I can see
I can just be me

All my life, all your life . . .
Now I know all I need is just to be . . .
Just be
Just be, just be (me), just be (you)
I wish I had known, it was all so simple
I didn't need you to take the ice from my heart,
all I needed was just to be.
Just be (me), just be (you)
Remember, just be . . .

Jacinto picked it up instantly, singing behind her as she gave him the words. One of his musicians drifted over and began to play the chords on the piano, then, because the generator was working again, the bass player plugged in his electric bass guitar and Bibi's quiet song was suddenly given a hard driving beat.

Oh my God. Of course! Bibi realized who Jacinto was now! She'd heard him a zillion times on the radio. How could she have been so dumb?

The shock of it ran through her, taking her back in time . . . she closed her eyes and went with the music . . . remembering how it had felt: her first gig at the House of Blues on Sunset in Hollywood, feeling the bass vibrate through her entire body, hearing the high whine of the guitar, trembling with excitement and fear, back in the fishnets and platforms, in silk and sequins, in love with life and music . . . she was the young Bibi just starting out . . .

When the music stopped it was like awakening from a dream, a dream she wanted so badly to live again.

Jacinto was standing by the piano talking to the bass guitarist, who was thunking out experimental chords. He seemed to have forgotten all about Bibi.

Unnoticed, Bibi took her guitar. She got up, and crept out of the room. The dog lumbered after her. She met no one as she walked through the hall and down the steps. Rain soaked her instantly. She opened the car door, threw the guitar into the back, helped Amigo onto the front seat, and drove quickly away.

Jacinto had *changed* her simple song, changed the rhythm, the emotion, made it sexy. It was no longer *her* song. It was *about* her, but now he'd made it his own. It was as though he had stolen it from her, and now probably she'd hear a slightly different version of it on the radio. She knew she should not have trusted him. She knew she should not have come tonight.

Chapter 37

Early the next morning, Bibi was in her bedroom under the turrets, getting dressed. The water heater wasn't working and her shower had been cold, and she was freezing. She quickly dragged on her favorite old black cashmere sweater. It was pilled and droopy but by far the coziest garment she possessed. It had seen her through good times when it was new and worse times as it grew older. Amigo had even been known to sleep on it, which was why it was covered in a sprinkling of dog hairs. Sweaters come and sweaters go, but some sweaters go on forever. It was like Linus with his security blanket; it comforted her. And after last night's foolishness with her song Bibi felt in need of comfort.

She stepped into her black sweatpants, dried her hair off with a towel, then went and sat on the window seat, combing out the knots and looking out onto the valley. Every leaf, every blade of grass seemed to gleam more brightly, revived by the last night's storm. The tree at the bottom of the hill marking the entrance to her road had been struck by a lightning bolt and had split in two. One half was blackened and twisted like a witch's tree, the other still stood, green leaves fluttering in the breeze. The three goats munched their way steadily across the grass and a couple of chickens, let out earlier from their coop, tottered in the ditch, their favorite laying place. Amigo sprawled on the terrace, too old to give chase and too content to even care. A bee buzzed against the open window. There was only the sound of the birds and the steady crunch of the goats. Bibi could even hear herself breathe.

She closed her eyes, letting her hair dry in the sun. Most days she loved this silence, felt protected by it, safe, but today it seemed oppressive. Today it reminded her she was alone when she should have been with her daughter.

She wondered for the millionth time if she had done the right thing, leaving her child. Yet how could she not? The scandal would have followed Paloma from school to school, city to city, country to country. Anyhow, nobody wanted Bibi anymore. She was a fallen star. She was bad news.

She thought about last night and Jacinto, and how he had taken her little song, and turned it into something bigger, like Leonard Cohen's "Hallelujah," repeating the refrain "*Just be (me), just be (you) I wish I had known, it was all so simple . . . and all I needed was just to be . . . Remember . . . just be . . .*"

Something scratched at the window. The bee fluttered in protest then flew off as another spatter of tiny pebbles hit. Kneeling on the cushion, Bibi stuck her head out, scanning the terrace below.

"Who's there?" she called, speaking Spanish of course. It was habitual these days. "Whoever you are there's an iron bell pull at the side of the door. You can't miss it. Why don't you use that instead of scratching my windows?"

There was no response. Suddenly nervous, she remembered the unlocked door. After all, she was alone.

Then a voice said, "Rapunzel, Rapunzel, let down your hair . . ."

Jacinto! She stuck her head out farther. He was looking up at her, one hand shading his eyes, smiling. In skinny beat-up jeans and a white tee, he looked good enough to eat.

"You *are* Rapunzel," he said. "I can tell by the long hair."

She kind of liked being compared with the heroine of a fairy story. "I think Rapunzel was probably a blonde," she said.

He laughed. "Okay, then I'd better leave, I'm not keen on blondes." He waved and turned away.

"Wait," she called.

He turned back and stood, legs apart, arms folded over his chest, looking up at her.

"Why did you come here?"

Frowning, he took a deep breath, appearing to think about it. He said, "I came because you ran away. You were upset and it was my fault. I came to say I'm sorry. I guess you didn't like what I did with your song."

"It's still my song," she said.

"And it will always be your song. I will not touch it again without your permission." He put his hands together, as though he were praying, and bowing his head, said, "I'm begging your forgiveness, fair lady Rapunzel. And begging you to at least invite me into your haunted castle for a cup of coffee, so we can talk. I'm really quite good with ghosts."

He looked so sexy standing there, and so apologetic . . . she could hear his voice, *"Just be me, just be you, just be."* He'd turned it into an anthem for the world, for everyone, girl or boy, man or woman, who had ever wondered about themselves, about who they really were. And hadn't everyone at some time in their life?

"The door's open," she told him, quickly pulling her still damp hair into a ponytail and smoothing down her sweater. She caught a glimpse of herself in the cheval mirror on her way out. Her face was scrubbed clean and the old black cashmere and sweatpants were covered in dog hairs. Too late to do anything about it now.

He was standing in her kitchen when she got downstairs, leaning nonchalantly against the sink, one leg crossed over the other, arms folded, completely relaxed.

He inspected her lazily. "You look wonderful like that," he said. "Better than last night."

She pulled a face. "Last night I looked like a fake Hungarian Gypsy girl. The real thing would have looked better, especially next to those smarty-boots French women."

"They weren't French, they were 'International,' which means they'd married rich men and showed up at a country-house party overdressed and in too many diamonds. French women would have been quietly chic. They always know how to dress for the occasion."

She had fixed coffee earlier, intending to have breakfast after her shower. She could feel his eyes on her as she poured some into a couple of pottery mugs with jolly pictures of roosters on them. "Sugar? Milk? And how do you know so much about French women, anyway?"

He refused the sugar and she took his mug and set it on the kitchen counter next to him, careful not to get too close, not to accidentally touch. She took her own mug and went and sat at the table.

Jacinto looked at her as she walked away, as physically aware of her as she was of him. "I like that," he said.

"What?" She put a hand up to her hair—was it falling down again?

"You put the hot mug right down on the table. Most women would have gotten a coaster."

Bibi shrugged, waving an arm at the table. "Have you *looked* at this table? It's been here forever and has probably seen more mugs of hot coffee and bottles of spilled wine than you or I ever have. It's too late for this table."

He walked across and ran his hand over the rough-hewn surface. "I love it, though. It's history. Like this place. Your castle."

"The Castello Adivino."

"The Fortune-Teller's Castle." He brought his coffee over and sat next to her.

Bibi tried not to stare at his biceps with the tattoo. She could see another circling his wrist, and one on his finger. Another disappeared from his neck into his chest under the plain white tee he wore.

He said, "So, Vida, you are a fortune-teller?"

"*Me?*" She threw back her head and laughed.

He thought she looked beautiful when she laughed. Her face became animated and she had small, very pretty teeth, white and even. And a soft mouth that curved up at the corners. *And pale lake-green eyes . . .*

"A fortune-teller?" Bibi said, amused. "I can't even predict my own fortune, never mind anyone else's. No, the castle was once owned by a woman said to have that ability, but that was long ago, lost in the mists of time."

He was still looking at her eyes. Those pale green eyes that were so hauntingly familiar, and the clue to her true identity. "Ahh, *the mists of time,*" he said. "You have a way with words."

"You know those are not *my* words."

"But the ones I sang last night were." He took a sip of his coffee, looking steadily at her. With her hair pulled back, her un-made-up face, without the contacts, the tinted glasses, she was who she was.

"They were Vida's words," he said, putting down the mug.

"And I am here to ask your permission to record them. I want to record 'Just Be,' Vida."

"You mean the way you played it last night?"

"Better," he said simply. "I want to add strings and a wailing baritone sax and trumpets. I only wish you would agree to sing it with me."

He waited for her reply but she turned her back, took her mug and carried it back to the sink, rinsed it under the tap and put it down on the draining board.

Bibi's heart was thundering under the dog-hairy sweater . . . how she *longed* to sing it with him, she could hear it now the way he'd done it, the way he would do it in the studio with strings, sax, and trumpets. Last night he had taken her little song and made it into something bigger, an anthem with the catchy hook.

The rooster outside the window cackled, no doubt after the hens again. "I don't sing," she said. "If you ever heard me you wouldn't even want me, I'm worse than the rooster."

"Rodolfo told me you'd sold other songs, I mean sold the performing rights, permission to record."

"Just three others. But not like this one, not the way you make it sound." She frowned as she thought about her previous songs. "My songs are small, intimate. I simply write the way I feel."

"About yourself. As I do. And as you obviously were with 'Just Be.'"

He went to stand next to her, catching her hands in both his.

"Vida, of the Castillo Adivino, I am going to tell your fortune. If you will not sing for me, at least give me permission to use what we did last night. We recorded it, you know, just casually, but it has a great basic sound, and there's your guitar solo in the middle, and a hint of you speaking the words in the background. I'd like to use that."

She looked worried and he squeezed her hands tightly. "I promise, you will be just background. Please say yes. Vida Hernandez?"

She gripped his hands as though he was saving her from drowning. "Yes," she said, simply. He pulled her to him. She thought he was going to kiss her hands but then his lips covered hers. Softly, slowly, he kissed her.

The sexual thud in the pit of her belly took her by surprise, the sexual awareness of him, his body next to hers. How long since she had felt this? She had never expected to again, and she *shouldn't* now . . . it was too dangerous . . . but oh she was melting into that delicious liquid sensual place she never wanted to leave . . . *This was a mistake, she was helpless with him, he was too strong for her, taking her over, she was ten years older than him . . .*

He took his lips away and she opened her eyes . . . *Oh my God! She had not put in her contacts, she had just gotten out of the shower, hadn't expected him!* He had to have noticed . . . yet he hadn't said anything . . .

He was smiling at her, that easy charming smile. "And now I'm taking you out to lunch to celebrate," he said.

"Where?" she asked.

"Wherever you like. Madrid? Málaga? Marbella? And we'll ask Rodolfo to draw up a contract today, I'll call my producer, we'll be in the recording studio tomorrow. Please, *please*, Vida, say you will come to the session, say you'll play guitar with me."

"I'll see," she said, but he'd seen her green eyes; he'd heard her song, maybe he knew who she was and maybe he was going to use that in the recording. But no, she could trust him, she could tell by the sincere look in his eyes. Yet hadn't Bruno had that same sincere look when he'd first met her?

She disentangled her hands, remembering that thud of sexual

frisson when Jacinto kissed her. She was attracted to him. More than attracted, she was captured by his energy, his life force. She had been like that herself, not too long ago, but the person she was then had become lost in the mists of time . . .

Hadn't she said those words just a few minutes ago? And now here she was back in the music biz, back in recording studios, back with a man who wanted her and whom she wanted. Back with a star.

It was all too good to be true. And she wanted to share it with Paloma.

Chapter 38

Barcelona

Mac had spent a sleepless night with Lorenza on his mind. After all, he told himself, how can a man walk into a room and find his past waiting for him, and looking almost exactly the way she had all those years ago, her eyes warm with memories, smiling and beautiful, sexy and available. Shared memories like theirs would never go away, even though he knew they should be kept as simply that. Memories.

He'd risen early, showered and shaved, managing to cut himself in the process. Blotting his chin he thought wryly it would look good with the black eye. He looked like a fighter, not a lover.

He got on the phone and ordered a rental car, then called Lorenza and got her housekeeper on the line. Buena said she would get the Señora right away, but he cut her off and asked her to give Lorenza a message saying he would drive to the bodega himself and to tell her he would arrive that evening.

Then he e-mailed Sunny and left a message saying he loved her and missed her. It was true. He did. He was careful, however, not to mention Lorenza. Sunny might not understand that she was in his past and her only role now was as Paloma's grandmother.

He made several other calls, one to a contact in Málaga, asking for information on problem boy, Antonio de Ravel. He'd also already checked Floradelisa and her life seemed to be an open book. But Jassy was something else.

He got Lev on the phone and discussed the possibility that Jassy was funding Bibi, for Paloma's sake, because there was no doubt Jassy adored her niece.

"That's if Bibi is still alive," Lev said. "And I'm beginning to doubt it."

"I'm not getting a single lead on her," Mac said. "How can a woman disappear so completely? Especially a famous one."

"Beats me," Lev said.

"There has to be some link. And that link could only be through the daughter she loved. I'm off to see Paloma now."

"At the Ravel bodega?"

"At the bodega."

"Watch out for that Lorenza," Lev warned. "She's quite a woman. But then you already know that."

As Mac clicked off the phone, he wondered how Lev knew about him and Lorenza.

He arrived at the bodega that evening after several wrong turns that had taken him miles—kilometers, he'd forgotten he was in Europe—out of his way.

He'd driven through endless fields of vines, heavy with bunches of still-unripe grapes. The headlights of his small rented Ford Fiesta picked up the startled glowing eyes of rabbits before they took off into ditches, tails bouncing, and for one incredible moment he thought he was being attacked when something swooped fast toward him, almost brushing the roof of the car with its wings as it soared suddenly upward. A horned owl beginning its nightly predator prowl.

The sky was clear, studded with a thousand stars that seemed brighter in the unpolluted countryside than they ever did in L.A., but nowhere did he see a sign with an arrow pointing the way to the Bodega de Ravel.

In the end he got there by mistake, simply by taking a left when he'd thought he should have taken a right, and found himself on a newly paved road, wide enough for two trucks to pass and with vines crowding to the very edge. Half a mile farther on was a long, low white house with dormer windows and blue tile roof, set in a wildflower meadow. A huge tree dominated the lawn. A table and chairs were set in its shade and a plaid rug with an open book lay on the grass, maybe forgotten by Paloma. He wondered what she knew about her mother that might give him a lead, if not to Bibi's whereabouts, then at least a clue as to who Bibi really was. Mac had found in the past that the most important thing was not what and where, but *who* you were. It had solved many a case for him.

Paloma had been watching out for him and now she flung herself under the portico and down the wide front steps into his arms. "*Mr. Reilly, Mr. Reilly!*"

He laughed as he caught her and swung her into the air. "Hey, it's *Mac*. Remember? And I'm glad to see you too, sweetheart."

"You came specially," she said, back on terra firma, looking up at him with those conker-brown eyes, so unlike her mother's that Mac wondered for a second exactly *who* her father might be.

"No thanks to you," he said, taking her hand and walking up the steps with her and into the house. "*You* didn't even ask me."

"But Jassy did, she told me she'd called you. And Lorenza asked too."

"Ah. The Matriarch," he said, looking for her.

Lorenza was not around but a little girl was; short, blue eyed, and blond pigtailed.

"This is my best friend, Cherrypop," Paloma told him.

"Pleased to meet you, Señor Reilly," Cherrypop said, speaking English. "My mother's from Brooklyn."

"Isn't everybody?" Mac said, laughing, because sometimes that seemed true. "And I'm pleased to meet you too, Cherrypop."

"Aren't you going to ask how I got my name?" She gave him a pert glance from those china blue eyes. "Everybody always does."

"Then I guess I've no need to ask, you're just gonna tell me."

Cherrypop pouted. She glanced at Paloma, then back at him.

"It's a long story," she said, just as Lorenza came down the stairs, barefoot, in a pale green caftan that skimmed her breasts and floated round her ankles, cool and elegant and simple all at the same time. Mac felt glad he had not made the drive alone with her. He didn't know if his resolve could have stood the test.

"Mac," she called. "I thought you must be lost!"

"I was, but remember I'm a detective, ultimately I can find anyone, anywhere."

"And you found *me*."

She came and put her arms around him, pressing her cool cheek against his. He breathed in the faint elusive flowery scent he remembered so well. He decided to buy Lorenza a gift; a bottle of perfume that came without memories. He'd heard Chanel No.5 was good.

He kissed her cheek and took a step back. "Another beautiful home, Lorenza," he said, glancing round the spacious hall with its polished wood floors and the big round table centered with an immense bowl of flowers, the wide low stairs and the raftered ceilings.

"De Ravel history is written in these walls," she told him. "As it is in the Ramblas house. But you know, of course, that the Ramblas house now belongs to Bibi, and to Paloma."

"Oh, but you can always live there, Grandma," Paloma said impulsively, making Lorenza smile.

She said, "Paloma, why don't you and Cherrypop show Mr. Reilly to his room, then we'll have dinner."

"Thanks," Mac said. "I could use a shower first though."

She met his eyes, smiling flirtatiously. He knew she was thinking what he was thinking and it wasn't good. Or was it? He took Paloma's hand.

"Okay, girls," he said, following Cherrypop, who hefted his Tumi bag and started up the stairs. "Let's go."

"You're at the end of the hall," Paloma told him, as they walked down a wide corridor, past her own room. "It's the biggest guest room. Lorenza keeps it for special people. Her room's at the other end." She pointed back, past where the staircase was, to a pair of double doors. "Of course hers is the biggest room of all. It used to be the place they kept cows, once upon a time."

"Eons ago," Cherrypop said, flinging open the door and then flinging Mac's bag onto a large tester bed, with silk gathered at the top into a sort of gilded wooden crown carved with vine leaves. Feminine, Mac thought, like Lorenza.

Cherrypop turned to look at him. "You still haven't asked about my name."

He laughed and told her he'd probably have lots of questions to ask her later.

"I know," she said, gazing at him, all solemn trusting blue eyes that Mac instantly suspected held more mischief than she was showing.

"Cherrypop knows why you're here," Paloma told him. "She knows everything and she says it's all crap about my mom being a murderer."

"I agree," Mac said, taken by surprise because this was the

first time Paloma had really addressed the question of her mother's guilt.

Paloma looked down at her feet. "I agree too," she said in a small voice. "At least, I think I do."

"Why don't we talk about it later," Mac said. "After my shower."

"And dinner," Cherrypop said, because she was starving.

"It's paella, the kind from Valencia, with chicken and bits of pork and shrimp and mussels," Paloma told him.

"I can't wait," he said.

And nor could Lorenza, who was pacing the floor, hands clasped together, brow knotted in a frown. Buena came in with two bottles of chilled white wine—a de Ravel white, of course, the one with the touch of fizz, typical of the area.

"You'll wear out that carpet," Buena said, watching Lorenza knowingly. She hadn't seen her like this in years, and she'd guessed why. Lorenza was no angel, and Buena knew there had been other men since Juan Pedro passed on. How could there not? She was a woman after all, and a beautiful and passionate one. Juan Pedro had loved her for it. You couldn't live in the same house as those two and not be aware of their lovemaking and their passion. It was the kind of thing servants always knew, just as she'd always known later, when Lorenza had taken lovers. The lover would sometimes join her here, as a guest, like this one tonight, though of course Buena understood Mac Reilly was not Lorenza's lover. Not yet anyhow, though she knew if Lorenza had her way he would be. But Mac Reilly was also here on serious business.

"Never mind the carpet, I'll wear myself out," Lorenza said, stopping in her pacing to look at Buena. "I've known him a long time," she added.

"You told me." Buena opened the bottles and put them in the ice bucket, along with a Fanta orange for the girls. Only one each, Lorenza was firm about that, especially after the story of Cherry-pop's baby teeth.

"He was special to me, all those years ago, Buena."

Buena pushed back her hair and skewered it more firmly with the pins. She smoothed down her blue cotton overall and folded her arms over her large bosom, looking at her friend and employer.

"I understand," she said simply. "And I can see you're jump-ing in with both feet. Be careful. And remember *why* he's here."

For a moment Lorenza had forgotten that Mac *was* here for Paloma; for a moment she'd thought he'd come to just see *her,* to be with her again.

She said, "He has a girlfriend. But I'm back in love with him, Buena. I want him. I *need* him. My life can begin again with him."

Buena adjusted the wine bottles in the ice bucket, worried. "He's different," she warned. "A man like that—he has his own way of life, his work. And anyway he already has a woman."

"Things can change," Lorenza said, thoughtfully.

And then Cherrypop burst rocketlike into the room, fol-lowed by a more sedate Paloma. "Here we are," she said. "And we're starving."

"Then go quickly and wash your hands," Lorenza ordered, pouring herself a glass of wine and sipping it gratefully; she'd need a drink to get her through the next hour or so. Then Mac walked in, long and lean in his eternal blue jeans, a chambray shirt, sleeves rolled, his black eye now yellowing and a cut on his chin. He was the best thing she had seen in years and she gave him a smile that dazzled.

"I'd forgotten you were so cute," she said.

"Not a word I'd ever use to describe myself," he said, accepting a glass of wine from Buena.

"Nor would I," Buena whispered to Lorenza. "He's too sexy for his own good. Or yours," she added. "And anyhow, I'll bet he's married."

"No, he's not," Lorenza whispered back, face turned from Mac, who was inspecting the room, which was furnished country-style, for comfort, with deep sofas and big chairs, a piano in the corner, exotic-looking paintings on the walls, and a large bronze sculpture of a herd of sheep, crowding on each other. Mac wondered if a group of sheep was called a herd; maybe he'd got that wrong.

"Anyway," Lorenza was still having a whispered conversation with Buena, "in life, and love, it's every woman for herself. I'm in love all over again, Buena, and I want him back. I'm declaring war on any woman he knows. And you know I always win."

Buena sighed loudly. She knew when Lorenza wanted something, nothing would stop her.

The children came back and Lorenza herded them, like the sheep, into a small informal dining room where the table was set with a wooden bowl of salad, and a large round cast-iron dish of paella, the yellowed rice firm and fragrant with saffron and crisp round the edges, that Paloma told Mac were always the best bits.

Buena filled their wineglasses, the girls had their Fanta orange with lots of ice and a straw—and Cherrypop told Mac the story of her name.

Then out of the blue Paloma said, "Mac, will you find my mom?"

"I'll try," he said, and she fell quiet again.

The remains of the paella were cleared away, slices of chocolate cake brought for the girls, a mousselike sorbet for Lorenza and Mac, who eyed the chocolate cake longingly. Sunny would have given him the cake, but then Sunny knew him. *Really* knew him, with all his foibles and quirks and moods and work ethics, as no other woman ever had. Not even Lorenza. They had been different people when they knew each other. There was more than twenty years of living coming between them now.

But he was here for Paloma and now he had a question for the girl. "If there was one thing, only *one* thing, you remember most about your mother, Paloma, what would it be?"

"Her singing," Paloma said promptly. "She sang all the time. Not just in the shower, y'know, but like *always*. And she wrote music, lovely songs. I can remember the words to some of them. She would never give up writing her songs, I know that."

Mac suddenly realized he had his link. He looked at Lorenza and said, "From children comes the truth."

Cherrypop stared at him. "What does he mean?" she whispered to Paloma, who shrugged, mystified.

Mac should have guessed. It was really so simple. Bibi's talent was too much a part of her. She might give up everything else: her home, her lifestyle, even give up her daughter, but she could never give up her music. It was *who* she was. Somewhere out there, Bibi was still working, she was still writing her songs, and somebody must be singing them. Somebody might even be recording them. Bibi's talent was not lost. If she were still alive, that is.

Chapter 39

Bodega de Ravel

After dinner, both the girls went off to watch TV. It was very late when Mac pushed back his chair. "Thanks for the wonderful dinner," he said to Lorenza.

"I enjoyed having you."

Lorenza didn't want him to go. She glanced out the open French door. A moon lit the vineyards. "It's such a lovely night, why don't we go for a stroll? I can show you my orchids. I grow them for exhibition, in a special temperature-controlled greenhouse. It was one of Juan Pedro's hobbies and I've kept it on."

"In memory of him," Mac said. He went and stood next to her, put a hand on her warm naked shoulder where the filmy caftan had slid off.

"Maybe tomorrow," he said, bending to kiss her cheek. That flowery scent was in his nostrils again. "I've got something I need to work on, calls to make." He straightened up and glanced at his Timex. It was late but he'd bet he wouldn't be waking Lev up.

Lorenza desperately wanted to keep him with her; she wanted more, she wanted so badly to have that special kind of love again, that overwhelming sexual feeling when a man put his arms around her and told her she was beautiful, that she was lovely, that he loved her, he would always love her. She was a woman suddenly madly in love again and she wanted her old lover back. It was as simple as that.

"Please?" she said, turning her face up to his.

Mac was looking at a lovely woman he cared deeply about, but time had moved on.

"You asked me to come here for Paloma's sake," he reminded her. "I think I might be on to something and I have to work fast, before Bruno Peretti shows up with a court order and takes Paloma back to California."

"Oh God! He can't do that!" Lorenza cried, shocked out of her love-dream.

"He might be able to," Mac said. "And I have to find a way to stop him."

Paloma and Cherrypop were sitting at the top of the stairs, eavesdropping. Giggling, they wanted to hear what grown-ups said to each other when they were alone.

"It's so romantic," worldly-wise Cherrypop said. "I mean, Lorenza's crazy about him, anybody could tell. Wouldn't it be wonderful if he fell in love and they got married. Then you could keep Mac all to yourself, right here at the bodega."

She beamed her toothy excited smile but Paloma was frowning. "Mac's in love with Sunny," she said. "And Sunny's beautiful, and she's kind, and . . ."

"And what? Anyhow I've never met Sunny so she doesn't count."

"Nor has Lorenza met Sunny," Paloma said, her loyalties suddenly divided. And that's when they heard Mac say that her stepfather could get a court order and take her back to California.

"*Oh my God,*" Cherrypop whispered. "He *can't* do that."

"No . . . please, *no* . . ." Paloma cried. Mac hadn't told her of that possibility; all he'd said was he would try to help, and now look what was happening.

She gripped her arms round Cherrypop's neck, so tight Cherrypop thought she might faint.

"What shall I do?" Paloma's voice was muffled, her face hidden in her friend's neck as though she wanted to disappear.

Cherrypop thought for a minute. It never took her long to make a decision. "We'll run away," she said.

"Where to?"

"Hmm, I don't know yet." She tossed her long blond braid back over her shoulder, and hunched over, elbows on knees, thinking.

"Don't you know anybody we could run away to?" Cherrypop asked at last. "I mean, like I have my uncle Julio in Murcia, but it might cost a lot to get there and anyhow he'd probably just send us back again, and then what?"

Paloma groaned. Lorenza and Mac's voices were coming closer. Mac was saying goodnight, heading for the stairs. The two shot up and ran into Paloma's room, where they threw themselves on the bed, scared.

"He almost caught us," Cherrypop said, still caught up in her idea of a pair of vagabonds running away. Or "on the lam" as she remembered they said in movies. It was all so exciting. Except the part about Paloma's horrible stepfather of course.

But Paloma had sat up straight again. "Maybe I should just talk to him," she said.

"The *stepfather*? You couldn't, he wouldn't even listen, besides he just wants your money. . . ."

"Not *him*. Mac, *idiot!*"

Despite the seriousness, Cherrypop giggled. "Aw, what the

hell." She yawned, suddenly exhausted. "Let's just watch TV. We can figure out what to do tomorrow."

Tomorrow seemed a long way away. Paloma turned on the TV and they sat cross-legged on her bed, watching. It was an interview show recorded a couple of months ago. They'd seen it before, but then Jacinto came on and sang. Paloma and Cherrypop thought he was wonderful. He was their favorite.

Chapter 40

Barcelona

Bibi was at Jacinto's house behind the glass partition of his private recording studio, wearing earphones and listening to him singing her song. The background music was already recorded; Jacinto's group had done a fabulous job, and strings and brass would be added tomorrow.

She leaned her head back, eyes closed, hardly believing this was her little song.

She loved it here, wrapped in the security of the small sound-proofed recording studio. Other than the sound engineer, she was alone with Jacinto. The song ended on a rush of exhilaration, a deep thrusting beat that at first had seemed out of place with her sensitive lyric, then quite remarkably had suddenly filled her quiet song with joy instead of pain.

"It's about finding yourself," Jacinto had told her earlier when they had gone through the lyrics together, this time with her tentatively singing along, deliberately keeping her voice small so he would not recognize her usual sweet throaty growl. "That's what you meant, isn't it?"

She admitted it was and he told her in his opinion finding yourself was not necessarily filled with pain. It could also be a joyous process.

"Who knows," he said, with a tender smile, "you might even like the new person you become."

Now, he stopped singing and silence filled the space. The melody still thrummed in Bibi's ears as Jacinto pushed his way through the glass doors, back into the sound booth.

"How was it?" he asked the engineer, who always worked with him and knew exactly what he was looking for.

The engineer made an affirmative circle with his finger and thumb. "Spot on. Five takes. Not bad for a last-minute setup."

"I think I've got one more to go."

Jacinto walked up to Bibi. He took her earphones off then took her hand and walked her through the swinging glass door into the recording area.

Bibi waited, bewildered, while he pulled up a stool, sat her on it, arranged a mike at the correct height in front of her, tilted it so it was close to her mouth.

"No. Oh no, I'm not going to sing," she said, shocked. "It's *your* record. I gave it to you, it has nothing to do with me."

"*Vida.*" He fell silent and looked at her.

She turned her head away. Of course he knew who she was, he had right from the beginning, and now he was asking her to sing. And she knew if she did, all would be lost. The new anonymous life she had made for Paloma with Lorenza and Jassy would be gone. Her daughter would no longer be the little Spanish girl with no ties to her mother's lurid past, no murders linked to her name, no suspicions and bad memories filling her mind. Just an ordinary girl, who had forgotten all about her by now.

"Vida?" Jacinto did not touch her, he did not take her hand, just leaned in close to her. She could feel his body heat, see the rise and fall of his chest, the deep ink-blue tattoo spiraling down where his shirt buttoned.

"I won't ask you to sing," he said, quietly. Bibi glanced nervously up to see if the mikes were off. The engineer had gone outside for a cigarette and they were alone.

Jacinto said, "I told you how much I loved the way you spoke your lyric, at Rodolfo's. You were just under my voice, a faint girlish echo. It gave another dimension to the song. I'm asking you to do that again. I want to catch the softness of your voice, the undertone of passion you so obviously felt and that came through in the words you wrote. Of course, I've given your song an upbeat almost Latin rhythm, I've given it a catchy salsa bridge, a hard bass line. I told you there'll be the strings sweeping in the background, and those almost Cuban-sounding trumpets, but it's *your voice* under mine that will make this record. Vida, I'm asking you, please, please, will you do it for me, one more time."

He took her chin and turned her face to his so that she was forced to look at him. "*Please*, Vida," he said. And then he whispered, "Your secret will be safe with me. You can trust me."

His breath was on her cheek, his lips hovered near hers, his eyes were hypnotic. He was so young, so beautiful, and so talented.

"I trust you," she said simply. He smiled. And then he kissed her.

It wasn't by any means a passionate kiss, merely a brush of his cool, firm lips against hers. And then he called the sound engineer back, fixed her mike all over again, and then for the first time in what seemed forever, but was in fact only a little over two years, Bibi was back recording one of her own songs.

A couple of hours later, when the recording engineer had left and the lights were dimmed, Bibi and Jacinto sat hand in hand in front of the big board, listening to the playback. Jacinto adjusted the treble here, the bass there, taking out an echo, leaving a space for the brass to come in. Then he sat back in the big leather swing chair next to Bibi's and together they just listened.

Her little song came roaring out at her, filled with raw energy, filled with joy, her own voice, breathy, sexy, underscoring Jacinto's rocking growl. It was so different from what she had intended; instead of a song about a woman filled with pain, it was a song for youth everywhere, for young people in search of themselves . . . and maybe finding it.

"Sweetheart," Jacinto said, as they sat on for a moment in the deep silence left when the record finished. "You are wonderful."

Bibi took a deep breath. It was time for the truth. "If you betray me, and tell the world who I am, you know you are guaranteed a hit."

"I'll never betray you," he said, without taking his eyes from hers.

She believed him, and hand in hand, they walked out of his studio and into the night.

Jacinto's house was surrounded by a garden with high walls to keep out fans and photographers. It was late and the moon shone its brilliant white light onto a narrow dark blue swimming pool that looked as still and deep as the bottom of the ocean. They walked to the edge, staring into its depths, then suddenly Jacinto tugged his shirt over his head and threw it onto the ground. He unzipped his jeans and pulled them off, balancing on the edge of the pool, laughing. He stripped off his undershorts and for an instant stood there naked.

"Last one in's a coward," he said, making a neat arcing dive into the inky water.

Bibi had time to notice that the swirling tattoo that began at his throat ended at his belly. And that there was another tattoo of a pierced heart just above his pubic hair, and that he had an erection, and that oh my God he was so beautiful and she was so turned on she almost didn't know what to do with herself.

Then it came to her; yes she *did* know. Of course she did! She *wanted* Jacinto. She wanted his arms around her, his body on hers, she wanted that erection beneath the pierced heart tattoo inside her. She wanted all of him and she wanted it now.

Jacinto surfaced and trod water at the opposite side of the pool. "Well?" he said mockingly.

One thing Bibi had learned in all those years as a performer, an entertainer, was how to strike a pose and look sexy. She did it now as she unbuttoned her shirt and let it hang open, half revealing her breasts. She slid out of her jeans, out of her neat white cotton little-girl underpants, suddenly embarrassed by them and wishing she had worn a sexy thong—which anyhow now she did not even possess. She stood for a second, hands held modestly over the red pubic hair she kept waxed in a neat strip, then in one quick move she threw off the shirt and dived into the pool.

He caught her underwater, kissing her, bubbles streaming from their noses until she almost had no breath left and they emerged spluttering, laughing, wrapped around each other, her arms entwined round his neck, legs around his hips. He had her buttocks in his hands, happiness and excitement in his eyes. . . .

She was drowning with pleasure as he let go of her and dived under, and she was laughing as she felt his mouth on her, his tongue inside her, his fingers holding her to him. She was drowning with pleasure as they made love in the water, on the water, under the water, and then on the grassy bank next to the water, holding madly on to each other, crazy for each other, with the heat of sex and the excitement of the long night and, for Bibi, the freshness of his young body after her long years of being alone, when she had not even so much as thought of another man.

High with pleasure and excitement and heat as she lay back, his mouth on her, then hers on him, devouring each other; her cries of excitement and his long final groan.

They lay, spent, still entwined, damp from the pool and from the sweet sweat of sex. Glancing at him lying on his back beside her, Bibi took in his slim young body, the flat abdomen, his lean flanks, the sweet round curve of his buttocks and the glorious darkness of his still-swollen penis that had transported her, along with his tongue, to unspeakable delights.

He was so young, she thought with a sudden pang. Only twenty-two. She was ten years older. My God, for the first time in her life she was "the older woman." It was almost funny and she smiled.

He turned his face to her and said lazily, "What's so funny, sweet lover?"

"You," she said. "Me."

"Bibi," he said softly.

"I am who I am," she said. "I'll just be me."

She looked at her new lover. This one she was sure would never betray her.

Chapter 41

With Ron at the controls of the Citation and a female copilot by the name of Betsy next to him, cute, blond, calm and collected and perfectly in control, the ride to Barcelona via Teterboro was uneventful. Apart, that is, from what was going on in Sunny's feverish brain.

Mac and the Matriarch! It sounded like a sitcom, only it was real and she was the joke.

Ron left the plane on autopilot and came to sit with her. The flight attendant kept the Cosmos coming until Ron finally said, mildly, "Don't you think three is enough, hon? After all, you're gonna have to deal with sober reality when you get off this plane." He wasn't always mild-mannered and could be very forceful; now though he was gentle because he knew she was unhappy.

"True." Sunny reclined her seat and curled up under the comforting blanket even though it wasn't cold. She was wearing the pink bed socks but not the matching eye mask. "What do you think he's up to, Ron? I mean, can he have fallen for her all over again?"

"He might have given it a passing thought," Ron admitted. "Y'know, old times and all that."

She curled deeper into her seat. It was extremely comfortable, dove gray leather with a Frette pillow and a soft gray blanket and her little pink bed socks.

"I remember girls in junior high in socks like that," Ron said. "You look about fourteen."

"I wish," she said miserably.

Exasperated, he threw his hands in the air. "For fuck's sake, quit it, Sunny. Mac's only met up with an old flame. It was all by chance, he didn't go out and search for her. Get yourself together, woman, and put on your best face. Because for sure, she will, and *she's* on her home turf. Goddamit, Sun, I thought you were a fighter."

"I am. I *am*." She sat up quickly, pushing her hair back, pulling her shirt down, sniffing away the self-pitying tears.

"I'm telling you, hon, you have nothing to worry about," Ron said. And when Ron told you something you believed him, unless you were the IRS, of course, but that was in the past.

"We'll be landing in an hour," he said, getting up and making his way forward. "I have a car waiting, we'll be at the hotel before you know it."

Sunny didn't know whether to be pleased or anxious. Of course Mac didn't know she was coming but now she was wondering if this surprise thing was such a good idea after all. A man taken by surprise—anything might happen.

Mac spent another restless night, much of it on the phone or e-mailing. Now he knew all about Antonio, knew the identity of his mistress and the fact that he kept her in an expensive apartment in Marbella. Mac doubted there would be enough left over for Antonio to be supporting his runaway half sister, and anyhow it was obvious from the contemptuous way Antonio had spoken about her at Floradelisa's, there was no love lost between them. He believed Floradelisa cared about Bibi, but she cared more about her niece, Paloma, and what was good for her.

Jassy was the only one who might have helped Bibi, but Jassy was the one who had also asked him for help. This family was getting him nowhere. Especially Lorenza.

He'd thought about Lorenza a lot in between calls, only too aware that she was just down the hall, behind that door. In bed. Asleep. Or perhaps awake, like him. He paced the floor. Of course he was tempted, what man wouldn't be, but he knew his biggest mistake in life would be to walk down that hallway and step through that door. The consequences would be terrible and there would be no going back.

He stood by the open window, quietly thinking about his life with Sunny, about how heart-stoppingly beautiful he found her and how she made him laugh; about their dogs and their Malibu home; about her cooking and her chronic untidiness that drove him crazy, about her body next to his in bed, or on the beach, or anywhere they could make love. He knew he could not live without her. He put Lorenza firmly back in the past and got on with the present. And his own life.

Of course he had to call Sunny again, longing for her, but all he got was her voicemail. He did not leave a message—he needed to speak to her, hear her voice. Sighing, he went back to his work. Paloma had to come first right now.

The only lead he had to Bibi was through her music. It was also the only way she could make money, unless of course she had money invested here in Europe, and nothing to do with the de Ravel vineyards or businesses. Ron Perrin was the man to ask about that but when Mac tried to get him in L.A., there was no reply. He sent an e-mail, asking him to call. Next he contacted a well-known L.A. money manager, one who specialized in show-biz and knew all about stars and their spendthrift ways and their big money. His name was Ted O'Mahoney and they had known each other, slightly, for years.

"Good to hear from another Irish-American," O'Mahoney said, when he took Mac's call.

"This one's hanging out in Spain."

"Lucky man. I hear the women are beautiful and the wine is good."

"Both are true," Mac said. "So, okay, Ted, this isn't a social call out of the blue, inviting you to lunch. I have a couple of questions for you, and I'll tell you up front, I'm talking about Bibi Fortunata."

Ted's astonished whistle came down the line. "I'm listening," he said.

The answers were what Mac had been hoping for. Yes, Ted said, Bibi could have money invested in Europe. He knew for a fact she worked with an investment broker by the name of Rodolfo Hernandez. "He's well known," he told Mac. "Runs an Andorran company, one of those secret tax-free investment businesses that makes him a fortune, I'll guarantee. Not that he needs it, I understand there's been money in that family for a couple of centuries."

"Then Hernandez lives in Andorra?"

"He'll certainly spend some time there, but it's not a place rich men choose to live, stuck away in the mountains between Spain and France, cold, no high life. No, I'm pretty certain your man would not be living there. Can't help you more than that, I'm afraid."

"But Bibi would have access to that money?"

"If she wished, yes. From what I know here, she hasn't touched a penny. Must think it's guilt money or something, you know, after the murders."

"Bibi didn't commit those murders." Mac knew it for certain.

"Then you know who did?"

"I'm working on it," Mac said. But in his heart he knew there was only one other person it could be. Bruno Peretti. The question was why did he do it? And how to prove it.

One thing he was sure of, it wasn't for Bibi's money. There would have been easier ways than murder for Bruno to get his hands on that, via the California court system. Peretti didn't love Bibi, he'd made that clear. Nor did he care about his stepdaughter. The question was—why?

At 9 A.M. there was a knock on the door. Buena came in carrying a tray. The smell of coffee wafted from the silver pot as she set it down on the table and removed the little knitted covers from two boiled eggs in pale blue cups, and the basket containing toast and small sugar-dusted rolls.

"Soft boiled, sir," she said, leveling a look at Mac. "The way the Señora says she remembers you like them."

If Mac was the blushing type, he might have blushed as Buena's penetrating dark glance took him in. He felt like a boy again, caught with a girl, except this time he wasn't tangled in the sheets and he wasn't guilty.

He smiled a thank-you, poured a cup of coffee, added a forbidden (by Sunny) two sugars, drank it down in a couple of gulps, and poured some more. He needed the coffee to stay awake.

Sunny needn't have worried. Mac was not at the hotel. But Allie was.

She was waiting in the lobby, a baseball cap pulled over her ponytail, trying to look inconspicuous behind a marble pillar because, even after all those years of fame, she still hated the celebrity thing fame had brought her. She spotted them as they came through the glass swing doors and ran to Sunny. They threw their arms round each other in a tight hug.

Allie said, "Haven't we been through all this last year in Monte Carlo? Only with the roles reversed? You running off, not Mac?"

"Almost," Sunny admitted. "The difference is Eduardo was never my lover."

Allie heaved a sigh. "True. But Lorenza de Ravel was never Mac's lover either. *Lorenza Machado* was. *And* that was more than twenty years ago."

"Oh shut up," Sunny said, managing a smile. "I'll bet he's with her now and that's not twenty years ago."

"So? You are here now, too. And you know what, you have nothing to worry about."

"That's what I keep telling her," Ron said, barreling toward them, head thrust forward, a smile for his wife on his face.

"Did I ever tell you you were beautiful?" he asked, burying his face in the nape of Allie's neck, where he said she smelled like new-mown hay.

"It's just that Jo Malone perfume," Allie told him, laughing. "Now, let's go to our suite, get you two cleaned up, then we'll find Mac."

"Do you know where he is?" Sunny asked, as they walked to the elevator.

"Oh, yes," Allie said, who'd made it her business, via the hotel manager, to find out. "I know exactly where he is."

It was late afternoon when Mac finally went downstairs, and Lorenza was nowhere to be seen. Paloma was though, and her friend.

"We waited for you to come down to breakfast." Cherrypop pouted accusingly. She thought Mac was glamorous, and even sexy. At least Lorenza certainly thought so, though he was a bit old.

"I was busy being spoiled," Mac said. "Buena brought breakfast to my room."

"Huh, she never does that for me," Paloma said, trying to pout the way Cherrypop did and only succeeding in making Mac laugh.

"Tell you what, I'm waiting for a phone call," he said. "Then I'm going to have to leave. Why don't we all take the dog for a walk, you can show me the vineyard."

"But we don't have a dog," Paloma said. "Lorenza doesn't like them. Of course I do, and maybe now I'm going to be living here she'll let me get one. Unless I can borrow Pirate, of course."

"You can borrow him any time you come stay with us," Mac said.

"You and Sunny?" Cherrypop had been hearing a lot about Sunny.

"That's right." Sunny was on Mac's mind a lot. If he hadn't got so much to do, he would have been on that plane hours ago, but things were coming together, he needed to be here.

"My stepfather had a dog," Paloma said suddenly. "A pit bull, old and mean, all he did was snarl and snap at me. He looked like Peretti. I always called my stepfather Peretti," she explained. "I never wanted him for a father. I never wanted any father, but especially not him." She eyed Mac hopefully, with those big brown eyes. "Though you would do, I guess."

"Only in a pinch," Mac said, patting her shoulder, and thinking about the young pit bull he'd seen in Peretti's Corvette, the night Peretti had decked him at Melvyn's. Paloma was right, Peretti did look like the pit bull.

"He called the dog Bach after his favorite composer," Paloma said. "He was always playing, like, kind of *funeral* music. He knew Mom hated it so I guess that's why he did it. He was always doing mean things like that to her. But anyway it caused problems with the neighbors because whenever he'd call for Bach, it sounded as though he was shouting 'bark, bark,' and the dog did."

Mac laughed. "What happened to it?" he asked, remembering the young dog parked in the Corvette.

She shrugged. "I don't know. It went everywhere with him. He always had it in the car when he went to a restaurant, or whatever. It was his shadow. He had it with him in Palm Springs, the night . . . well, *that* night."

Of course Paloma meant the night of the murders. When Peretti was in Palm Springs with his old dog and Bibi was home in the Hollywood Hills with Paloma. It seemed everybody in this case had an alibi, even the dog.

Just then, Lorenza made her entrance.

Mac could not fail to notice that she looked all long brown legs in her white shorts and that the shirt tied under her breasts left an alluring brown gap any man would want to put his hands around. Not him, of course.

"There you are." She smiled at him. "I had some business to take care of, sorry I'm late."

"You're not late, he just came down. Buena gave him breakfast in bed." Paloma ran over and took her hand, holding it affectionately to her cheek.

Lorenza wished she had been the one giving Mac breakfast in bed. She had spent the long night torn between keeping her memories and never running after a man, and longing to run down the corridor to him, into his room, into his arms. Now, looking at him, she knew that's exactly what she should have done. She had missed her golden opportunity and knew it might never come again. Unless she arranged it, that is. A woman like her was never short of inventive ways to catch a man.

"Anyway, Mac's late," Cherrypop said. "He's just coming down from breakfast and we already had lunch. Anyhow, I'm starving again."

Lorenza laughed. She really loved those two children. She was glad Paloma was here with her and that finally, she could protect her from that bastard of a stepfather. She needed to ask Mac what was going on, if anything. Maybe the famous detective wasn't going to solve this problem after all.

"Girls, I have to talk business with Mac," she said. "Why don't you go for a swim, or play tennis." They ran off, delighted, and she said to Mac, "I'll have Buena fix some sangria, there's nothing like it on a hot afternoon. Come, let's go sit on the grass, in the shade, then we'll talk."

The plaid rug was still there, under the tree, and Lorenza collapsed gracefully onto it, giving Mac that seductive smile again. "Tell me all about Sunny," she said, taking him by surprise.

"What do you want to know?" He didn't like talking about Sunny to Lorenza.

"Who she is. What she looks like. Is she in love with you?" She paused and gave him that long keen look again. "More importantly, are *you* in love with her?"

"Lorenza. Please." Mac sat on the rug next to her. "I can't talk to you about this, it's none—"

"None of my business. But, don't you see, I'd like it to be my business."

"It can't. I can't. My lovely Lorenza, I will always remember you—*us*—but time and life have moved on." He didn't want to talk about Juan Pedro, and nor did she. She was concentrating on Mac and Mac was concentrating on Sunny, wishing with all his heart he could get on the night plane and in a few hours be with her. Why hadn't she called him, anyway?

Buena walked across the lawn toward them, carrying the jug of sangria and two big round goblets. They fell silent while she put the tray down then poured each of them a glass, making sure the lemon and orange slices floated on top.

"This is our Spanish specialty," Lorenza told him as Buena handed him an icy goblet. "Red wine—our own, of course—lemonade, a hint of brandy, fruit . . . perfect in this heat."

She fanned herself, watching as he tasted it. "Good," he said. Then, "Back to the real business of Paloma. Lorenza, I have to stop Peretti from coming here, and I have to stop him from finding Bibi. Tell me, do you know a man named Rodolfo Hernandez?"

She sat up straighter. "Of course I know Rodolfo. He was a good friend of Juan Pedro's, he's managed our business affairs for decades. But don't tell me Rodolfo has something to do with Bibi's disappearance." She was genuinely shocked. "He's an honest man, noble, the best," she added fiercely. "Rodolfo would never do anything wrong."

"I'm not suggesting he has, only that he might be able to help." Mac was not about to tell her he thought Juan Pedro's old friend might indeed be helping his tragic daughter. That was what friendship was all about. He asked Lorenza if she knew where he lived and she told him no, but she had the address and number of his office in Andorra, and that of his offices in Madrid.

"He's an important man in the financial world," she said, thoughtfully. "He must have known Bibi since she was a child. He was much closer to Juan Pedro in those early days. Before my time," she added with a rueful smile.

Sometimes, like now, Mac had to really like Lorenza. It had nothing to do with him loving her all those years ago, that was simply pure youthful passion—or impure, as it turned out. But there was a fierce element of goodness in her that emerged when she was thinking about Paloma, and not about herself.

She reached for the jug of sangria and topped up their drinks. "I'll go get those numbers for you," she said, getting gracefully to her feet and striding, fast, long-legged in the shorts, back to the house.

She was gone a long time. Mac checked his watch. He needed to make that call to Rodolfo Hernandez as soon as possible. He guessed Lorenza must have gotten waylaid by some vineyard business or other. He drank the sangria down and lay back on the plaid rug, thinking about Bruno Peretti and how he could get to him before he got to Bibi, and how he could nail him for the murder. What he needed was a motive. He needed to know exactly *why* Peretti had done it. One thing he was sure of, it wasn't simply for the money. He would have been better off staying with Bibi and taking her to court for every cent he could get. Murder was not the solution.

It was pleasant in the shade, watching leaves fluttering over his head giving a brief glimpse of sky here and there, blue as Sunny's eyes. *No,* wait a minute, Sunny had brown eyes, golden-brown eyes . . . his own eyes closed and fatigue, sleepless nights, and jet lag took him over.

Paloma and Cherrypop were hanging out her bedroom window, watching him. Actually, they had been watching him and Lorenza. "You wait," Cherrypop had told Paloma, "she's gonna kiss him any minute."

"No!" Paloma exclaimed, horrified.

"That's what grown-ups do," Cherrypop added. "Besides, she's so hot for him." She had heard her mom use that expression and kind of liked it—hot for him—sounded like sunshine on a warm day to her though she guessed it really meant sex. Not that she was exactly sure what sex meant either but it was endlessly fascinating to grown-ups so it must be interesting.

"I wonder when we'll feel like that," she said to Paloma, who was kneeling on the window seat cushion, still peeking at Mac.

"Like what?" Paloma adjusted the tiny binoculars Jassy had given her when she was in her bird-watching phase. They were so small you could have watched many birds through them, but Jassy was never practical.

"Y'know, *hot*?"

"I don't want to ever be 'hot,'" Paloma said firmly.

"My friend . . . my *other* friend . . ." Cherrypop adjusted her words hurriedly so as not to offend her friend Paloma. "Anyhow, my friend at school said it's when boys want to get into your underpants."

Paloma turned to look at her, surprised. "Why on earth would they want to do that?"

"Because that's what boys like." Cherrypop was an authority now.

"That's weird," Paloma said, returning her loving gaze to Mac. "I do believe he's sleeping," she said finally. "He hasn't moved in the past half hour. Uh-uh, here comes Lorenza."

Cherrypop joined her on the seat cushion. She hung her head out the window too.

"I bet she's gonna kiss him. You know, like Sleeping Beauty."

"That was the prince waking the princess. Women don't do the kissing anyhow. Men do it."

"How do you know?" Cherrypop asked, adjusting the short cheerleader skirt her mom had brought back from the States last year. Her knees were starting to hurt and this game was getting boring.

"Everybody knows that."

They fell silent, watching Lorenza lope barefoot over the grass. When she reached the plaid blanket, she stopped and looked down at Mac, lying on his back, eyes closed, sleeping the sleep of pure exhaustion.

Without another moment's hesitation Lorenza lay down next to him. She moved closer, turning her body sideways, fully stretched out alongside him. She put her head on his shoulder, snuggling into him, then she gently placed her leg over his, crooking her knee so that it came in intimate contact with him. Sighing, she smiled. She was where she belonged, back in Mac's arms.

"Oh my God," Cherrypop said. "Did you just see what she did?"

"Oh my God, I do. I *did* see." Paloma and Cherrypop looked at each other, stunned, then turned to look out the window again, at the big black limo slowly making its way up the drive.

Chapter 42

Bodega de Ravel

The long black Mercedes sped silently up the two-lane private road and then there the house was, low and white and serene in the evening sun. In front was a huge tree, cork oak, said Ron, who knew about these things since he had become a winemaker.

A table was placed in its spreading shade with a tray of glasses and a frosty-looking jug containing what Sunny thought looked like sangria, the winey/cognac mixture that was truly Spanish. The chairs had been pushed back and a plaid blanket was spread on the ground. And on that blanket lay Mac, on his back, eyes closed, seemingly fast asleep. And with his arm around a woman. Her head was tucked into his shoulder and her leg flung across his body. *Exactly the way Sunny always did with Mac when they were in bed. Together.*

"Don't look," Allie said quickly. "It's all a mistake, I know Mac can explain."

"*Oh, God,*" Sunny said as the car pulled up in front of the house and Ron got quickly out and marched back over the lawn to the shade tree.

"*Oh, God,*" she said again, rolling down the window and

turning to watch. Mac was scrambling to his feet, a surprised smile on his face.

"Well, if it isn't my old friend Ron," they heard him say, as he grasped Ron's hand and slapped him on the shoulder.

"Yeah," Ron said. "In fact I've come specially to meet *your* old friend."

Lorenza quickly took in the limo with the blackened windows. She guessed Sunny had arrived to corral her love, and took it smoothly in her experienced stride. She got gracefully to her feet, gave Ron a warm smile, and offered her hand.

"I'm so glad to meet you," she said. "Yes, I *am* an old friend of Mac's. And I'm sorry you caught us napping, a little too much sangria I'm afraid."

More like too much Lorenza, Ron thought, recalling her long brown leg flung over Mac as he dozed.

Back in the limo Sunny grabbed Allie. "Maybe we should just leave," she said, suddenly calm. "I mean, is this it? Is it over between us?"

Just then an excited shout came from the steps, the front door was flung open, and Paloma and Cherrypop came racing to see who had arrived.

"Oh, it's *you!*" Paloma shrieked as Sunny rolled down the window. "It's *you!* You're really here. Did you bring Pirate and Tesoro?"

"Not this time," Sunny said, smiling in spite of everything because who could resist such a wholehearted welcome.

"This is Cherrypop," Paloma said quickly.

"And this is Allie," Sunny said.

"Oh my God." It was Cherrypop this time. "*Oh my God,* you're . . . the *movie star.*"

"Not anymore," Allie said modestly.

Looking out the window she saw Ron walking toward the car with Mac and Lorenza de Ravel, who looked stunning in white shorts with a white shirt knotted under her breasts, leaving an enticing slice of bare brown midriff that exactly matched the color of her long brown legs. Her flip-flops were white and so were her sunglasses, which Allie thought a bit of a cheap touch. In her experience only hookers and teenagers ever wore *white* sunglasses.

She turned and quickly checked Sunny out: a simple blue chambray shirtdress, perfect for the country, just above the knee, with legs that were certainly as good as Lorenza de Ravel's; a simple string of pearls that nowhere matched the triple row of large ones around Lorenza's long neck; soft white Gucci moccasins, and her trademark red lipstick.

"You can take her on any day," she whispered in Sunny's ear.

"And I might have to," Sunny said, watching Mac slip his hand under Lorenza's elbow as they approached.

"Look, look, Mac! Look who's here," Paloma yelled, excited.

Mac peered in the car window. He saw Allie, and Sunny next to her, and straightened up. He took a step back. "Sunny, am I glad to see you. The cavalry's here," he said to Ron, grinning.

"I certainly hope we got here in time," Allie said, as Mac opened the door and she stepped out.

"Trust me, Allie, you did," he said, but it was Sunny he was looking at, over Allie's shoulder. He saw from her frozen face she did not believe him.

"Welcome to the de Ravel bodega. Welcome to my home." Lorenza's voice came from behind Mac. "But of course, I *know* who you are," she said to Allie, looking pleased. "I've always admired you, and now I get to meet you and you're even more beautiful than on-screen. Your husband told me you're old friends of

Mac's. How on earth did you find him, out here in the country-side?"

"He's not the only detective around," Ron said as Sunny emerged from the limo, swinging her long legs out gracefully, knees together, then standing in one smooth elegant motion to her full height that, she was pleased to note, was at least a couple of inches taller than Lorenza de Ravel, who was at least twice as beautiful as she'd expected with that cloud of dark hair floating around a face that was not perfect but caught the eye with its drama.

"Hello," she said, looking in her rival Lorenza's clear dark Spanish eyes.

Mac jumped in to introduce them. "This is Sunny Alvarez. Lorenza de Ravel."

"Sunny's the one who looked after me in Malibu after I almost drowned," Paloma cried, rushing at Sunny and entwining her in a tight embrace.

"Of course," Lorenza said. "I remember. You told me how kind Sunny was to you. And Mac has told me all about you too," she added, smiling at Sunny. "Please, let's go into the house and get you something cool to drink. Allow me to make you welcome. Any friend of Mac's is also a friend of mine."

Sunny's eyes met Allie's as they walked behind Lorenza into the house, with Paloma tagging alongside, clutching Sunny's hand. Sunny knew Allie was thinking the same thing she was. What *exactly* had Mac told Lorenza about her? That she was his? And he was hers? And never the twain should part? Or was it "never the twain shall meet." Oh what the hell, she'd got it wrong again; she never could come up with the proper quote in times of emergency, though she *was* good at finding bodies now and then.

Right now she'd quite like to find Lorenza's body, at the bottom of the stairs for instance, in this lovely house where

everything gleamed and shone, perfectly kept, perfectly flowered, perfectly scented with beeswax and jasmine and a faint
whiff of winter wood smoke.

"Sunny?" Mac said, giving her a tentative smile.

Lorenza caught it and quietly excused herself, calling to
Buena as she strode down the hall to the kitchen.

Chapter 43

Mac went and stood next to Sunny.

"I didn't expect you." He clapped a hand to his head and groaned because the minute he said it, he knew it was the wrong thing.

Sunny didn't bother to say *obviously* he didn't expect her, since it was the obvious thing to say. Instead, she stood aloof, her nose pointed in the air.

"Please, Sun, baby," Mac said. "I'm here to find Bibi. Nothing else, I promise you."

Allie and Ron moved discreetly away. They wandered through the living area onto the terrace and looked interestedly past the wildflower meadow at the rows of vines climbing the hills into the sunset.

"I'm glad." Sunny moved a step away from Mac.

It was the first time he'd ever seen her like this: stiff, uncaring, her face turned from him.

"It's not the way it seemed, Sunny, I promise you. I simply fell asleep. I didn't even know she was there."

"Oh, she was very much there." Sunny lifted her long dark hair from her neck, holding it up as though she felt hot. Mac poured her a glass of the iced sangria Buena had brought in from outside.

"This will cool you off," he said.

"It certainly didn't cool you off." She looked over her shoulder at him, eyes snapping.

"Sun, I promise you, it was nothing."

"It's not 'nothing' when *we* sleep like that. *Me* with you . . . my leg over *you*."

"But then we're in bed, we're naked, we love each other, you always sleep like that, I love the way you feel, pressed against my body, so soft, so . . . so *you*, Sunny. It's only *you* I care about, I promise . . ."

"At least she had her clothes on."

"Of course she had! I've never seen her without her clothes."

"Oh yes, I believe you have," she said.

"Look, it was years ago, we were just kids, in love with love and life. I admit we couldn't get enough of each other, and then it was over. I haven't even thought about her in years, and she certainly never thought about me. She was madly in love with her husband."

"Unfortunately for me, he's dead," Sunny said, just as Lorenza appeared carrying a tray laden with a frosty ice bucket containing two bottles of wine.

Chapter 44

Lorenza paused for a second, taking in the scene. She had taken the opportunity to change and instead of the white shorts and shirt, was now wearing a soft flowery pink summer dress that caressed her curves, light as a lover's hand. A deep V-neck displayed her pretty cleavage and ruffled cap sleeves looked girlish and sophisticated at the same time. She had on high-heeled strappy sandals that showed off her legs and she'd brushed her dark hair into a face-framing cloud that fluttered as she walked toward them.

She smiled. She could imagine the conversation that had just taken place.

"I thought we should start with a tasting of our de Ravel Sauvignon Blanc," she said, smiling innocently into Sunny's eyes. "It's a favorite of mine, and I'm sure we have the same taste."

Sunny wondered whether Lorenza's remark had a deeper meaning; did Lorenza mean they had the same taste in men? She suddenly felt a little travel-stained in the creased chambray shirt-dress, and she hadn't failed to notice that Lorenza had taken advantage of the break to freshen up her lipstick and her perfume. She knew that scent . . . what was it? Versace, of course. She'd never liked it.

She looked at Mac, who had gone to open the bottles of wine. Lorenza waited by his side, holding out a glass, which Mac filled. She walked across to Sunny who was still standing at the entrance to the living room.

"Please, my dear Sunny, *do* come in and make yourself more comfortable. And *do* taste this wine, it's beautifully chilled and you look so hot. I'm sure you will feel better, especially because it has that little sparkle to it that women are always looking for."

Coming in from the terrace Allie heard Lorenza. "Shit," she muttered to Ron. "This time the cavalry is really needed."

"I'm a winemaker too," Allie said, striding rapidly over to where Lorenza was standing, next to Mac, of course, holding another glass for him to fill. Not that the bastard couldn't have held the glass himself and filled it, Allie thought, hiding her scowl behind a smile as Lorenza turned to her.

"I didn't know you had a vineyard," Lorenza said, surprised.

"Not many people do, yet," Ron said. "Allie won't allow her name to be used, she wants to do it the hard way, no strings pulled. And she's doing very well, thank you very much."

"How wonderful," Lorenza said. He was obviously so proud of her, she was impressed. She thought regretfully about Juan Pedro and sighed. "I know how hard it is for a woman in the wine business. Please, try my small offering, it's not a grand wine but it has a kind of delicacy I think you might enjoy."

Allie accepted the glass, looking over at Sunny, who was still standing where she had left her, a glass clutched nervously in her hand too, and looking as if she thought its contents might be poisoned. Allie wondered for a minute whether it was; it wouldn't be the first time a woman had tried to drug her rival in order to win a man, but she dismissed that thought quickly.

Mac had put down the wine bottle and gone over to Sunny. He took the glass from her, put it down on a nearby table, and clasped her by the hand.

"Please, excuse us for a moment," he said to them. "Sunny and I have things we need to discuss."

Allie caught Lorenza's frown. She hadn't lived in Hollywood and been a movie star for nothing; she'd learned a lot about women in her career and she knew that, whatever the reason— love, lust, past memories, loneliness, opportunity and a hard dick, or the fact that Lorenza's love for Mac had never died—she meant business. She was out to get Mac and it was up to Ron and her to protect Sunny from Lorenza.

Lorenza poured herself some wine and took a sip. "I don't blame you, if you hate me," she said with a serene little smile. "After all, Sunny is your friend. And so is Mac. I hate to come between a man and a woman, but the truth is, everyone is free, and everyone has a choice. Mac and I were lovers, young lovers it's true, but we've never lost that certain feeling, that . . . passion."

Allie looked steadily back at her. She knew Lorenza wanted her to ask if she and Mac were lovers *now* and she was damned if she would, but her heart ached for Sunny because she suddenly suspected they were. How else that intimacy of that little scene, her leg thrown over him, his arm around her as they slept. At least Mac slept. She wasn't sure about Lorenza.

"I understand," was all she said finally.

"I'm glad you do," Lorenza said in a matter-of-fact tone.

And with that she walked to the window, where she stood looking at Mac and Sunny in the shade of the tree.

They were close, not touching, but Sunny's body language did not bode well. Mac was doing all the talking, running a distracted hand through his hair. Allie glanced at Ron. They both thought this looked like a man pleading his case.

"As he fuckin' should," Ron muttered. He'd never have believed it about Mac if he hadn't seen it with his own eyes.

"We'd better get Sunny out of here," he said abruptly to Allie. "We should never have come."

Lorenza turned away from the window, her fuchsia lipstick perfectly in place, her cloud of dark hair swinging as she strode, so gracefully, toward them. She was a woman in love as she had only been twice in her life and she could not let this one go. Mac meant so much to her, more than these people would ever understand. She wasn't wicked, she was just in love. She would fight for him to the end.

She said, "I do hope you'll all stay for dinner. Buena is preparing roast chickens, and I promise they're like no chickens you've ever tasted. And I'm sure by then, it'll be time for some champagne."

"Not a shot, ma'am," Ron said abruptly. "But thanks for the offer." And, grabbing Allie by the arm, he marched her to the door.

Allie dumped her wineglass on a handy little highly polished table on the way out. "We're leaving?" she whispered, astonished. "Just like that?"

"Damn fuckin' right we are. I'm not allowing that woman to patronize Sunny. We're getting her out of here. Right now." He gave Allie a keen sideways glance. "Don't you see, Lorenza de Ravel has her sights on Mac? That woman is zoned in and she wants what they had before. And the way they were, in that embrace on the blanket when we drove up, she might be getting it."

"Oh God," Allie said, thinking of Sunny's possible heartbreak to come.

She had never seen Ron like this before, full of barely contained anger, a bomb waiting for the fuse to go off. The sad thing was the anger was directed at his good friend. Ron was right though. She understood that as she marched across the lawn at his side. He was not going to allow Sunny to be humiliated if he had anything to do with it. As for Mac . . . well, that decision was up to Mac.

Chapter 45

Mac said, "Sunny. Please. I promise you it was nothing. I wasn't even aware she was there. I was outside alone, having a glass or two of that sangria—Jesus, I didn't know sangria was so potent. Between that and the jet lag and that I can't sleep without you, I was so wiped out I must have fallen asleep. I swear to you, Sunny, it wasn't the way it looked. Lorenza must have come out and seen me sleeping, and lay down next to me . . . ."

"*On* you," Sunny said, still with ice in her voice.

"I wasn't aware of that."

"I'll bet it was just like old times."

Mac ran a despairing hand through his hair. He shook his head. "I don't know about old times. Oh God, well yes, when I met her again, of course I thought about old times. How could I not? Yes, we were lovers, and yes I did love her then. Didn't I tell you there was only one other woman I'd ever loved? Until I met you?"

Sunny's whole body seemed to sag and tears shot from her eyes, like tiny bullets of rain, aimed at him. "That's the whole point," she wailed. "I heard it in your voice on the phone . . . that's why I came . . . and look what I found. I was right, wasn't I?"

She'd wanted so much to believe him, yet she had seen what she had seen, an intimacy that only happened between lovers.

Mac was looking at her, eyes all blue steel and anger. Anger at her? Anger at Lorenza? Anger at himself?

"I would never betray you, Sunny," he was saying, but she was looking past him, at Lorenza standing on the terrace, arms folded, watching them. And at Allie and Ron marching across the grass toward her. *Mac wouldn't lie to her . . . he just wouldn't . . .*

"Sunny!" Ron called out, and Mac spun round to look.

"Mac," Sunny said, putting her hand out to him.

Then there came that familiar low vibrating rumble. *His phone.*

Without even thinking, Mac's hand went to his pocket. He took out the phone, glanced at the readout.

"Lev?" Mac said.

The fuckin' phone! Sunny had always heard about "last straws." Now she knew this was it. She ran to Allie, stumbling into her arms as Ron hustled them both quickly toward the car. The driver saw them coming and already had the door open.

Sunny huddled in the backseat, head thrown back, eyes closed as the car purred off. But she had to look. She had to see if Mac had gone back to Lorenza, who was waiting for him on the terrace.

But Mac was still standing under the tree, phone in hand, looking after her, dumbstruck. And then he was yelling.

His voice calling her name echoed after her as the car drove quickly away.

Chapter 46

Trujillo

Bibi was alone at the Castillo Adivino, the "Fortune-Teller's Castle." She wondered if the fortune-teller would have been able to predict the events of the past few days, and how her life would change.

She was sitting on the high-backed old green velvet sofa. Amigo lay next to her, though she'd had to haul him up this time. He was getting so rickety, he simply didn't have enough push left in his legs.

She was playing Jacinto's CD with the volume turned up so high, it bounced off the walls: Jacinto's rocking growl and her own voice, a breathless sexy whisper underneath. *"I don't need you to take the ice from my eyes . . ."* Her words. But Jacinto had done exactly that. He'd taken the ice from her eyes and from her heart.

She flung herself back against the worn velvet cushions, legs slung over Amigo, who merely opened one eye to check, then snuggled back down. Their voices soared overhead and Bibi's world seemed to tremble all over again as she thought of her young lover, remembering his body on hers; in hers; the sweetness of his mouth, his energy and pleasure and their laughter.

If only, if only, she thought, coming back to her senses. She understood there was no future there. She had made the record with him and she knew it would be a hit, Jacinto's records always were, but she was professional enough, expert enough to know it was special when the music spoke to you like this. Yet she could have no part of it. She was back in the castle, anonymous once again in her secret life as Vida Hernandez. A woman with a past and no daughter.

"Bibi?" A shout came as the door was swung open and Rodolfo poked his head around it. "My God, I can't even hear myself speak," he yelled over the billowing music.

Bibi sat up and turned it off. "It's Jacinto's new CD."

"So I guessed. Of course, that's you in there."

He came and sat next to her, shunting the dog over as Bibi swung her legs down to make room for him.

"Did I do the right thing?"

"You mean, will you be recognized? It's possible, but who could prove it? Besides, Vida Hernandez's name will be on the record, as the writer. Jacinto told me you didn't want any credit for the voice. Am I wrong, Bibi, or did he understand why?"

"He guessed," Bibi admitted. "I don't know how, but he did."

"He knew it at my place the night you played your song. Your music has an identity. It could only be you."

"Oh, God," she said, worried. "What now?"

"There's something else," he said. "An American detective called my office making inquiries about you. Of course my staff told him nothing. Everything there is confidential and he respected that. I myself did not speak with him, but what he wanted to know was whether I still handled your business affairs. He was informed only that confidentiality was the essence of our business."

Rodolfo spread his hands wide and added with a shrug, "Remember, this detective has nothing to do with your recording with Jacinto. It's something that had to happen sooner or later, and of course Lorenza is behind it. She's looking for you."

Bibi clutched the old black cashmere sweater round her neck, suddenly cold. The music had ended and the castle was silent but for Amigo's labored breathing. Automatically, she put out a hand to stroke him again. *Poor Amigo. Poor her. Poor Paloma.*

"Lorenza always cared about Paloma," she said. "After all, Paloma is Juan Pedro's granddaughter."

"Paloma also stands to inherit your share of the de Ravel business and fortune. Peretti is still Paloma's legal stepfather and I heard he's after that inheritance and he'll do anything he can to get it. Including forcing Paloma to go back and live with him."

"Jesus! No." She spoke so sharply the dog lifted its head to stare at her, unnerved. "He can't do that. Paloma *belongs* to the de Ravels."

"Bibi, I've thought this over very carefully. I know Lorenza hired this detective to find you. Paloma needs *you* back in her life. You can fight Peretti, in court if necessary. You'll be fighting for Paloma, for your own child. You cannot allow him to take her. You'll have to face up to the past, after all you were never charged with the murders, only accused. You have to come forward, you have to claim your rights as a mother again."

Rodolfo threw his arms wide, startling the old dog again. It gazed, wounded, at him, and he stroked its black and white fur comfortingly. "Do you have any choice, Bibi?"

"I didn't kill those poor people. Don't you think I've asked myself—you can't know how many hundreds of times—who could have done it and why? And still I have no answer."

"Then I suggest you ask this detective. He's quite well known."

She glanced inquiringly at him.

"His name's Mac Reilly."

Bibi closed her eyes, recalling the TV show, *Mac Reilly's Malibu Mysteries.*

"Of course," she said. "He's good, *simpatico* . . . I mean there's something *real* about him."

"He's good at what he does. Lorenza chose well. So? Will you see him?"

Bibi closed her eyes. The castle was silent. The music was gone. Jacinto was gone. Her carefully structured new existence was in jeopardy. Her life was falling apart all over again.

"Rodolfo," she said. "Do you think Mac Reilly could find who the killer is?"

"You'd have to ask him that question," Rodolfo said.

Chapter 47

Barcelona

When they got back to their suite at the hotel, the phone was ringing. Allie plonked herself onto the sofa next to Sunny and they sat, staring blankly at Ron as he picked it up to answer.

"If it's Mac, I can't even speak," Sunny said, but Ron shook his head, listening. He held out the phone to her.

"It's Paloma."

"Oh, God, I'd forgotten all about Paloma. That poor kid, how could I?"

Watching as Sunny took the phone, Allie thought of course Sunny could, under the circumstances, but she said nothing, listening.

"Paloma," Sunny said. "I'm so sorry I left like that, without even telling you."

"It's okay," Paloma said hurriedly. "I *know* why you left but it's not the way you think. I saw it all. It wasn't Mac, it was all Lorenza, she thinks she's in love with him and she wants him to love her but he doesn't, he loves you, I know it, Sunny, I saw it *all*."

She paused for breath and Sunny said, "What do you mean, it was Lorenza?" She sat up straight and looked, eyebrows raised, at Allie, listening while Paloma told her the whole story. She had no doubt Paloma was telling her the truth.

"I'll never forget you and Mac that day in Malibu," Paloma said passionately. "You were so wonderful and I saw your ring and I saw the way Mac looked at you, and I know I'm only a kid but I can tell when somebody loves somebody. I've seen enough movies on TV," she added, making Sunny laugh.

"When you left, I told Mac what happened. He ran after you as you drove away. I know he's coming to get you, to explain. Will you let him, Sunny? *Please.* I couldn't bear to lose you *too.* Besides, I *need* Mac."

Sunny didn't know whether to laugh or cry, perhaps she was doing a bit of both. "Don't worry, sweetheart," she said, "you won't."

Paloma made her promise to call and Sunny rang off. She told Allie and Ron what had happened and Ron shook his head.

"I acted too hastily," he said. "But you have to admit it looked bad."

"*Tell* me about it," Sunny said, her spirits back up again. "And just wait till I see that Mac Reilly, I'm gonna kill him."

"Please don't. You need him." Allie scooped up her bag, kissed Sunny on the cheek, took her husband's arm, and walked to the door. "And I'll bet he'll be here any minute." She looked at Ron, the man she loved and who made it all possible for her. "We're out of here," she said. "You lovers will need to be alone."

Sitting there, alone, in the big hotel suite in Barcelona, Sunny thought about what had happened in the last few weeks and how her life and Mac's had changed. The past had caught up with them, and when she thought about it, she remembered she had a past of her own. What woman her age didn't? Mac never asked her about the men she'd been involved with, only the one she had once contemplated running off with in Monte Carlo, and *that* had been a mistake. The trouble was Mac's past had come back to bite them. Somewhere along the line, they had almost lost each other. Trust was a deal breaker. Lose it and things would never be the same.

Mac didn't knock, he just strode into the room, hair wild from running his hands through it, battling the hellish Barcelona traffic, taking longer than he'd wanted.

"You're late," Sunny said.

"You know I always get lost without you to navigate."

"I know. I was lost too."

She got up as he came toward her, put his arms round her, and her body sagged into his in relief.

"It was torture," she said, not crying because she needed to be happy again in this moment; she wanted to remember it, to never put herself or Mac through this again.

"Oh God, I love you so much," Mac said. "How could you even think I could be without you?"

Sunny couldn't help saying what she said next; after all she was a woman, and she was a jealous one. "She's beautiful," she said.

"I don't care. I only want to see you. *You* are all that is beautiful, what we are *together* is beautiful."

Sunny unwound her arms from round his neck and, taking his hand, led him to the bedroom. He kicked the door closed behind him as she took him to her bed, stripping off her crumpled chambray shirtdress as she went, lifting one foot then the other, out of her lilac lace boy-shorts panties, the kind Mac liked so she always wore them for him. He took off her bra and then stripped off his jeans and shirt and threw them onto the floor where they tangled in a pile with her underthings.

She hooked her hands through the band of his undershorts and pulled him to her, slipping her fingers inside to touch him. His hands were on her breasts, kissing them, then his fingers were enmeshed in her long dark hair. "Black as a wing," he whispered, remembering. They were naked and loving each other, only now with an extra shot of passion because they had almost lost each other, and love like theirs should never be thrown away so carelessly, or simply handed away to another woman.

"Sunny," Mac said, much later. "Will you please marry me?"

He was lying next to her, flat on his back. Sunny opened her eyes. She stared blankly at the ceiling for a moment, then said, "You mean *now*? Right this minute?"

"Any time you say. I want to be your husband, your mate, your lover, and I want *you* to be my wife, my mate, my lover. And my assistant private investigator."

Sunny giggled. She leaned on her elbow, looking admiringly at him. "Anyone ever tell you, you are a beautiful man?" she asked, then shrieked, realizing the implications of what she had said. "No, no, oh *please*, don't answer that."

"No one ever did," Mac lied valiantly, making her laugh. "Anyhow," he said. "*Will* you marry me?"

"What if the phone rings?"

Their eyes met. "So what if it does?"

"So, will you answer it?"

"Never," he said.

And so of course the phone rang.

Chapter 48

Turin, Italy

Lev Orenstein stared, puzzled, at his iPhone. He'd never known Mac not to pick up his calls. He left a message. "Call me. It's urgent." Then he went back to his sidewalk café.

His double espresso waited at the table along with Gus, his man in charge of movie star Carole Brightwater's protection detail. Right now, though, Lev wasn't so concerned about Carole Brightwater, who anyway was yesterday's news and needed so little "protection" even the paparazzi had given up on her. What was more interesting, and what he urgently needed to communicate to Mac, was that Bibi Fortunata's husband was sitting at the next table and he was giving Carole the come-on.

Lev didn't give a shit about the come-on, but he could not allow Carole to be picked up by Peretti, because Mac had him in his sights as prime suspect in the Hollywood double murder. Mac had no evidence but Lev had always found gut instinct a valid place to begin investigations.

He'd noticed Peretti watching Carole as she'd flaunted her way across the street to the café in her flouncy Dolce & Gabbana skirt and settled herself, amidst a flurry of shopping bags, at the table next to him.

Peretti was now ignoring Carole, a little too ostentatiously to be true, and had gone back to his phone call. Lev and Gus at the next table acted like they weren't with Carole, and in fact Lev was not. Gus was his man in charge and Lev had only come onto the scene after Carole had changed her plans, dumped the golf pro in Dublin and taken off for Italy. She'd ended up in Turin because she said she had friends in the Fiat family and wanted to visit. In Lev's opinion she'd be safer with Fiat than Peretti.

Carole's champagne arrived and she took a sip, then from her Hermès Birkin bag removed a tiny green alligator case with an oval mirror, took out the lipstick it contained, and carefully reapplied it. Lev knew she was looking at Peretti in the mirror, and he also saw Peretti knew who Carole was.

Peretti was good-looking, hard faced, pale eyes, self-assured, sexy, untrustworthy. Lev agreed with Mac. He wouldn't trust him even to pick up the check for Carole's drink. He'd already run a few lifestyle checks on Mr. Perettti and found a small-time Ponzi-schemer who'd gone through Bibi's money so fast no one could ever keep track of it. And now Mac believed Peretti wanted more.

Carole flipped her green alligator lipstick case shut, glanced at Peretti, caught his eyes. She put the lipstick back in her Birkin bag and looked back again. Peretti gave her a long knowing look out of the corner of his eye. Then he smiled, a kind of slightly jaw-dropped coming-on-to-her half smile. Still looking at her, he moved his tongue suggestively out the side of his mouth, licking his lips. Jesus, Lev thought. Was he just licking his lips? Or was he thinking about licking her! He thought the latter.

"Grab her," he told Gus. "Tell her it's an emergency. Get her out of here and away from him."

Gus was six-five and big with it. A couple of strides and he'd inserted himself between Carole Brightwater and Peretti.

"Emergency . . . danger . . ." he said to her, in a surprisingly soft voice for such a large man. He scooped up Carole's shopping totes and her Birkin bag, put a hand under her elbow, lifted her out of her seat, fast-walked her to the waiting chauffered town car, pushed her inside, slammed her door, and got in next to the driver who immediately took off.

Peretti's hand, clasped to a bottle of ice-cold Peroni beer, was still in the halfway position to his mouth. Stunned, he put it quickly down and scanned the neighboring tables, eyes narrowing as he looked at the tall bald guy in the aviators and floral Tommy Bahama shirt. The guy was cool, busy on his cell, not a care in the world.

He had no idea what had just happened, but he didn't like it. He got up to leave.

In fact Lev was on the phone summoning another of his men on the Brightwater detail, the one sitting at the very last table at the sidewalk café.

"Follow him," was all he said. Then he got on the phone and tried Mac Reilly again.

Chapter 49

Barcelona

There was a smile on Sunny's face as she snuggled up to Mac. She was vindicated. For once he had not answered that troublesome phone, for once he had said the hell with the rest of the world, this is about us. For once it was only them. Somehow now, though, that bothered her. It just wasn't *normal*.

She sat up in bed and turned to look at him. His eyes were closed.

"My future wife," he murmured, grabbing her. "Just promise you'll never, *ever* leave me."

The phone buzzed again. He opened an eye and looked at her. She lay back, and put a pillow over her face. "So okay, answer it," she said.

Her voice was muffled and Mac laughed. He didn't bother to check, he knew who it was.

"Lev," he said.

He was wrong. It was a woman's voice, quiet. "Mr. Reilly?"

"Yes," he said.

"This is Bibi Fortunata."

Mac was silent, floored for once.

Sunny had the pillow over her face but of course she was listening. She heard the long silence. It took something drastic to shut Mac Reilly up, and she sat up and stared at him.

He stared back at her, then he said very gently, as though speaking to someone who might be ill, or frightened, or possibly both, "Bibi. I'm so glad to hear from you. I know your daughter, and I have to tell you she misses you and loves you very much."

Bug-eyed, Sunny knelt on the bed, clutching the pillow to her chest.

"Paloma is the reason I'm finally making contact," Bibi said. "Rodolfo Hernandez said you were looking for me. He told me Peretti is trying to get custody of Paloma, and he wants to get his hands on the de Ravel businesses, take charge of Paloma's share."

"I'm here to prevent that happening," Mac said. "But I can do it if you are willing to give up your anonymity and face the past."

There was a long silence, then Bibi said, "I'm scared. I know the police will dig up that tragedy and maybe this time they'll arrest me for the murders, and Paloma's life will be ruined all over again."

"Not if I have anything to do with it, it won't. Bibi, I must talk to you about Peretti, about exactly what happened the night of the killings. I'll meet you anywhere, just name a place. You can trust me," he added.

She hesitated only for a moment, then, "The Ramblas house," she said. "In one hour."

"I'll be there. And you can't know how glad I am to hear from you," Mac said.

"To know I'm alive, you mean?"

"If only for your daughter's sake, yes."

She said, "I'm asking you, *begging* you, please, not to tell Paloma. Not yet."

"I definitely won't tell her," Mac said. "That's her mother's job."

He said he would see her in an hour, then turned and looked at Sunny.

She was still kneeling on the bed, jaw dropped, eyes bulging. He held up his hand, palm out. "Please, please don't say 'oh my God.'"

"Oh my God," she said. "It was *her.* The famous long-lost Bibi."

"Alive and kicking and worried about Peretti and her daughter."

"I don't blame her."

Sunny was already off the bed, picking up their cast-off clothing as she headed for the shower. "When are we leaving?"

"Immediately."

She turned and gave him a radiant smile. "Chief Assistant Private Eye reporting for work. Oh my God, I can't believe this just happened," she added, as Mac checked his messages.

He got the one from Lev, in Turin, frowning, just as the phone rang again.

"About fuckin' time you answered," Lev said. "Things are happening you need to know about."

"I just got your message."

"Well, here's another, so listen up good. Last night a woman's body was fished out of the river here. She has been identified as Teresa Peretti."

"As in 'Peretti'?"

"The same. Not only that, buddy, she is Bruno Peretti's wife."

"Ex-wife."

"There was no divorce. She was a devout Catholic."

Mac restrained himself from saying "oh my God." "She jump? Or was she pushed?"

"Who knows? You wanna bet on Peretti? Not only that, my friend, after I saw him in the café today I had him followed. He got on a flight for Barcelona. You'd better keep an eye on Paloma, this man's dangerous."

"How could he expect to get away with killing the ex?"

"Trouble is, mad men have no moral standards," Lev said, grinning despite the circumstances. "Because he's friggin crazy, that's why. There's no police involved; a poor woman jumps in the river and ends it all. Who really cares?"

"And an undivorced wife would mean he was not legally married to Bibi."

"A bigamist."

"And therefore could not legally adopt Paloma. By the way, Bibi just called," he added casually.

"And you answered," Lev said. Mac could tell he was laughing. "So now you've got your hands full. Bibi's back from the dead. For the moment," he added, thinking of Peretti. "So where do we go from here?"

"I'm willing to bet he's on his way to grab Paloma. He's still her stepfather and he can still do it."

"Better take care," Lev said. "Call me."

Chapter 50

Sunny had been standing by the bathroom door, listening to Mac's end of the conversation. "What?" she said, when he'd finished.

He quickly brought her up to date on the Turin happenings, and the dead wife. "Peretti's on his way to get Paloma," he said. "And he can still do it. We have to get her out of the bodega, hide her somewhere."

"We'll go get her then," Sunny said.

"I have to meet Bibi in" —he checked his watch—"forty minutes. Sunny, *you* are gonna have to go and get her."

Sunny thought for a quick minute, about returning to the bodega and Lorenza.

Mac read her thoughts. "This is not about you and Lorenza. It's not about me. It's about that child."

"Why can't Lorenza just get her out of there, take her somewhere . . ."

Even as she said it, Sunny knew that was not fair to Lorenza. Mac was in charge of Paloma's safety. The responsibility was his, and therefore now hers as well.

"Chief Assistant PI," she said. "Okay, I'll do it. But I'm taking Allie with me. Moral support," she added.

Mac went over and kissed her. "I trust only you, Sunny. You can do this. Just get that girl and go anywhere but here. Then call me."

"Why not just call the police?"

"I can't, yet, because of Bibi. I promised to do nothing until we talk."

"So, do I tell Lorenza about her?"

"Absolutely not. I'll call and let her know you are on your way, and so is Peretti, and she's to hand Paloma over to you for safekeeping. Okay?"

Sunny wished he didn't have to call Lorenza, but she got on the phone to Allie and said she needed her. And that Mac needed Ron to accompany him on an important mission.

"How important?" Allie asked. Having just gotten out of the shower, she was comfortable in a bathrobe, hair pulled back, and looking forward to a room-service grilled chicken sandwich— with fries—and a glass of wine, and she wasn't exactly eager to get on the road again.

"You and I have to go to the bodega," Sunny said.

"Shit," Allie said, stunned.

"To get Paloma," Sunny told her. "Peretti's on his way. We're the rescue detail."

"What about the great detective?" Allie's doorbell rang. It must be her sandwich. Ron went to let in the room-service waiter, who then rattled around, setting up the table, as Ron's phone rang.

"The great detective has a secret rendezvous. He's calling Ron right now. He needs him."

"I'm beginning to wonder what you two would do without us," Allie said, but she could tell from Sunny's voice it was urgent. "I'm bringing my sandwich," she said. "We can eat it in the car."

*   *   *

Fifteen minutes later they were sitting in the back of the black limo, doing just that.

"I hadn't realized how hungry I was," Sunny said, taking a huge bite. "I'm starving."

"So what were you two doing all this time, anyway?" Allie asked with a knowing grin.

"Mac's been talking to Bibi," Sunny said, casually, and Allie almost choked on the chicken.

"You're kidding me," she said. "*Bibi*?"

Sunny put a warning finger to her lips, even though the window between them and the driver was closed.

"He's gone to meet her and he's asked Ron to go with him."

"You mean Ron knew and didn't tell me?"

"No, no . . ." Sunny filled her in on what was going on. "We can't say anything to Lorenza," she added. "And especially we can't tell Paloma, not until Bibi is reunited with her."

"Bibi wants that?"

Sunny shrugged, she didn't know. "That's what Mac is talking to her about. She's still scared she'll be arrested for those murders, still afraid for Paloma. She doesn't want her to suffer anymore."

"That kid has surely suffered enough."

Allie took another bite of the sandwich. It didn't taste that good anymore. "And anyhow, what about Lorenza?"

"Mac told me he would call her, tell her just to hand the kid over to us, it was urgent, and that we would take care of her."

"Let's hope she agreed," Allie said, thinking not only of Paloma, but of Sunny, about to face her rival again.

"It doesn't matter," Sunny said, reading her mind. "It's not about me and Lorenza and Mac. It's about that child."

Allie squeezed her knee affectionately. "You're a good kid yourself, y'know that?"

"I'm the Assistant Private Investigator," Sunny said, and despite everything, they burst out laughing.

Chapter 51

Bodega de Ravel

Lorenza had the door open before the limo even stopped, which meant Sunny was able to get a good look at her rival. Lorenza was wearing white, chiffon, for God's sake; long and soft and flowing and about as feminine as you could get. Her hair lifted in the breeze as she waited on the steps for them to get out of the car. Even from this distance Sunny could tell she was perfectly made-up, perfectly groomed.

"Fucking perfect," Allie muttered. "Don't you hate it when the hostess says just show up casual and then she's in silver and sparkles?"

"Give her a break," Sunny muttered back. "The only sparkles are the diamonds." And they were, big beautiful diamonds. In her ears.

Watching Sunny climb from the car, Lorenza put a hand to her neck, feeling for the pearls, but she had chosen not to wear them tonight. They were Juan Pedro's pearls and this was not about Juan Pedro and her. She missed them, though. And quite suddenly, with a stab of grief, she also missed her husband. There had been other lovers. Not "lovers" exactly . . . well, there were some she'd thought perhaps she'd been in love with, for a while, and who she still thought of with affection and still counted as friends. But ultimately it ended because either she was too selfish, or too full of her memories, or too much her own woman, and she had always been the one to move on. Except with Mac.

"Welcome to my home again," she said, holding out her arms so Sunny had no choice but to air-kiss her.

Sunny remembered the perfume. Versace. She'd always thought it a cheap scent.

"Mac called to say you were on your way." Lorenza embraced Allie too, and Allie thought, even close up, Lorenza looked stunning. She smoothed back her own long blond hair, remembering her scrubbed-clean un-made-up face, not even her eyebrows for heaven's sakes, and blondes always needed their eyebrows.

"This is not about us, or Mac," Sunny said, standing in the big hall with the big round table with its big urn of fresh flowers and the scent of beeswax and jasmine and smoke from a long-dead winter fire. "It's all about Paloma."

Lorenza looked at her. Jeans, of course. American women always wore jeans. An apple green cashmere cardigan, buttoned to the neck. A beautiful mouth, slicked with a bright red lipstick, she thought jealously, only a woman as sexually lovely as Sunny Alvarez could wear successfully. And a pink heart-shaped diamond on her engagement finger.

She said, "I know. Mac told me it was urgent." Suddenly afraid, she reached for Sunny's hand. "Is she in danger?"

"Not yet. But we must act quickly."

Lorenza said, "I told her to pack a small bag, said she should wait in her room till I come and get her."

"We have to leave right away," Sunny said, but looking at Lorenza's troubled face she suddenly felt sorry for her.

"I know how much you love Paloma," she said, catching the glimpse of panicked tears.

"I need to go with her," Lorenza said. "I can't just let her go like this God knows where, out into the night . . ."

"It's okay. Allie and I will take care of her."

"But Mac should be here. *Where is* Mac?"

Allie prayed Sunny wasn't going to blurt out that Mac was with Bibi. She needn't have worried, because Sunny said something completely different.

"I know this is not the right moment, when everything is so urgent," she said carefully. "But I want you to know I understand how much you loved Mac. And I know how in love he was with you. I envy you that time, being young together, and I know first love is the one you never forget. But time has moved on, Lorenza, for all of us. We're at the same place in our lives. We're more than simply lovers, we are a team. He thinks for me, I think for him. I know him better than anyone and he knows all my faults, all my vanities, all my insecurities . . ."

Lorenza nodded. "I understand," she said, lifting her chin high so her dark hair clouded round her lovely face. "And I was wrong. When Mac came here I thought, perhaps . . ." She shrugged and her lovely white chiffon gown slid farther off her smooth shoulders. She put up her hand again, seeking for Juan Pedro's pearls. "I loved my husband the way you love Mac," she said. "I read his thoughts, anticipated his needs, helped with his daily business problems. And we were lovers. In the best possible way, I loved my husband physically. The way I see you do Mac. There was always that bond between us, and it had nothing to do with the lovers I'd had before Juan Pedro, and has nothing to do with the lovers I've had since Juan Pedro. For me, my husband will always be my love. It's as simple as that. When Mac came here, I was a woman clutching at straws, hoping to find something we once had but that no longer existed. I was a fool, Sunny Alvarez. And a guilty fool because a woman always knows there is a moment, a single moment when it could have moved forward, I could have done the wrong thing. . . ."

She was thinking of that long night with Mac in his room down the hall, her knowing he was there, his presence like electricity transmitting itself to her, her sexual longing for him, for his arm around her.

"Thank God, it never happened," she said, meeting Sunny's frank gaze.

Sunny had to admire her, for baring her soul could not have been easy. And she liked her for her honesty.

"I know," she said gently, thanking Mac in her heart for being strong against the temptation of a lovely woman, an old lover, who had wanted him so much. He had remained true. The bonds of truth had not been broken.

Woman to woman, now she and Lorenza faced each other, in that beautiful hall with the scents of jasmine and the big bouquet of flowers and old wood smoke from the big fireplace.

She remembered Paloma. "We must leave at once," she said, coming instantly to her senses.

"But where will we go?" Lorenza asked.

Allie caught the "we." "You must stay here," she said. "Ron told me Mac's putting guards on the bodega in case Peretti shows up, though he doesn't believe he will. Lev Orenstein's taken care of it."

"Paloma's not leaving without me," Lorenza said fiercely. "She's *my* grandchild."

Of course Sunny knew Paloma was really Juan Pedro's granddaughter, but this wasn't the moment to go into that, and besides, she could see Lorenza cared deeply.

"Can I come down now?" a small voice said suddenly. Paloma was at the top of the stairs, clutching a small Barbie-pink bag, stuffed to overflowing with important things, like a special whistle she'd won at the funfair in Malibu, the cardigan Sunny had given her that day on the beach when she'd almost drowned, as well as the Missoni scarf, plus video games and her iPhone, a very old baseball cap commemorating Barcelona's Olympic Games in 1994 that had belonged to Juan Pedro, and a plastic bag of junk jewels she'd decided she absolutely couldn't live without.

"Anyhow, where are we all going?" she asked, chirpily, longing to run down and hug Sunny and Allie, but waiting obediently for Lorenza to give her the word.

Lorenza looked at her, then she said fiercely to Sunny, "I know *exactly* where we'll go. And I'll drive. Wait here while I get changed." And lifting her skirts, she took the stairs two at a time, stopping only to hug Paloma and tell her she could wait with Sunny and Allie downstairs.

"Where are we going? Sunny?" Paloma asked again, wrapped in a bear hug.

"Lorenza said she'd take us somewhere special. I'll bet you're going to like it."

"I know we're leaving because of Peretti, he's coming to get me, and you and Mac and Lorenza are not gonna let that happen. Right?"

"Right, baby," Sunny said, just as Lorenza came dashing back down the stairs. She'd changed into black leggings and a white sweater and, like Paloma, clutched a bag overflowing with hastily packed necessities. Her hair was pulled back in a bun and she wore Juan Pedro's pearls. She needed them for moral support.

She'd already warned Buena what might happen and Buena had gone to stay with Cherrypop's family, out of any danger.

"We'll take my car," she said, herding them quickly to the big BMW SUV. "And I'm driving. I know the way," she added, catching Sunny's worried look.

Telling Paloma to sit in the back with Allie, and making sure she fastened her seat belt, Lorenza got behind the wheel. Sunny climbed in next to her and Lorenza started up the powerful engine.

"So," Sunny said, as the headlights cut the darkness of the country night. "Exactly where *are* we going?"

"I've always found," Lorenza said, negotiating the turnoff onto the road leading to Barcelona with practiced ease, "that the best way to get lost is in a crowd. That's why we're going to the biggest, grandest hotel on the sea, right here in Barcelona. We're going to eat paella at one of those waterfront restaurants where Paloma can watch the boats coming in and out. It's always music and bustle there at night, people eat so late."

"You're kidding me," Paloma cried, thrilled with this sudden treat.

"No, she's not," Sunny said, smiling at Lorenza. "Your grandmother knows exactly how to make you happy."

And she knew Lorenza was right, they could get lost in a crowd.

Chapter 52

Barcelona

For Bibi, the Ramblas house had always been "home." She was born there, had been Daddy's spoiled little girl there, and had returned, a woman, to attend her father's funeral. True, her life was separated from the de Ravel family's; her home had become Hollywood, her life meant being on the road for months, touring, or long periods of solitude, writing; of recording, and managing things, or being managed by others. And it had meant being mother to Paloma.

They were in the car, at the gates, and while Bibi hid her face, Rodolfo talked to the old man *guardien*. She remembered him being younger, a proud man always with his ratty mixed-breed Jack Russell, of which the current one, already poking its nose up at the car window, was probably a descendent.

Rodolfo knew the *guardien* too, from all those years visiting Juan Pedro. Now he explained they needed access to the house, that other people would be arriving and he was to let them in. He called off his dog and gave Rodolfo the key, touching his blue beret in respect.

When Rodolfo opened that massive front door and turned on the lights, for Bibi it was like stepping back in time. She could almost hear her own shrill childish voice calling for her sisters, hear herself yelling *Papa, Papa,* when her father returned home in the evenings; hear the maids singing in the kitchen as they prepared for a dinner party; hear her sisters squabbling over their home-work. She could smell the churros Floradelisa always sneaked in after school; see the sunlight slanting over the old wood plank floors, breathe the hot sweet smell of summer jasmine, and the appley scent of crackling winter log fires. Closing her eyes she saw her father's face as clearly as if he were there with her. Now, at this very moment, when she needed him. It was then she knew she had done the proper thing, in coming "home."

"You know something," she said to Rodolfo, who was looking anxiously at her. "In all the years I lived here, we children were never allowed to go into those old theater boxes. The boiserie doors were kept locked and a maid was permitted in once a week, to dust and polish. I always wanted to see what my small world looked like from up there, from that box, looking down to where the tiny stage was before it was destroyed centuries ago by fire."

She smiled as she turned to look at him. "I always thought if only I could get in there, I might see the ghostly 'diva,' in her big swooping hat, maybe catch the glitter of her diamonds, even a smile."

"It's an old wives' tale," Rodolfo scoffed. "No one ever really saw the diva, she was invented because with a house this old, with its history, naturally it should have a ghost. I think now we can lay that myth safely to rest."

"Let's go up there anyway," Bibi said, taking his hand for safety because nothing he, or anyone else, could say would ever convince her there was no ghost.

The boiseries were the painted wooden doors and they were not kept locked anymore, since there was no longer any need to keep out inquisitive children, who might have leaned over the balcony and fallen. The old plush upholstery on the banquettes emitted a puff of dust when Bibi sat down, leaning her arms along the padded rail, beneath which the tiny golden cherubs with wings waved their golden trumpets. The dust smelled of old perfume and cedar sachets to keep out the moths; of fancy paper programs announcing the evening's players, many of whom Bibi had heard were scandalous young women wearing little but tights and a corset half hidden under a tumble of hair. If she closed her eyes she could see them now, strutting prettily to the music . . . and, now she thought about it, not so far off from what she herself had done on stage. Perhaps, after all, she had inherited something of the old house's past and its ghosts, and brought it with her into the present. And now, with Jacinto's new recording, maybe even into a future she had not dared to believe she might possess.

And if it were not for Paloma, she would not. She would not even be here. She would have stayed alone at her castle, keeping to herself, just her and Amigo. She would have always been within reach of Paloma in an emergency. "A matter of life and death," she had promised herself. And now that matter of life and death was here. Mac Reilly said Peretti was on his way to take Paloma. Her daughter was in danger.

She was brought abruptly back to the present when Mac Reilly walked into the hall, without knocking. She leaned into the shadows, taking him in, as he stood, glancing round.

Rodolfo hurried to introduce himself and the two talked quietly, then Mac glanced her way.

Bibi thought he had a particularly penetrating look, it was as though when his eyes met hers, he instantly knew her, knew all the thoughts going through her head.

He gave her a small bow, respecting all her confusion and fears, and the fact that she was finally home again, in this house where she had lived as a child, and that now was hers.

"I want you to know there's no need to be afraid for Paloma," he said. "She's on her way to somewhere safe, with people I'd trust with my own life, as well as hers."

Bibi sagged back with relief. "I believe you," she said.

Mac thought he would never have recognized Bibi Fortunata, this slightly built woman in jeans and a black sweatshirt, mouse-brown hair dragged into a ponytail, pale un-made-up face. But there was something compelling about her, a quality that forced you to look at her, to take notice, and of course the clear direct gaze of her lake-green eyes would always tell you this was the star, Bibi Fortunata.

She threw her arms round him and he smiled. Like mother, like daughter; impulsive and warm and generous with her hugs.

"Where is Paloma?" Bibi asked, still afraid.

"It's better you don't know. Later, we'll talk about her."

Rodolfo took Bibi's arm. "Come on, *querida,* let's go sit in your father's study. I'll get some drinks and we can talk there."

Bibi took a seat next to Mac. She hadn't taken her eyes off him. "You said you could help me."

"I can, on condition you'll agree to return to the States and face up to the police. Only this time I'll be with you, and I've already told them what I believe happened." He put up a hand when he saw her panicked face. "No. I did not tell them you were here in Spain, nor that I was meeting with you. Only you can give that go-ahead. But first let me tell you that Paloma is well, she's a great girl, and a credit to her mother."

He filled Bibi in on his first encounter with Paloma on the beach in Malibu, and about Jassy's phone call, and then his meeting with Lorenza.

"The Matriarch," Bibi said, managing a smile, because it had always seemed such a ridiculous thing to call a woman in her forties "the Matriarch."

"Coincidentally, she was an old friend," Mac said, because he thought he'd better put Bibi in the picture for future reference. "Paloma is living with her at the bodega."

"I know," Bibi said. She always knew where Paloma was.

"You mind if I ask how?"

"Jassy," Bibi said simply. "We never saw each other, Jassy and I, and she never knew where I was, but she talked to Rodolfo and he told me. Jassy cared. I'll never forget the day she came and took Paloma away, the look in Jassy's eyes. She knew she had to do it and it hurt her almost as much as it hurt me. But it had to be done."

"And now it has to be undone," Mac said. "And to do that, we have to clear your name. I believe Peretti killed those two people. What I can't explain is *why* he did it. Not only that, he has an alibi for that night; he was at home in Palm Springs."

"Peretti always had a answer for everything," Bibi said bitterly.

He leaned toward her, searching her face. "Bibi, there has to be something you remember, some strange thing about that night, or about Peretti's behavior, even before that . . . something— anything—however small and unimportant it might have seemed at the time. You have to search your memory, think back to that night, put yourself back there in time, in that place. Remember, however small a detail, it could mean something to us. To Paloma's future."

Bibi closed her eyes and leaned back against the sofa cushions. She tugged the scrunchie from her ponytail, and let her hair fall free, shaking away the lurking headache.

She remembered she'd had a headache that night when she'd gone to visit her friend Brandi. Her head was pounding so badly then, she had not even taken a sip of the wine, the Sauvignon Blanc that was her favorite. She could picture the scene quite clearly: Brandi sprawling on the white sofa in her small apartment just off the Sunset Strip, her physical assets lavishly displayed in a leopard-print low-cut top and skin-tight leggings.

"I don't know why," Bibi said, puzzled, "but somehow I'd never thought of Brandi as a tart, I mean she always showed up in regular clothes, y'know, a cami and a cardigan, a pair of expensive pants, gold hoops and a lot of gold bracelets. That kind of Beverly Hills housewife look. Though of course I knew she was no Beverly Hills housewife, just an aspiring actress. At least that's what she told me."

"She invited you over?"

Bibi looked at him, startled, she'd thought he'd known all the circumstances. Which of course Mac did but he wanted it from the horse's mouth. "Oh, no. I'd found out about her and Wally. . . ."

"Your boyfriend," Mac said helpfully.

"You might call him that. Anyway, I'd found out and I was in a tearing rage, humiliated, ready to kill her. . . ."

Rodolfo said quickly, "She didn't mean that."

"I understand," Mac said.

Bibi shrugged. "Anyhow, by the time I got there and saw her, looking so . . . so well, *unremarkable,* and kind of slutty, all that anger had drained away. I really didn't care. I didn't care about Wally either. I was sick of both of them. And especially of Peretti.

"And then Brandi said she was fucking Peretti too, and I just stood there, looking at her, and I knew it was true. It was Peretti who'd told me about her and Wally, and now she was telling me about her and Peretti, and I was thinking why am I involved with these corrupt people? Why do I even *know* them? If it were not for Peretti I would never have called them my friends. And my daughter, my poor little Paloma, has this man for a stepfather, and she's met these immoral evil people in *my home,* her *own home* . . ."

"So you didn't put anything in Brandi's wine?"

"I was angry, Mac Reilly, but I'm no killer. And by then I didn't care who Brandi was screwing, or Wally, or Peretti. I just wanted out. And that is what I did. I turned and walked out."

"What's your last memory, before you walked out on Brandi?"

Bibi thought for a minute. "That she had been drinking. Before I got there, I mean. The wine bottle was almost empty and her glass was half full. I remember the lipstick on the rim."

"And you did not drink any wine?"

"Nothing."

"So you just went back home?"

"I drove back, alone. Yes."

"What car were you driving?"

"The dark gray Lexus SUV I always drive. The blue Bentley was Peretti's idea. He was always flashy, always trying to make an impression, the kind of man who over-tipped the maître d' and was abusive to waiters."

Mac knew exactly the type she meant.

"So, where was the Bentley that night?"

Bibi frowned, trying to remember. "I guess it was in the garage. The house had three garages, each quite separate. It was an old house and that's just the way things worked out garage-wise."

"So you didn't actually see the Bentley when you returned from Brandi's."

"No. I did not." Bibi sighed. "But I already told the police that."

"I know, I know." Mac patted her hand consolingly. "Have patience with me, we're getting somewhere with this. So, the Bentley might have already been gone. The wine was already drunk. And where was Peretti when all this was going on?"

Bibi shook her head, mystified. "He said he was in Palm Springs, with the dog. That bastard old pit bull," she added, frowning at the memory.

She suddenly sat up straighter. "You know something weird, though? The next morning—the morning after the murders—I got a call from our local vet. He told me they had the body of a dog there. A pit bull. Someone out hiking in the hills behind my house had found it and brought it in. It had been mauled by coyotes. He traced it to Peretti through a microchip in its ear. He wanted to know if Peretti would come and claim it, or should he dispose of it. I gave him Peretti's number in Palm Springs and told him to ask him."

"This is the dog who was Peretti's shadow," Mac said. "The dog who never left his side. Without whom Peretti never made a move."

"Yes," she said simply.

Mac knew Peretti was there at the Hollywood house the night of the murders. He could have done it. What he did not have was a motive, and he asked Bibi for that now.

"You must know the reason he'd kill your lover, and his woman," he said. "You know Peretti well enough to understand his every move."

Bibi's eyes widened as she thought about what Mac had said. "I always believed Peretti was mentally disturbed," she said finally. "The sudden rages, the screaming and shouting, followed by terrifying silences. He was jealous of my success, jealous that I was the one in the limelight, the one treated like a star." She shook her head. "I'm not saying that to show off, Mac Reilly, it's simply the way it was and Peretti couldn't stand it. He couldn't stand being Mr. Bibi Fortunata. He wanted to be who I was, and he wanted my success and my money. And he told me so. He told me he'd only married me for what I *was,* not *who* I was, that I was really nothing."

Mac understood the psychology of a man like that. He'd wanted her to suffer for a lifetime. He'd wanted to see her ruined. His satisfaction would come from seeing her jailed for life, her beauty gone, her talent destroyed. Peretti was a sociopath, a killer in disguise as a well-heeled man about town.

There was no doubt Peretti still burned with that anger and hatred for Bibi, and since Bibi had disappeared, the only way he had left to get at her, was through her daughter Paloma.

It was Bibi Peretti really wanted to kill, but he'd come up with an even better way to destroy her, and get his hands on her money. Peretti knew that once he got Paloma, if she were still alive Bibi could be forced out of hiding, and this time he'd make sure she ended up in jail for two murders. And he'd get away scot-free.

Chapter 53

Rodolfo went to sit next to Bibi, on Juan Pedro's sofa, where the fat old cat Magre used to snuggle against his master, right up until the night he died. There was no sadness in this room of Juan Pedro's, only a sense of ease, of a contented man who'd left a legacy of a life well lived, a man who loved his children, difficult though they might have been, and who had dearly loved his wives, but most especially, in the end, Lorenza.

Rodolfo looked at Bibi. She was leaning forward, chin in her hand, lost in memories too.

"How I wish my father still was here," she said, taking Rodolfo's hand and gripping it tightly. She met his eyes, both remembering. Then she turned to Mac.

"I trust you," she said finally. "I'll go back with you to Hollywood, face the police again. I'll do whatever you say, but first I must see my daughter. I have to be with Paloma, to explain, so she'll understand why I did this to her."

"Paloma will understand," Rodolfo said. "She's very like her mother, that girl."

Bibi smiled for the first time that night. "And maybe her father too," she added quietly.

Mac caught what she said. Paloma's father had never been mentioned up to now. It was simply taken for granted there was no father, at least no one who counted enough in Bibi's life to let him near her daughter. He wondered again how Bibi had ended up with a maniac like Peretti. Any other father would have been better. The story of the Russian dancer absconding from the ballet company was obviously one of those myths Bibi invented to keep the truth a secret. And that was her privilege. Until, of course, her daughter started to ask questions, as one day she would, and wanted to meet her father.

Mac got Sunny on the phone. "Where are you?"

"Barcelona, in a hotel. Actually we're eating paella in an outdoor café, watching the boats, and the flamenco dancers. It's great fun."

"Sunny!"

"Ooops, sorry. But Paloma is having a good time, she's safe, right here with me and Ali. And Lorenza."

Mac put Lorenza out of his mind for the moment and brought Sunny up to date on Peretti. "I spoke with Lev," he told her. "He alerted the Turin cops, who've already alerted the Spanish Guardia. They'll meet the flight and arrest Peretti. And now Bibi wants to see her daughter. She needs to explain."

"A reunion!" Sunny whispered into her phone because she didn't want the others to catch what she was saying, not until she had it all fixed, about Bibi and Paloma.

"I want you to bring Paloma here, right away," Mac said. "Later, I'll take Bibi back to L.A. to face the past. I'll be waiting for you, outside the house."

"We're in Lorenza's car, she says the guardian knows it, he'll let us in," Sunny said.

"I just want you and Paloma. No Lorenza. Okay?"

Sunny nodded into her phone. She understood, but she didn't quite know what to say to Paloma. "What shall I tell her?"

Mac said, "Tell her you're taking her home, and I will be waiting for her."

Chapter 54

The old house was so silent you could hear every clock tick: the French ormolu on the mantel, the gilded Venetian one in the salon, the British grandfather with the solid brass movement, made in England a hundred and fifty years ago.

Bibi thought the minutes had never gone so slowly. Every second seemed an eternity.

Mac waited outside. Rodolfo stood by the window, looking at the dead fountain illuminated in the faint bluish light from the moon. He turned abruptly away. "I'll wait outside with Mac," he said.

"No! Rodolfo, please don't leave me."

"I thought you'd want to see her alone, it's such a private moment, so important in both your lives."

"I *need* you," Bibi said simply, and he went over to her and took her hand in both his, and kissed it.

"I'll never leave you, you know that," he said, just as tires scrunched on the gravel. There was the sound of doors slamming, women's voices. And a child's.

Bibi's face lit with a mixture of panic and happiness. Now the moment was here, she didn't know how to handle it. She said, "Rodolfo, whatever shall I do?"

"Listen to what she has to say," he advised. "Explanations will

not be needed, all Paloma wants right now is her mother back."
He patted her hands again and went to open the door. "And the
father," he said, turning to look at Bibi. "Maybe it's time now, that
she knew about him."

Mac and Sunny were standing on the steps, with Paloma between them. There was a smile on the child's face and she brimmed
with excitement about the daring exploits of the night: running
away, the hotel, the boats and flamenco dancers, the paella.

"Rodolfo," she cried. "Are we having a party?"

"Kind of," Mac answered for Rodolfo. "Go with Rodolfo,
sweetheart. He'll take care of everything now."

Paloma turned to him, suddenly panicked. "Oh, but no, *you*
are taking care of everything," she said. "You promised to find my
mom. *You promised.*"

She clung to him. His eyes met Sunny's across Paloma's ragged
red head.

"Remember, I always keep my promises," he said, and unraveling her arms he gave her a little push toward Rodolfo, who grabbed
her hand, took her inside, and closed the door.

Sunny sank onto the steps. Mac sat next to her. Allie and Lorenza waited in the car.

"I don't think I can bear the suspense," Sunny said.

Mac put an arm around her. He kissed her cheek. "It'll be
okay. Trust me." And finally reprieved from his silence, he got on
the phone to his friend at the L.A. police department, and began
to fill him in on his strange story of Peretti and Turin and the arrest, and the dog and the Hollywood Hills murder.

Paloma was still clutching Rodolfo's hand when she walked
into her grandfather's old study and saw Bibi standing there. There
was an explosion of happiness inside her head, her brain seemed

to go on "hold," rainbows of colors flitted before her eyes. Her heart thudded, her knees shook, but she did not cry. She clapped a hand over her mouth to stop the scream, stood rooted to the spot, then rushed into her mother's arms.

She's grown, Bibi thought. She's not the same little girl I left. How could she be, she's nine years old now and there's a big difference between seven and nine. Inches taller, and skinny with it. But she knew her daughter, knew the fresh smell of her skin, her carrot-red hair, she *knew* her as only her mother could. There was no going back now, only going forward, together, she and her girl, forward with the truth. With honesty. With love.

"I knew you would come back for me," Paloma murmured into Bibi's comforting bosom. "I *knew* you would never leave me for good. Moms just don't do that. Ever."

"Never," Bibi agreed. "And I'll never do it again." There were no tears, only happiness. "It's all so clear now, what has to be done," she said.

Paloma lifted her head, and leaned back to look at her. "It's all because of Mac Reilly," she said, still gripping Bibi tight. "I knew that day on Malibu beach, if anybody could find you, it would be him."

Chapter 55

What Bruno Peretti was thinking on the plane to Barcelona was that he'd lost his cool. For once, he had acted on pure impulse instead of a well-thought-out plan. He should have come directly to Barcelona, gotten the kid, and gotten out. He could have done it so easily, because he was still her legal stepfather, and so far the Ravel family had not taken out any court orders against him. They'd had no need, he'd simply disappeared into the woodwork, out of their hair, out of Paloma's life, out of Bibi's life, wherever the hell she was, because if anybody had ever done the perfect disappearing act it was Bibi.

Dead or alive, though, he would get her, eventually. Bibi would end up in that jail, along with the killers and other criminals. His life would begin all over again, and this time he would be on top. *He* would run those de Ravel vineyards, make an international name for himself. He'd send the kid to boarding school in Switzerland, or England, or somewhere; away from Hollywood, that's for sure. This time he would be the star.

First, though, he had to find out where the kid was. He'd already checked and knew she was no longer with Jassy. He guessed Lorenza de Ravel had taken over the responsibility. He would head first for the Ramblas house. Then, the bodega.

He was quite surprised, therefore, when the plane taxied to the gate and two plainclothes detectives came on board and arrested him for the murder in Turin. He was handcuffed and accompanied off the plane flanked by a pair of Guardia, the Spanish cops.

It could, he guessed, be called "a new beginning." He laughed to himself as he walked across to the police van and got in. He told himself he'd get Bibi yet.

Chapter 56

Malibu

A couple of months later, sitting on Mac's deck watching the ocean, with Tesoro snuggled so deeply into her lap she might never be able to remove her, Sunny thought it seemed as though Barcelona had simply transferred itself to Malibu for the wedding.

Mac was sitting next to her, feet propped, as usual, on the deck rail, hands behind his head and a smile on his face. Pirate leaned his gruff, ugly face adoringly on Mac's knee.

"How did we ever manage in Barcelona without the dogs?" he asked, lazily scratching Pirate's head.

"You mean you could have coped with Tesoro as well as Peretti?"

Sunny was laughing at him, but Mac didn't care. "Laugh all you want, future wife," he said, not moving an inch, even to grab her and kiss her.

"Not much time left to be a bachelor," she agreed, sticking her bare feet on the rail next to her fiancé's.

"Jeez," he said. "Blue toenails."

"That's the 'something blue.'" Sunny stared admiringly at her perfectly pedicured feet. "Y'know, the 'something borrowed, something blue' they always say you must have at weddings."

"Especially your own wedding." He gave her a mocking glance out the corner of his eye.

"Oh, my God, it's now!" she said.

Mac groaned and put a lazy hand over her mouth.

"I know, I know, sorry. I'll never say oh my God again, but oh my God, Mac, it is just a few hours away, and we'll be married."

"Man and wife," he agreed. "Do you have a dress yet?"

"Do I have a dress!" In fact Sunny had quite a few dresses, at least two of which she'd bought expecting to get married a couple of times previously. Always to Mac, of course. But now it was about to come true.

The wedding was to take place at 6 P.M. Right here on the beach in front of the house. Bridal planners were busy setting up chairs adorned with fronds of wildflowers and grasses, arranging rows of votive candles in sea-blue glass jars, smoothing the sand where a small gazebo was set up, draped in pale blue chiffon and tied with white roses. Two stakes were being driven into the ground near the gazebo where Pirate and Tesoro would be tethered for safety's sake, so there'd be no jumping up and ruining the bride's dress, which waited, pristine in its blue plastic garment bag, in Mac's bedroom. A mere column of cream silk-satin, soft on the body as the summer breeze. Of course Sunny would go barefoot.

Caterers were barbecuing shrimp and grilling soft-shell crabs; yellowtail sushi was ready to be sliced; buffalo chicken wings—Mac's personal request—would be broiled later. There would be ribs and salads and corn on the cob, and everything beachy and simple they had been able to dream up. And lots of champagne, of course. Sunny's favorite.

She would have one bridesmaid. Paloma, in an ice-blue cotton sundress, and with her now slightly longer hair brushed into a neat buzz cut. And two maids of honor. Allie and Bibi. Ron was to be Mac's best man. All was in order.

Sunny glanced at Mac. She squeezed his hand. "Hey," she whispered, leaning closer and disturbing Tesoro, who grumbled through her teeth. "There's nothing for us to do."

Mac turned and smiled. "I know it." He got up and removed Tesoro from Sunny's lap, then took her hand.

"Come with me, future wife," he said, leading her, smiling, to the bedroom.

Four hours later, the barefoot bride walked down the scratchy wooden steps to the beach, a bunch of wilting peonies clutched in her hands and a smile of such joy on her face, people commented it looked as though she was lit from within with some special radiance. Her slender satin dress slid smoothly over her long golden legs, and she wore a gardenia in her long black hair. Paloma preceded her, scattering rose petals with one hand and holding Tesoro on the leash in the other. The dog had a large pink bow tied round his neck—Mac's assistant Roddy's touch— that it was trying desperately to scratch off. Paloma tied the dog to the stake by the gazebo, where Mac waited for his bride.

Bibi walked behind Sunny. Her hair was back to its glorious natural red—natural, that is, with a little help from her hairdresser friends until it grew back in completely, and she wore a short dress, simple and pink because Sunny said pink clashed so beautifully with her hair.

Of course people turned to stare; everybody knew the story of Bibi's redemption and was curious, but she no longer cared. Bibi had found out how to be her own woman. Her song "Just Be" had broken the spell that seemed to hang over her all her life, and Jacinto, who was sitting in the front row, turning now to smile at her as she walked down the sandy path, had not only made her dreams come true, he had made new dreams for her. At this moment, she was happy. She had learned the hard way that it was rare anything lasted forever. She hoped it would but she would take what happiness she could, while she had it, and enjoy it.

Allie followed, long blond hair smooth as silk, her strapless turquoise cotton dress matching her eyes, eyes that were brimming anyway, because she was just so happy for Sunny and Mac, her dearest friends. And happy that Ron, her husband, was there standing up for Mac, the man who'd saved their lives. This was one of the best days of *all* their lives.

Mac watched his love, his woman, his life, stepping barefoot with her blue toenails across the sand toward him. He had never seen her look so beautiful, except maybe a few hours ago when she had lain naked and passionate in his arms, love and lust and promise in her eyes.

Mac had refused to tie Pirate up, and the dog was sitting next to him. He gave Mac's hand a loving little nudge. He was wearing a blue eye patch over the dead eye socket, and a blue satin bow held back his scraggy gray fur. Mac thought his dog had never looked more handsome. But that's love for you.

Jacinto, cool and rock-star sexy, sat next to Jassy in the front row. She was in what Galliano had described to her as "beach wedding couture," which meant clouds of fine gray silk exactly the color of the mist hanging over the ocean and with a scrap of red net and a feather on her upswept blond hair. She had never looked lovelier.

Rodolfo and his partner William sat on her other side, both handsome and cool, along with Floradelisa, trim in a white linen pantsuit. Only Antonio was missing. And Lorenza, of course, though Sunny had been careful to invite her.

"I think you will be the most beautiful bride," Lorenza replied, sending a gift of an antique Spanish silver bowl. "And a wonderful wife and darling companion for Mac. I wish you both well, and hope I will always remain your long-distance friend."

Both Mac and Sunny hoped that too.

Then there was Lev, ugly-attractive, and for once not in a Tommy Bahama tropical shirt, but in plain dark blue, still with the aviators, of course. His shaved head gleamed under the cool gray evening light and there was more than one woman in the audience giving him an appreciative eye.

Sunny's mom and dad were there of course; the handsome Mexican, who ran his ranch near Santa Fe, and his hippie flower-child wife, still with those bangs like a seventies model, wide blue eyes and a matching blue voile caftan, hung around with a dozen shell necklaces in honor of the beach occasion. More family, more friends, all close, all connected, all loving.

It was, Mac thought, looking at his bride as he slid the plain gold ring on her finger, a perfect wedding.

"Finally," he said, leaning in to kiss her.

"Finally," Sunny said.

And then Tesoro broke free from her bonds, galloped into the gazebo, and bit Mac on the ankle.

Chapter 57

Bibi finally took the advice Rodolfo had given her that night in Barcelona, and talked to Paloma about her father. First, though, she talked to her friend, Sunny.

It was a couple of weeks after the wedding and Mrs. Sunny Alvarez Reilly had just returned from a honeymoon in Mauritius, where the brochures had proven correct, and the Indian Ocean was blue and transparent and soft as chiffon on the skin, and the sand was white and the snorkeling filled with fishes of every shape and wondrous color imaginable. There were daiquiris with little paper umbrellas in them, and grilled fish for dinner, and a wide, wide bed, hung with soft white muslin to protect them from the night breeze that lifted her hair as she clasped her lover in her arms.

"It was everything a honeymoon could be," she told Bibi.

They were in Malibu, sitting on the deck, huddled in sweaters because the ocean mist had come in. Still, they loved the salty smell of it, and the way it clung to their hair and their cheeks.

"Homemade moisturizer," Sunny said, with a grin.

"The best," Bibi agreed.

Mac and Paloma had taken the dogs and gone to pick up

pizzas and also a bottle of Pimm's, the British drink that, mixed with Vernors ginger ale, and with cucumber and a sprig of mint, had become Sunny's current favorite.

"Though maybe it's more of a red wine night," she said with a slight shiver.

They were both on the old porch swing, swinging lazily back and forth, but Bibi leaned closer to her. "Sunny?" she said. "I have to tell you something. Actually, I want to *ask* you something."

She was absolutely serious and Sunny stopped swinging.

"What's up?" she asked, suddenly alarmed. "It's not about Paloma?"

"Well, in a way, yes, it is. But it's really about her father."

This was out of left field. Sunny sat up straighter and listened.

"I never talked to Paloma about him, not because he's bad, like Peretti, but because . . . well, you see it's because he had his own life. He was happy in that life, and I . . . we . . . what happened between us was not a great romance, a falling in love, a 'live or die' affair of the heart. Oh, it *was* love. I loved him so much, but then you see, I always had. And he's always loved me. Since I was a child."

"Then he's an older man?"

"To me, he was. And now he is. You see I knew him all my life. He was a friend of Juan Pedro's, a good friend, younger than my father of course, but to a child he was old. He was always there for me, he followed my career, gave me financial advice, advised me about the wrong turns my life was taking, always remembered my birthday. . . .

"And then Juan Pedro died. I hadn't seen that much of him in those last years, I was busy and Juan Pedro had married again. Our separation made no difference when it came to his death. I was devastated. I couldn't function. All I wanted, after that funeral that Lorenza tried so hard to make a joyous celebration of his life, was comfort. I needed love. And Rodolfo gave that."

Bibi leaned back in the porch swing, waiting for her reaction, but her friend simply stared out at the ocean, saying nothing, waiting for her to go on.

Bibi said, "It was so gentle, so simple, so warm, so *necessary*, so real; the most loving experience of my life. It was over before it even began. A tender moment between two people who had always loved each other, and always would. Rodolfo had his life partner, and his own life. And I had my work, my talent, my hectic other-worldly ridiculous way of life that I thought so important. Until I found I was pregnant.

"I didn't tell Rodolfo. I couldn't interrupt his life, and he loved William so much, they were a team, partners for life. I wanted him to think it was somebody else's child. And I wanted the baby so badly, I wanted to keep the memory of our night together. Had it been a boy I would have named him for Juan Pedro, but I got my dear little girl, and that's when I finally told Rodolfo.

"Of course he is a man of honor. Not only that, he was thrilled, he had never in his life expected to be a father. I gave him permission to tell his partner, his true life love, William." Bibi shrugged, looking anxiously at Sunny. "And so they both became long-distance fathers. Except Paloma never knew, and nor did anyone else."

"The Russian dancer absconding from the Kirov . . . ?" Sunny said.

"I had to say something," Bibi explained.

"You bet you did," Sunny said. "But what you told me is wonderful, Bibi. It's about true loving and caring and tenderness, and Paloma is the result not only of that night, but of all those long years Rodolfo looked after you, and cared about you."

Bibi said, "What I'm asking you is, should I tell Paloma? She's gone through so much, I'm afraid for her."

"How can you *not* tell her? Of course, you *should*. *Of course* she should know Rodolfo is her father. My God, all these years she must have wondered, and then to get stuck with a crazy killer like Peretti. You *owe* it to Paloma to tell her. And you'd better get on the phone right now, and tell Rodolfo you are stepping up to the plate. You are telling Paloma the truth."

"What truth?"

Paloma stood in the doorway, two pizza boxes balanced in her hands. Pirate, drooling in anticipation—he loved pizza—stood on one side of her, and Tesoro, who had become her devoted slave, sat neatly on her other side, still on the new pink lead Paloma had bought her. Officially, Paloma now shared Tesoro with Sunny. That was their deal. And sometimes she was allowed to borrow the Chihuahua on weekends or, like when Sunny had gone off on her honeymoon, even for a couple of weeks.

Now Paloma said, "What secrets are you two talking about?"

Sunny walked over to her, took the pizza boxes from her, and carried them into the kitchen. "Your mom wants to talk to you," she said, heading off Mac who was just closing the front door with his foot, also balancing a box, this one containing the Pimm's and the ginger ale, and a couple of extra champagnes.

He raised his brows as Sunny shoved him toward the kitchen. "What's up?"

"Secrets," she said. "Or at least one secret. A very important one."

Mac put the box on the kitchen counter and took the pizzas from her. He turned the oven on to four hundred and ten, took a baking sheet from the drawer, unpacked the pizzas and put them on it. He liked his pizza hot and crispy, never microwaved.

"I'll bet I know what it is."

"Bet you don't," she said, smugly.

"You mean about Rodolfo being Paloma's father?"

"Oh my God," she gasped, making Mac frown. "But how did you know?"

"I guessed, that night in Barcelona when Bibi and Paloma were reunited. Something Rodolfo said, then I noticed the way he looked at Bibi, and the tenderness in his eyes when he saw Paloma. He took that little girl's hand like she was the fairy princess and led her into that house and to her mother."

"Oh my God," Sunny said again. "Ooops, sorry. I promise I'll never say that again."

Mac was pouring champagne. "A celebration is called for," he said, handing her a glass. "But anyhow, later, Rodolfo told me."

"He *told* you!"

"He asked me to keep an eye on Paloma, make sure she wasn't harmed by all the terrible publicity, keep her away from it all. He said he would take her back to Spain with him but he knew Bibi couldn't bear another separation. I don't think he ever really believed she would tell Paloma, though. And now, I guess she has because Paloma has a right to know."

Sunny glanced apprehensively out the window. She saw the lounger had stopped swinging. Then she saw Paloma get up. She saw Paloma take Bibi's hand and walk toward the open French doors.

Sunny stopped herself from saying "oh my God" just in time and instead said tersely, "Here they come."

Paloma was first. "Guess what?" she said, her face filled with excitement. "Rodolfo is really my dad. He always has been, I just never knew. And guess what that means? Now I have two real dads, because William will be my daddy too. And we're going back to Spain to live in Mom's castle, as well as Barcelona, and

I'll go to the same school Mom went to, in Las Ramblas, and you will come and visit any time you want."

"We'll be a real family," Bibi said, putting her arms round her daughter and hugging her. "Isn't that the best news of all?"

Sunny thought it was the best news since her honeymoon in Mauritius.

Epilogue

After Bruno Peretti was arrested by the Guardia, he spent a couple of months in a tough Spanish jail before being extradited to the U.S., where he was taken to Rikers Island. The story of his arrest and Bibi's innocence was big, for a while, the way those notorious stories are, and the public came out in Bibi's favor, horrified by her long ordeal, and the enforced separation from her daughter.

The public and the media soon lost interest in Peretti while he languished, complaining, and arrogant as ever. It was his arrogance, not a judge and jury, that gave him a death sentence.

Peretti was stabbed to death with a tool made from a sharpened plastic toothbrush. No one confessed, no one knew who did it, no one mourned him.

Lorenza shocked everyone by suddenly marrying an "old flame," a man she had dated over the years. He is ten years younger, handsome, of course, sexy, of course—he'd have to be to keep up with Lorenza. And rich enough to keep her in comfort if she needed it, which, being the businesswoman she is, she certainly does not. The Marqués de Ravel wines are a global success, their price point making them perfect for the mass market. And they are good quality too. Lorenza sees to that. When she thinks of Mac, which of course she does every now and then, it is with regret. Does she regret her attempt to steal him back from Sunny? Not on your life, she doesn't. But if she couldn't have him, then Sunny Alvarez will make him a good wife. And she will keep her memories, and the thought of what might have been, that night with Mac at the bodega. If only . . .

And of course, Mr. and Mrs. Reilly, Sunny and Mac, are now living in almost perfect harmony, in his little shack on Malibu beach, where he is almost coming to terms with the fact that she will say "oh my God" every time she is surprised or shocked; and she is coming to terms with the fact that the phone will always ring bringing more trouble, and that Mac will always answer it. The Chihuahua Tesoro, and Mac's dear scruffy mutt Pirate, will at best remain friendly enemies, but hey, nothing's perfect.

Or is it? Sunny asks herself, sitting with Mac on that deck overlooking the Pacific, with the sun going down and the dogs behaving themselves, and a glass of champagne in her hand. Maybe she's wrong, and life is perfect after all.

Here is a sneak peek at
Elizabeth Adler's new novel

A Place in the Country

Available June 2012

chapter 1

Caroline Evans was having a day out from her rented London flat, driving through rainy Oxfordshire with her fifteen-year-old daughter slumped in a silent sulk next to her.

They had taken in Oxford, "city of dreaming spires," which seemed to have more traffic than a motorway in rush hour, plus a couple of thousand young people smoking and drinking coffee and hanging about outside pubs. Issy ignored it all but Caroline had fallen for the rain-slicked courtyards and the ancient colleges half-hidden behind tall gates that had been there long before Henry's time. That would be Henry VIII, who, Caroline now figured couldn't have been all bad, despite the six wives. After all, her own husband had had two, and that was before her.

"A serial husband," she had said doubtfully when James told her he was going to marry her, though she was longing to say yes because she was so besotted by him she couldn't see straight, even with her glasses on.

Forget charming the birds; James Evans could, and did, charm everyone. Caroline remembered thinking it was okay about the other two wives, she would be the last wife. That's what James told her. And she'd believed him. She was twenty-two.

Now she was thirty-eight and an ex-wife, with a teenage daughter whose name was Isabel, always known as Issy, who some days talked to her and some days did not; who looked mostly like her father; and who, Caroline suspected, was smoking. However she did not yet have a tattoo, or at least not one in any place visible to her mother.

"Oxford's a lot different from when I was a girl," she said, maneuvering the old Land Rover bumpily out of the city and onto the A40, toward Cheltenham, though she had no specific destination in mind.

"Of course it is. That was a long time ago." Her daughter turned to look at her. "You should wear lipstick," she said. "And mascara."

Caroline sighed, remembering not so long ago when her child had thought she was perfect. She fiddled in her handbag for the lipstick and Issy told her she shouldn't do that while driving. It seemed she could do nothing right.

"Bloody rain," Issy said, looking at the wipers sloshing water sideways across the windscreen.

Caroline glanced sharply at her, then caught the sign for Burford and swung right into one of the prettiest high streets in the Cotswolds. Picture perfect, lined with small shops selling the usual souvenirs and postcards, but also art galleries and antique stores, bakeries and tea shops, as well as trees dripping onto the umbrellas of the few hardy citizens who waded through the puddles, heading for shelter.

Caroline slammed on the brakes as a car pulled out in front of her. "Look, we've got a parking spot. We were meant to stop here. Let's have tea."

Issy's sigh matched the stoop of her shoulders as she clambered unwillingly out of the car and stood in the rain, looking, her mother thought with a twinge of pity, utterly helpless and defeated in her new Marks & Spencer parka. Rain slicked her brown hair and there was a look of sadness in her brown eyes. It had been there ever since they'd left Singapore a year and a half ago, and Caroline did not know what to do about it.

Now, though, she grabbed her hand firmly and hurried her across the road into the nearest tearoom. As they climbed the stairs and took the last available table, she wasn't thinking about the strawberry cream tea she would order for them both, she was thinking of James, wondering, as she had so often, if she had done the right thing, leaving him.

"Mom." They had just sat down and Issy got up again. "I'm going downstairs to look at the shop."

The tearoom was over a junky jewelry-souvenir shop. "Okay." Caroline watched her go.

The tea came, carried on a plastic tray decorated with birds of the region, by a young woman not much more than her daughter's age, but who at least smiled at her and said it was the Earl Grey you wanted, Madam.

Caroline said it was and the girl put the tray down, arranged the small flowery cups in front of her and indicated the two-tier china cake stand with its nicely browned scones and a choice of small cakes; éclairs, fruit tarts, and iced buns. There was a dish of strawberry jam and a deep bowl with cream so thick you could stand your spoon in it.

"Perfect, thank you." Caroline found herself smiling as she poured pale tea into the flowery little cup. She had been brought up in London, an English girl who'd married and gone to live in Singapore with a husband she loved, a daughter she adored, a beautiful penthouse home with a view of the river and the city and its twinkling nighttime lights.

"Best of both worlds," James said, when they first looked at it. They were young marrieds; he American in his early thirties, successful in hedge funds and investments, and so attractive and charming he didn't need a penthouse to feel on top of the world. And she was so hazy with love and sex she couldn't think of anything else.

That was then. *Now,* was this rainy English day, a steamy little tea shop, and an almost silent daughter who finally came back, taking the wooden stairs two at a time. She sat down, took a scone, sliced it neatly, slathered it with jam and a dollop of thick cream, took a too-large bite, then picked up her phone and began texting.

Who she was texting Caroline didn't know. Still, she took a scone, and smiled. "This is the best," she said hopefully.

"Yeah." Issy's thumbs were busy but Caroline noticed she was also watching her as she struggled to arrange cream on top of the crumbling scone without it collapsing entirely in her hand.

"You should cut it into two pieces," Issy informed her.

"You sound just like my mother," Caroline said, making Issy smile. It was the first smile Caroline had seen all day.

"Here, this is for you." Issy pushed over a small package, wrapped in pink tissue paper.

"*Really?* For me?"

"I said so, didn't I?"

She looked away and Caroline knew she was embarrassed and thought she was being loud, and that everyone was looking.

"A present," she said, unraveling the pink tissue. "Ohh, Issy, how lovely."

It was a tiny brooch, junky, cheap but somehow sweet. She ran a finger over the fake silver. Fake or not, she would always treasure it. "A little bird, on the wing," she said.

"Sort of like us. Birds on the wing, never alighting anywhere."

"You mean us not having a real home anymore?" Caroline felt that clench in her heart again. "We'll get one, soon. I promise you."

Her voice sounded more confident than she felt. Money was tight, to say the least. When she'd married James, she had been young, she hadn't known any better and had signed that prenup, which of course meant that all she'd gotten from the divorce and sixteen years of marriage was a very small lump sum, and child support until her daughter became eighteen.

She glanced round the small tearoom at the other people; ordinary people, mackintoshes and parkas steaming over the backs of their chairs in the heat wafting from a long white radiator under the already steamed-up windows. People, Caroline thought, whose lives were all set; who had a pattern, a routine, and probably not a care in the world as they ate their scones and jam and cream and talked about the rain, as the English always did because it always rained anyway.

"Come on, have that last chocolate éclair, why don't you," she said briskly, pulling herself together. "Then we'll get out into the country-side, see a bit more of the Cotswolds."

Issy gave her that world-weary fifteen-year-old shrug. "Whatever," she said, which Caroline guessed meant she agreed.